I0760840

TRILOGY OF EVE BOOK THREE

DAWN OF EVE

PAM GODWIN

Editor: Lesa Godwin, Godwin Proofing
Interior Designer: Pam Godwin
Cover Artist: Okay Creations

Visit my website at pamgodwin.com

The Trilogy of Eve must be read in order.

Dead of Eve #1
Blood of Eve #2
Dawn of Eve #3

ONE

Dawn
Twenty-Two Years Post-Apocalypse

Hunger leaked into his eyes. I knew that look. Knew it and felt it as if I were staring at my reflection. Except where his need to tear open my throat stemmed from bloodlust, my hunger was methodical and honed through training. I was bred to kill.

The frigid wind lashed my cheeks and gnawed at my fingers. I tightened my grip on the nocked arrow, the bowstring stretched beside my face. Heart thundering, breaths quickening, fueled by adrenaline, fear, excitement, I adjusted my aim to his head. *Eliminate.*

Fifteen feet away, the hybrid blinked glassy eyes at the fire-red braid that had fallen from my hood. If he took a step, I would release the arrow, and he knew it.

"Daughter of Eve." He spat the words, but a tincture of dread serrated his voice.

Of course, he knew who I was. Not because these creatures put up posters of my face with the headline *Daughter of Eve—Do not bite.* But because my golden eyes and crimson hair were dead giveaways. Also, human women didn't leave their heavily-guarded sanctuaries without an army of men. They were too rare and crucial to the continuation of our species.

But I wasn't a normal human woman.

My mother had delivered me into this wretched existence

with a promise—a promise to the world that I would make it a lot less wretched. *No pressure.* So while our women remained protected and hidden behind barricaded walls, I fought in the open. While they produced life, I took it away.

Humans weren't the only species that subscribed to the prophecy of Eve. The hybrids believed I was put on this planet to eliminate them. But they didn't know my weaknesses, didn't know how very human I was. In fact, the hybrid staring at me now had no idea that if he drained my blood, he would live and I would die.

Bundled in layers of tattered clothes, scruff on his jaw, pronounced cheekbones, and tangled hair, he looked like a desperate twenty-year-old man. But he was more monster than human. The fangs pressing against his lower lip were all the proof I needed.

I released the arrow, and he dropped to the ground. Crimson splattered the pristine snow, the arrow protruding from his eye socket.

With a sigh of relief, I yanked the feathered shaft from his skull and scanned the Yukon landscape for the next threat.

The low sun reflected off a blanket of glittery white. Beyond the frosty tundra lay forested wilderness and mountainous terrain bristling with evergreens. Branches sagged beneath heaps of snow, creating deep shadows beneath the canopy. The perfect place for hybrids to hide.

"Dawn!" Eddie bellowed from a distance behind me.

Dammit, why was he still here? I'd given him an order.

"Hurry the fuck up!" His voice echoed across the wintry plain. "More are coming."

There were always more. Even in this forsaken part of the world, hybrids outnumbered humans.

An arctic gust shivered through me, cutting into my bones despite the fur pelts and heavy boots. Another violent tremor attacked my body, and I swore I felt my arteries ice up.

Canadian winters could bite my bony ass. I didn't leave the Nevada desert and travel all this way to freeze to death. Or bleed to death. Odds were on the latter, given the silhouettes emerging from the tree line about a mile away.

"Return to the women," I shouted over my shoulder. "Get them to the camp. I'll catch up."

If I ran, I would lead the hybrids to the survivors we'd just taken from them. I needed to end this here. Now.

My teeth chattered, and my hands burned against the unholy chill in the air. I was outnumbered, physically weaker and slower, and exhausted from the endless shivering. But I was the supposed prophecy, the one who would save humanity. I had a helluva lot of shit to do before I died.

"Come on, suckers." I trained the arrow, waiting for the hybrids to reach my forty-yard range limit.

Eddie's boots crunched across the frozen ground behind me, approaching rather than retreating.

He never listens.

I was the leader of the Resistance, the highest human position in the new world, feared by every man, woman, and hybrid. Except Eddie. Thank fuck for that, because that would be weird.

Stopping at my side, bow at the ready, he flashed his don't-be-hatin' grin. The one that glimmered in his brown eyes and softened his sharp cheekbones.

"You're disobeying me, you bastard." I smiled to myself and pulled back the arrow, training it on the first of six approaching hybrids. Almost within range. "Seriously, Eddie. I need you looking after the women."

The bitter cold had chafed his mocha skin and cracked his lips, but he looked as fearless and handsome as ever in his ink-dyed leather hides. The threaded seams stretched around his muscled arms, and the tailored fit accentuated the sex appeal that seemed to affect every woman but me.

"They're in good hands." He breathed in, out, mirroring my position with his bow.

The four soldiers who accompanied us on this mission were more than qualified to lead twenty survivors to camp. But they weren't Eddie.

"I gave you an order." Without shifting my cheek from the

bow, I slid him a sidelong glare.

"Not leaving you, Red."

His rumbling tone was casual, his grin playful. But I knew my best friend better than anyone. He would die for me without hesitation.

I needed to remind him I was in charge. "If you don't—"

"Your threats mean fuck-all compared to what your fathers will do to me if I return without you."

Yeah. There was that. No human alive would risk disappointing the three legendary guardians. Not even me, their only child.

The chance to argue my position disintegrated as the hybrids moved into shooting range. Six males, armed only with their agility and fangs. Killing one close up was a pain in the ass. But forty yards away? They moved faster than the speed of an arrow. To accommodate for that, I tried to predict which direction they'd weave and released the shot.

It sliced through the air behind them. *Son of a bitch!*

Steadying my breaths, I fired five more, hit a leg, a torso, but failed to land a kill shot. With their fast healing abilities, the only way to take one down was to damage the brain.

"They're not coming closer. We need to move in." Eddie volleyed another arrow.

His target ducked, and the shot sank into a snowdrift. My pulse elevated.

The hybrids stayed back, maintaining a range that would force us to blow through our ammunition. Once we ran out, they would attack.

Eddie's quiver held about twenty arrows, same as mine. Probably enough to take down half of them, but not all six. Time for a different strategy.

I dropped the bow, unbuckled the quiver's strap, and secured it to his back.

"What are you doing?" He pulled back an arrow, eyes on the threat.

"Cover me." I whirled away, racing my crazy ass straight toward the horde.

"Oh, fuck no!" He continued to yell, but the roaring wind and clomp of my boots on the hard-packed snow muffled his voice.

With each step, my insides coiled tighter and tighter. I was a better archer than him, but one of us needed to be the bait, the blood-scented distraction that would trigger their instinct to chase. I was immune to their venomous bite. Eddie was not.

The hybrids formed a menacing wall of muscle and fanged smiles. They might've been mindless with hunger, but they were intelligent creatures, educated in survival and weaponry, their mental capacities equal to humans. Add to that their superior strength, speed, and health, and I was, without a doubt, the underdog. One sharp fang in my jugular and I'd bleed out like any other human. Which was why my stomach felt like a boulder and why Eddie was screaming and sprinting after me.

Without slowing, I wrapped a scarf of wolf skin around my throat and gripped the dagger hidden beneath the folds of my fur cloak, the hilt scratched to hell and worn down by my mother's hands. It was one of the few keepsakes I had of hers. If I lost it, I would never forgive myself.

Locking my fingers around it, I lurched to the right and hauled ass. The hairs on my nape lifted as the hybrids pounced after me. I had no hope of outrunning them, but they were most definitely distracted.

Eddie's arrows riddled the snow around me as he raced to take down my pursuers.

I slid to a stop, spun around, and lunged at the first male. With brute force, I buried the blade in his temple, the steel sinking through bone thanks to hours of sharpening. As he slumped to the ground, I held on to the hilt, yanked it free, and turned toward the next attacker.

Fangs filled my vision, followed by the hungry eyes of a hybrid. He clutched my shoulders and wrenched me against his chest. No amount of writhing and stabbing would break his iron hold.

An arrow flew past my head, and he swerved to evade it. His pupils dilated with the instinct to bite, but he seemed to be restraining himself, his pale face taut with uncertainty.

Despite the rumors, I wasn't poisonous to them, evidenced by the countless bite marks marring my body. Though my blood didn't kill them, no one had ever bitten me and lived long enough to debunk the popular legend. Thank fuck for that, because in his moment of indecision, one of Eddie's arrows sliced through his skull.

I shoved him away and released a ragged breath. Another dead hybrid lay a few feet away. Three left. Where—?

Something fast and huge slammed into my side. The air whooshed from my lungs, and my back crashed against the ground, jolting unbearable agony down my spine. Shit, shit, shit. I couldn't lift my limbs, couldn't breathe.

Hands, legs, and heavy bodies pinned me down. All three of them were on me, scrambling over each other like a pack of wolves. I angled my head and found Eddie crawling to his feet about twenty yards away, his bow nowhere in sight. Fuck, this wasn't good.

Tangled in fur pelts, I dodged a mouthful of teeth, swiped the knife, and sliced through a throat. Blood sprayed everywhere, but the fucker didn't slow, snapping his jaws inches from my face and clawing at my chest, feral in his need to feed.

I kicked my legs, trying and failing to ward off the other two while making fumbling stabs at one near my neck.

Fingers pawed at my lower body, separating the layers of fur. No, no, no! Images of them biting, raping, and killing me propelled me to kick harder. Frigid air penetrated my suede leggings as I tried to squirm free.

Blinding pain exploded through my inner thigh, vicious and all-consuming. I screamed in anguish, tears burning my eyes. I'd been bitten.

With one hand around the male's throat, I slashed the blade at the others, twisting and jerking my leg from the fangs, certain a chunk of my skin had been ripped off in the process.

The scent of iron invaded my inhales and roiled my stomach. I couldn't wrestle away, couldn't stop them if they tried to bite again. They were too fast, too strong, too fucking relentless.

Panic rose, sharp and crippling. What if this was it? My final fight? The end of the prophecy? The extinction of mankind?

I gritted my teeth and swung the knife with every ounce of vigor I had left. I missed, adjusted, and tried again and again, grunting as I pierced the back of the hybrid's head.

He fell off me, and my energy drained, trickling away with the blood seeping from my leg. It was all I could do to fight off the remaining two, my movements defensive, desperate. And waning.

The air stirred with an incoming arrow. The hybrid at my throat fell limp, a feathered shaft sticking out of his head. *Oh sweet mother, thank you.* Only one left.

He crawled up my body, fangs gleaming. A teenage male with hypnotic blue eyes. Arrows pelted the ground around us, but he nimbly veered side to side, taking a shot in the arm and flashing me a pained smile.

In the next breath, he yanked me to my feet. With my chest against his, he whirled around in a macabre dance, using me as a damn shield against Eddie's barrage.

The movement sent shock waves of pain through my leg. I bit down on the inside of my cheek, my attention clinging to the knife where it still protruded from the skull at my feet.

When the arrows stopped flying, the hybrid lowered his greedy gaze to my throat.

I jerked just as his mouth made contact, and his teeth hit my shoulder. But the thick furs prevented him from breaking skin.

With a guttural growl, he grabbed my jaw and shoved down the scarf. My heart banged against my ribs, and my lungs labored for air.

"Dawn!" Eddie ran closer, circling a few feet away with an arrow poised. "I can't get a shot."

I hated the terror in his eyes. Hated that I couldn't hide the fear in my own eyes.

The hybrid held me in front of him, knowing Eddie wouldn't risk hitting me. I continued to kick and thrash, but no matter how hard I tried, I couldn't break free. I needed the knife.

He dipped his head, going for my throat again. My heart rate skyrocketed, and I tucked my chin, my focus landing on the arrow jammed in his bicep.

I reached for it, twisted it free, and jabbed it into his eye socket. Not hard enough, evidently, because he was roaring, clawing at it, still fucking breathing. But it was enough to make him stumble. Enough for Eddie to deliver a deathblow, his arrow piercing the center of the hybrid's forehead.

The body crumpled to the ground, and the sudden release of tension in my muscles sent a wave of dizziness through me. I swayed, shook it off, and staggered over the snow to collect my mother's dagger.

Eddie caught me around the waist, holding me up. "Swear to Eve, you're going to give me a fucking heart attack."

"You know I don't like when you use my mother's name like that." I gripped his arms for support.

He cupped my cheek with icy fingers, lifting my gaze to his. Nineteen years of love and loyalty shone in his eyes, and I knew mine returned the sentiment.

"Thank you." I squeezed his wrist and stepped back, searching the bodies for the knife. "I was kind of getting my ass kicked, so it's a good thing you stayed, huh?"

A smirk touched his lips as he strapped my quiver and bow to my back.

I spotted the dagger and returned it to the sheath at my hip, feeling a thousand times more relaxed now that I had it back in my possession.

As we collected the arrows, each step spiked a blaze of agony through my thigh. I kept my expression neutral, but Eddie, being Eddie, didn't miss a beat.

"You're hurt." His gaze swept over my body, pausing on

my wounded leg.

"I think half my thigh was chewed off."

"Want me to look at it?" His dark brows pulled together, expression creased with worry.

"I'll check it out."

I couldn't imagine living in a world where I wasn't nursing at least one injury, but since I hadn't face-planted yet, the bite probably wasn't as bad as I thought. Regardless, it was going to be an agonizing three-day walk back to camp.

"I kept one of the horses." He rubbed his hands together, huffing breaths on his fingers.

He should've left all the horses with the women. Having just been rescued from a hybrid breeding facility, they were in no shape to walk over frozen terrain. With the women doubled up, there were just enough horses to go around.

I snatched the last arrow from the ground and limped away, headed in the direction of the others. They were probably an hour ahead of us.

"Don't get all pissy." He jogged after me. "One of the girls refused to ride, so I made a judgment call. A damn good one given the way you're wobbling."

"Always taking caring of me." My lips rose despite the sweat beading across my brow and the chill on my skin. I felt miserably weak and sick to my stomach. "What would I do without you?"

He stepped in front of me, concern etching his face. "I'm going to go get the horse. Wait here."

"'kay." I plopped down, knowing he wouldn't leave me unprotected for longer than a few minutes.

Tucked beneath the fur cloak, I bandaged the wound with scraps of hide and devoured a stash of dried meat. Eddie returned, and for the next hour, I rode behind him on the horse, feeling marginally better, a little stronger and more alert. Despite the jarring ride, keeping weight off my leg and racing toward the rest of our group seemed to do wonders for my mental state.

Following the tracks they'd left in the snow, we galloped

over barren tundra for miles. As we reached one of the abandoned villages we'd passed through several days ago, Eddie slowed the horse.

"What is it?" I leaned around him and glimpsed movement up ahead. "Is that our group?"

"Yeah." He guided the horse along a row of crumbling shacks. "Why would they stop here? They should've kept going."

"Maybe they needed to rest?" The tingle along my spine disagreed. Something was wrong.

I grabbed the bow from my back and positioned an arrow. The wound in my thigh protested as I used my legs to balance on the horse.

"Approach cautiously," I whispered, tensing against every crunch of the horse's hooves.

The wind was too quiet. The gutted shacks, the falling snow, the silhouettes moving just beyond the hill—it was all too fucking quiet. A lump formed in my throat.

A moment later, the faint aroma of burning wood reached my nose. "Do you smell that?"

Our soldiers knew better than to start a fire. The smoke alone would draw hybrids.

"Yeah," Eddie said. "But I don't see smoke."

At the top of the hill, I peered around his broad shoulder and gasped.

Our four soldiers and the twenty women we rescued sat around a doused fire pit, licking their fingers and eating…something. A quick scan of the perimeter revealed the carcass of a mountain goat, the bones picked cleaned and organs gone. Dread filled my insides.

"Shit." Eddie pulled the horse to a stop. "Don't they know?"

Apparently not. I focused on the soldiers' teeth, relieved to find them straight and human. The women we'd rescued were all in their thirties and forties, which meant they were born pre-apocalypse, had been cured by my mother's blood, and were immune to the spider venom. In other words, they were human and couldn't be turned. But if I didn't protect them, they would be recaptured, held until they gave birth, and slaughtered.

Lowering the bow, I slid to the ground, whimpered against the pain in my leg, and staggered toward them. "There are no mountain goats in this area. Not for miles."

Two dozen startled eyes found mine, mouths paused mid-chew. Starvation lined the hollow indentions of their cheeks and bony frames, their desperation to eat heartbreaking.

"The goat was running that way." One of the soldiers pointed at the tree line in the distance. "I think it was lost. Couldn't pass up food like that."

"Someone put that animal here." A shiver licked my spine, and my pulse sped up. "It's a trap to keep you in place. We need to go, right fucking now."

The women glanced around, clutching their pregnant bellies as the soldiers scrambled to their feet. But it was too late.

A stampede of footfalls sounded in the valley behind me, racing over the snow at inhuman speeds. They were coming.

TWO

The distant rumble echoed through the frozen valley. I nocked an arrow, spun toward the din, and drew a shivery breath.

A dark smudge of silhouettes emerged on the white horizon between two rocky peaks. At least a dozen hybrids. My heart rate quickened.

The surrounding mountains, though miles away, created an echo chamber, magnifying every sound. The hybrids weren't as close as they seemed, probably several minutes away by foot. That gave me just enough time to lose my shit or pull it together.

My pulse leapt in time with the throb in my leg as I raced toward the cluster of horses and scanned the saddle packs for our arrow supply. Eddie beat me there, grabbed the largest quiver, and added it to the one on my back.

"What's your plan?" A winter storm churned in his expression. "I hope to Eve you're not going to—"

"I need you to lead the women to our camp." I pivoted toward the survivors, relieved to see they hadn't moved.

Twenty pairs of wide eyes stared at me. Shoulders hunched, hands gripping swollen bellies, they probably thought I rescued them so I could kill them. Maybe I should. Pregnant women were a precious commodity, but these women had been bitten—bites that had turned their unborn children into hybrids.

I pointed at three of the four soldiers, and in a few clipped commands, I sent the men away on horseback with instructions to circle back for the women in twenty minutes. The fourth soldier, Jeremy, was our best rider, so I kept him with me, directing him to mount a chestnut mare.

My injured leg twinged as I climbed on behind him. "Everyone else, lay on the ground. On your backs or sides. Eyes closed. Pretend you're dead. Hurry." My hands shook as I waited for the women to obey. "Good, now don't move. Don't lift your heads. Don't fucking breathe—"

"Dawn…" Eddie charged toward me, his jaw a stone block of stubbornness.

"That includes you." With one hand on the bow, I clutched Jeremy's waist with the other and narrowed my eyes at Eddie.

I hated leaving him short a horse. Unless they squeezed three to a saddle, a few women would have to walk.

Eddie lowered to the snow-covered ground, stretched out on his back, and set his bow beside him, his furious gaze locked on mine. "You really think they'll believe you slaughtered the women?"

"Yes." If I was wrong, Eddie would be on his own and outnumbered. A lump sealed my throat.

We'd traveled to this arctic land to take down the northern breeding facilities. As passionately as the Resistance wanted to save human women, it wasn't a stretch to believe we were just as eager to exterminate their infected offspring. In truth, we killed the babies as soon as they were born. It was the best way to stop the spread of infection. The mothers were our priority.

"Don't move until it's safe." I thrust a finger at Eddie and filled my eyes with a soul-deep command. *Don't you dare fucking die.* "Then head straight to camp. Don't stop to rest until nightfall."

His face hardened, his six-foot frame rigid as steel, but he gave a tight nod.

The horse side-stepped, twitching with nervousness. I squeezed my thighs around Jeremy's hips as he tangled his hands in the flaxen mane and turned us toward the hybrids.

The bloodsuckers sprinted out of the valley and across the open tundra, too far away to see us.

"Which way?" Jeremy glanced at me over his shoulder, his expression as pale as his white-blond hair.

The hybrids approached from the north. I'd sent our soldiers south. Dense woodland lay to the east and west. Our camp was east.

"West." I pointed an arrow at the thickest section of evergreens about a mile away. "There."

With a kick, he spurred the horse into a full-speed gallop. The frigid wind knocked the hood off my head and stung my eyes. I clung to the folds of his wolf-skin coat and tensed against the heavy burden of quivers banging against my back. Carrying about fifty arrows might've been enough on a lucky day, but I'd have to shoot backward. With frozen fingers. On a moving horse.

My insides knotted.

The path Jeremy chose led us closer to the attackers. Two, four, six…eleven male hybrids sprinted toward us, fur pelts flapping behind their leather-clad legs and eyes on the people I'd abandoned in the distance. I forced myself not to follow their gazes.

Positioned between the hybrids and our group, Jeremy veered west toward the trees. I gripped hard on the bow, still out of range to make a shot. *Come on, you fuckers. Follow us.*

They slowed, faltering, their heads ticking between me and the group I left behind. I stole a backward glimpse at Eddie and the others, and my chest pinched. Bodies scattered the snowy ground, unmoving, vulnerable. They looked dead.

My muscles tensed with the urge to turn back. When it came to Eddie, my training and instincts always got twisted up. First lesson my fathers taught me was not to get attached to people, but I'd known Eddie since birth, born one day apart. We grew up together, fought together, and dammit, we would die together.

Neither of us are dying today.

The glacial air bit at my cheeks as I unraveled my braid and let my fire-red hair sail behind me like a flag. Even if the hybrids suspected the women weren't dead, they'd already implanted their infected seed. I was the bigger prize.

Although my father, Michio, had slain the nutjob responsible for the apocalypse, the Drone's fanatical plan to replace mankind with a *perfect* species lived on through his creations. His divine race of bloodsuckers had one objective: transform every human into hybrid.

According to the prophecy, only one thing could stop them.

Me.

The daughter of Eve.

But I was just a nineteen-year-old human girl. It might've been laughable, except every hybrid and human believed it. Even I struggled to refute it. My mother's valiant life, her ultimate death, my very existence—all of it had been foreshadowed by a dead child. My half-sister, Annie. She never specifically said I would be a superhuman badass, but my fathers had assumed I would have some kind of genetic alteration like my mother. Well, that didn't happen, and it sucked.

The hybrids sped up, but their trajectory swerved left, headed straight toward me.

"Holy shit!" I hugged Jeremy's back. "It worked. They're coming."

"A little soon to celebrate." His breaths huffed in white clouds as he leaned forward, kicking the mare into top speed.

Hybrids sprinted faster than horses, but a horse could run longer distances and excelled at navigating rugged terrain. We just had to wear the hybrids out.

And slow them down.

I twisted at the waist, positioned an arrow, and let it fly. Blood pumping, mind focused, I fired at our pursuers for the next two miles. In the distance, Eddie and the women grew smaller and smaller until the horizon swallowed them completely.

Releasing a huge breath, I continued to volley arrows. By the time we made it to the tree line, I'd only taken down two hybrids.

"Duck." Jeremy swerved the horse.

I bent just as a decapitating branch whipped past my head. "Thanks."

For the next hour, Jeremy sped us through the thick foliage, announcing when to dart and weave as I flew through my arrow supply and eliminated two more hybrids.

Daylight waned, and the shadows crept in around us. It didn't take long for nightfall to cloak the woodland.

My hands turned to ice, my wounded leg pulsed from straining those muscles, and I swear to all that was holy, my nipples were so hard from shivering it felt like they had cut through the suede strap that bound my breasts. But somehow, we maintained the lead. Maybe because we weren't dodging arrows or climbing over fallen trees. I had a new appreciation for a horse's long, powerful legs.

Seven hybrids remained when I reached for an arrow and found none.

Fear spiked through my blood. "I'm out."

The hybrids were gaining, no more than thirty yards away. I swapped the bow for my mother's dagger.

"Dawn..." Jeremy said slowly, voice deep and cautious. "I think we have another problem."

He steered the horse between skeletal trunks and bent down as if trying to see through the shadows of the evergreens ahead.

"What?" I squinted at the trees, my shoulders prickling as the trailing footfalls grew louder.

He broke through a thicket of pines and jerked the horse to the side, narrowly avoiding a collision with a towering wrought-iron fence.

"What the—?" I hooked an arm around his waist and held tight. "Follow the perimeter. Maybe there's an opening."

The hybrids stayed on our trail as we sped alongside the fence. It was at least ten feet tall, commercial grade, definitely pre-apocalypse, and topped with coils of barbed wire.

Why was it in the middle of nowhere Canada, blocking my escape route? More importantly, where did it fucking end? There was nothing but more trees and snow on the other side. For some reason, my intuition screamed at me to run far away from this man-made structure. But there was nowhere to go. We sure as hell couldn't turn back.

"I see a gate." Jeremy freed a long blade from the sheath on his leg. "Fuck, it's not open. There's no latch."

As far as I could see, the fence didn't end in either direction. When I peeked behind us, my pulse went ballistic. We had about ten seconds before the hybrids were on us.

"Go faster!" I dug my fingers into his waist.

"It's opening!"

"What?" I leaned around his shoulder.

The gate stopped its creeping movement, leaving a crack just big enough for a person to slide through. The wind must've moved it.

"Think we can push it with the horse?" He slowed as we approached.

"We don't have time. If the horse doesn't fit through—"

"Get ready to jump."

We stopped a few feet away. The moment our feet hit the ground, the horse raced off, spooked by the approaching hybrids. I shoved Jeremy through the opening, and the gate didn't give. Why was it stuck?

I followed him through and tried to shove it closed while holding tight to the knife. "Shit, it won't budge. Come on, you bastard."

Was it mechanical? Electrical? Technology was nonexistent so far away from human sanctuaries. Whatever it was, I needed the damn thing closed!

Jeremy slammed his shoulder against it, but the hybrids were already here, seconds from slipping through the gate.

"Run!" Adrenaline surged through me as I took off through the trees with Jeremy at my side.

A few paces in, I expected to be tackled to the ground,

held down, bitten—

"Daughter of Eve!" One of the hybrids shouted. "Come back here."

I turned just as the gate snapped shut, locking the hybrids on the other side. How was that possible? Was someone operating it?

Relief loosened my shoulders, but vanished just as quickly. There were only three sets of eyes glaring through the rungs.

"Some of them slipped inside." *Four hybrids.* My heart jackhammered as I grabbed Jeremy's arm and weaved through the trees.

Branches tore at my face and clawed at my fur pelts. Grinding snow crackled beneath my boots. The trumpeting *coo-cooo* of an owl echoed overhead, and behind me, the tread of feet was muffled, farther back. Were the hybrids toying with us?

I ran faster, my legs burning with exertion and the cold seeping into my bones. The chill was the worst, the full-body trembling heightening the dread, the terror. It was such a raw, helpless feeling. I couldn't shake it. Couldn't catch my breath. I longed to be anywhere but here. Like back at camp with Eddie and my fathers. Warm and safe. *Please don't let me die here.*

With my fingers locked around the dagger, I ran as hard as I could, glancing over my shoulder at the pitch-black woodland and yanking Jeremy forward when he tripped. Clambering over the trails, pulse racing, breathless and terrified, I was just buying time. The hybrids would catch up. We couldn't run forever.

"Is that—?" Jeremy pointed his blade at something up ahead.

The forest ended abruptly. We shot into a moonlit clearing, and there, just a few yards ahead sat a sprawling mansion. My breath froze in my throat.

I didn't stop running as I took in the multiple stories, stone foundation, solid roof, heavy front door, all of it was maintained by…someone. That someone was home, given the candles flickering behind the unbroken windows. And the mechanical fence. And the way the front door was cracked open, just like the gate.

"I don't like this." Goosebumps engulfed my arms.

Jeremy pulled me forward without slowing his gait. "Could be a wealthy recluse. Maybe they want to help."

That front door looked a whole lot like salvation, but as I raced toward it, doubt poured in.

I knew people lived like this once. Rich folks who preferred isolation and wilderness. But twenty-two years after the apocalypse, it was all we could do just to stay alive. No one retired in well-kept mansions. Definitely not humans. We congregated in packs, built fortresses out of scrap metal, and survived through *strength in numbers.*

Hybrids wouldn't live here either. They were too busy hunting and feeding and overrunning the planet. We were at war. Everyone was struggling. This preserved mansion was unnatural.

A few feet from the door, I skidded to a stop. Jeremy halted beside me, and we both turned at the sound of footsteps.

One male hybrid strolled across the clearing and tilted his bald head, his fangs stark in the moonlight.

"Who lives here?" I backed up a step, searching the darkness for the others.

"Maybe the devil." The hybrid glanced up at the estate, his expression unreadable.

He prowled closer, his strides slow. Taunting? Or being cautious? Did he know who was inside? Was he trying to trick us into entering or scare us into running?

I tightened my grip on the knife and took another step back, pulling Jeremy with me.

"Could be the beast that created us all," the hybrid said, shifting his gaze to the door and stopping a few yards away.

A tremor skated down my spine. The Drone was dead, and there was no such thing as a devil or a beast or whatever he was implying. He was fucking with us. If we fled, he and the others would catch us. If we made it inside and barred the door, we might survive.

"We're going in," I said under my breath, second-guessing my decision immediately.

It was freezing cold outside. No way was the door left open by accident.

Jeremy stiffened beside me. "Okay."

We turned as one, ran up the short flight of stairs, across the porch, and through the door. As I slammed it shut, I glimpsed the hybrid in the clearing. He hadn't moved.

My legs felt weak as I bolted the door. Four bolts, made of heavy metal and seemingly impenetrable. As I engaged each one, the cylinders echoed loudly, ramping up my pulse. If the residents didn't know they had intruders, they certainly knew now.

Turning, I found a large sitting area, a grand staircase, another sitting room through the doorway on the right, and three corridors that led deeper into the house. Strategically placed candles on the walls and tables illuminated the rooms in a soft glow.

Jeremy held the blade out in front of him in a white-knuckled grip. "Where are they?"

"Maybe it's just one person. Someone more afraid of us than we are of him."

Then why were the hairs on my neck standing on end?

A hint of staleness clung to the air. Thick layers of dust and cobwebs covered the furniture, wood floors, and unlit light fixtures. And the silence…sweet hell, it was eerily quiet. So quiet the absence of sound rang in my ears.

"Hello?" My voice resounded off the crusty, cracked wallpaper.

The answering silence shivered my skin. I hadn't even taken a step from the front door, and I wanted to turn around and run out.

"What's your gut telling you right now?" I flexed my grip on the knife.

"That it's safer in here. And warmer."

It was definitely warmer. There must've been a fire burning

somewhere. Or maybe it was the lack of gusty wind. Ironically, I was trembling harder in here than outside.

"Okay." I swallowed past a knot of fear. "I'm going to go look—"

Something shifted in my periphery. Something low to the floor in the sitting room on the right. My mouth went dry.

"Did you see that?" I nodded at the wide doorway.

"No." Jeremy's voice wavered. "What was it?"

The floor creaked, the disturbance coming from around the corner in that second room. A chill tiptoed over my shoulders. I didn't move, didn't blink, as I waited for another sound, questioning whether I'd imagined the first one.

Minutes passed. The silence persisted for an eternity. The kind of terrifying silence that locked up the joints and stopped the heart.

"Stay here where I can see you. I'm going to peek around the corner." I adjusted my fingers around the knife and crept toward the sitting room.

Sweat gathered between my breasts, and my heart thundered louder than my footsteps. I rounded the corner, and a quick scan of every nook and shadow confirmed no one was there.

The room held all the same lavish furnishings. Ornate chairs and lamps and fancy impractical things. The couch alone looked like no one had sat on it in years. Blankets of dust covered the floors, tables, and seats. No fingerprints, footprints, or buttprints. Nothing had been disturbed.

"I think I saw something." Jeremy stepped forward, eyes glued straight ahead and blade held up, shaking in his hand.

His next step shifted him out of my field of view, blocked by the wall between the rooms.

"We need to stay together." My nerves rioted, sparking tingles beneath my skin. "Come ba—"

A shadow slithered across the floor by the front door. What the fuck?

I stepped toward it, turned the corner, and met Jeremy's stark eyes across the room. "What's wrong?"

"I think—"

Something lunged from the floor in the shadowed hallway, swept his legs out from under him, and knocked him flat on his back.

He screamed in agony, and his blade skittered under the couch. I bolted toward him, lungs heaving and boots slipping on clumps of snow. I couldn't make out what attacked him, couldn't stop it from dragging him down the corridor on his back like a rag doll.

He twisted onto his stomach and scraped his fingers over the floor, his eyes locked on mine, silently begging. My stomach clamped. Nausea rose. I propelled forward, stumbling, reaching, separated by the length of the hall as he was ripped into another room. Legs first. Then his chest. The last thing I saw was his horrified expression before blood sprayed from the doorway. His severed head rolled into the corridor.

"Noooo!" My hand flew to my throat, my entire body frozen in shock and unholy terror.

For an eternal heartbeat, I stared at the head, shaking all over and gasping for air. *This can't be happening. This can't be happening.*

I turned and ran, frantically searching the floor for movement while slashing the blade around me.

Two steps from the door, a sting burned through my neck. I pawed at the hurt, and my fingers brushed…something…*shouldn't be there. Why do I feel funny?*

Sudden dizziness sent me stumbling backward. A heavy weight invaded my limbs, and black spots flickered across my vision. My knees wobbled as I yanked the sharp object from my neck and held it close to my eyes, squinting through the blurriness.

A dart.

My face turned ice-cold. The floor rose up, and everything went black.

THREE

I woke in a fog of disorientation, my muscles so sluggish I couldn't move despite the panic gripping my body. Lying on my side with my cheek against a soft surface, I fell back on my training. Eyes closed, breaths even, I feigned sleep and gathered my bearings.

Silence spread over me like a corpse, chilling in its stillness. Or maybe it was the air. The subterranean temperature pressed against my exposed face and arms, the rest of my body swaddled in furs. I'd been unconscious long enough to generate a cocoon of body heat, but it didn't stop my insides from trembling.

My hands lay motionless in front of me, one on the bedding, the other curled against the cold hard floor. A damp earthy scent tickled my nose, conjuring images of underground caverns, deeply-dug graves, and dark enclosed places.

My pulse roared as I fought to keep my eyelids closed and relaxed. Was I still in the mansion? A basement? My cloak, tunic, and boots had been removed. Suede still bound my breasts. The medallion I never removed hung against my sternum, the chain secure around my neck. But I couldn't tell if the soft hides against my lower half were my leggings or whatever had been wrapped around me.

I couldn't feel the weight of my mother's dagger or the familiar wood of my bow. Holding my breath, I listened again. Nothing. Who or what was I up against? I'd been drugged, my fathers didn't know how to find me, and Jeremy was dead.

Jeremy. Fucking hell, I couldn't block out the image of his severed head.

Since implementing the Resistance at age fifteen, I'd lost numerous soldiers, too many friends to count. But Jeremy's death was still too fresh, too raw, every vivid detail violent and crippling. The shifting shadows, the speed and viciousness of the strike, his terrified eyes—all reminders that I was on my own, unarmed, and at the mercy of the mysterious thing that had butchered him.

I swallowed back a helpless sob, my jaw locked in grief and loss and utter fear.

Stop it!

My head was still attached to my body. I was still alive. I could still escape the nightmare I'd ignorantly walked into.

Once I was certain I'd regained some strength, I drew a fortifying breath and cracked open an eye. A hazy glow drew my gaze to an electric bulb in the rafters. Where the hell was I? I'd seen electric lights before, but only in well-established settlements like Arkendale and Hoover Dam.

I blinked to clear my vision, and a bare foot came into view. A man's leg stretched along the concrete floor within arm's reach, covered in black cotton pants. He sat with his back to the opposite wall, the other knee bent, eyes closed. My heart stuttered.

Ropes of muscle defined his arms, his pale chest cut with deep indentions of brawn. His torso was hairless, scarless, his skin tight and smooth. Almost too smooth, like polished marble. Too perfect. *Hybrid?*

I jerked my attention to his mouth, to the full lips that neither smiled nor scowled. Was he asleep? Hiding fangs? Waiting for me to wake? None of that made sense. If he was human, he wouldn't have closed his eyes and let his guard down with a stranger. Maybe he knew who I was? If he was a hybrid, he would've fucked me or killed me while I was unconscious.

Without moving or breathing, I allowed myself another

second to absorb the beautiful bone structure of his face and the sweep of black hair across his brow. Strong nose, masculine jaw, not a hint of stubble. He was devastatingly gorgeous.

An inexplicable desire to see his eyes fluttered in my chest, the feeling both unnerving and strangely exciting.

Was he the one who shot the dart in my neck?

Yanking my gaze away, I scanned the room for a weapon and an exit. Four concrete walls, wood rafters embedded in concrete overhead, and two doors made up the confined space. One doorway was doorless, revealing a bathroom just large enough to hold the toilet and place to stand beneath the shower head.

The other door was a solid steel barrier. No cracks to let light in, no hinges, no locks or knobs.

No way out. My heart slammed out of control.

With soundless movements, I sifted a hand through the furs, knowing full well I wouldn't find anything useful. I'd been stripped of weapons. But other than the dull throb in my thigh, I didn't sense any new injuries.

I glanced back at the man, and my breath caught.

Eyes, the color of a lightning storm, glowed with iridescent streaks of silver and ice. They were impossibly clear, faceted like diamonds, and ringed with lethal confidence. My throat went dry.

As he stared at me, nothing moved. Not his chest to allow respiration. Not his lashes to enable blinking. I might've thought he was dead, except his crystal gaze was very much alive. It invaded my skin and fucked with my breathing. No, it didn't just invade. It attacked. In that deadlock of eye contact, I questioned my fate, my purpose, and everything I thought I knew about myself and the world.

I was captivated, offended by my own stupefaction, and terrified down to my basest instincts. I simply lay there, irrationally paralyzed as he consumed me with a single look. This man, a stranger, might've been an enemy, if he was even a man at all. Yet my instinct to kill wasn't triggered.

At gut level, I knew he wasn't a hybrid. But he wasn't human either.

"Show me your teeth." Sweat broke out on my forehead.

He studied me with those monochromatic eyes that were neither white nor gray. When he finally blinked, they flickered through every shade of electricity. "Show me yours."

The guttural resonance of his voice pulsed through me, an endless echo that compelled my lips to pull back from my straight human teeth. Hybrids couldn't retract their fangs, so now that he knew I was human, what would he do about it?

He inclined his head, not a hint of surprise in his ethereal expression. He looked at me as if he didn't just know who I was but knew my very soul and intended to shred it on a level I didn't even know existed.

"Your turn." I lifted on an elbow.

The twitch at the corner of his mouth twisted and taunted before stretching into a smile that separated with intimidation. A smile that revealed bright white teeth and the irrefutable twin points of elongated canines.

My pulse detonated as I shoved off the furs and leapt into a crouch, balancing my weight on my uninjured leg. Surrounded by concrete walls without a weapon, I had no way of defending myself, no way to escape.

Was he the captor or a captive like me? Did it matter at this point? *He has fangs!*

With my fingers curled in the bedding beneath my feet, I braced for a fight to the death.

He rubbed a palm along the thigh of his outstretched leg, his other arm draped over his bent knee. I should've expected his control. He hadn't bitten me while I slept, hadn't shown any interest in closing the distance between us.

"What are you?" My back bumped the wall as I poised on the balls of my feet.

"I'm the same as you."

He wasn't human, not with those freaky translucent eyes and the all-knowing way he watched me.

"We're not—"

"We're both fighters." His gaze traveled over the band of suede across my breasts, down my bare arms, and lingered on the chewed-up hole in my leggings.

I didn't have to look to know the leather strip I'd tied around my wound had been replaced with a dry cotton bandage. Who had tended my injury? Him? Someone else?

"We both bleed." He drummed his fingers on his leg. "We both dream and fear and fuck."

Heat tinged my cheeks. "Are you a hybrid?"

"Are your fathers hybrids?"

If he knew who I was, he'd know my fathers had fangs. But they were human, immune to the infection because they'd consumed my mother's blood.

I squinted at him. "Are you human?"

He made a sudden jerking motion that sent me lunging toward the door. I slammed my shoulder against the steel and swept my hands along the edge where a handle should've been.

"We can't get out." Sitting in the same place, he licked a fang and huffed a laugh. "Do you always spook so easily around humans?"

"You're not human." I pressed my back against the door. "Who brought me in here?"

"How red is the hair on your cunt?" He flashed a razored grin. "As red as your face?"

The fire in my cheeks spread to my neck. "Who drugged me?"

He shrugged and rested his head against the wall with a sparkle of amusement in his eyes.

"Are we in the basement of the mansion?" I glanced at the rafters. "Who lives here? What do they want?"

"I have questions, too, but while I watched you sleep, I seem to have forgotten all train of thought but one." His gaze burned white-hot. "Has the prophesied daughter ever been fucked?"

I clamped my jaw shut and balled my hands.

"Yes or no." He tipped his head. "Has the notorious Dawn

of Eve ever been impaled by a cock?"

My nostrils flared as anger seared through my chest.

"Oh, now don't give me that look. The entire world is dying to know the status of your hymen."

Who the fuck was this guy? No one would ever say that to me. No one would dare. I'd created the Resistance, rallied thousands of soldiers, took out all the breeding facilities in America, and just decimated the last nest in Canada. Hybrids fought me, but they did so with fear. Because they knew that someday I would win back mankind's freedom.

Freedom to come out of hiding. To walk down the street without weapons. To rebuild cities and create music and art and follow dreams. Someday, humans would return to the life our ancestors enjoyed.

But first, I needed to escape this room.

"How did you end up in here?" I straightened, arms at my sides and muscles burning to strike.

"A dart in my neck."

I searched his translucent eyes for the truth and felt a gravitational pull to keep looking, an insane urge to fall deeper, to sink further into the brilliant shards of light.

With great effort, I refocused on his shoulder, breaking the trance. "Were you one of the hybrids that chased me here?"

Confusion creased his beautiful face. Such a human expression.

"How long have you been here?" I kept my gaze on his shoulder.

"A day. Maybe two."

Not the answer I expected. I didn't trust him. "What's your name?"

"Salem."

I'd never heard of him, not that I'd expected to. "Your full name."

He shook his head.

Why wouldn't he tell me? Did he not know?

Surnames were no longer relevant. Since men outnumbered women five to one, most of us had one mother and multiple fathers. So we took our mothers' first names. Eddie of Shea, Dawn of Eve…

"Salem of…?" I raised a brow.

Refusal twisted his lips into a smirk, the fucker.

"Were you born with fangs?" I kept my voice steady, despite the uneasiness tingling my skin. "Or were you bitten?"

"Born this way, sweetheart." His gaze made a leisurely descent to my mouth, and his fangs indented his lower lip. "If you come closer, I'll let you touch them."

No fucking way. I furrowed my brow. If he entered the world with those teeth, then his mother had been bitten while pregnant. The venom would've altered his mind while he was in utero, and he would've been born a hybrid, mindless in hunger. By puberty, he would've become a raping, killing man-eater on a mission to wipe out humanity.

Yet he hadn't made a single attempt to spread my legs and chew on an artery. What the fuck was he?

Provoking a creature I shared a cage with wasn't the smartest strategy, but I needed answers. "Are you defective?"

"Are *you*? You're supposed to be mankind's savior. Yet here you are, trapped with a man who can snuff out your existence in the span of a heartbeat."

If that was a threat, why hadn't he already killed me? I didn't believe a word he said, but if he'd truly been born with fangs, I could deduce his age and possibly his bloodline.

Twenty-two years ago, an airborne virus mutated the human race. The aphids were the first wave.

If he'd been alive when the virus first hit, he wouldn't be alive now. No one under the age of twenty survived, and every woman mutated into a nymph. Except my mother. Through some genetic anomaly, she evolved into something unexplainable and unique—a human ladybird, the aphid's predator, the Mother of the Living. Most referred to her as a goddess.

Two years after the apocalypse, she'd cured every living woman. When she became pregnant with me, she obliterated the aphids. That might've given mankind a fighting chance to repopulate, except the Drone had already created a new species. The spiders were the second wave.

Women didn't start giving birth in the new world until nineteen years ago. Very few gave birth to human children. The hybrids were the third wave.

Like those I rescued from the breeding facilities, every woman over the age of twenty-two had been cured and therefore, carried my mother's healing blood. But their offspring did not. Human women were captured by hybrids and used to breed more hybrids. For nineteen brutal years, hybrids dominated the planet.

"You're nineteen." I stared at the man with spider-like fangs.

"I'm twenty. Five months older than you."

Icy coldness hit my core. I wasn't shocked he knew my age. The day of my birth had been a monumental moment in new world history. It was the day of Eve's death. The day the prophecy was fulfilled. What chilled me to the bone was *his* age. I wasn't the first child born in the new world, but those who came before me were only a month older.

Arkendale was home to the first flood of women my mother had cured. They were the first to establish a human settlement and the first to become pregnant, making Arkendale a turning point for the human race. One month after those unprecedented pregnancies, my mother became pregnant with me.

"You're lying." I narrowed my eyes. "Even if you were born in Arkendale—"

"I've never been to Arkendale." His gaze traced my rigid stance and flicked back to my face. "You need to loosen up." He patted the floor beside him. "Sit down. I won't bite, Dawn of Eve."

"We've already established you know my full name." Tension knotted my shoulders. "Seems only fair that I know yours."

"All right." He leaned forward, elbows braced on his knees, and pinned me with his stormy eyes. "Salem of Elaine."

My breath hitched. "Elaine? No, that's…not…"

A storm of denial and rage swelled inside me. *Elaine's child would easily be five months older than me.*

But it was too coincidental for Elaine's missing child to show up here, in this room, in fucking Canada of all places.

"Ah, so Michio told you?" A sick kind of pleasure lifted his cheeks. "Then you know about his relationship with my mother."

"Relationship?" Beneath the calmness of my voice, I boiled with ferocious protectiveness of my father. "Elaine raped him. Repeatedly."

"Ain't that a bitch?"

Bang bang bang went my heart, that wretched sound. "My mother found Elaine in the mountains months before Arkendale. She cured Elaine. Protected her. And Jesse, my—"

"Your biological father."

"Yes. Jesse's friends took care of Elaine."

"They fucked her, you mean." His lack of emotion sent a chill across my skin. "She said I look like Tallis, your father's Australian friend. I wouldn't know because Tallis died before I was born. Because the Great Eve failed to save him."

I knew the story, every gruesome detail. "My mother tried to save him. She *did* save Elaine. And you know how Elaine returned the favor? She teamed up with the Drone and turned against my entire family!"

He shrugged a shoulder.

Fuck him. I could still feel the pain in Michio's voice when he told me how his body had been controlled by the Drone, how he couldn't lift a finger to rescue my mother, couldn't protect himself from Elaine.

I glared at that vile bitch's son. "Michio was locked in a room, mentally aware but unable to command his muscles, while your pregnant mother violated him over and over. *For months.*" Feral hatred simmered my blood and growled through my voice. "Where is she?"

No one knew what happened to Elaine or her unborn child. Other than my mother, Elaine was the only woman

Michio had ever bitten—a bite that had been against *his* will. It was unknown what the effects would be on her unborn child.

Salem sure as fuck didn't look human. It wasn't the fangs so much as those unnatural eyes, the way they diffused the passage of light, deflecting logic and hypnotizing to the point of confusion. Distorted, blinding, hot-flashy kind of confusion.

Was hot-flashy right? I didn't know, but holy shit, I felt things—powerful, irresistible impulses throbbing frantically between my legs. I didn't just want to touch his fangs. I wanted to taste them. The consuming ache in my pussy begged me to crawl onto his lap and grind against the hard length outlined by his pants. The sparks in his eyes emblazoned the world in licking, biting, thrusting lust. Nothing mattered but the need to make him my first, my last, and my everything in between.

It's a trick. It's a trick. Snap out of it.

I sank my teeth into my lip until the taste of blood coated my tongue. Until my vision cleared and my body cooled. "You're bewitching me."

"I'm not, but I gotta say… Virginity has never smelled so desperate." His timbre vibrated through my womb. "So fucking exquisite. Before we get out of here, I'll have you writhing on my cock, clenching around me, and begging until your voice is gone."

"Um, yeah…good luck with that." I blinked hard and pointed my glare on his bare feet. "Where the fuck is your mother?"

The air shifted, and in the next breath, he was on me. Trapped between the wall and the large muscles of his chest, I couldn't pry my wrists from the shackle of his hand at my back, couldn't turn my head away from the grip of his fingers on my jaw.

"My mother is dead." His heart thumped against mine, his erection jabbed against my thigh, and his fangs teased the delicate skin on my neck.

"H-how?" I dug my fingernails into flesh, ripping at the muscled terrain of his forearm.

He pressed his teeth against my jugular. "I tore out her throat."

FOUR

"*Why* did you tear out your mother's throat?" I drew in a jagged breath, pinned between the wall and the hard length of Salem's body. "Was it a hunger thing or a she's-a-vile-bitch thing?"

"Does it matter?" He pinched my neck between his teeth, biting hard enough to spark pain without breaking skin.

"Yeah, it really does, seeing how your fangs are digging— For fuck's sake, are you licking me?" I stiffened beneath the wet heat of his tongue, bracing for an impending puncture. "For the record, I'm not a vile bitch."

He hummed, a deep pulsating rattle against my throat.

"Stop licking me." My voice was strong, unwavering, despite the sinking dread in my stomach.

Not only had I been captured by an unknown monster, I was confined in a room with a bloodsucker. Every nerve in my body demanded I shove, kick, and inflict unholy hell. But if I moved, my jugular would not fare well.

"Let's just…think this through for a second." I swallowed against his aggressive nips. "Maybe our captor locked us together so we'd kill each other." I twisted my wrists at my back, causing the shackle of his hand to clench tighter. "We should work together, find a way out."

"Maybe our captor's a voyeur and wants to watch me fuck you." He sucked on the tendon straining in my throat. "We should have sex first *then* find a way out."

"I'm serious." I bucked my hips, panic surging as I inadvertently bumped the swollen length between his legs.

"Get off me!"

He tightened his grip on my hands and jaw, his breaths quickening, growing deep and urgent. The sound of hunger.

"Do you always play with your food?" I quivered beneath the stinging scrape of his fangs.

"Only when she smells like desperation."

"I'm not—" Something flickered in the corner of my eye.

Wavy lines illuminated in his throat. What the fuck? I stared harder, certain I was seeing his veins. They were…*glowing.* Pulsing. Shimmering like tributaries in the moonlight.

A dull throb lit at the base of my skull. Was I hallucinating? I tried to angle my head for a better look, but the hand on my jaw prevented me from moving.

The longer I strained my field of view, the sharper my eyesight became. Arteries spiderwebbed through his neck, bulging red and blue beneath porcelain skin. I tracked the pump of blood through each bend and branch, spellbound by the ferocity in which it flowed. Was he doing this on purpose? Somehow altering his physiology to scare me?

My vision zoomed in. I didn't know how, but the network of capillaries magnified until all I could see was a matrix of swirling blood cells. And something else. Something that didn't belong.

Silver particles glimmered in his veins. The cellular flecks floated together, wriggling and *alive*, forming wormlike structures that grew brighter, denser, as they sped through the vessels toward his chest. I should've been horrified by the microscopic sight, but instead my mouth watered, and a rapacious urge came over me. I wanted to put my teeth on his throat, sink into an artery, and extract every venomous ribbon.

What?

"Salem." My voice cracked. "There's something in your throat."

He stilled. "What did you say?"

"Something really fucking weird is slithering in your

veins."

He jerked, moving his neck into my direct line of sight. When my eyes refocused, I couldn't see arteries or silver worms or anything abnormal. Had I imagined it?

No way. I was *not* seeing things. "How did you make your skin transparent?"

Releasing my wrists, he gripped his throat, mouth parted, forehead scrunched, *distracted.*

I dropped to the floor and swept out a leg to knock him off balance. He stumbled, eyes wide, and I pounced.

Years on a battlefield had given me deadly strong fingers and hands. As I wrestled him to the floor, my unbending grip stayed close to his joints—wrists, shoulders, pelvis—but fuck me, he was slippery. Every time I maneuvered him into submission, he twisted free, slamming me against the concrete and shoving me against the wall.

Shit, okay, I was weaker, definitely slower, but I made him work for it, deflecting bites and landing blows. My reflexes kicked in, every muscle firing the way my fathers had trained me. I timed my punches, moved my body like water, and linked my state of mind to my breaths.

Using Salem's center of gravity against him, I redirected most of his strikes as we rolled through the room in a tangle of arms and legs. The heave of our grunts echoed off the walls, our fists smacking flesh and knees digging into muscle.

Pain exploded in my thigh, followed by a warm gush from my wound. I bit down on my cheek, tasted metal, and swung toward his face.

He dodged, slipped past my guard, and flipped me on my back. He wasn't even winded as he pinned my arms above my head and leaned in. "What did you see in my neck?"

I gulped for air, searching for arteries that were no longer visible. "Your veins? Your blood? I don't know! You tell me."

"My veins?" He winged up a black eyebrow and used the weight of his body to flatten me to the floor.

The concrete chilled my sweaty back, but the heat pouring

off him was burning me up. "Get off me, you heavy bastard."

Twisting beneath him, I tried to free my arms from the clench of his fingers. But my struggling was a wasted effort, one that felt a whole lot like foreplay. Every lift and roll of my hips rubbed our lower bodies in a dirty dance. With only a thin swath of suede between our chests, my damp skin slid intimately against his, making this the most body fluid I'd ever shared with another person. *Or animal.*

It should've repulsed me. Should've convinced me to stop squirming. But holy merciful Mother, my blood fevered and my pleasure centers went berserk. The smothering weight of his rock-hard torso, the twitch of his erection against my pussy, the taunting smile all over his breathtaking face made my libido purr and my heart roar.

I needed to exorcise this shit before I did something stupid like devour his mouth, because seriously, his lips—all pink and pillowy—looked good enough to eat.

Forcing my body to relax, I reined in my runaway pulse and steadied my voice. "What do you want?"

He dipped his head, bringing the intensity of his faceted eyes closer, closer, the view so damn sparkly and fathomless, so enthralling and... *wrong.* I forced my gaze to his pale shoulder.

"Has your cunt ever been this close to surrender?" He ground his cock against me.

"This isn't surrender, baby." I squeezed my legs together, trapping his muscled thigh, and grimaced at the sting in my injury. "It's resistance."

"Ah, yes. Dawn of Eve, leader of the Resistance." His eyes bathed my face in blinding heat. "You've been resisting your entire life. Waiting. For me."

"Wow." I let out a strained laugh. "Since you have me all figured out, you can return to your side of the room now."

A devilish grin took hold of his mouth. "No resistance is impenetrable, sweetheart."

I pressed my lips together, certain he wasn't talking about my army. Why wasn't I more pissed off? He was disrespecting me, violating me, fucking restraining me. I wasn't this woman, this confused creature who lay beneath a man while warring with the desire to taste his filthy mouth.

He squeezed my wrists, holding them with superhuman strength against the cold floor above my head. "Tell me why you're a virgin."

No sense in denying what he'd already figured out. But should I answer him? Only my fathers asked about my virginity. They questioned me as a doctor, a priest, and an overprotective dad, always in the interest of guarding their daughter's emotional and physical health.

I settled on the truth. "Been a little busy. Fighting. Protecting innocents. Killing bloodsuckers. No time for—"

"Breeding?"

"Yeah. *That.*" I glared at him, wrestled against the pull of his magnetic eyes, and quickly turned my head. "Is that what *you* do? Breed human women?"

I stared at the cracks in the wall and let my focus drift to the fringe of my vision, trying to recreate the indirect view I'd had of his throat. Sinews strung tight in his neck, his skin an opaque sheath of white. No glowing veins. No wriggling silver organisms.

"I'm not a hybrid." His chiseled jaw tightened in my periphery.

"Then what are you?"

"I could ask you the same question." His thigh flexed between my legs. "Look at me."

"Hell no."

"Are you scared, my little fighter?"

"Don't confuse my distrust with fear." I pulled in a breath and released it slowly. "I'll make a deal with you. Explain the hocus-pocus bullshit you're doing with your eyes and see-through skin, and I'll look at you as long as you want…until we get out of here."

The scent of leather and pine wafted from his skin as he pressed impossibly closer. "It's not me."

"What's not you? Are you telling me you're not

controlling your own body?"

"I'm telling you I'm not tricking you with my eyes, my blood…or whatever it is you're seeing."

Did I believe him? I shouldn't, but something in his voice made me consider alternatives. "We were drugged. Maybe it did something to our—"

"It's you."

"What?"

"*Your* golden eyes are seducing *me*." He cocked his head. "*You* are the one seeing things in my veins."

I immediately rejected the accusation, every part of me coiling in defense. But a niggle of doubt worked its way in. Wasn't this what my fathers and I had been searching for? An idiosyncrasy that defied science? A quirk in my genetic makeup?

"Okay, let's say you're right—which you're not." With a steeling breath, I bore my gaze into his. "What do you see?"

"Yellow leaves in autumn." His breath whispered across my lips. "Blooms in a sunflower field. Wings of a swallowtail. The golden—"

"That's not what I—"

"Shut up." His pupils widened, swallowing the metallic shards of his irises. "The golden sky at dawn. Enchantment. Beauty. In its rawest, purest, most dangerous form."

Seductive warmth electrified my core. Evidently, I was a sucker for pretty words. "But what do you *feel* when you look at my eyes?"

"You already know."

The inch of space between us charged with ionized air, crackling static across my skin. How could this be *my* doing when everything I felt was a response to him? The press of his thigh between my legs made me tremble. The heat of his breaths caused my ribs to expand. His cock, stiff and pulsing against my pussy, produced a throb that was so sharp and greedy I wondered if I'd torn an inner muscle.

I let my gaze wander over his masculine jaw, razored teeth, straight nose, and complexion that was as pristine as fine china. Inky black hair lay in sexy finger-raked clumps, neither too long nor too short. When did he find time for a haircut? Now that I thought of it, there wasn't a hint of stubble on his face. It made him look boyish and innocent. Until I looked at his eyes.

Raw sexuality emanated from the depths. Dark. Voracious. Bold. I imagined his fingers pulling my hair. Our bodies naked. Grinding. The smacking sounds of pounding flesh. The walls of my pussy stretching around him. Teeth in my neck.

I blinked, blew out a breath, and blinked again, but the erotic sensations lingered, demanding and insatiable. Why had I even let my mind go there? With *him*? Was this what he felt when he stared at my eyes? If so, why hadn't he tried to fuck me? I didn't believe for a second he was protecting me from himself.

If he thought my blood was poisonous, he was probably protecting himself from *me*.

"Do you bite during sex?" I pressed my shoulders against the concrete, aware my nipples were trying to cut through the band of suede across my breasts.

He smirked. "If you want my cock, all you have to do is beg."

"I want you to give me some breathing room so I can figure this out."

His gaze drifted to our hands above my head and returned to my face. "Don't move."

At my nod, he released my wrists. His fingers tiptoed down my arms and rested on my cheeks.

"I've heard rumors." He searched my face, his expression contemplative. "When your fathers bite, it's sexual, for them and whoever they're feeding from?"

"They only bite each other."

"So it's true?"

"Yeah." I pulled my arms down and stretched them along on the floor at my sides. "They keep their fangs to themselves. The outcome is too intimate."

I'd wandered into their bedroom too many times as a child and found them entwined, nude, always with their fangs buried. As far as I knew, they'd never brought a woman into their bed, not once since my mother. They were nothing if not stubbornly faithful to her and one another.

"When hybrids bite," Salem said, "they don't experience arousal."

True, because the venom altered that part of their brains, separating bloodlust from sexual lust.

"But they still feel something," I said, "because they're driven to breed. To *rape*." My muscles hardened, instincts engaging. "What about you? If it looks like a hybrid, walks like a hybrid, bites like a hybrid…"

"I might be like your fathers." He lifted, just an inch, and a chill seeped between our bodies. "I've never forced a woman. I've also never encountered one who tried to entrance me with her eyes."

"I'm not."

"Nor am I entrancing you."

We regarded each other, breaths colliding in a heady cloud of suspicion and desire. There were so many things going on in his gaze, his pupils flickering at the center of ductile silver disks that seemed to flex with the light. And deeper, beneath the reflective metal of his eyes, loomed a blizzard of emotion.

He was as powerless as I was to ignore the intoxicating energy enveloping us. It overtook my senses, coaxed my hands to his sculpted pectorals, and lifted my mouth, my lips hovering a hair's breadth from his.

"You're not a hybrid." I'd never wanted to be this close, this intimate, with anything that had fangs.

"I'm a deviation." A frown creased his brow. "Like you."

"But this attraction…" I shook my head, tried to clear it. "It has to be the dart. Whatever we were injected with is fucking with our senses."

He slid his hand down my throat, a slight tremor in his fingers. "Or this is something else entirely."

Something organic? Some kind of incorporeal force coming

from within us, from whatever made us different? It made me nervous, cagey. I needed space.

I pushed against his chest. "I don't trust you."

He nodded, but the flash in his eyes said he'd just accepted a challenge.

"What happens to the humans you bite?" I asked. "Do they grow fangs?"

"Never." His eyes hardened. "When I bite you, you'll orgasm harder than you ever have, but you won't grow fangs."

"We need to find a way out of here." I glanced at the steel door, the only thing that should've been holding my attention in this spartan room.

His nostrils flared. "You're bleeding."

My leg?

I didn't have a word for how quickly he moved. One second he was in my face and the next he was on my thigh, the bandage ripped away, and his mouth sealed to my injury.

"Please, don't bite me." My breath rushed out, my entire body frozen beneath him.

His eyes lifted to mine, shining like vivid bits of colored glass as he swept his tongue around my wound. My mind revolted at the sight of him licking me, but my body gravitated closer, into the storm of his gaze, pressing against his blood-stained lips.

"The human mouth is dirtier than a latrine." I gripped his hair, a pointless attempt to pull him away.

He smiled against my flesh. "So I'm human now?"

"No, I…I don't know."

A deep groan rumbled in his chest, and he tore at the hole in my pants until my leg was bare from the thigh down. The feel of his body against my skin produced a sharp ache below my waist. My heart thundered, and my fingernails bit into my palms. I wanted him closer, so close that I'd feel more than just the warmth of his mouth.

His complexion seemed to darken with each passing second, his eyes flashing through a kaleidoscope of colors. Was my blood doing this to him? How long had it been since he'd fed? He wasn't sucking, simply cleaning my injury. Why did that disappoint me? Why did I want so badly to feel him drawing on my veins?

A loud electric buzz startled me out of my trance, followed by the vibration of metal. The steel door slid slowly sideways as if hung on a track controlled by mechanical gears. My muscles tensed.

Salem sat back on his heels, gaze on the door and expression unreadable. He wiped an arm across his lips. "Stay back."

But I was already moving, scrambling to my feet, hell bent on fighting my way out of this room.

The steel barrier inched away, revealing more steel behind it. *Bars.* A gate? *Fuck!*

Torchlights danced along a stonewall that butted against another wall on the left. We were at the end of a corridor that tunneled to the right and out of view. Did it lead to the surface? Deeper into the bowels of this nightmare?

I slammed into the gate, gripped the rungs, and shook it with all my might.

"Dawn, get back." Salem grabbed my arm, the urgency in his voice spiking the hairs on my nape.

I let him pull me away just as a swirl of shadows crept across the floor on the other side. *Multiple* shadows. And the sounds… Nails scraping concrete. Low throaty snarls. Clanging chains.

"What is that?" I whispered, backing up until I bumped into Salem's chest.

"Dinner."

His arms wrapped around my waist, holding me to him as something came into view in the hall. Hands. Then three tiny bodies. Sweet fucking hell, they were toddlers, no older than two or three, crawling along the floor in ragged, dirty clothes. Pale skin, bright eyes, sweet faces.

Salem would have to step over my dead body if he intended to feed from them.

Everything went still—their tiny fingers freezing on the floor, their eyes unblinking, the rattle of chains around their necks falling silent. My stomach hardened, and Salem turned to stone against my back.

Something was wrong, so very very wrong. It wasn't just the abhorrent age of the children or the chain leashes hooked to metal collars around their necks. It was the way they peered through the vertical bars of the gate, drooling from fanged mouths and staring up at me like *I* was dinner.

FIVE

"Salem…" I whispered beneath my breath, but it came out too loud, prompting a chorus of growls from the hybrid children.

My shoulders bunched, and my nerves fried with agonizing dread. Any second that gate would open, and I would have to use my hands to break their tiny bodies. Unless they broke me first.

Salem shoved me behind him, pressing my back against the farthest wall. "Don't move."

I opened my mouth to agree and slammed it shut at the sight of his throat. Holy shit, his veins… The labyrinth of vessels fanned down his neck, his chest, reaching toward his heart. With each breath he took, the vascular bundles gleamed brighter, clearer, in a striation of red and silver.

"Look down." I pointed a shaky finger as adrenaline surged through my own blood. "You see it, right? Your veins are glowing through your skin."

He stared at his torso, brushed a hand across his pecs, and the silver things fluttered through his blood. He shook his head, brows pulling together.

Could I see something he couldn't? Was I losing my mind?

Behind him, the hybrids attacked the gate, snapping monstrous teeth and stretching thin, pallid arms through the six-inch gap at the bottom.

Salem prowled toward them, shoulders squared, the muscles along his spine flexing. Luminous veins spread from beneath his sooty hair, stretching outward from the base of his skull and feathering down his back. But it was the transformation in his demeanor that alarmed me the most. He seemed to grow taller, harder, more aggressive. What the fuck was he doing?

He reached the gate, let out a cruel, feral snarl, and lunged. The babies cowered, their tiny human cries raising bumps across my skin. But their fear was fleeting. They slammed against the gate with renewed ferocity, climbing over one another and craning their necks to fix their rabid stares on me.

I tried to step back, but my heels hit the wall. I wanted to sink into the concrete and escape on the other side. I'd never killed a child—hybrid or otherwise. I would if I had to, but the thought made my stomach fold in on itself.

Salem crouched in front of the gate, not a twitch in his muscles as the hybrids hissed and spit inches from his face. "Close your eyes, Dawn."

Nope, not happening. For all I knew, he was one of them. At this point, I wasn't sure I should blink.

Without a backward glance, he reached through the rungs, snatched the chains connected to their collars, and gathered them in both hands. The leashes snapped taut, leading into the darkness, and Salem pulled on them, wrestling for slack against whoever held the ends. The metal links slid through his hands, but he held on, fighting with the unseen force.

The hybrids fell upon his arm, sinking their teeth into his flesh. I flinched, panicking. What was he trying to do? Pin the hybrids to the rungs? It wasn't a bad idea. If they were restrained, we might have a fighting chance when the gate opened. But they were biting him!

My muscles burned to go to him. I shouldn't, and I wouldn't if I had any common sense.

I must've gotten hit on the head when I was captured, because my legs started moving, sprinting across the room. I grabbed the leashes through the bars, barely dodging a fang.

Sliding my hands over his, I held tight, and together we wrenched the leashes through to our side. The creatures lunged for me, but Salem knocked them back, taking more bites to his arm. My fingers ached from clenching, and the rusty links tore at my palms as I tried to evade those lethal mouths.

Salem hissed at the hybrids, his arm shredded in bloody bites. They didn't back off. They couldn't, not with the tug-of-war on their tethers.

While I wrestled the chains, Salem reached farther through the rungs. Before I could question him, he wrapped huge hands around their heads and bashed them violently against the bars, over and over.

The sound of crushing bone simmered bile in my chest. My stomach twisted on the verge of emptying. Logically, I knew they were a threat that needed to be eliminated, but as their faces bled and buckled inward and their little bodies slumped, all I saw were children. *A dead child is a dead child.*

Except they weren't dead. The blunt impact had stunned them, but already their limbs were twitching, rising, reanimating with vicious intent.

Salem used that window of recovery to pound his fists into their skulls. One by one, he smashed brains and bits of bone into the concrete, each blow splattering more gore and cracking a fissure of anguish inside me.

Achy pressure invaded my jaw. I clenched it, tightened my fists on the chains, and hooked them around a rung for leverage against the opposing force at the other end. Now would've been a good time to close my eyes, but I couldn't look away from the horror and destruction exploding in front of me.

Salem slammed his fists hard and repeatedly with a savagery I would've never been able to inflict. I wanted to stop him. Stop the wet meaty thuds, the coppery scent of blood, the tiny faces collapsing into flattened pulp. It was more than my heart could handle. But there was no place for that kind of sensitivity. Not in this room. Not in this cruel world.

I pretended my eyes didn't itch and burn, pretended my throat wasn't swollen with heartache, and hung on to the chains until he decided they were dead.

He pulled his hands back through the gate and pried my numb fingers off the chains. The reins snapped out of reach, and the carnage jerked like gruesome marionettes on wires, the collars still attached to their necks.

I covered my mouth with my forearm and fought the urge to puke. The leashes scraped across the concrete, dragging away the remains and leaving behind a red slick trail. Tremors attacked my limbs as the scrape of chains faded down the corridor and fell silent.

"Who are you?" Salem shouted, gripping the rungs and rattling the gate. He threw his body into it and raised his voice. "What do you want?"

Footsteps approached, confident, unhurried. The tread of boots. Rubber soles.

My knees locked up, my entire body frozen as I stared at the corridor a few feet away. Salem was either stupidly brave or just plain stupid, because he pressed his cheek against the bars, trying to get a glimpse of whatever was coming.

"Can you see anything?" I whispered.

He shook his head without lifting his gaze from the hall.

The footfalls stopped just out of view, and something skidded across the blood-smeared floor. The corner of a brown object slipped under the gate.

I unlocked my joints and stepped to the side, peering around Salem's broad frame. A cardboard flat sat in the corridor, filled with hunks of meat, cooked rice, bottled water, and...*bandages?* I didn't realize how hungry I was until the aroma of fire-roasted fish teased the air. The smell also made my nausea a thousand times worse.

"Show yourself," Salem said, his voice low and dangerous. Fists wrapped around the rungs, he shoved against the gate. "Fucking coward!"

As the footsteps retreated, I stared at Salem's back, mesmerized by the dimming flicker of his veins. The smaller capillaries farthest from his core vanished first, and the fade-out swept inward until his skin was once again a blank canvas.

"Salem, your back." I squinted harder, questioning my

damn eyesight. "Your veins just disappeared."

Was it an illusion? Some kind of mutation connected to his emotions or to the vicinity of our captor? Maybe I'd been injected with a chemical that controlled my vision?

He glanced at his chest and returned his attention to the corridor. "I don't know what it means."

An electric buzz sounded overhead. With a grinding rattle, the door emerged from the frame, sliding out of the wall and forcing Salem to release his hold on the gate. Would it crush him if he hadn't moved?

"The food." I jerked forward.

He hooked a finger in the cardboard lip and yanked the tray into the room. Then he fought the door, shoving with contracted muscles. It didn't stop moving, didn't budge an inch. He jerked his fingers away just as the exit sealed shut.

The horror of the past few minutes hung in the air. Every breath tasted stagnant and disease-ridden, magnifying the dread curdling inside me. Salem took a step toward me, but whatever he saw in my expression made him stop just out of arm's reach.

For a breathless moment, we stared at each other, his gunmetal eyes searching mine. Trust wasn't the word I'd use to describe the sensation that pulled me toward him, but fuck me, he was the only potential ally I had in this nightmare.

"That was really fucked up." I stepped closer, scanning his flawless face for a hint of humanity.

Please don't let him be okay with what just happened.

"I told you to close your eyes." He stared down at his mangled arms, his gaze turning inward, unreadable.

I didn't expect tears of remorse and any obvious sign of emotion, but he seemed…dazed, unsettled. That was a whole lot better than indifference.

"Our captor is a hybrid," I said with ninety-nine percent conviction. "*Captors,* I'm guessing, since hybrids never work alone."

Were they watching us now? I glanced around the room, probing for cracks or holes in the walls and ceiling. Everything was sealed up. I wasn't even sure how we were getting air. There was no way we were being spied on.

"Hybrid? How can you be so sure?" He walked around me and entered the small bathroom. "Because humans don't keep hybrid children as pets?"

"Exactly. It's too dangerous." I stayed on his heels, itching with nervous energy. "Most human mothers kill their hybrid infants within days of birth. If they don't—"

"The child kills her." He pinned me with a lethal glare.

His mother had given birth to a fanged child. Whether it'd been circumstance or her own free will, she hadn't killed him. That outcome hadn't ended in her favor.

Fighting the compulsion to fall into his gemstone eyes, I refocused on his chewed-up forearms. Beneath the congealing blood, the bites appeared to be closing. Regenerating like a hybrid. *Like my fathers.*

Reaching around him, I cranked the shower handle on the wall. The pipes groaned and spit water from the shower head. I quickly rinsed the blood splatter off my hands, not surprised by the chill. Hot water from a tap required a level of engineering that was only found in organized settlements. I should've been resting in a place like that now, with Eddie and my fathers.

As I turned back to Salem, I spotted two stained pieces of cardboard and empty water bottles on the floor beneath the sink. Previous meals he'd been fed?

"How old were you when you killed your mother?" I asked.

"Twelve." Looming over me, he didn't move to rinse the blood.

"If you lasted twelve years without biting her, what happened? Did she do something to you?"

His jaw went rigid, his gaze cryptic. If the topic of his mother was off-limits, why had he mentioned her death earlier?

"Can you see my veins now?" He lifted his chin.

I took in the thick column of his neck, defined shoulders,

and wide chest. Standing at least eight inches taller than my five foot four frame, he was ruthlessly beautiful, every ripped inch of him commanding and seductive—the essence of pure alpha. The mystery behind what he was and what he was hiding only made him more captivating. I wanted to learn him, his body and his mind. I needed him on my side, this man who wielded such cold-blooded strength.

I had to tilt my head back to study his throat, straining to see the vascularity beneath thick ropes of muscle in his neck and torso. I concentrated, mentally flaying his perfect skin and imagining the circulation of his blood. No matter how hard I visualized it, I couldn't make it appear.

"You look normal," I said. If the definition of normal was imposing, terrifying beauty. "I *know* I saw something crawling through your blood, something silver and alive."

"Well, I can't see it, and your ability—if we can call it that—seems flaky." Skepticism flattened his tone. He raised a red-stained forearm and held it inches from my face. "Can you see silver things in the blood on my skin?"

The splatter looked like drying paint, drippy at the edges with clots around the fading punctures. Having spent a lifetime immersed in bloodshed, I shouldn't have had a reaction to it. So why was my stomach cramping? My pulse humming? Fuck, my teeth ached.

My teeth? I crashed my molars together, tried to override the strange pang with a deliberate one.

The dull throb persisted in my gums, pooling saliva in my mouth and making me crave things. Just a taste of his blood. A lick to quench this ungodly hunger.

"Dawn." He grabbed my hand—the one I'd unknowingly wrapped around his wrist—and wrenched it away. "For the fuck of Eve, snap out of it!"

"Do *not* use my mother's name like that." I pressed the heels of my hands against my pounding head and slowly the ache in my gums receded.

"What did you see?"

"Nothing." I lowered my hands and fixed my gaze on the

wall.

"That wasn't *nothing.*" He held his arms beneath the spray of water. "You were digging your nails in and licking your fucking lips."

My mind ran in circles. What the hell had possessed me to touch him? It was beyond disturbing that I didn't even realize I was doing it. I was certain I'd seen something in his veins earlier. Was it the sedative we'd been injected with? The Drone's venom? Didn't matter. I'd seen it twice and couldn't see it now.

"I'm beginning to question your street cred." He rubbed at a stubborn patch of blood on his arm. "How would the world react if they knew the fearless leader of the Resistance was mentally unstable?"

Fuck him. I didn't give a shit what he or anyone else thought of me.

Water swirled in shades of rust down the drain between our feet. When the last of the blood washed away, only the faint dots of healing skin remained on his arms, and even those were vanishing before my eyes.

He shut off the faucet and shook out his hands on his way out of the bathroom. I lingered in the doorway as he lowered to the floor and dug into the piles of food with his fingers. There were no utensils, nothing that could've been used as a weapon.

"That could be poisoned." I folded my arms across my chest and tried not to think about the brain matter stuck to the bottom of the cardboard.

"If our captor was going to poison us, he would've done it with the darts."

"Did you see him? Or are you just assuming he's male?"

He twisted the lid off an old, flimsy water bottle. "Just a guess."

I'd made the same assumption. Less than twenty percent of the human population was female. A grim percentage considering there were about a hundred hybrids for every human. Half of the hybrids were female, but female hybrids didn't leave their nests. Their sole purpose in life was to breed, breed, and breed again.

"You said you've been in this room a day or two." I stared at his arresting profile. "Who carried me in here?"

"The door opened, and a dart shot through the crack." He swallowed a gulp of water and nodded at the bedding. "You were there when I woke."

"Is this the first time you've been fed?"

"The third time. The food always arrives the same way on a tray like this about every ten hours or so, by my estimation."

"The hybrid children—?"

"They came the prior times but never attacked the gate like that. They wanted *you.*"

And Salem had killed them. To protect me?

My insides fluttered with that pull again, the demand to go to him so deep and confusing. I followed it out of curiosity, *not trust*, and sat with my injured leg stretched to the side, facing him with the cardboard tray between us.

"Where were you when you were captured?" My stomach growled at the intoxicating aroma of juicy seared meat.

"I was looking for shelter and stumbled upon a mansion. I assume we're in the basement." He lifted a hunk of fish to his mouth. "The dart hit me as soon as I stepped inside. What about you?"

"The same. I had a soldier with me, and he was…" My ribs squeezed. "He was decapitated by…I don't know. It moved too fast. Do you think it was…?" I turned my head toward the door.

"A hybrid child?" He swallowed a mouthful of meat. "They're deceptively fast and strong. Decapitation would require little effort."

I shivered. "Have you killed one before today?"

"No." He scooted the cardboard toward me until it bumped my leg. "You?"

"Nope." I picked at the boneless fish, the meat falling apart as I lifted a pinch to my mouth.

The flavors exploded on my tongue, smoky and sweet with

hints of lemon and ginger.

"You like it?" He watched me as if memorizing the bliss on my face.

"Yeah. We should probably savor it. Since you killed his pets, I doubt we'll get another meal."

"Maybe I did exactly what he wanted. He left the food after I killed them." He gestured at the tray. "And bandages."

"True." I wondered if the bandages were meant for Salem or me. "Do you think he knows you heal quickly?"

Shrugging, he plucked a clump of rice from the pile and popped it in his mouth. "Want to know what I think?"

He flashed a fanged smile, one that suggested his thoughts had nothing to do with the conversation.

I narrowed my eyes. "If it has to do with the scent of my virginity or the color of my pussy hair, keep it to yourself."

"For a virgin, you have a deliciously dirty mouth."

"Yeah, well…" I scooped a bite of rice. "I was raised by three men."

"One of your fathers is a Catholic priest."

"Roark?" I choked on a starchy swallow. "If you heard him talk, you'd question how I turned out so reserved." A pang twisted in my chest. I missed him so much. "Anyway, I grew up with men—*soldiers*—training, traveling, fighting side by side. There's no room for girly sensitivities in a testosterone-filled army."

"Yet you never gave it up to one of your soldiers."

"No."

I'd fantasized. Oh boy, did I ever. I'd bunked with men for years, watched them bathe in rivers and work out half-nude and drenched in sweat. It was torture on my hormones, but there wasn't a human man alive who would touch me and risk the wrath of my fathers.

I stared at Salem's soft lips. How many women had he kissed? Fucked? How many hearts had he broken? As dangerously attractive as he was, I bet he knew the female form with practiced intimacy.

At first glimpse, he didn't look like the rugged barbarians

who fought at my side. His clean-shaved jaw, aristocratic features, and neatly trimmed hair evoked images of a civilized coupling, one where he wooed and coaxed with refined patience. But his polished appearance was deceiving. The crass way he'd spoken to me, the barely restrained hunger in his eyes, and the unapologetic air of brutality he carried in his posture—all of it promised a hard, rigorous fucking. He would pin me in place with an unforgiving grip, drive his teeth into my flesh, and thrust with inglorious abandon.

My inner muscles tightened, and my nipples hardened beneath the bandana. Here, locked in a room with the most gorgeous man I'd ever seen, I didn't have my fathers' threats to protect me. Didn't have the distractions of Resistance missions and battles. For the first time in my life, I was idle, weaponless, and hyper-aware of my gnawing sexual hunger.

As that realization dug in, I busied my trembling hands with the food, dividing the piles in half.

"What were you going to say?" I directed my gaze around the room, anywhere but at the mouth-watering man in front of me. "Do you have a theory on why we were captured?"

"I think our captor knows we're both different."

My reputation as the prophecy preceded me, but… "How would he have known *you* are different?"

"I've been in Canada for a few years." He chewed a bite of fish, swallowed. "Maybe he was watching me. I have the teeth and speed of a hybrid, but I can control the hunger." His crystal eyes found mine. "I think he locked us together to see what would happen."

"Sex." My voice was as bold as the fire flaming my face.

"Yes. *Sex*." The solicitous sound of that word on his tongue produced a warmth of moisture between my legs.

If I were imprisoned with him for any length of time, it could happen. I could have sex with him and find out what all the talk was about. As far as attraction went, I'd never been so distractingly affected by a man. It wasn't just his sculptured gladiatorial build, masculine bone structure, or enthralling eyes. It was the way he looked at me as if he'd just found something he'd been craving his entire life.

If that was the case, how lucky for him. And convenient.

"You live in Canada?" I narrowed my eyes.

"Near the southern border of Alberta."

"That's a really far walk." Like fifteen-hundred-miles far. "What were you doing in the middle of nowhere Yukon?"

He draped an arm over a bent knee and leaned forward, his gaze predatory. "I was tracking someone."

Ice slid down my spine. I didn't need to ask. The answer pulled up the corners of his lips.

"Me." I gritted my teeth.

"You."

SIX

I wasn't an expert on stalking, but over the years, I'd put some arrows in a few creepers—both hybrid and human. The pressing question wasn't how Salem knew who I was or even *why* he was following me. Though I was terribly curious about the latter.

Forcing myself to remain seated on the floor, I looked him directly in the eyes. "How did you know where to find me?"

It wasn't like I advertised my travel schedule. I strategized missions in the murky hush of abandoned buildings, temporary camps, or—on rare occasion—at home base in Hoover Dam. Those meetings included only my fathers or my most trusted soldiers in the Resistance.

"You crossed through my territory about a month ago." Salem watched me from inches away, his eyes aglow with an unnatural inner light that swirled his irises like molten glass, wickedly hypnotic…

I blinked, breaking the spell. "You have a territory? Who the hell are you?"

"I'm no one." He leaned back and picked at the dwindling pile of meat, chewing and swallowing as if to draw out his damn answer. "I made a place for myself. It's out of the way. Fortified against intruders. Big enough to share with some friends who look out for me as I do for them."

"What kind of friends? Humans? Hybrids?"

"Hybrids."

"How?" I stood and tugged on what was left of my one-legged pants. "You can't be *friends* with hybrids."

"*I* can." He leaned back against the wall, wearing an amused expression. "When they can't impregnate or turn you, they're really quite amicable."

He couldn't be turned into a hybrid. The implication of that was mind-boggling. My fathers and I couldn't be turned because we carried my mother's immunity. Over the years, Michio had experimented with our blood, trying to develop a vaccine. It seemed to work on the few humans he tested it on, but eventually their bodies rejected the antivenom and shut down. None survived.

I paced the concrete room, covering the length in just a few strides. "Obviously, you're immune to the hybrid's bite. I mean, you just got bitten and nothing happened. But you have hybrid friends? That's just… I don't understand. Do you hang out with them?"

"Sometimes."

I rubbed my temples, struggling to imagine hybrids doing anything but raping and killing. "What do you do with them? Drink whiskey and trade world-domination tactics over a buffet of human throats?"

His eyes narrowed but maintained their lustrous glow. "Judgey isn't a sexy look on you."

"Judgey?" I stabbed a finger toward the door. "A hybrid child decapitated my friend! What do you think your hybrid *buddies* would do to me?"

He shrugged. "Maybe you should be more receptive to people that are different than you."

"They're not people!" Anger inflamed my face as I pointed at the scars on my throat. "Do you how I got these? And this? And this?" I gestured at each faded mark in turn, on my chest, midsection, and arms. My entire body was a tapestry of dental records. "Oh, and how about this one?" I positioned my injured thigh beneath his nose.

"Love bites?" A smile struggled on his lips until it split into a deep, rumbling laugh.

Heat raced over my skin and gathered between my legs. I couldn't ignore the enticing, palpable, sinfully sexual way his laughter affected me. But I didn't have to like it. "You know what? Fuck you."

"Judgey *and* bitchy." His expression sobered, his voice low and clipped. "Sit the fuck down and finish eating."

"No." I crossed my arms over my chest. My defiance felt a little bratty and a lot stupid, but I didn't care. "You still haven't explained your stalking."

He nudged the tray of food toward me with his foot and reclined lower against the wall, eyes hooded. His posture reminded me of Jesse—the bored slouch, hands casually clasped across his stomach, expression slack. My dad did that whole devil-may-care thing whenever he wanted me to think he wasn't paying attention. But I knew damn well he was always listening, watching.

I sat beside the tray and snatched the bandages and medical tape. The wound on my thigh wasn't festering. No pus. A little pink at the edges, not the angry red of infection. Satisfied it was healing, I wrapped my leg.

"My *friends*..." Salem arched a brow as if waiting for me to interject.

I pulled my lips tight, refusing to give him the satisfaction of another argument.

"My friends spotted a redheaded human woman riding through Alberta." He huffed a laugh. "I didn't have to be a wizard to know it was you, Eve's infamous daughter, leading her gang of human rebels into Canada. How many breeding facilities did you take out?"

We'd leveled all four of the known nests in Canada, but I wasn't about to acknowledge my objectives or successes to him. He was a stranger, and that made him a threat. Not to mention the twin blades of pearly whites hidden behind his lips.

But he hasn't bitten me.

I wanted to trust him. This wasn't my usual *oh-I-hope-he-doesn't-kill-me* predilection. I felt an all-encompassing desire to count on him, to foster that dependency into something profound and long-lasting. As fucked up as that was, my need to believe in him went beyond my ability to tamp it down.

There was no sparkly-eyed thralldom going on here. I wasn't even looking at his eyes. No, I was staring at a panorama of airbrushed skin, flat pale nipples, and a rippling terrace of muscle with *V*-cut indentions that drew an arrow downward, down, lower… Yeah, right there, where my imagination ran wild. Thin cotton pants sat low on his hips and outlined just enough bulge to guarantee his tantalizing masculinity didn't stop at the waistband.

A fever spread through me, firing up my pulse. Why was I so recklessly drawn to him? Out of the hundreds of men I'd known through my life, why Salem? Because he was spectacularly, unequivocally, drop-dead gorgeous? Was I really that shallow?

"I'll take your refusal to answer my question," he said, "as an admission of guilt."

Wait. What was the question? Oh, right. "Are you saying you approve of the breeding facilities?"

"I don't give a shit how hybrids multiply or at what length the Resistance will go to stop them. As long as the politics and the fighting stay the fuck away from me, I'm happy to spend the rest of my life in my little piece of utopia, isolated and oblivious."

"Utopia? On *this* planet?" I gaped at him. "You're caged in a…a…prison, captured by a psychopathic hybrid. Probably multiple hybrids, who targeted me because of my position in the Resistance. Who knows why you're in here, but you are. That puts you balls-deep in this great big unhappy world, lover boy."

"I like when you call me that." He licked his smiling lips. "Especially when you're talking about my balls."

"You're impossible." I touched icy fingers to my warm neck, hoping it wasn't beet red. "Did you listen to anything I said?"

"Yes, and if I hadn't given in to my curiosity, I'd be at home right now, with a luxurious bed to sleep in and a plethora of delectable food to eat. Comfortable and happy.

But you decided to come to Canada and pass through *my* territory." His head canted as he studied me with an intense expression. "I've heard a lot about you over the years. A lot of speculation about the mystical powers you inherited from Eve."

All folklore and bullshit. The only things I inherited were her golden eyes and crazy stubbornosity. "So you decided to check out my *powers* for yourself? See what all the hoopla was about?"

"Yep."

"You realize that without a small army you wouldn't have been able to get within forty yards of me." I would've put an arrow through his eye the moment he tried to approach, and that was if he managed to breach my camp. "Yet here you are, conveniently sequestered for some unforeseeable future *with me*. Lucky break. Too fucking lucky. I think you set this whole thing up."

"You call *this* lucky?" He swept out an arm, indicating the single pallet of bedding, the cardboard tray of food, and the steel door. "You should think through your accusations before flinging them around." He dragged a hand down his face. "You're goddamn exhausting."

"*I'm* exhausting?" Frustration flared through me. "Let's see…you've flirted and postured and laughed and begged for sex—"

"I do *not* beg."

"—and admitted you're a stalker—"

"Dammit, woman. I'm not—"

"But not once have you proposed an escape plan." I pursed my lips. "If you were truly captured and locked away from your beloved utopia, why are you so nonchalant?"

"Maybe because I spent the first fucking day wearing myself out trying to escape this fucking room."

Oh.

Not good.

The gravity of the situation sank my stomach like a lead weight. If he couldn't escape, I couldn't escape. Whether he was a hybrid or a human with extraordinary physiology like my fathers, the simple fact was I needed him to be my reinforcement. If... *when* I managed to get out of here, I faced an unknown enemy on the other side of that door. *Without my weapons.* A wingman with fangs would be invaluable.

I bent over the cardboard tray and finished off the fish and water with a sickening sense of dread, knowing my next meal depended on the whim of my captors. "If they want us alive, maybe they won't starve us."

"Unless this is a test to see how much we can endure, what we can survive. No doubt they've heard rumors about the prophesied daughter. Maybe they want to learn your secrets, see if you have any powers they can use before they kill you."

The fish soured in my gut. Unable to look at the greasy, blood-stained cardboard any longer, I carried it into the bathroom and added it to the pile beneath the sink.

A toothbrush and baking soda sat on the vanity, along with a bar of handmade soap that looked creamy like goat's milk. I sniffed it, and the aroma of pine tinged my nose. "If they're going to kill us, why on Earth would they provide soap?"

"Maybe," Salem said from the other room, "the last prisoner brought it in."

I shivered. There was no mirror or anything sharp or breakable that could be fashioned into a weapon. I returned to the room, sat on the thin pallet of furs, and glared at my pants. I needed to make the legs the same length, for no reason than to busy my hands.

"When the door opens again," I said, pulling at the seam on my ankle, "we should try to have a civil conversation with them. Maybe they'll explain what they want."

Salem nodded, his shiny black hair falling across his brow. He watched me from across the room as I fought the stitching in an attempt to remove the remaining leg of my pants.

"If that doesn't work..." I lowered my voice to barely a whisper. "I can pretend I'm dying or something. Maybe that'll lure them in here."

"I like that idea." He shifted to his knees. "I can pretend

I'm fucking you to near-death." His pupils dilated. "Or *not* pretend."

My blood heated. "That's not what I—"

He moved, and in a flash, he was crouched a breath away with his hands over mine on my ankle. The heat from his body filled me with equal parts shock and arousal. I tried to jerk free, but he countered my retreat, his fingers shackling my leg.

"Relax." He stared at me with the intensity of a hungry hunter. "I'm just going to fix your pants."

My breath fled slowly, raggedly. I pulled my hands away and rested against the wall, letting the concrete support my back and cool my skin.

Locking his eyes on mine, he dipped his head and bit through the stubborn threads around my ankle. His exhales seared across my flesh, making me shiver. He didn't look away as his hands ripped the suede upward, opening the seam along my calf, the inside of my knee, my thigh, and—

"Whoa." I gripped his fingers. "That's high enough."

He inched closer, smoothly maneuvering into a kneeling position between my legs. "Here?"

I pried my gaze from his voltaic eyes and stared at the hand on my thigh, the placement of his fingers aligning with the shearing job he'd done on the other pants leg. At my nod, he tore the soft leather away and set it aside, leaving me dressed in an acceptable pair of suede shorts.

Acceptable if I weren't imprisoned in arctic Canada.

"We can use the scraps," he said, "to dry off with after our showers."

I was hoping we'd escape before that doorless, wide-open shower was mentioned. Not that I'd ever had the luxury of modesty. I'd bathed in lakes and communal showers with my soldiers, washing and watching each other's backs in the interest of time and safety. But I had a sneaking suspicion Salem would turn shower time into an opportunity to watch my back *and* my front, up and down and side to side.

Thankfully, the toilet sat around the corner, but sound

traveled. After a day or two of digested food, our intimate situation would become a whole lot more intimate.

Until then… I blew out a breath. "So we wait."

He settled on the furs next to me, stretched his legs alongside mine, and looked at the door. "We wait."

And so began my time in Purgatory.

We passed the hours with easy conversation. I explained what I saw in his veins and my speculations about what we might've been injected with. He remained convinced that my x-ray vision had nothing to do with our captors and everything to do with the prophecy.

My eyes grew itchy with fatigue as I talked, sticking to safe topics like my fathers. Every man, woman, and hybrid knew of the legendary guardians. Stories reveling how they'd protected my mother and killed the Drone had spread from camp to camp for twenty years. As Salem asked questions, I separated the embellishments from the facts, sharing what my fathers had told me growing up—the accounts of their lives in the old world and their adventures with my mother after the virus.

Salem and I skirted around sensitive subjects, such as his mother, the Resistance, and the hybrid war against humanity. He spoke a lot about his utopia, how it was built underground and out of view, and how dozens of hybrid males lived there harmoniously, keeping to themselves without violence or mayhem, reaping what little scraps of happiness they could find.

"I'd have to see it to believe it." I covered my bare legs with a fold of the fur bedding to ward off the chill in the air.

"When we break out of here, you should come visit."

My stomach hardened. "I don't think so, Salem."

"Why not?"

"A lone woman among hybrids?" I laughed, mirthlessly.

He turned to face me, his shoulder resting against the wall and eyes fierce. "You would be under my protection."

His *protection* needed a good test drive before I would ever consider his offer. What I wanted to do was bring him to my fathers and let Michio prod and poke him with needles.

Michio had studied me like a scientific specimen my entire life, trying and failing to derive a cure for the hybrid infection from my genetics. But something had changed since I arrived here. I felt…*different.* Definitely more sexually aware. Damn Salem and the audacious impact he had on me. Was this a sparks-flying-in-lust kind of thing? I didn't know, so I chalked up my strange feelings to sexual inexperience.

It was the other stuff that was breaking my brain, like how the hybrid children had seemed to only attack Salem because he was in the way in their attempts to get to me. If Salem were human like my fathers, they would've gone for his throat. More importantly, there was my reaction to his veins, his *blood.* Why had I felt such a visceral desire to bite him? That was just…no. Way too ugh-ish to comprehend.

I needed Michio to analyze my reactions with his medical mind. And I needed Jesse and Roark to tell me everything was going to be okay. I needed to get the fuck out of here.

As the hours ticked by, I grew less chatty, withdrawing inside my head and battling my coiling edginess. I'd never been this inert for this long. I'd never been *imprisoned.*

Salem must've been imperceptibly bridging the space between us, because when I turned my head, he was right there, his breath on my face and his gaze overly bright, so damn overwhelming.

"You need a distraction." Devious insinuation glimmered in his eyes.

I groaned. "Don't say it."

He leaned in so close his mouth brushed my ear. "Nothing is more distracting than a cock tearing through your hymen."

An appalled wheeze crawled up my throat and burst past my lips in a snorting cackle that quickly transformed into full, unrestrained belly laughter.

He laughed with me, not quite as hysterically, but the sound of his levity was euphoric, infectious, and straight-up sensual. It was then that I knew, without a doubt, he would seduce me. It was already happening—the tingle in my chest, the hitch in my breaths, and the wet throb between my legs.

Should I push him away? Hide my reactions? Wedge a wall between us? I didn't trust him, but beyond that, there was no reason I couldn't just straddle his lap and fuck him to exhaustion. My nipples tightened at the thought, my entire body painfully aware of every inch of his.

I would probably fumble through my first time, but how complicated could it be? After listening to my soldiers drone on about positions and techniques, I understood the mechanics. Then there were all the awkward conversations with my fathers. Michio, instructing me on the importance of safe sex. Roark, explaining the emotional connection that should come when two or more bodies are joined. And Jesse, carrying on as if I were asexual, declaring, *You are not having sex. Ever.*

My takeaway? A level of trust was needed for such an intimate act.

Trust. That slimy little sentiment wormed its way into my softer parts, but I was nowhere near ready to accept it. Hell, I didn't even feel safe enough to fall asleep with Salem in the same room. I'd been nodding off for hours, fighting it, unwilling to put myself in such a vulnerable position.

How long had I been in here? There were no windows, no visible skyline to mark the passing of time. I'd arrived here at night, right? My internal clock told me it was nearing dawn.

Beside me, Salem launched into a conversation about the scarcity of good hunting knives, his timbre flowing through me like my dad's Irish whiskey, smooth and drugging, lulling me into a stupor.

I hummed and grunted at the right parts, but my mind was slipping. I straightened my spine against the wall, wriggled my feet, rubbed my gritty eyes, but my body refused to work with me. My eyelids weighed a thousand pounds. Falling. Blurring. Blink, blink, blink…

I woke to a galloping sound. *Lub-dub. Lub-dub. Lub-dub.* It echoed through my head as I lay on my side, my cheek pressed against a hard, warm surface. What the hell was that noise?

Lifting my head, I realized I'd been sleeping on Salem's chest. I no longer heard the unnaturally loud *lub-dub*, but I could guess the source.

Veins spread down his neck, growing thicker, brighter around his heart, and teeming with silver ribbon-like organisms. My gums tingled, and greedy warmth gripped my core.

My gaze flew to his, and when I found him watching me, my hunger for him compounded.

"What's wrong?" He raised up slightly, his elbows braced on the floor behind him.

An electric buzz snapped my attention to the door. With a mechanical groan, the steel barrier slid open.

SEVEN

Heart racing, I scrambled to my feet and darted for the door. By the time I reached it, the solid steel had slid halfway open, revealing the closed gate that barred the opening. Beyond the rungs waited an empty corridor. Flames swayed on the wall torches, the air disturbed by whatever had just fled. *Dammit!*

"Come back!" I gripped the gate, pressing my face in the narrow gap between two bars.

The door sank into the groove in the wall and shuddered to silence. A cardboard tray waited inches from my feet, the scent of grilled oysters and chili peppers flooding my senses.

I held my breath and listened. For a fleeting moment, I swore I heard the faint retreat of footsteps.

"I just want to talk." My voice boomed through the stillness. I couldn't see around the corner, couldn't see shit from this angle. "Please. Just tell me what you want."

Salem slipped around me, bending to drag the food and water beneath the gate and into the room.

The veins beneath his skin became evanescent before my eyes, vanishing like wisps of vapor. The phenomenon had to be correlated to the retreating footsteps. Whatever or whoever had just been here was linked to him. It was the simplest explanation.

I returned my attention to the hall, determination girding my tone. "Hello? Do you know who I am? You don't have to show your face. Just talk to me. We can work something out. I have resources, people at my disposable who can give you whatever you need."

Within reason. My fathers would probably sacrifice a village of human women in exchange for my life, but I would *never* offer that.

Warm skin skimmed against my back, and my heart sputtered. Salem rested a hand on my hip, his other on the rung above mine. As he pressed forward, his brick-hard body forced me closer to the gate, caging me in.

"Hey, out there." His breath rustled my hair. "Can you bring a flask next time? I'm not picky. Just fill it with the hardest stuff you got."

"Unbelievable," I muttered. "Why not request a mint for your pillow, too? Oh, wait. We don't have pillows."

"You don't need a pillow." He dipped his head and nuzzled my neck, spreading goosebumps down my spine. "You slept like a log on my chest. A drooling, snoring log."

"I did not sn—"

The gears overhead buzzed, and the door shimmied into motion. *No, no, no!* I grabbed the steel edge and tried to shove it back, but it powered toward me with mechanical force.

"You're wasting your time." He grasped my hips. "I've already tried that."

I swatted his hands away. "We have to do something."

My lungs seethed, every cell in my body raging for freedom. Desperation drove me to fight, my arms burning and my feet slipping along the concrete in my useless attempt to overpower the door. As the view of the corridor shrank, the air grew thinner, my hope crushing beneath the weight of steel.

Despair crept in, and on its heels came an explosion of fury. My gut simmered, my heart pounded, and a guttural roar barreled from my throat. I fucking lost it.

"You dickless motherfucker! Are you afraid of a human girl?" I wedged into the crack of the closing door and pounded on the gate, shaking with full-body tremors. "I know you can hear me. Are you so despicable you're ashamed to show yourself?" I frantically slapped at the steel, the pain only further enraging me. "I bet your face is covered in boils and your fangs are so rotten your entire body is rancid. Do hybrid children cover their eyes when they see you?"

"That's enough." Salem hooked an arm around my waist and yanked me back just as the door sealed shut.

Red bled through my vision, my temper plunging somewhere between delirious and spastic. In a fit of swinging arms, I jerked in Salem's hold until my feet no longer touched the floor.

"You have nothing to say?" I bellowed at the door, kicking wildly with my back pinned to Salem's chest. "That's bullshit! If the world decides to give itself an enema you better take cover, you son of a bitch, because you're the lowest hanging excrement. The dirtiest, most parasitic ass-clinger. To call you an infection would be offensive to all the honest diseases. You're worse than a hybrid, because a hybrid doesn't pretend to be what it's not. You're a fake. A lousy wannabe scourge that cowers in a hole. A toxic, *dead* asshole! You aren't even—"

"All right, stop." Salem covered my mouth with a hand, his chest heaving against my back. "So much for civil conversation."

Was he laughing at me? I slammed an elbow against his stomach, and he coughed out a runaway chuckle.

How would I break out of here? What the fuck was I going to do? I wrenched his hand from my mouth, bucking and wheezing in his constrictive hold, suffocating, and powerless to stop the moisture burning my eyes.

Eddie would arrive back at camp any time now, and my fathers… Sweet unmerciful hell, I couldn't even think about the looks on my fathers' faces when they realized I wasn't with him. Their retaliation against my captors would be a slaughter of hellsblood and damnation, but they would have to locate me first. That was the bitch of it. I'd run off into the arctic nothingness, where it snowed hourly, where my tracks would be buried, where they would never find me.

I was on my own. *With Salem.*

Turning in the steel bands of his arms, I let my gaze flit up his chiseled torso and linger on the smooth, vein-less column of his neck. "We're not getting out of here."

"We will." He touched a knuckle to my chin and lifted my eyes to the startling silver of his. "We just have to give them what they want."

He stroked his thumb along my bottom lip, and my skin heated beneath his hungry gaze.

"Is sex the only thing you think about?" My voice was tight, my emotions stretched on a live wire, seconds from spilling down my face.

"I'm thinking about the clues, Dawn. The toothbrush, the soap… Why would they concern themselves with our hygiene?"

"Maybe they plan to sell us to the highest bidder."

"They put us in here with one bed," he rasped, his timbre low and gravelly.

Awakening pulsed between my legs. "Maybe there's a shortage of furs."

"Tonight's dinner…" He slid his fingers across my cheek and into my hair. "Oysters, chili peppers, and pine nuts. All aphrodisiacs."

"Oh." My heart rate sped up, and my insides liquidized.

No edible sexual stimulants needed here. I was already a trembling heap of weak knees, heart palpitations, and boob sweat. Maybe it was the lingering adrenaline from my tantrum or the realization I might never escape this place.

Why would our captors want us to have sex? Was this some kind of breeding experiment? I wasn't convinced there was some grand, premeditated plan. They couldn't have known I would be in this area, stumbling upon an abandoned mansion alone.

But I wasn't alone.

The raw desire darkening Salem's face twisted my desperation into a different kind of need. I wanted him to ease my torment, devour my fears, and make all this go away. If he let go of me, I might just fall on my back with my legs open. My fathers would be so proud.

Salem didn't release me and instead spun us around until my back met the wall. The hand in my hair held tight, and his lips lowered, hovering a kiss away.

"Your eyes are addictive." His voice whispered through me, licking my nerve endings. "Sometimes I see sparks of emerald, but the gold dominates, the color so blinding and painful it's like staring into a lost sunrise after twenty years of darkness."

My heart swooned and dipped, and I mentally smacked it back where it belonged. My emotions were all over the damn place. Two seconds ago, I was spitting and roaring. Now he was all sweet-talky and seductive. I didn't know how to respond to his compliment, so I said nothing.

Breathing was already a challenge with his half-naked body wrapped around me. He was just so beautiful. Seductive, preternatural, *he-can't-be-real* kind of beautiful. Glossy black hair and dense fringes of black lashes were a striking contrast to his complexion. How was his skin so pristine and luminous? There were no creases around his eyes or blemishes or freckles, as if he'd never seen the sun, never labored in harsh weather. Did he wear a wide-brimmed hat, long-sleeves, and live under a rock?

He must've worked out regularly in a sunless cave for all the muscle he flexed against me. Bulging biceps, powerful shoulders, every ridge and valley sharply cut beneath satiny flesh. I lifted a hand to his chest and stroked a solid pectoral, awestruck by his radiating warmth.

He stared down at me with lids half-mast, his grin stretching across his face with devilish arrogance. "You've thought about having sex with me."

My veins hummed, but I refused to feed his ego. "Not as much as you think about having sex with yourself."

His fangs peeked out, pressing against his lip as he glanced around the room. "Since we're sorely lacking privacy, you'll have a front row seat. You ever watched a man stroke one off?"

Never, but living among virile soldiers, I'd heard the late-night grunts, the smacking sounds of beating meat on nearby bedrolls. I might've been a virgin, but I wasn't sheltered.

"Do what you have to do." I tried to sound indifferent. "Just don't look me in the eye when you do it. That would be weird."

"I'd rather watch your hand." He shifted closer and touched his forehead to mine. "While you're fingering your wet pussy."

I grasped for a retort, but his hulking presence zapped my brain cells. The way his fingers glided to my neck, holding me in place. The feel of his cock swelling against my hip. The acceleration of his breaths fanning my face. He was an intoxicating high, a tranquilizer for doubt, his demeanor potent and his almighty size crowding in and taking up space.

"This room is too small." I clutched his biceps, pushing him away, pulling him closer—I couldn't decide.

"We can make it work." His mouth floated over mine, near enough to feel the zing of fleeting contact.

"You're going to kiss me."

"You're not going to stop me."

As if his voice held divine authority and his words were a magical incantation, I parted my lips. The movement brushed our mouths together, sending an electric shock across my skin. He held that moment in suspension, staring at me. I stared right back.

This wasn't witchcraft or glamour. It was simple, raw, carnal desire, a natural attraction between a man and woman, necessary for the survival of my species. Except my lips were on fire. I was on fire. The world was on fire, and I was in a new kind of hell.

"Salem…" I stretched up on tiptoes, seeking relief.

With a deep growl, he lifted me up the wall, wrapped my legs around his hips, and seized my mouth. There was no tender exploration or coy nips and pecks. The moment I surrendered, he claimed me with bruising aggression. His tongue chased mine, his lips firm and combative. It was primitive and frenzied, vibrating with all the components of a first kiss—the distrust, the nervousness, the reckless hunger.

I followed his lead, my tongue riding with his and my thighs clenching around his waist. Heads slanted, fingers grabbing, we rocked together in a tousle of limbs and tongues and teeth…

Fangs. The razored tips grazed my lips, but I didn't taste blood, didn't feel so much as a prick. His mouth glided along mine, his tongue furiously lashing and rolling, but somehow he kept his teeth sheathed.

He didn't show the same restraint with the rest of his body. Grabbing my hair at the scalp, he wrenched my head back and deepened the kiss. His other hand palmed my ass, his fingers working into my butt crack, dipping downward, and pressing roughly against the seam of my shorts—the only thing stopping him from penetrating my pussy. Grinding against my front, he thrust his erection between my legs like he was trying to rut a hole through our clothes.

Maybe this was a bad idea. I didn't know him, couldn't trust him. But strangers had sex all the time, and dammit, I wanted this. *Him.* I wasn't bold enough to reach into his pants and take it, but I refused to shove him away and sabotage the one pleasurable thing in this hopeless situation.

I stabbed my hands in his hair and pulled, holding him to me as I dipped my tongue and bit his lips. He groaned and drove his hips faster, harder, his fingers digging between my thighs, punishing my swollen flesh.

I cracked open my eyes and found his shut tight. His inky brows pinched together, his expression taut with pain, as if he were losing his footing. I loved that. I needed him on my level—shaky, off-balanced, and diving straight toward undone.

Liquid heat coursed through my body, melting my insides and chilling my skin. Sweet mother, I'd never been this hot and itchy and so incredibly turned on. I squirmed against him, panting, needing more, cursing our clothes, and aching for his fingers on my nipples, my inner thighs, and deep inside my pussy.

"Dawn." He pulled back to meet my eyes. "Do you want me to fuck you?"

I choked on a breathless gasp. "You're giving me a choice?"

"I'm giving you time." He cupped my face. "I'll work up to it and break you in slowly. Or…" He touched his mouth to mine, his voice thick with arousal. "I'll pull down your pants right now and fuck you."

As his words sank in, I lowered my feet to the floor and rested my head against the wall. "You said slowly, not gently."

"I won't be gentle." He stroked a finger across my swollen lips. "Was that your first kiss?"

"Yeah." My voice croaked, and I cleared it. "How'd I do?"

"You were a little overzealous with your teeth."

"What?" Embarrassment tightened my jaw.

"I can teach you how to control that drooling problem."

Oh my fuck. Seriously?

His gaze glimmered with laughter.

I punched him in the abs. "You're such a dick."

His amusement faded, and his pupils darkened, the silver of his eyes sharpening. "You're exquisite." He traced a finger around the corners of my mouth. "If that kiss was any indication, I'm not sure I'll survive your sweet ginger cunt."

Damn his filthy mouth. I liked it way more than I should have. "We may not survive this prison."

His arm fell, along with his expression as his gaze flicked to the door.

Way to ruin the mood. I reached for his hand and squeezed. "Food's getting cold."

"Yeah." He stepped away, dragged the tray to the pallet of bedding, and sat with his back against the wall.

We ate in silence, but as we chewed each bite, we shared a curious, exploratory conversation without words. Every stolen glance had its own language. Each brush of our fingers communicated interest. Slowly, our bodies shifted closer, drawn together by mutual attraction and the simple need for affection.

Eventually, he reached over and pulled me across his lap. I reclined in the cradle of his thighs, my back against his chest, with his arm around my waist. Supported by his strength and the choice he'd given me, I felt safe, all things considered.

Strange how a kiss had taken me from cagey and suspicious to cautiously friendly. Was I letting my guard fall too quickly? I hadn't given him an answer about sex. But rather than fall on me like a hybrid, he absently caressed my hair, his cock softening and tucked away in his pants.

That was good. It would give me time to think. And agonize over those thoughts.

Swallowing the last oyster, I shifted to lay my cheek on his chest. "When I woke earlier, I could hear your blood pumping."

"You were sleeping on me." He slid the empty tray away and wrapped his arms around my hips, pulling me closer in the *V* of his legs.

"I can hear your heartbeat now, but this was louder, sharper." I drew a squiggly line down his neck with a finger. "I heard the circulation of your blood in my *head.* It was like a megaphone or…I don't know, like I was inside of you."

His hand clenched and relaxed in my hair. "You don't hear it now?"

"No. I think the appearance of your veins, the sound, is linked to whoever is bringing our food." I sat up, shivering against a chill of excitement. "What if we unlocked a latent ability? If I can sense hybrids, that would be…" I blew out a breath. "Too unreal."

"Unreal?" He touched my chin, tilting my gaze to his. "Your mother sensed aphids, right?"

"Yeah, but that was different." I touched my midsection. "She felt them here. When she became pregnant with me—"

"She wiped them out. *You* were the source of that power." He dropped his hand, his expression unreadable. "Or so they say."

That was a rumor I couldn't refute. I'd given my mother an

extraordinary gift. Then I took it away, along with her life, when I drew my first breath. My chest squeezed. I would never look into her eyes, never feel her arms around me, never hear her voice. Instead, I spent the past nineteen years watching my fathers grieve while I hovered on the outskirts without any real sense of the woman they mourned with every breath.

"Seems to me," Salem said, "you've been hiding a handy power."

"Handy for you?" I searched his prismatic eyes. "You're friends with hybrids."

"No, I have friends who happen to be hybrid. I'm impartial to their genetic makeup. Do you trust the humans you encounter simply because they're human?"

"Everyone is an enemy until proven otherwise." I twisted to face him, folding my legs in the space between his. "What are you?"

"I'm not your enemy."

"That's not what I'm asking."

"You want to know if I'm human or something else?" A muscle bounced in his jaw. "I don't know the answer."

I touched his hairless face and caressed the tension there. "Do you know why the Drone made Michio bite Elaine?"

"He wanted to take control of the child in her womb." He shifted his head and kissed my fingers. "He wanted to control *me.*"

I nodded. "But since Michio consumed my mother's blood, it made his venom ineffective. The Drone wasn't happy about that and bit Elaine himself, only to discover Michio's bite had made you immune to the infection." With a surge of boldness, I touched the sharp tip of Salem's fang. "Michio would shit a brick if he knew you had these. He always believed Elaine would give birth to a human child."

Grooves formed between his brows. "Did the Drone bite other women?"

"No, and neither did my fathers. Their bite results in infertility—not exactly something they want to spread to our endangered species." My mind swam through the repercussions. "Your mother was bitten by the Drone and cured by the blood of Eve. That made her a rarity. Like Michio."

"Wouldn't that mean I have the same genetic…whatever as Michio?"

"Maybe? When Michio bit Jesse and Roark, he passed on his unusual traits to them. It would make sense that he passed the same to you through your mother." I gripped the medallion that hung from my neck, tracing the embedded treasures—Jesse's turquoise stone, Roark's rosary bead, Michio's fang. "My fathers are human. They just happen to have hybrid speed, healing, and…" I waved a hand at Salem's mouth.

He flashed his fangs. "There's your answer."

"Does that make us siblings?"

He squinted at me darkly. "Fuck no."

Laughter bubbled past my lips. "I'm kidding." I desperately wanted him to be like my fathers, because the alternative meant I'd just shared my first kiss with a genetic unknown. "But I've never seen veins glow beneath my fathers' skin. Why is it happening now? Is it a timing thing or a *you* thing?"

He shrugged. "Hell if I know."

"Now I'm dying to know if it extends to others. If I can see veins in my soldiers, I could keep one of my men—"

Fingers dug into my hip.

"—at my side and use him as radar when hybrids approach."

A growl erupted in Salem's chest.

"What?" I arched an eyebrow.

He grabbed my neck with a possessive hand, his expression tight. "If you want those men to live, you will *not* talk about keeping them anywhere near you."

"You're jealous." I narrowed my eyes.

He stood abruptly, taking me with him. "I'm tired."

Setting me on my feet, he strode into the bathroom and around the corner. The trickling sound of him peeing produced a pinch in my bladder. I'd been ignoring my own need to pee for hours.

As I listened, my mind took a salacious detour filled with images of his pants pushed down around his thighs, his balls hanging freely, and his cock in his hand. A curl of heat spread through me, descending, throbbing…

Stop it, you hussy. He's peeing!

When he stepped into view and turned on the shower, his back was to me—his stark-naked, glorious backside. I stifled a moan and bit the inside of my cheek.

Salem wasn't just handsome. He was built like a primordial god of darkness. Standing over six feet, he raised his arms to wet his hair, the black strands turning impossibly blacker, so shiny and thick between the rake of his fingers.

His broad back tapered into a narrow waist, muscled ass, and long powerful legs. The pallor of his skin should've given him a sickly appearance, but in the name of all that was holy, the man couldn't look sick if he tried.

The Resistance soldiers were dark-skinned, tanned, or freckled and sunburned. They bore numerous scars, their bodies weathered by hardship, tattooed with ink and death, and covered in hair. In comparison, Salem looked like a timeless Adonic statue, carved to perfection, immaculately refined, far surpassing handsome and ascending directly toward angelic. A dark angel, made of brawn and nocturnal beauty.

He didn't glance back at me as he lathered soap down his chest. I knew the water was frigid, but he seemed completely unaffected by it, his hands moving over relaxed muscles and flawless skin. He was so delicious to look at my entire body ignited. Should I stop gawking and turn around? Would he offer me the same courtesy?

I wobbled on a tightrope of indecision. I could make an issue out of our nudity. I could shower when he slept, demand he face the other way, dance around with my hands covering all the vulnerable parts. But why? I didn't behave that way with my soldiers.

Because this was Salem. Our mutual attraction was blatant.

Sex was inevitable.

Even more reason to shed this irrational modesty.

With a steeling breath, I reached behind me and untied the bandana that supported my breasts. Keeping my gaze glued to the back of his head, I pushed down my shorts. The chilly air prickled my naked skin. Hyper-aware of every scar, freckle, and imperfection on my body, I stepped toward the bathroom and stopped.

Tension flexed across his shoulders, but he continued washing as if I weren't standing there with my nipples as hard as pine nuts. He hadn't turned around, but the fucker *knew*.

I clenched and unclenched my hands and strode into the bathroom.

EIGHT

Salem didn't acknowledge my naked walk into the tiny concrete room. He didn't turn his head or utter a sound when I used the toilet and cautiously approached his beautiful backside. Pressing my nails into my palms, I sucked in a fortifying breath.

A mist of icy droplets stung my skin and tightened my nipples. Keeping his back to me, he lowered his arms, then his head, and a skitter of goosebumps rose along his spine.

"Are you finished with the soap?" My teeth chattered, and I hadn't even stepped beneath the spray yet.

"I'm going to turn around." His deep timbre warmed my prickly flesh. "Don't run."

I laughed nervously. "Where am I going to go?"

He grunted a noise that sounded like a chuckle, and slowly, tauntingly, pivoted to face me.

His gaze landed on mine. "Feeling brave?"

"Feeling dirty." I choked on the unintended innuendo. "I mean *grimy*. It's been a few days since I've bathed."

Eeesh. Now I just sounded gross.

A smile sparkled in his eyes, but his expression was tight and severe, the cords in his neck straining, like he was fighting the urge to look down. Anticipation slammed my heart against my ribs. I wanted him to look, to take his eyeful and get this over with—whatever *this* was.

We stood in a gridlock of eye contact. As the seconds dripped by, I vacillated between hot flashes and cold chills, my entire body pulsing with awareness and swaying toward him.

He must've noticed, because his nostrils flared and his gaze broke away, traveling downward.

I stared at the sharp lines of his face as he leisurely examined me from tits to toes. On his second pass, he lingered on the juncture between my legs. My inner muscles spasmed. His jaw set. My breath picked up, and so did his. I flexed my hands.

A smirk sneaked over his lips. "Bright red."

What did he expect? The hair on my head was as red as a ladybug's wings.

I followed his gaze to my pubic hair, but my focus landed on the trim black patch of *his*. My lungs buckled. Had I imagined him hairless down there? Yeah, maybe. If there was hair anywhere else below his neck, I couldn't see it. Not that I was looking at anything but the massive erection pointed at me. We stood so close, if I released the clench of my abs, the flared head of his cock would bump my stomach.

I'd seen every shade and size of human and hybrid genitalia. Most of the older ones, the human men born in the old world, were circumcised—such a barbaric thing to do for a supposed civilized society. But the males in my generation were uncut. Like Salem.

Pale skin stretched tightly over engorged steel that looked too heavy and swollen to stand up. But there it was, growing thicker and jerking upward as I stared with wide eyes. While I'd never seen a dick this close up, I knew with certainty his would forever be my benchmark to which others were compared.

Mother of mercy, he would split me in half with that thing. Yet the thought of him inside me aroused a hunger so deep I throbbed to sink my fingers between my legs and rub fast and hard until I screamed in relief.

This was madness. I wasn't a stranger to self-pleasure, but I'd never considered touching myself while someone watched. Salem had put the idea in my head, and now it tantalized me so much I couldn't stop my hand from creeping down, over my naval, through my curls—

"Fuck, Dawn." His arm flew out, and he clutched the edge of the sink beside him. "You're killing me."

I snapped my gaze up and gasped. His fangs had lengthened, sharpened, his mouth parting to accommodate the ivory blades. I couldn't see his veins, but my gums ached in mutual hunger. If I were alone, I might've bitten my own wrist just to soothe the discomfort.

Where the hell did that thought come from? Was he somehow projecting his feelings to me? No, this…whatever this was felt like it was coming from a place deep inside me. A confusing, irrational, *instinctual* place.

He lowered his head, his eyes burning with silver flames as he studied me from beneath sooty brows.

"I was going to wash you." He grabbed my arm and pushed the soap against my palm. "But I'm not…" He released me, stepping back and bumping into the sink. "I need to…take the edge off…before I…"

I didn't need him to finish that sentence. His muscles bunched, his face taut and feet planted wide, like a man facing battle. He stood tall and commanding as his gaze devoured my form, each sweep returning to my hand where it hovered over the ache between my legs. But he was unraveling, evidenced by the heave of his breaths, the bob of his Adam's apple, and the shaking in his fingers as he gripped his erection.

With a backward step, I slipped beneath the icy water, hoping it would jolt some sense back into me. The brutal cold only made my nipples pucker tighter and my body tremble. When the frigid water soaked through my hair and hit my neck, I gasped. His liquid-metal eyes zeroed in on my mouth.

"I don't want to hurt you, but dammit, you're testing me. You're…" He fisted his length in a white-knuckled grip. "So fucking…" His hand made a swift stroke. "Insanely." Stroke, stroke. "Beautiful."

His heated words shocked my heart, but what left me paralyzed was the brazen way he began to viciously fuck his hand. This man knew no boundaries, and his confidence promised a surfeit of sexual experience.

I won't be gentle.

He could introduce me to things I would've never consented to had we met under different circumstances. But here we stood on neutral turf, naked and needy with nowhere to go, no excuse to hide.

My hands moved with purpose, rubbing the soap across my skin, through my hair, and between my legs. I wanted to be clean for no other reason than to please him. Maybe that was wrong. Heaven help me, the Resistance soldiers would clench their intolerant assholes if they knew what their leader was contemplating. A bloodsucker was an enemy. Intimacy with an enemy was forbidden. And forbidden was wrong.

I didn't care.

I needed to stop thinking in terms of wrong and right. My mother had fanged lovers. *Three of them!* She'd feared Michio the first time she saw his altered canines, had even hurled knives at him. But in the end, she'd clawed through the Drone's mental barricades to save Michio's life.

Salem snarled past clenched fangs, his hand flying over his cock with brutal speed. Abs contracting and hips thrusting into each downward stroke, he stared at my pussy like he was seconds from eating me whole.

Behold the incarnation of danger in all its infernal glory, a predator on the cusp of breaking his tenuous leash, his focus centered on his fluttery-hearted prey. My stomach hardened, and my pulse elevated, but beneath the fear surged a rush of raucous energy. I lived for adventure, and nothing was more thrilling than crashing through barricades on a fast horse and flinging arrows at that which I feared most.

And I knew exactly which horse I wanted to ride.

I let the soap thunk to the floor, blindly reached behind me, and shut off the water. His strokes faltered then sped up with renewed fury. Excitement blazed in his eyes, the heat in them chasing the chill from my skin.

A hard swallow, two steps forward, and I sank to my knees with my mouth an inch from his cock.

"Give it to me." I slid trembling fingers along his, closing over his grip.

"Take it." Ruthless fists ensnared my hair, holding me captive as he thrust between my parted lips.

His broad head punched the back of my throat hard enough to make my eyes burn. I choked, and my hands shot to his thighs, pushing him away as I tried to control my gag reflex. He was too invasive, too big, far more than I'd expected. What was I thinking?

He held me immobile, his fingers twisting in my hair and stinging my scalp as he hammered against my throat over and over. I gulped for air, whimpered, and writhed, my knees slipping painfully on the concrete. The more I fought, the harder he drove his hips, as if my struggling excited him.

Bite, bite, bite whispered through my mind, but I slapped it away. I'd put myself in this position because I wanted to pleasure him, not castrate him.

I tightened my hands around the flanks of his thighs and relaxed my jaw, my throat, and finally, my fingers. Timing my breaths with his thrusts, I stopped fighting, stopped thinking, and let him guide me through my first blow job.

His hands shook as they supported my head, and the trim of his hair brushed my nose with the scent of musk and man. I lost myself in the feel of him stretching my mouth, sliding over my tongue, and embedding my taste buds with the salty essence of his skin.

Soon, my throat grew numb. The pain was still there, but something else bloomed at the edges. Maybe it was the thrill in unfamiliar intimacy or the feel of his powerful body beneath my hands and between my lips. Whatever it was turned my muscles to jelly and melted my insides into a pool of throbbing heat.

I instinctively swirled my tongue and tightened my lips, carefully guarding my teeth as I sucked. Oh man, I didn't know what I was doing, but I'd practiced in my head a million times over the years. *Suck, lick, watch the teeth. I've got this.*

"Fuck." His hips jerked, and his chest vibrated with an

agonized moan.

The sound was diabolical. His scent—intoxicating. His cock—heavy, throbbing, weeping sinfully in my mouth. He slowed for a moment, and I lapped at the glans, humming. He shifted his feet, spreading wider, and burst into rapid, furious thrusts. All I could do was hold on. His urgency slammed into overdrive, each thrust making me hotter, more soaked between my legs, and oh-so quivery in all the right places.

Soft thumbs stroked my temples, at odds with the cruel drive of his hips. "Damn you and your greedy mouth."

His thighs shuddered beneath my hands, and he rammed deep, stopped. Balls pressed against my chin, he dropped his head back and released a loud animalistic groan.

Salty ejaculate coated my tongue. I swallowed, shocked by the quantity, the curious taste, and the realization that I wanted to do it again.

He slipped from my mouth, and I wriggled my aching jaw. He hadn't caught his breath, but his fangs seemed smaller, less threatening. He gripped my elbow and helped me up, his hooded gaze lazily moving over my body like lava.

"You've never done that before?" Disbelief rasped through his voice.

"No." My lips thinned with irritation.

I was starting to resent the prospect that he'd shared all kinds of intimacy with however many others. Meanwhile, every step I took with him felt like a momentous discovery. It put me at a vulnerable disadvantage, making him more significant to me than I was to him.

But that wasn't the only thing twisting me into an agitated state. The molten heat pounding between my legs hadn't ebbed. My skin felt hypersensitive. My nipples jutted hard and painfully, and the flames burning inside me roared with a vengeance.

He rested his ass against the edge of the sink and pulled me into the spread of his legs. His erect cock lay between the press of our lower bodies.

I tried not to stare, but he looked unbelievably harder.

"Didn't your, uh...release take the edge off?"

"Normally..." He glanced down, brows pinching. "It would." When he lifted his head, his eyes flashed with an efflorescence of blinding white. "Your fucking mouth had the opposite effect."

I didn't like his accusatory tone, but a smile twitched on my lips, because *wow.* High five to my oral skills. Who knew?

With a strangled growl, he grabbed my neck and caught my grin in a demanding kiss. I melted against him, and the world narrowed to the heat of his mouth and the hammer of his heart. Logic fled, consequences evaporated, and desire took over in a collision of tongues and dueling breaths.

Strong fingers seized the backs of my thighs, and the floor fell away. The walls spun around me as he moved with superhuman speed, out of the bathroom and through the main room. As though a mystical force kept our lips joined, the kiss didn't falter when my back hit the bedding on the floor. He followed me down, chest to chest, the weight of his body blanketing me in a heavy comfort.

With my legs closed and trapped between his thighs, I explored his mouth for an eternity. Despite the swollen erection against my belly, he seemed content to do the same, licking and sucking, with his fists in my hair and hips rocking with greedy enthusiasm.

The erratic tempo of our breaths saturated the room as I swept my hands down his muscled back and gripped his gorgeous ass. The air deserted my lungs. Holy shit, he was hard. *Hard everywhere.* The feel of his chiseled body and the sounds of his groans smothered me in desire.

I wanted...I *needed...* "Salem."

He broke the kiss and rose slightly, straddling my hips. When our eyes connected, I indulged in the luminous pull of his, and my heart took off in a tailspin.

"My turn." Each word was full of gravel, tumbling from fanged lips.

His gaze drifted south, tracing my parted mouth, the bob in my throat, and the heave of my breasts. He lowered his head, and my nipples throbbed. He drew one into his wet mouth, and my entire chest caught fire. The sucking sensation roused a vigorous pulse in my womb, like an invisible string connected his lips to my deepest, most ravenous hot spots.

He slid down my legs, kissing and licking erogenous zones I didn't even know existed. I arched my back, shuddering against the overload of stimulation. My hands clutched at his shoulders, and my knees shook against his calves. Sweet fucking fuck, his skilled tongue seemed to know every locus of pleasure, dipping into the curves of my waist, trailing around my hipbones, and swirling in the valley of my compressed thighs.

He's going to kiss me there. The thought hijacked my brain and froze my lungs. *Don't freak out. Don't freak out.*

Eddie's veterinarian mother, Shea, gave me regular vaginal exams to spare Michio that awkward task. But that was different. Like, *why-am-I-thinking-about-that, it's-not-in-the-same-galaxy* different.

Salem gripped my knee and leaned to the side, tugging my leg out from under him. I tensed with uncertainty, but he overpowered, opening me up to his searing gaze.

"What do you think, oh golden-eyed savior of mankind?" He pressed his nose against my cleft and inhaled. "Are you ready to come on my tongue?"

My heart did this *skippy dippy fuzzy woozy* thing, and I wheezed a strained laugh.

Positioning his shoulders between my thighs, he met my eyes. "Breathe."

"Yep. No problem." I exhaled sharply and fisted my hands in the furs beneath me.

Without looking away, he dragged the backs of his fingers down my naval and through my red curls. He did it again and again, each time teasing a swelling scorch of need toward the place I needed him most. I tried to hold still, but my hunger was so sharp and impatient I squirmed beneath his touch, whimpering on the verge of begging.

His formidable jawline tightened, the curve of his lips

flattening in a fierce line. Rebellious black hair hung in wet strands across his knitted brow, and his luminous eyes narrowed with concentration as they lowered.

He shifted between my legs, one hand sliding up to cup my breast while the other sank out of view. Heat brushed my sensitive slit. His fingers. Slipping through my drenched folds. Circling my entrance. Stretching and spreading my arousal. Lighting me from the inside out.

"Your cunt is so…*small*." His voice was a silken whisper. "So fucking wet."

He breached my opening. One finger. Two. Biting pleasure tore through my body, and I moaned, heart thundering. A storm in my chest. Bolts of lightning across my skin. Then his lips, strikingly hot and wet. A suction of sweltering heat. Gliding and sucking. When his tongue dipped, I cried out and grabbed his hair.

He caught my hands and pressed them against the bedding at my sides.

"Don't push me." His gaze sharpened. "Unless you want my bite"—he rolled his tongue around my clit and sucked—"here."

I bucked my hips against the sensation, writhing at the thought of his fangs sinking into my engorged bundle of nerves. Slick heat rushed between my thighs, the sudden need for his bite so insanely potent it made no sense.

His breath vibrated across my skin, and I knew he felt the answering quiver in mine. He watched me with an intensity that sharpened his fangs and flared his nostrils.

If he wanted to bite me, why was he holding back? He'd already consumed my blood when he licked my wound. Was he worried about draining me? Something else? I'd survived numerous bites without infection, but he wasn't a hybrid. When Michio had injected me with his venom, I had no reaction. But Salem was…I didn't know.

Blood as an essential food source was a conversation we needed to have. *Later.*

I shook my head.

Something flickered in his gaze. Disappointment? Relief? "Then don't move."

NINE

With my fingers buried in the furs, I closed my eyes and tracked the smooth slide of his jaw against my inner thigh. The hot sweep of his breath along my drenched flesh. The curl of his tongue deep inside me.

When his lips found my clit with delicious precision, my eyes shot open and my ass flew off the floor. He caught my hips, pressing me down and holding me in place as he licked and sucked and drove me out of my mind. Tingling urgency swelled in my core, growing bigger, stronger, racing my heart, and riling my nerve endings.

His thumbs joined in and parted my folds, teasing the breach of my body. Strong fingers framed my mound as he glided those thumbs in a sensual stirring motion, up and down and around my opening, gathering moisture and kneading in tandem along either side of my clit. I groaned against the incredible sensation, and he released my bud, dipping, stirring, only to return and massage it again. Catch. Release. Stroke. Repeat. His expert caress stole my breath, the pressure ruthlessly precise, the technique indescribable.

I strained toward his touch, needing him closer and *inside.* Then he was there, penetrating me with wicked strokes, fingertips, knuckles, rubbing my channel into a fit of spasms. As his tongue plunged and flicked, I wanted to howl with demands. *Faster. Rougher. Deeper. Now.*

"Whatever you're doing…" I sucked air and ground against his mouth. "Don't stop."

"Beg." His rogue smile twitched against my pussy, the

fucking sadist.

"Please!" punched past my lips, but my tone sounded like *Now!* I softened my voice. "Please, keep going. Right there, right there…"

Holy hell, I was a breathy, gooey puddle of need. His erotic kisses shattered my reserve, turning me into a wanton creature. I didn't care. I loved the way my body felt beneath his mouth, loved how his eyes burned when I moaned. And I loved the fragile precipice he dangled me on. I clung to the edge for infinite moments in pure bliss. Until he ran his tongue up my center and latched onto my clit.

I exploded. Pleasure unlike anything I'd ever experienced released forcefully and violently through my body, surging white-hot electricity to my fingers and toes. I screamed through the shock waves, my voice unrecognizable, spine arching, and muscles clamping around his fingers.

He groaned against my sensitize flesh and continued to fuck me with his fingers, his lips moving faster, more aggressively against my clit. I bucked and thrashed. It was too much, too soon. But he didn't ease up, didn't give me a second to bask in the aftermath.

He didn't relent through the next climax either. Or the one after that.

His endurance was boundless, his energy inhuman, and he proved it by holding me in a state of ecstasy for hours. His mouth did insidious things to my focus. A mouth made to gratify the drives of womanly hunger. I lost track of time and orgasms. My brain melted into mush. My body lolled, sated and buzzing, and still, he didn't slow.

Sprawled beneath the relentless tongue on my breast, I touched his chin and tipped his face up.

"Enough, Salem." My voice was raw, hoarse from screaming. "What're you doing?"

"Enjoying your gorgeous body." He licked my nipple. "Passing the time in the best way possible." A kiss to my breastbone. "Breaking you in."

"Congratulations." I dropped my arm from his face, too

damn exhausted to hold it up. "I'm broken."

"No, you're not." He slid up my chest, his talented hands roaming my body as he buried his nose in my neck. "I haven't even fucked you yet."

I groaned. "Damn your superhuman stamina."

"I've never heard a complaint."

Tension shot through my jaw, and I shut my eyes, cursing my irrational jealousy.

He cupped my face, nudging it until I opened my eyes. "One more."

One more orgasm? "No, Salem, I can't. You sucked me dry." I threw my arms and legs around him like a dying monkey and pulled until he let his weight fall against me. "Let's snuggle. And sleep. Lots and lots of sleep."

"You can sleep…after you suck *me* dry." He broke my embrace and climbed toward my head. "Open your pretty mouth."

He straddled my shoulders, and his cock jutted above my face, so swollen and red I felt a pinch of guilt. He'd stroked and licked me through countless orgasms—hours of rippling pleasure without biting me, fucking me, or taking his own release.

I might've been seconds from passing out face down in a drool of contentment, but he'd more than earned a hard suck and swallow.

He gripped the base of his erection and stared down at me, his face glistening with a sheen of my come.

"You have a little something…" I directed my gaze at his mouth. "On your…" Jaw, lips, cheeks, everywhere. The sight was disturbing and so fucking erotic.

He swiped a finger across his chin and licked it clean, eyes closing and dark lashes flickering against his skin. "You taste like honey and ripe—"

"If you're going to say—"

"Virginity." His eyes flashed open, brighter and hotter than ever.

"Is that right?" I raised a brow. "You eat a lot of virgins?"

"No." He angled his cock toward my mouth. "You're my first, but don't worry. Virginity is curable, and I intend to cure you in every way imaginable."

His timbre enveloped me like a cold dark night as he slid his fist from root to tip, adding pressure toward the head. Beads of pre-come welled in the slit, and he smeared the salty fluid across my lips.

I opened my mouth. In surprise? Invitation? Certainly not to speak for I had no words.

His lips parted, fangs elongating, and gaze sparking with hellfire. A beast on the edge of starvation.

"When we get out of here…" He notched the head of his cock between my lips, his voice thick with arousal. "I'm going to keep you."

Before I could argue about my place in the world, he dropped his hands to the floor above my head and thrust.

I gripped his ass, my fingers digging into stone as he worked his cock in my mouth, his strokes long and rhythmic. The groaning noises he made were enough to relight my weary fire and coax my tongue into action.

Flat on my back with him kneeling over my head and fucking my face was an unsettling position to be in. He could get carried away and pound my skull into the concrete. But he didn't. The drive of his hips was softer this time, more careful and controlled, as if he knew exactly what he was doing.

He's probably done this a thousand times.

"Cup my balls." His command sounded like a plea, whispered on pained breath.

I shifted a hand around his thigh and reached between his legs from the front. Tentative at first, I slowly massaged his sac, feeling my way around the soft hairless skin and marveling at the weight and shape. *Momentous discovery.* Salem was full of them.

"Dawn…"

Looking up at his eyes, those electric silver eyes, I grunted a *'uh?* around the plunge of his cock.

"Tighten your fing—"

I squeezed.

"Ahhh." His hips moved faster. "Fuck, yes, just like that."

Emboldened, I moved my free hand to the base of his shaft. With a tight fist, I jacked him off while sucking and licking the broad head. He groaned and squeezed his eyes shut, his chest heaving and thighs shaking. Oh, he liked that?

His thrusts slowed to lazy nudges, and for a moment, I thought he was going to hold still and let me take over.

Braced on an arm above my head, he reached down with the other hand and curled his fingers over mine. Then he showed me what he wanted—a tighter grip, twisting strokes, hard tugs—all while I cupped his balls and sucked on the tip. *I think I got it.*

His hand returned to the floor above my head. The muscles in his abs bunched and rippled as he held himself immobile, mouth parted, watching me with a nerve-wracking amount of intensity.

"You look so fucking sinful with your lips around me." His hand moved to the suction of my mouth, and he trailed a knuckle over the hollow of my cheek. "Most beautiful view I've ever seen." His eyes lost focus, his expression tightening. "I'm going to come, baby."

I moaned and sucked harder, twisting my wrist and kneading his balls. He roared, every inch of him turning to steel as he spilled down my throat. I stared up at him with a smile in my eyes and swallowed every drop.

His cock slid out, replaced with his lips in a blur of movement. His naked body covered mine, breaths ragged, as he ate at my mouth. He kissed me deeply, tenderly, straight into a dead-to-the-world coma.

I woke sometime later to the amplified sound of his blood pumping. At some point while I'd slept, he'd pulled on his black cotton pants, but I was still naked, wrapped in warm furs and Salem.

Lifting my cheek from his chest, I wasn't surprised to find a tracery of glowing veins in his neck and torso. I glanced at the door, certain our captors were headed our way.

"Food's coming." I stroked my hand over the vascular pattern of interlaced branches around his heart, mesmerized by the brightening blood flow and the metallic substance worming through it.

Voracious heat pierced through my stomach and stirred through the roots of my teeth. I craved him, *his blood*, but until I understood what was happening, I wasn't going to mention it to him.

He glanced down at his chest. "You see my veins?"

"Yeah, but…" With each caress, the arteries pulsed harder, brighter, gravitating closer to his skin and reaching for my hand. I coasted my fingers down his torso and produced the same effect everywhere I touched. "Can you feel that?"

"Feel what?" He watched my hand with an absorption that illuminated his eyes.

"I can see those silver ribbony things in your blood. I hear your circulation, and when I…" I skimmed my hand across his chest, awe-struck by a bizarre feeling of power. "When I do this, your veins flutter and stretch upward, like a…magnet? I can't sense them by touch, but holy shit, Salem. How can you not feel that?"

An electric buzz sounded, and the steel door slid slowly into motion.

His wide-eyed gaze flew to mine. He almost looked…scared. Not of the door. Scared of *me?*

He jerked out from under me and rolled me to my back. "Pretend you're sick. Dying," he whispered at my ear. Then he rushed for the door.

TEN

Pretend you're sick. Dying.

Eyes closed, I lay still on the pallet of bedding and produced the best weak sounding moan I could muster. If our captors believed the ruse and wanted me alive, they'd rush in, right? My muscles tensed to fight.

"Come back! She's sick!" Salem rattled the gate. "I don't know what's wrong with her." The sound of his pacing footsteps drifted across the floor. "She's vomiting. High fever. Convulsions. I don't know. She's not lucid. I think it's the bite on her leg. It looks infected."

My thigh twitched, but the wound felt fine. It seemed to be healing properly.

The door buzzed, the gears kicked in, and the groan of steel sliding back in place marked a wasted effort.

His breathing picked up, and the gate clanked against whatever part of him he slammed into it. "Don't fucking leave me in here with a rotting corpse!"

Not a thought I wanted to entertain. I peeked an eye open and craned my neck.

He angrily grabbed the waiting cardboard of food and yanked it into the room. When the door sealed shut, I pulled on my shorts, tied the band of suede around my breasts, and slipped into the bathroom to brush my teeth. As I spit the baking soda in the sink, he approached my back.

His hand roamed down my spine with familiarity, and his other plucked the toothbrush from my fingers. Neither of us spoke while he cleaned his teeth. We settled on the pallet of bedding and ate in silence. Roasted beets, some kind of fire-grilled game, and bottled water. At least they fed us well, but I didn't taste the food. I felt numb.

I finished my portion of the meal, telling myself we would break out. Some way or another, I'd see my fathers again.

"Before the door opened," I said, "you looked scared. Why?"

He stroked a finger along his eyebrow, studying me. "You said you can make my veins…flutter? That's pretty alarming, Dawn, because I don't feel shit."

I broke eye contact and pressed my lips together.

"Hey." He touched my chin and lifted my face to his. "You don't scare me. You made my veins move. I'm still alive. We're good."

"*Good* isn't the word I'd use." I pointed a look around our cell.

"Tell me something." He pulled me across his lap, covered our legs with the bedding, and leaned against the wall. "Something personal."

"Personal?" Sitting sideways on his thighs, I rested my head on his shoulder. "Like what?"

"I don't know." He pinched a lock of my hair and coiled it around his finger. "Tell me about someone you care about, your greatest joy, your happiest and worst memories. Tell me anything."

I drew a breath as my mind darted to the one thing that encapsulated his list. "I had a dog."

"A dog?" His hand stilled in my hair. "*The* dog?"

"Darwin. I assume you heard stories."

"I heard about a German Shepherd that saved your mother from starvation, aphids, werewolves, and led your fathers to her prison in Hoover Dam."

"Werewolves?" I laughed. "It was a lion."

"Is the dog…?"

"He died." August 15 at 6:10 AM. Just as the sun rose over Hoover Dam. "I was ten. We were alone on our morning walk through the garden, the one where my mother died."

"The legendary place of your birth."

I nodded, my chest squeezing. "He hobbled over to the spot where she..." I cleared my throat. "The residents built a memorial in the garden where she passed. There's a fountain and benches. A wooden statue carved in her image, surrounded by flowers and keepsakes—blades, figurines, jewelry, things that people, vagabonds from across the country, have made for her in veneration of her life."

Uncomfortable with the wavering sound of my voice, I rubbed a hand on my thigh and pulled in a steadying breath.

He wove his fingers around mine. "You grew up there? At the dam?"

"Near there. My fathers had a yacht on Lake Mead, a few minute's ride by speedboat. But as I got older, we spent more time at the dam and less time on the yacht. Scarcity of fuel made transportation harder, and all my friends and teachers lived within those walls. So when I was nine, we made a permanent move to the dam. Darwin died a year later."

"Old age?"

"Yeah. He..." My breath shuddered as old wounds pulled open. "He went silently, sweetly. Just walked over to the statue of Eve and lay down, eyes closed with his gray muzzle resting on the statue's carved feet. It was perfect, really. The sun was just rising. The air was warm and scented with blooming flowers. And I was with him, stroking his head as his last breath slipped away." I attempted a small smile, but my eyes burned, blurring with moisture.

Salem's thumb caught a tear that sneaked down my cheek. Then he cradled my face between his hands and rested his forehead against mine.

"My fathers...they...when they showed up, it was horrifying to watch." I curled my fingers around his wrists. "It was the only time I've ever seen them cry."

My fierce, intimidating protectors. Bent over in devastation. Eyes swollen, shoulders hunched, clinging to one another as if they were reliving my mother's death all over again.

Salem held me against his chest and stroked my hair. Long minutes whispered by before he spoke. "I had a friend. He was like a father to me."

I didn't move, didn't breathe, longing to glimpse something vulnerable in this confident, dangerous man.

"His name was Wyatt. One of Elaine's countless lovers." Salem fidgeted with a knot in the furs. "He was different from the others. Protective. Kind. *Fatherly.*" The last word was a raw whisper, full of hurt and resentment.

I was afraid to ask, but the pinned line of his lips suggested he wouldn't continue.

"What happened to him?" I leaned closer and touched the hard line of his jaw.

"Elaine killed him. Cut his throat in his sleep." His expression was blank, his voice monotone. "She didn't like the attention he gave me. I should've ended the jealous bitch then, but I was only eight. Too young to survive on my own."

Yet he'd killed her when he was twelve? Still too young to be an orphan in a vicious, desolate world.

"I'm so sorry." I offered him the same compassion he'd given me, my forehead against his, my fingers stroking his neck. Then I kissed his lips and leaned back. "When you were twelve—"

"Enough about Elaine."

Okay, fine. I wouldn't push. *For now.*

He regarded me in a stretch of silence, his eyelids descending lazily over dilated pupils. "Your lips are stained red, like...blood."

I touched my mouth. *The beets.* Then I touched his. Not a tinge of red in sight. "How long can you go without blood?"

"Depends." His tongue darted out and licked my fingertip.

"On?" I pulled my hand back and shifted on his lap.

"Exertion. Loss of my own blood. Sex."

I suddenly felt the urge to scoot away, but that was ridiculous, given my hungry curiosity for the topic of conversation. "Sex?"

"I can't fuck without biting."

"Can't?" I narrowed my eyes. "Or won't?"

"Can't. I have immaculate control of my appetite. Except when I smell blood." His voice dropped to a vibrating rumble. "And during sex."

I glanced at my injured leg covered in furs and returned to him. "Do you drain your…fuck buddies?"

"Never."

So a sip then? That was how my fathers fed on one other. *In the privacy of their bedroom.* I wrinkled my nose at the thought of them in the heat of the moment. Not an image any daughter wants to have of her parents.

Effectively turned off, I climbed to my feet and rolled my neck. "Wanna spar?"

I needed to keep my strength honed and my mind focused, because eventually we *would* bust out of here, and when we did, it would no doubt be a fight to the death.

"Spar?" A devilish grin swept over Salem's face. "Ready to cry your pretty eyes in defeat?"

"Pfft." I shook out my arms and flexed my hands. "You're going down."

He tilted his head, smiling. "In what world do you think you can beat me?"

"In the world of badass women, lover boy. I'll give you a tour." I crooked a finger at him. "On your feet."

Our sparring session lasted five minutes, and I was certain he gave me those minutes out of the hustling depths of his heart. The joke was on me, because the moment he decided to end it, I was chest down, nose smashed against the concrete, with my hands pinned behind my back. He hadn't even broken a sweat, where as I was soaked to the bone. In that way, he was just like my fathers. They never let me win.

But it was a productive way to whittle away time. So over the next few days, we sparred often. We also worked out. Crunches, lunges, sit-ups. Salem found great pleasure in using my body to do his bench-pressing and curls, the show off.

The meals arrived on a rotation, every ten to twelve hours.

We experimented each time with his veins, testing the way they fluttered beneath my hand and stretched toward my movements. He seemed frustrated by the fact that I could see a part of him he couldn't. Or maybe he was just frustrated in general. He never got his flask of liquor, and our captors never spoke or showed themselves. It was as if we were imprisoned by ghosts.

We showered daily and washed our scraps of clothes with a shrinking bar of soap. I used the bar sparingly, fretting over the inevitability of having nothing to clean with. It was such an inconsequential worry in the scheme of things. But being confined to a concrete room made a person stew about all kinds of shit.

Salem stewed about the hybrid children he'd killed, but not in a regretful way. He was contemplative and curious, sharing his speculation that they'd come from the breeding facility I'd infiltrated the day I was captured. It made sense. There had been no babies or children there. They had to have gone somewhere—somewhere close like this mansion, given the harsh Yukon climate.

I spoke often of Eddie's mother, Shea, regaling Salem with stories about her spitfire personality. She'd been my mother's best friend and raised me as one of her own. I loved her the way I loved her son—deeply and unconditionally. My mood darkened when I thought about Shea, Eddie, and my fathers, but Salem always seemed to notice, redirecting the conversation in a lighter direction.

We slept a lot. The dungeon chill chased us beneath the furs with our bodies pressed together, seeking each other for warmth. Sleeping with him in such an intimate embrace was hell on my emotional fortitude. I held up those walls of distrust to protect myself, but hour by hour, day after day, he butted his sexy self into the cracks of my fracturing defenses.

I blamed my weakness on his mastery of my body. He knew how to kiss me, touch me, and make me crazy and stupid with need. He brought me to climax every waking hour like it was his mission in life. We showered. We ate.

Then his mouth was on me again. But he didn't fuck me, no matter how many times I begged. It was baffling, unexpected, and motherfucking frustrating.

It put me in a brooding flux of introspection. If I removed sex and captivity from the equation, how did I feel about him? I spent a lot of time waffling between being narrow-minded, open-minded, and a million minds about it. But the truth was I liked him. I'd certainly grown dependent on his company. Even more troubling, I realized I cared about him on a terrifyingly soulful level.

"What are you waiting for?" I asked ten days later.

Ten days was our estimate based on the number of cardboard trays accumulated beneath the sink.

He stood before me, head lowered, eyes up and firmly fixed on mine. His shoulders were back, arms at his sides, his stance powerfully fierce, and his expression ten shades of smug after just handing me my ass in a wrestling match.

"I know you want me." I circled him, panting through labored breaths. "You've been hard as a rock for ten days." I stopped in front of him and glared at the ever-present erection tenting his pants. "What gives?"

He smirked.

"We're probably going to die in here." I anchored my hands on my hips. "I don't want to die a virgin."

I sounded crazy. Was this what idleness did to people? Was I losing my mind?

"You won't." He folded his hands behind his back, watching me intently.

"Won't what? Die in here? Or die a virgin?"

"Neither."

Same song we'd danced to for days. I turned away and glowered at the steel door. Over the past week, I'd resorted to a screaming tantrum of colorful insults every time it opened. I was ready to unleash some more vulgar yet ever-so-heartfelt words for our captors.

"When is your next monthly cycle?" he asked at my back.

Holy shit. "Pregnancy?" I whirled on him. "That's what

you're worried about?"

"Answer the question."

"I don't know." I pushed a hand through my hair. "I'm not regular, but it's usually every two to three months. I probably have a month before my next one." Fucking hell, would I still be in here then? "Why?"

"Two reasons. One, you'll bleed and the scent..." His eyes flashed. "I won't be able to control myself. Two—"

"Wait. Back up. What happens when you lose control? Be specific."

"If you're bleeding between your legs?" He stepped toward me, his gaze lowering to my suddenly-too-short shorts. "I'll start there. Licking. Sucking. Biting."

I stumbled back, my mouth gaping.

"Then I'll suck on one of those plump veins in your delicate neck." He took another step, and his fangs jutted between his teeth. "I won't drain you, not even close. But I'll most definitely fuck you until you can't walk."

A gulp hung in my throat. "And the downside?"

"The second reason for my question about your cycle. I've never fathered a child. I don't even know if I'm fertile." He backed me against the wall and skimmed his hands around my waist to grip my butt. "How do *you* feel about giving them a child?" He nodded at the door.

Images flashed through my mind of a redheaded toddler with fangs, wearing a collar and crawling on a leash.

I shuddered. "Ten days ago, you were all... How did you phrase it? *I'll pull down your pants right now and fuck you.*"

"Ten days ago, I didn't know you, didn't give a shit what happened to you after I got off inside your tight body."

Ouch. Well, that was honest. And not all that different from my feelings about him when we first met.

"My fathers are infertile," I said. "Jesse wasn't—obviously—until Michio bit him."

"Maybe I am, too." He gripped the back of my knee, hiked my leg up, and pressed his erection against my core. "Maybe my seed won't take. Maybe we'll escape before we find out. The *maybes* have been a tiresome weight on my mind, but you know what? I want you. I want you so fucking badly, damn the risks. Damn this fucking prison. Damn the whole miserable fucking world, because none of it is as agonizing as being with you without *having* you."

How could he say such disastrous things and make them sound so damn perfect? I was so knocked off balance and tongue-tied he might as well have aimed an arrow at my heart and let it fly.

"What will it be, Dawn?" He braced a forearm on the wall above my head and touched his lips to my ear. "Is it worth the risk?"

In the face of human extinction, pregnancy was a reward, not a risk.

Outside of concrete dungeons, I was pro-reproduction. All the way. I knew some human women resented being thought of as an incubator, and I understood that at a gut level. Sex for the solitary purpose of pleasure was an awesome notion, and most women indulged in that, but there was no birth control. One did not even consider such a crazy concept.

STDs were the least of humanity's problems.

Salem and I could bust out of here, smash the boil-covered faces of our captors, and fuck each other's brains out in a river of their rotten blood. Sign me up for that scenario. It got me laid. I loved when human women got laid. Because hello? A dying race! To save!

But pregnancy within these walls? I dropped my head against the concrete. "Fuck."

"Is that your answer?"

"No. Yes." *Idon'tknowIdon'tknow.* I needed to gather my wits, which was damn hard with his lips tickling along my shoulder, tongue swirling against the arch of my neck. A delectable shiver tiptoed across my skin. "Make me a promise."

His mouth stilled on my throat, and his cock jerked against me. "Anything."

"A lot of things can happen in nine months. Promise me

one of those things will be our escape."

He feathered a hand up my back, released the tie on the bandana, and yanked it from my chest. "I pro—"

"Don't just say it." I batted at his wandering fingers, heart pounding. "*Mean* it."

"I promise you." His expression darkened. "We're getting out of here." He gripped my shorts and shoved them to the floor. "But I'm fucking you first."

ELEVEN

The wall at my back chilled my nude body and added little support for my wobbly legs. I clutched Salem's shoulders as his dark promises deposited a lump in my throat.

I won't be gentle.

I can't fuck without biting.

I'll most definitely fuck you until you can't walk.

The lustrous silver of his eyes lured me in like a moonlit tide. My impulsive tendencies didn't always work in my favor, but I knew in my gut I wouldn't regret acting on the reckless, unpredictable, blistering desire I felt for him. No matter how scared I was, intuition demanded I give myself to him. Whether it was the glowy-vein thing or our insane attraction to each other, we were connected on a level neither of us could ignore. Call it fate, prophecy, pheromones, whatever. This was happening.

He stroked a finger down my breastbone, pausing at the curve of my breast. I swore his hand trembled before he dipped lower and traced the jut of my hipbone. And lower still, ghosting knuckles along the inner flesh of my thighs.

He brushed his lips against my throat, whispered at my ear. "Part your legs."

"*You* part my legs."

His fingers shifted, clamped onto my clit, and tweaked it. *Hard.*

A hot flush quivered low in my belly. I scooted my feet apart and dropped my hands to the sculpted indentations of his hips. "We're going to do this standing up?"

"If that's what I decide." He scraped a fang along the juncture of my shoulder and neck.

"It's gonna be like that, huh?" A silly comeback, considering we both knew he would be leading me through this.

"Exactly like that." He sank his hand between my legs, coaxing me open and exciting my inner muscles.

I followed the low waistband around his hips to his back, caressing beneath the cotton and savoring the muscled curve of his ass. With every stroke he made through my folds, I grew wetter, more feverish, silently begging him to ease in.

But there was no easing. His fingers impaled me, pinching delicate tissues and eliciting a foreboding burn.

I yelped, rose up on tiptoes, and adjusted my grip on his glutes.

"Fuck, you're tight." He dropped his forehead to my shoulder and twisted his hand, sinking deeper inside me. "If you bleed on my dick, I won't last."

I'd thought about that. His fingers had penetrated me countless times, but his shaft would be an invasion of epic proportions.

Shifting my grip to his biceps, I lowered my gaze to the hand stirring merciless pleasure between my thighs. "Will I…tear during sex?"

"If your hymen's still intact." He slipped his fingers out and swirled upward to circle my clit.

I gasped, my legs shaking against the onslaught of sensation.

"I haven't felt a barrier." He probed me again, roughly, cruelly, knuckles buried, while his rock-hard chest trapped me against the wall. "As athletic as you are, you probably tore it long ago." His smoldering eyes found mine. "You're soaked. Feel that? Your tiny little pussy sucking on my fingers?"

Ahhh, his naughty words, his ruthless touch, the hunger in his eyes… I slid out my tongue to lick dry lips, but he beat me to it, sinking wet fingers into my mouth and shocking my taste buds with the tang of my arousal. His fangs lengthened, his breathing quickened, and his grip on my waist dug in.

When I tightened my lips and sucked, he yanked his hand away, shoved it between us, and pushed the front of his pants down just enough to free his swollen length. With taunting strokes, he rubbed the broad head against my slick flesh. My eyes fluttered shut, my entire body trembling with nervous excitement.

"Look at me." His syrupy timbre snapped my eyes open.

My breath dissolved. It was impossible to not stare at him like he was a sex object. *Or a sex god.* The translucent embers of his eyes glowed against a flawless complexion. His sexual confidence was palpable, radiating from him in waves of heat. Layers of muscle flexed against me, hard-packed strength carved into a physique made for fucking. He was the kind of man who seduced and ensnared, seized and conquered. Because he could. He could do whatever the hell he wanted. And right now, he wanted me.

His erection throbbed, hot and hard, against my pussy. He bent his knees for a better angle, working the tip around my slippery opening. This wasn't the position I'd imagined. I was too short, my legs weak and unsteady. I didn't know where to put my hands, didn't know what the hell I was doing. The floor would've been ideal. I could barely remain vertical, and he hadn't even fucked me yet.

"Salem?" I rested a hand against the taut tendons in his neck. "I don't think—"

He crashed his mouth against my lips, grabbing my neck as his tongue rubbed and lashed and owned. Holy hell, he'd been holding back. I felt his urgency in the wild, brutal edge of his kiss and in the frantic jab of his dick against my sensitive flesh. He consumed me with a passion he'd never shown before, his mouth hard and bruising, scorching a trail of fire to my core.

The wall vanished from my back, and the room spun around me. In the next heartbeat, I lay on the pallet of furs, spread beneath his vibrating body. He kicked off his pants, grasped the backs of my legs, and pushed my knees toward my head, opening me in the most vulnerable way.

With a ringing roar in my ears, I locked my hands on his shoulders and pressed my back against the floor, welcoming the support. I would've sighed with relief if I had any air left in my lungs.

Lining up his cock, he met my eyes. The only warning he gave me.

Sharp penetrating pain speared my pussy, and the force and depth in which he thrust stopped my heart. My mouth hung open in a silent shriek, my fingers locked on his shoulders as a blaze of fire devoured my inner walls and raced up my spine.

Buried to the root with an iron grip on the backs of my thighs, he held still, choked, "Deep breath."

Was he talking to me or himself? I was pretty sure my lungs had collapsed beneath the inferno in my body.

He stared at where we were joined, his fangs indenting his bottom lip as he inhaled.

I found my breath. "Is there blood?"

"No." When his gaze reconnected with mine, his eyes were volcanic, and the muscles in his face twitched with tension. "Do you feel…any changes?"

Other than the searing fullness stretching my body beyond capacity? I knew what he was asking. Did sex with him unlock another weird ability? His veins remained invisible beneath his skin. I didn't feel any cravings for blood, didn't have the sudden urge to tear out his jugular. Nothing was amiss, and the uncomfortable pain slowly began to sink into a warm, languid fever.

When I shook my head, his focus zoomed in on my throat. Then he kissed a path there, across my cheek, over my jaw, his fangs sharp and menacing as they dragged down my neck. My insides quivered, and my blood sang, surging toward my heart and skyrocketing my pulse.

He jerked his hips, gliding his length along the raw tissues inside me. Then he kicked into a pounding fast rhythm, releasing my legs to fist my hair and pull painfully at the roots. With my head angled to the side and held immobile between his hands, he pressed his teeth against my jaw, his breath seething with desire.

He didn't just fuck me. He burrowed inside me with total engagement of his being, embracing me with every tendon, bone, and molecule in his body. He possessed me physically and emotionally as if I were an extension of himself. I felt stripped of more than just clothes, as though every secret part of me was exposed and at his mercy. The intimacy was beautiful and terrifying, inflaming a desperate need to deepen the trust and hold on to the connection with teeth and nails.

"You feel unbelievable." His syllables blended together, smooth and velvety like the lips on my cheek. "Your body was made for me. I can't get enough." He hammered faster, harder, his fangs scraping across my jaw, voice breathless. "The grip of your narrow little cunt is driving me fucking insane. I need…I have to…feed."

I moaned a garbled *yes* and stabbed my fingers in his hair, digging against his scalp. He nipped and kissed my jaw, hands clenched around my neck, and in my peripheral vision, his eyes illuminated beneath hooded lids.

Then his hands slipped over my breasts and wedged under my back. His thrusts sped up, lunging deeper inside me as he stretched his jaw over my throat.

Scars from a dozen bites tingled on my chest and arms, the remembered pain shooting tension through my neck. I anchored my feet on the floor and forced my fingers to relax in his hair. I felt so fucking fragile and small beneath his powerful body and lethal teeth. But I also felt safe. *He won't hurt me.*

Everything narrowed to the firm lips on my throat, tugging, nibbling, his tongue flicking across delicate skin. Then his breath evaporated, and a sharp piercing burn ripped through my neck. The pain was shocking yet finite as a torrent of longing so hot and intense rushed wetness between my legs.

A low guttural groan reverberated in his chest, and his hips slowed to a rocking grind. He suckled and swallowed, producing a strange melting sensation in my body. Venomous heat spread through my veins, warming my chest and throbbing my teeth. The drugging sensation was so immensely demanding it smothered me in a haze of hunger. I wanted to come. I needed to bite.

Perspiration formed on my skin. The room bled red. Sound slipped away, leaving the humming swish of his blood. And the scent of iron, warm and thick. The flavor, bold and rich, on my lips. I tasted his blood? *Impossible.* But I needed to. I needed to sink my teeth and alleviate this starving ache.

I bucked my hips and angled my mouth toward his neck. His hand caught my jaw, holding it in a vise as he drew from my vein and fucked me into submission.

"I need…" My voice sounded distant and reedy, weighted with lust.

His free hand reached between us and rubbed my clit with expert strokes, momentarily clouding my craving for blood. I shut my eyes, relaxed into the pull of approaching bliss, and when the orgasm hit, I felt it so acutely my back bowed and a scream shattered my vocal chords. I locked my legs around his back and met his furious thrusts, reaching, gripping, and vying for control.

He yanked his fangs from my neck and threw his head back, following me into madness. My name poured from his bloody lips like a plea, his breaths ragged and muscles stark with tension. Then he collapsed on my chest and buried his face in my neck, his tongue roving over the puncture marks.

"Best thing I've ever experienced." His mouth moved against my skin, his fingers lazily curling through my hair.

His neck was so close I could taste his coppery essence. My mind and body refused to ignore it. Fuck, my teeth hurt. Just a bite. A little turnabout was fair play. I angled my head, pressed my teeth against his throat—

"Fuck!" He jerked back. "What are you—?" His eyes locked on my mouth and widened. "You're bleeding. You're—" He pressed a finger on my lip and inched it upward. "Shit!"

He pulled out of me and fell back on his ass. Dread sank in

my stomach as I tentatively moved my tongue, catching it on a razored point. My hand flew to my mouth, and the rushing roar of my heart filled my ears.

I scooted until my back hit the wall, putting space between me and the intoxicating scent of his blood.

He pulled on his pants, watching me cautiously. "Do you feel stronger, faster?"

"I don't know. I'm…" *Stunned.* I touched my canines, probed at the sharp tips, and held my hand in front of me.

Blood. That was what I'd tasted. I'd fucking bitten myself, and now that my senses weren't overloaded with sex and bloodlust, I felt the twin indentations against my lip when I closed my mouth.

"How?" He wiped his mouth with the back of his hand and stared at me with wary astonishment. "Was it…did it happen when we started fucking or when I bit you?"

I replayed the past few minutes in my head and remembered the moment I tasted blood. "When you bit me."

We stared at each other, the silence thickening until he broke it. "What are you thinking?"

"You told me your bite wouldn't turn me."

"This wasn't me, Dawn." His voice deepened, clipping with anger. "I've bitten countless human women and they've—"

"Stop."

"—never grown fangs!"

Furious desperation blazed in his glare. I swallowed the bait, internalized it, and decided I believed him.

"I've waited my whole life for some kind of genetic alteration to happen, but *not* fangs. I would've never imagined…" I waved a shaky hand at my mouth. "How the hell does this save humanity?"

His jaw tensed. "Maybe your bite alters hybrids."

"Like a cure." I pulled the pelt of furs over my nudity, shivering against the cold and the racing direction of my thoughts.

How could my fangs cure the hybrid infection? It wasn't

like I could bite the entire population. But maybe I only needed to bite a few, and it would spread?

He rubbed his neck, and a tenebrous storm swept across his expression. "I don't like this."

I trembled in a fog of utter shock. "If I had to make a ruling, I'm eleven percent this is a good thing and eighty-nine percent this is a *what-the-almighty-fuck-I-don't-know* thing."

"Eleven percent?" He narrowed his eyes. "Explain."

"I'm hungry, Salem." I glanced at his beautiful throat. "Fangs would allow me to—"

"No." He pointed at me, voice stern.

"Just a taste."

"No tasting." He took a step back.

"Why the fuck not? You just *tasted* me."

"I unlocked this…thing in you." He gestured at my fangs. "We don't know what'll happen the other way around."

"Why would you think—?"

"Your mother…" He gripped the back of his neck and paced the far side of the room. "She destroyed the Drone's *monstrous* creations. Creations like *me*. She shared their strength and speed and blew them to hell with a thought."

"The aphids. Not you." I gritted my teeth and flinched against the prick of my fangs. *Fuck!*

He watched me with shadows of distrust behind his luminous eyes. "We need to test your strength."

"Now?"

Just as the word left my mouth, he was on me, chest to chest, my back to the floor, and his hands around my neck. I couldn't breathe past the stranglehold. Black spots invaded my vision. My fangs pierced my lip and filled my mouth with blood. I couldn't shove him off, couldn't pry his hands from my throat. *Let go, let go, let go.*

He did, leaping up and back across the room. "Human strength." His voice was even, unruffled, *relieved.*

"Go to hell." I gripped my throat, gulping for air. "Don't ever do that again."

"We need to get out of here." He turned toward the door.

"What are you going to—?"

Bang. Bang. Bang. His fist pounded on the steel. "Let me out!" He raised his voice to a volume that rattled the rafters. "I fucked the crazy bitch, and she turned into a fucking hybrid. Get me the fuck out of here!"

I gaped at him. "Are you serious?"

He glanced at me over his shoulder, put a finger against his shushing lips, and winked.

I rolled my eyes. Our captors didn't come when he said I was dying. I didn't hold on to any hope that they'd rush to protect him.

Gliding my tongue over my new teeth, I acquainted myself with the angled edges. I continued the oral exploration while pulling on my shorts and tying the makeshift bra around my chest. Lifting my head, I caught the glow of his veins out of the corner of my eye. My breath hitched.

"Salem," I whispered. When he looked my way, I pointed at his chest and mouthed, *They're coming.*

I scanned the concrete ceiling, embedded wood beams, and single electric bulb as I'd done a million times over the past ten days. There were no cracks or peep holes anywhere in this cell block. No way our captors could spy on us.

An electric buzz signaled the impending movement of the door.

I met Salem's eyes. "It's too soon for a food delivery."

He backed away from the door, angling in the opposite direction of where I stood. Should I go after him? Pretend to attack him? We hadn't discussed a fucking plan.

The gears groaned, and the door shimmied opened an inch, another inch, and stopped. My heart crashed to a halt.

I stole a glance at Salem, but his attention was on the door, his back straight, expression severe. I followed his gaze, my pulse throbbing in my throat.

Something moved in the dark crack. Small and indiscernible, it hovered at chest height, glinting in the light. Metal?

The next few seconds flashed in a blur. A pop sounded.

The air whistled. Salem shouted and lunged for me. His body slammed me to the floor and pain jolted through my back. What the—?

He sprawled across me, the tension draining from his muscles and a dart protruding from his shoulder. A chill tore up my spine, and I jerked to run for the bathroom. But he was too heavy to move off me, and I was too slow. Another pop had already rent the air.

A prick stung my thigh. I reached down, bumped the dart in my leg. Queasiness surged. Vertigo spun me into groggy confusion. I fought it, fumbling in slow motion. So heavy. Too fuzzy.

Fuck you, Salem, and your stupid ideas.

The lights went out.

TWELVE

My legs were on fire.

I clawed my way out of the dazed space between unconsciousness and awareness, mentally probing my body. The prickling scorch of a thousand needles attacked my face and hands, and a knot of nausea twisted my stomach. Why was I burning? Where was I?

I lay still on my back and listened.

Nothing. But the nothingness sounded different, vast, as if it stretched out around me for miles. And the air felt sharper, fresher. Brutally cold. A waft of alpine tickled my burning nose. Not burning. *Freezing.*

I cracked open an eye and met pitch-black darkness. Where was Salem? My pulse kicked up. *Don't panic.*

My fingers curled into frigid, powdery…snow? My breath rushed out, and my head spun through the weight of lingering sedation. Warm softness covered my upper body and feet. I felt around with clumsy movements and found familiar textures on my body—my cloak, medallion, boots, shorts. Holy shit, my bow!

A branch snapped in the distance, and something skittered overhead. My heart catapulted to my throat. I was outside. At night. Drugged. In shorts.

How did I get here? Were my captors nearby? Salem? Everything I'd had with me when I was captured had been returned, except…

I pawed through the folds of furs, frantically searching for my mother's dagger. When I found it buckled to my hip, relief escaped my cracked lips in a plume of condensation. An answering breath sounded a few feet away. Salem?

Rolling to my side, I strained my eyes and spotted an obscure human-sized smudge lying in the snow.

"Salem?" I whispered.

The shadow stirred. "Dawn?"

Oh, thank fuck. I crawled toward him, scraping my exposed legs through the wet snow and shaking violently.

My vision adjusted on the silhouettes of surrounding trees and the trail of footprints heading off to the right. Were we still in the Yukon? How long did a sedative last? They couldn't have transported us far. Unless they'd tranquilized me more than once.

I reached his leather clad body and rolled him to his back. He wore a long black coat buttoned down the front, leather pants, and heavy boots. Beside him sat a huge backpack and a strange wooden club with a curved neck and a spiky bulb at the end.

Hooking a finger beneath the collar of his trench coat, I tugged it down. *No veins.*

"Am I glowing?" He opened his starlit eyes and stared up at me.

"Uh, just your eyes. Damn. You could light up the sky with those peepers." I glanced around, my heart rate accelerating. "I just woke. I don't know where we are. Looks like the Yukon. We're alone, but who knows for how long."

"Shh." He cupped my cheek and gave me a small smile. "You okay?"

"Frozen to the bone." I shivered to the point of pain. "A little sluggish. A lot confused. You?"

"Same." He sat up and started to topple over, catching himself on a braced arm. "Whoa. I think I need a minute."

"Why are you waking after me?" I maneuvered my numb legs into a crouch, pulling the cloak around my bare skin. "Doesn't your body recover quicker?"

"It should've…no, wait." He dropped his head in his hands. "I came to…I was being dragged face down through the snow and…fuck!" He reached back and rubbed his shoulder blade. "They shot me more than once."

"Did you see them?" I glanced at the tracks and counted two sets of footprints. "How many?"

"It was dark. I only remember flashes. Snow. A pair of boots. The sting in my back." He looked around. "Any idea which way—?" His gaze landed on my crouched position. "You're still in those shorts."

"Yep. I'll be dead from hypothermia in a few hours." My teeth chattered. "Got any extra room in your pants?"

"You already know the answer to that." His eyes glimmered as he grabbed the backpack. "This is…" He dug through it. "This is *my* backpack. It doesn't make sense. They let us go? Put clothes on us?" He pulled out a hunting knife and stared at it in shock. "Why would they return our weapons?"

"They want us to live?"

"So they tossed us out in sub-zero temperatures with no food or shelter?" He removed a pair of fur-lined leather pants. "Put these on. I'll find something to hold them up."

A few minutes later, he led us in the opposite direction from the boot tracks. A rope belt held my borrowed pants in place, and fur gloves and a hat from his backpack added extra protection from the cold. On his mission to stalk me, he'd come prepared, where I'd run off into No Man's Land, leaving all my supplies behind with Eddie. *Stupid, impulsive me.*

Clutching my mother's dagger, I plowed through the snow, weaving around low-hanging branches and feeling my way through the dark. I didn't have a single arrow and needed to fashion some as soon as we found shelter.

He squinted at a compass from his backpack, but we didn't have a starting point. We'd been dropped in a frozen forest without a map or a smack on the ass.

"You know what's bugging me?" He stopped, waiting for me to catch up.

"My shorter legs?"

"No, baby." His leather-gloved hand lifted my chin. "I love your legs."

I pressed a kiss on his palm, expecting him to flinch away from my teeth. Instead, he pulled my head against his chest and wrapped me in a warm embrace. Maybe he could sense my bloodlust had taken a nosedive in lieu of a more pressing need—*surviving the night.*

"What's bugging you?" I mumbled against the chest straps of his backpack.

I could think of a thousand things. Why did our captors free us? Because we had sex? Because I grew fangs? Why not just kill us if they didn't like the outcome? Or maybe we gave them exactly what they wanted? What if I was pregnant? What if my fangs are meant to destroy humanity, not save it? *Don't think about that.*

"I don't want to freak you out." He nudged my face up, warming my cheeks with his gloved hands. "But are you sure you're okay? You don't feel any bites? No pain from a possible…from forced entry?"

Rape. The hairs on my nape stood on end. "Let's keep moving." I trudged ahead, concentrating on twinges or discomfort I might've overlooked. If I'd been raped, would I feel raped? "Other than your bite on my neck, I don't feel anything suspicious."

"If our captors were hybrid," he said, "why didn't they bite you?"

The hybrid venom mentally programmed the infected with an uncontrollable need to bite humans and impregnate women. If I were still human—*Scratch that. I* am *still human*—they wouldn't have been able to stop themselves from fucking and feeding on my comatose body.

I rubbed my arms beneath the cloak. "Maybe my fangs deterred them." I threw him a sideways glare. "You did tell them the crazy bitch turned into a hybrid."

He kept his eyes straight ahead, and the corner of his mouth twitched. "I promised you I'd get us out of there."

"About that…" I stopped, tilted my head. "How did you

know that would work?"

He looked around, scrutinizing the woodland shadows. "We're not doing this here." Without a backward glance, he sped up his gait.

"Not doing what?" I chased after him, tightening my grip on the dagger. "You know something, don't you? What are you not telling me?"

"Let it go, Dawn."

"No—"

He whirled on me and caught my throat in a punishing grip. "Daylight is coming." He stabbed a finger toward the right. "If we don't find a place to bunker down…" His expression tightened with an unusual mix of pain and ferocity. Just as quickly, his face softened. "I know you don't trust me—"

"I do." I pried at the fingers on my throat. "When you're not fucking choking me."

His hand loosened but didn't release me. "You *don't* trust me, and we'll talk about that. We'll talk about all of it as soon as we're safe."

He dropped his arm and strode away, leaving me shaken and speechless.

Assuming we were still near the Yukon River in Canada's far north, there would only be about four or five hours of daylight. But how did he know what time it was? I stared at the canopy of branches overhead and the black sky peeking through. It could've been nine at night or nine in the morning. My sense of time and direction was fucked up beyond recognition.

The wide hump of his backpack faded into the darkness, and the dense shadows of undergrowth crept in around me. I missed the warmth of sunlight on my face, the scent of it on my skin, and the profound sight of it destroying the gloom of night. *Dawn.* The word my mother whispered on her dying breath. The last thing she saw before she gave me her life. A life I wouldn't squander.

Salem wanted us to find safety, and that took priority over

his secrets. I didn't trust him with intel regarding Resistance missions, didn't trust that his actions were in favor of humanity's future. But I trusted him with my life. I believed, in the depths of my soul, he would protect me.

We plodded side by side in silence through the endless timberland. He stole glances at the eastern horizon but stayed on a southern course, according to his compass. I kept my eyes peeled for signs of my fathers. They would be frantically hunting for me. Could they be looking in this very forest? I'd been missing for at least ten days. Their concern must've been eating them alive. I watched for breaks in the tree limbs and stacked stones—any of their trademarks indicating they'd passed through the area.

I left my own breadcrumbs by knotting branches on trees I passed and bending them in the direction I traveled.

"What are you doing?" Salem eyed my hands.

I tied off a black spruce limb and folded it until it bowed with the end aiming southward.

"It's something Jesse taught me." I released the branch and continued walking south. "When I'm lost, I bend the branches to point like arrows along my route. If one of my fathers sees it, he'll know which way I went."

"And if there are no trees?" He sounded skeptical.

"We have distinctive trademarks for every situation."

"Do they actually find you through these trademarks?"

"Always." I drew in an unsteady breath.

The Yukon spanned over one-hundred-thousand square miles. Finding me was like finding a needle in a mountain of pine needles. But Eddie knew I'd headed west—the opposite direction of our camp.

"If our captors dumped us near the mansion," I said, "We're west of my camp, a three or four day walk maybe."

"What kind of camp?"

"A small barricaded town. A few people lived there when we found it. We've been helping them fortify their walls, and in exchange, they let us use it as a temporary headquarters for the past couple months."

He nodded and continued walking. I didn't question his decision to venture south. The footprints in the snow where we woke trailed north. Mission number one was putting distance between us and our captors. Once we gathered our bearings, I would go east, back to my temporary hub, with or without Salem.

My chest clenched at the thought of separating from him. I forced it out of my mind, refusing to focus on what-ifs.

"What is that?" I nodded at the odd wooden club in his hand.

"It's a totokia club." He held it in front of me, giving me a closer view in the dark. "Sometimes mistaken as a pineapple club."

It reminded me of an ostrich, with the long neck curving into a round head and a pointed beak. Except the head bristled with wooden thorns and the beak sharpened into a lethal spike.

"Does it have a story?" I asked.

"My friend, the man I told you about, Wyatt..." He tipped the club upward to rest on his shoulder as he stepped over a fallen log.

"The man who was like a father to you."

"Yeah. He was an antique dealer before the virus and had this club in his collection. When he gave it to me, he said it was from the Fiji Islands. See the spike? It was designed to puncture a neat hole through a skull. The bulky head puts weight behind it, so when you drive the spike through bone, you don't need a long warning swing. The natives were known cannibals. You can imagine its usefulness."

"That's, uh..." I coughed against my fist. "Disturbing."

"But effective." He slid me a fanged grin.

"Well, you're probably not going to need it out here."

I hadn't seen a hint of life in the however many hours we'd been walking. I'd kept a watchful eye on his neck, waiting for the phosphorescent veins to appear. Not that I expected to encounter a random enemy or wandering vagabond. The Yukon had been sparsely populated in the old world. It would be exponentially barren now.

"Do you know how many people died in the last world war?" I paused to knot and bend a branch that hung in my path.

His eyebrows scrunched. "I'm going to guess it was a lot."

"Over sixty million." I brushed the snow from my gloves and caught up with him. "That was three-percent of the world population in 1940. Do you know how many died when the virus hit?"

"Humans?"

"Yes, Salem. How many *humans* died in those first few weeks?"

"Ninety percent." His focus drifted over the trees, his gaze distant.

"Yeah. That's over six billion people. Gone. Just like that." I stared at the frosty skeletal terrain. "There's not very many of us left, especially not out here in this arctic hell. The chances of us running into someone who could help—"

"Look." He grabbed my hand and pointed at a dimly lit clearing up ahead. "Maybe we'll see a landmark or something to guide us."

We rushed forward and slammed to a stop.

A river stretched out before us, about forty-yards wide, frozen over, and glistening beneath the moonlight.

My heart jumped with excitement. "Is this—?"

"The Yukon River? Yes." He pointed north at a fuzzy mountain peak against the paling gray skyline. "If that's Midnight Dome, we're just south of old Dawson City."

My mind darted to images of the map I'd studied for months. We were farther north than I'd thought, but I knew how to make it back to camp from here. Only a five-day walk. A grin spread across my face.

He turned me toward the steep rocky bluff that towered over the opposite shore of the river. "There's a cave in there. See it?"

The limestone karst was a majestic depiction of erosion by wind, ice, and water. Shadows clung to the porous ridges and jutting overhangs, but the angle of the moonlight revealed a skinny crack in the rock-ribbed veneer. If the river hadn't been frozen, it wouldn't have been accessible.

He tested the surface of the ice with a stomp of his boot. "It's at least a foot thick. Should be safe to walk on." He speared another glance at the eastern horizon.

Given the fading hues of the sky, the sun would rise any minute and illuminate a snow-glazed landscape blotted with spruce trees and divided by the frozen river. A river that would lead me southeast, directly back to camp. A flutter lifted my chest.

"I'm going to cross first," he said. "When I make it halfway, follow my path."

As he ventured out on the ice, I gathered four flat stones and stacked three of them on the shore where he entered. I placed the fourth stone beside the pile at a one o'clock position—the direction of the cave.

"Dawn! Move your ass." He stood at the center of the river, tall and fierce beneath the heavy weight of the backpack.

"Will your cannibal club put a hole through the ice?" I strode across the surface, aided by the grippy soles of my boots. "We could do some ice fishing."

He wove his hand around mine and led me to the cliff. "I'm better at hunting beaver."

"Was that an innuendo?"

"No." He huffed a laugh. "Trapping a beaver is a helluva lot easier than spearing fish."

"Beavers don't like to be trapped."

He shook his head, grinning at me. "*That's* an innuendo."

I lifted a shoulder, sharing his smile.

Up ahead, the craggy flank of the cliff gave way to a fissure and hopefully, a cave within. He crouched down and ducked his head inside the two-foot wide crack.

"Salem." I pulled on our laced fingers. "What if an ice bear lives in there?"

"Then we eat it." He shrugged off the backpack, removed

a kerosene lantern, and lit it with a built-in striker.

I stared, wide-eyed and impressed. What else did he have in that pack?

"What?" He looked at the lamp and back at me. "I make my own kerosene with oil shale and—"

"I do, too, but you seem to have an endless supply of handy stuff. It's curious, that's all."

"I live in this terrain, remember? I also knew that tracking you—"

"Stalking."

"*Tracking*—"

"Trapping beaver." I pinned my lips together, fighting laughter.

"Fuck." He broke first, laughing and rubbing his head. "You win. I knew that *stalking* and *trapping beaver* wouldn't be a weekend trip. I set out with a season's worth of supplies."

"All right, you dirty boy scout." I nodded at the cave. "Carry on."

Rather than crawling through the crack, he rose to his full height and tugged me against his chest.

"I've been meaning to tell you." He kissed the corner of my mouth. "Your fangs"—a kiss on the other corner—"are sexy as fuck."

When he leaned back, an invasion of frostbitten air rushed over my lips. I wanted his mouth back. And his hands, his teeth, his cock… I wanted all of him joined with all of me in a warm cocoon of bliss.

"You're not afraid I'll bite you?" I reached out and fidgeted with a button on his leather coat.

"I recognize the levels of bloodlust. Right now, your body needs sleep and food."

He turned back to the crevice and ducked inside, pulling me along with a grip on my hand. The dusky glow of the lamp guided us through the narrow opening and into a yawning space the diameter of our concrete prison in the mansion. I buckled my mother's dagger on my hip and turned in a circle.

The limestone walls percolated with moisture. Soft white minerals formed drippy deposits on the low ceiling, and an abandoned fire pit sat next to the narrow entrance.

Setting the lantern on the floor in the center of the space, he squatted beside the pile of petrified wood and picked through the ash and timber.

I folded my arms across my chest to ward off the chill. "Do you think someone stays here?"

"In the old world, troglodytes inhabited this area. I suspect they all mutated or died twenty years ago."

"Troglodytes?"

"Shaggy beards. Anti-modernization. Mushroom-picking, cave-dwelling hermits."

"Sounds lonely."

"There's freedom in the wilderness, right?"

"Is that what you think?" I longed for civilized society, surrounded by growing families and people I could depend on.

"No." He brushed his hands together and stood with his head lowered to avoid a bump on the ceiling. "I appreciate the finer things in life."

There was a wealth of knowledge to pull from that statement, but I had more important things to focus on. "Let's get a fire going. We need to go catch something to eat."

"The wood is too wet." He stared at the pale band of light on the rocky floor of the cave opening. "I can't use it for a fire."

"Okay, well, we have daylight now. Grab your hunting knife." I strode toward the crevice that led outside. "There's plenty of firewood around here. And I need some hardwoods and fletching to make arrows."

"Wait." He grabbed my arm and yanked me toward the rear of the cave. "You're not going out there without me."

"I wasn't. I thought…" I narrowed my eyes at the strange look on his face. "What's wrong with you?"

He stepped back, planting his boots in a wide stance, as if to block my escape.

"What are you doing?" I didn't like the sudden rigidness in his posture.

"Before our captors brought you in…" He squared his shoulders and gestured at the floor. "Sit down."

"I don't want to sit down." My nerves were fraying, every part of me desperate to hear the rest of that sentence. "Keep talking."

"They aimed a tranquilizer gun through the crack in the door, but before they fired it, a male voice spoke to me." His jaw tensed in the glimmer of the lantern. "He said, 'Fuck the daughter of Eve and you'll be freed.'"

Anger spiked through my veins, and my hands fisted at my sides. "That's why you—?"

"No! Listen." He raked a hand through his hair. "At first, yeah, I wanted to fuck your hot little body and collect my get out of jail free card. But within hours, you changed everything."

"I don't understand." My stomach knotted, my voice sharp and ugly. "What did I do exactly?"

"You…*glowed.* Intensely and brightly. I thought it was your eyes bewitching me, but it's you. Your inner strength, remarkable beauty, sassy comebacks—the whole fucking package." He stepped closer, pausing within arm's reach. "You made me care about you. Fucking you in exchange for freedom no longer mattered. *You* mattered, and I wanted you on *my* terms, when you trusted me enough to want me in return."

As I absorbed his words, I shifted to put space between us. He moved in, pressed my back against the wall, and framed my face with gloved hands.

My fists relaxed, and my breathing slipped into a defeated rhythm. "Why didn't you tell me?"

He touched his brow to mine. "I didn't want you to give me your virginity for any other reason than because you wanted to."

I understood that, but the omission still left a vexing burn. "What was your plan after you notified our captors that you fucked the crazy bitch? The deal was they would free *you*, right?"

He lowered his hands to my waist and squeezed. "I intended to throw you over my shoulder and fight our way out."

"By taking a tranquilizer dart in the back?" I arched a brow.

"I didn't know what kind of gun it was." His nostrils flared, and his eyes burned silver. "I acted on instinct. If you'd been shot with a bullet—"

I pressed my fingers against his lips. "Fair enough."

We could talk circles around *would'ves, could'ves, should'ves,* but we'd end up in the same place—cold, tired, and hungry. I didn't know if I believed him. I didn't know why our captors wanted him to have sex with me. We'd played into some mindfuck game that I couldn't begin to figure out with an exhausted brain.

Right now, we were alive, and we would stay that way if we found food and remained focused. We had four, maybe five hours of daylight to catch something to eat, and I would need every one of those hours to find a breathing carcass in this wasteland, as well as the supplies to fashion enough arrows to last me the five-day walk back to camp.

I ducked around him and headed for the mouth of the cave. "Unless you have any other omissions you'd like to share, let's go foraging."

"I can't." The guttural growl in his voice stopped me in my tracks.

"Why not?" I turned around.

He was crouched in the deepest part of the cave, forearms resting on his thighs, head lowered, and metallic eyes cutting through the dark. "I can't go outside."

"What? You were just out there. You're not making any sense."

His gaze shifted to the ground behind me. I pivoted, searching the sunlit rock floor for clues. Then it hit me.

Pale, luminous complexion. No creases around his eyes.

No blemishes. No freckles. *As if he'd never seen the sun.*

"Sunlight," I whispered. "You can't be in the sun?" I spun back. "Are you allergic?"

"Something like that."

"How bad? What happens?"

Did he get a burn? A rash? Did his skin swell up?

He rose in a fluid motion and prowled toward me, sliding a glove off one hand. When he reached the band of light striping the threshold of the cave, he veered around it and lowered on his haunches behind the wall of the opening, his entire body blanketed in shadows.

I clutched my throat, warring with the urge to tell him he didn't have to prove anything. But selfish curiosity held my voice hostage.

His face tilted downward as he flexed his gloveless hand. Then he stretched out his arm and held his fingers in the light.

Blisters bubbled, dried, and cracked like parched earth in a fraction of a second. He hissed past clenched fangs as his skin sizzled and smoldered in wisps of smoke, shriveling, baking, and dissolving to ash over bone.

"Salem!" I screamed in horror, my stomach hardening into ice. "Stop!"

The exposed muscle in his fingers flexed as he curled them into a fist. He yanked his hand back, tucked it to his chest, and lifted electric eyes etched with pain. "This is why I killed Elaine."

THIRTEEN

A swamping wave of denial and confusion crashed into me. *Sunlight turns him to ash.* I felt a pressing need to sit down before I fell down. *He's trapped in eternal darkness.* My legs gave out as I plopped hard to the ground and dropped my throbbing head in my hands.

This is why he killed Elaine?

Heavy black boots appeared beneath my face, inches from the sunlit opening of the cave. I lifted my head.

Salem held his charred hand behind his back. The other he offered to me, palm up and concealed in leather. "Come sit with me in the dark."

The pain had retreated from his eyes, and in its place was crystal-sharp vigilance. Did he think I would run? That I was afraid of him?

His expression was carved in stone, his body dangerously still, as if he were braced to chase me—directly into the sun if it came to that.

I clutched his gloved fingers and stood. "I'm not running from you."

"Nor am I running from you." He glanced at my fangs.

Good grief. He still thought I was going to bite him? Then what? That I'd kill him with my inexperienced bloodlust? I pressed my lips together and steeled my spine. We had a lot of shit to talk about.

Leading me to the darkest corner of the cave, he released my hand to snag the backpack and club. Then he sat with his back to the wall and pulled me onto his lap.

His leather coat and trousers creaked as I set my bow aside and settled against his rock-hard body. Despite the layers of clothes between us, I felt his warmth and strength everywhere, the image of his nude physique forever branded in my mind. He must've spent an absurd amount of time building those powerful shoulders, curved biceps, and *V*-shaped abs. There wasn't an ounce of fat beneath all that rippling muscle. He was inconceivably gorgeous, formidable and agile, with the stamina of a horse. Yet something as essential and benign as the sun reduced him to ash.

"Let me see your hand," I said softly, reclining against his chest.

"It'll heal."

I removed my borrowed fur gloves and held out my palm.

He drew in a breath and rested his wrist in my hand. The lantern bathed his raw bubbly skin in a deathly glow. Though the tissues were rapidly stitching back together, it must've been excruciating to endure. I stole a glance over my shoulder and found his eyes closed, brows pinched, and his head tipped back against the wall.

This is why I killed Elaine.

"You blame her for this?" I balanced his forearm on my knee, preventing his delicate flesh from bumping anything.

"Elaine? No. The Drone made me what I am when he injected her pregnant body with his experimental venom. I ki—"

"Wait. He injected her with something other than his bite?" My stomach cramped. Whether it was nerves or hunger, I pretended to ignore it.

"Elaine let him do whatever he wanted to her. She hoped to give him a perfectly engineered child, the Prince of his chosen race. The Drone died before I was born, but she still hoped." He made a fist, stretching the newly formed skin across his knuckles. "The brainwashed cunt was disappointed the first time she took me into the sun. I'm surprised she didn't just let me disintegrate and toss my ashes into the wind. But then she wouldn't have been able to use my *condition* as punishment over the next twelve years."

My breath caught. "What do you mean?"

"We lived all over North America, moving from place to place."

Running from my father? Michio had searched for her for years, driven by revenge. But it was as if she'd vanished from the earth.

"She hated that we could only travel at night," he said. "It was inconvenient that we could only bunker down in dark places. She hated me for that. Hated that my weakness made me imperfect. Whenever I misbehaved… Hell, even when I didn't, she shoved me outside and held me in the sun long enough to ensure I felt her resentment down to my bones. Literally."

I covered my mouth, and a knot of anguish coiled in my gut.

"During one of those punishments," he said quietly, "I tore out her throat."

Twisting on his lap, I straddled his hips and cupped his strong neck. "I hope she suffered."

He touched his lips to mine so very lightly. The tender caress was fangs in the heart, desperately feeding from my soul. It was painful and beautiful and poignant.

"Our captors could've dumped you in daylight." I rested my forehead against his.

"They could've killed you while I was drugged."

"They could've sniffed my panties." I pursed my lips.

"They better not have—"

"Maybe they sniffed yours?"

His shoulders twitched beneath my hands, and a moment later, a gorgeous grin cracked his face.

I traced the sensual curve of his mouth. "Come back to my camp with me. Michio's there, and he might be able to—" I stopped myself before I made promises I couldn't keep. "He can run some genetic tests. Maybe there's something…I don't know. Before the virus, he worked in a lab with the Drone. They were close once and knew the intricacies of each other's work. Maybe he can explain your reaction to sunlight?"

"You're asking me to enter the domain of the great warriors after I deflowered their precious daughter?" He laughed mirthlessly. "They'll castrate me."

"They'd have to get through me first."

"Fierce." He stroked a thumb across my cheek.

"Stubborn. I'm not ready to let you go."

"Good thing, because I have no intention of letting *you* go."

"Stalker," I whispered against his lips.

The fingers caressing my face felt soft and warm and…healed. I clutched his wrist and held it in the lamp light. Pristine, porcelain skin wrapped his large muscled hand, tipped with perfectly trimmed nails. *Incredible.*

"That was fast." I laced our fingers together and met his eyes. "How much sun exposure can you withstand before…"

"It only takes seconds to burn past muscle and bone and reach my organs." He stared at our hands, expression unreadable. "There were times when I was younger…it took weeks to heal my insides. I didn't think I'd survive those injuries. My worst incident was from five of the most grueling seconds of my life. One glance at the sunrise and…" He closed his eyes, his brow rutted with pain.

"You've never seen the sun." My heart ached.

His eyes opened and roamed over my hair. "I imagine it looks a lot like this." Lifting a fiery lock, he tenderly stroked the strands. "And this." He traced a finger around one of my eyes and lingered on the outer corner. "*My* Dawn."

Your eyes are addictive…so blinding and painful it's like staring into a lost sunrise after twenty years of darkness.

The words he'd spoken right before my first kiss hit me with stunning impact. I wanted to warm him with my mouth and give him a breath of light in his cold, dismal world. But what if I accidentally bit him? Would he even take the chance? My chest clenched at the thought of never kissing him again.

I sneaked my hands beneath his coat, trailing fingers over

the wool that covered his flat abs.

He stared at my mouth, his gaze losing focus. Then he blinked, and his face was all sharp lines, his eyes lucent shards of need. "We're stuck here for about four hours. I have a small ration of food—"

I slipped my hand lower, and when I brushed the hard swell in his leather pants, raw desire pulsed through my core. "I want to kiss you. I want—"

He captured my mouth in a delicious slide of lips, his tongue teasing the seam and his arms snaking around my back. He angled his head and dove in for a deeper kiss. Reluctantly, I pulled back, unsure how to maneuver around my oversized teeth.

I pressed my tongue against my fangs. "You said no tasting, but if I scratch you with them—"

"Shh." He nibbled on my lower lip and licked the upper one as his hands sifted through my hair. "If you nick me, don't suck on the cut. I'll know if your bloodlust rises."

The danger was the hollow points of my fangs and whatever I might inject him with. He was stronger than me. Strong enough to stop me.

His fingers tightened around the roots at my scalp and pulled. "Give me your mouth."

I lifted my chin and gave him more than a kiss. With every lick, nuzzle, and caress, I offered a piece of my heart. I felt myself falling and stretched out my arms, not to stop it from happening, but to absorb the collision and embrace him with the entirety of my being.

He kissed me savagely, dizzyingly, his hands pulling roughly on my hair. I attacked the buttons on his coat and spread it open, snuggling into the steely heat of his wool-covered chest. He slipped his tongue between my lips, and I ate at his mouth with mindless hunger.

The rich taste of iron slid down my throat, and I knew I'd pricked him. But thoughts of fangs and blood weren't ruling me now. I wanted his cock, and I rocked against it to show him how much. Oh. My. Hell. He was so fucking hard.

Straddling his hips, I pushed against his chest and angled him away from the wall until he lowered his back to the ground.

He stared up at me, lips parted and those vivid silver eyes penetrating me with desire. Greedy need vibrated beneath my skin, and my insides melted into one huge throb between my legs.

His fingers plucked at the clasps on my cloak, and a moment later, the heavy fur slid to the ground.

"I'll keep you warm." He untied the bandana around my chest and pulled off his wool sweater. "Take these off before I rip them." He yanked at my borrowed trousers.

I stripped them quickly, trembling less from the cold and more from the flickering flames in his eyes as they licked over my nudity. With my knees on either side of his hips and cushioned by his coat spread open beneath him, I feathered fingers down the chiseled ridges of his torso, lingered on the button on his pants. The sight of his arousal straining the leather rushed adrenaline through my body, burning me up and racing my pulse.

When his length sprung free, he gripped the base and rubbed the broad head around my entrance. "Always so wet."

"Always so hard." I flattened my palms against his chest and leaned over him. "Fuck me like this…with me on top."

His fangs lengthened, and mine ached in kind. With a hand on my waist and the other on his cock, he drove his hips upward and impaled me to the hilt. A string of breathy moans cascaded between us. Eyes locked, we moved together, slowly, then faster, causing every charged cell in my body to merge between my legs. The feeling of fullness was electrifying, the gliding strokes sinfully addictive.

The wintry air needled my skin, but as I pushed up and rode his cock like I knew what I was doing, my blood started pumping and heating my body. His hands were everywhere, cupping my breasts, tweaking my nipples, massaging my clit. He was all powerful thrusts and grunting need, and I was consumed by it. I'd intended to fuck him, but being on top didn't give me any more control. He held me where he wanted me, led the pace, and set the balance of pain and pleasure.

The blissful sensation of his caresses eclipsed the hammering pressure against the back of my pussy. Soon, all I felt was his trembling urgency and the singe of his gaze. My pulse thundered as I looked into those eyes. I wanted him to own my lips, my desperate noises, and every spasm in my pussy. I wanted him to look at me like this forever, like I belonged to him in every way.

When he grasped my neck and trussed up a breast for the strike of his fangs, I sank into his hold. My eyes fluttered shut as his bite seared my nipple, seeped into my veins, and galvanized my senses.

"Come with me." His mouth left my breast and caught my lips in a brutal kiss that sent us spiraling off the cliff.

Bright light burst behind my eyelids, zinging fiery sparks across my skin. My stomach tightened, and my teeth ached. When I tasted his blood, my orgasm intensified. I wanted more and broke the kiss to go for his neck.

The hand on my throat shoved me back. He hissed through his release, his pupils dilated in the faint glow of the lantern. A bead of red dotted his lip, beckoning me with an inconsolable thirst.

I strained against his grip, possessed with the need to lap at the well of blood. In a blur of movement, he flipped us, pinning me beneath the weight of his body, his fist around my throat and his cock buried to the root, spilling wet warmth inside me.

"Breathe." With a swipe of his tongue, he erased the blood from his mouth. His free hand brushed the hair from my face, soothing my frenzied breaths. "Good girl. Now another one. Pull it deep into your diaphragm."

His gravelly voice was hypnotic, his masculine scent a drugging comfort. I listened to his repeated instruction, breathing, relaxing, soaking in the protective warmth of his body. Eventually, the roar in my ears fled, the throb in my teeth ebbed, and my muscles slackened.

He rolled us to lay on our sides, face to face, his thigh wedged between my legs and the leather and fur of our coats wrapped around us.

"Will it always be like that?" I snuggled closer against his chest. "The overwhelming need to bite during sex?"

"It is for me." He rested his lips on the crown of my head. "You won't be able to stop me from biting, but *I* can stop *you*."

Didn't seem fair, but I accepted the circumstances. While I was immune to a hybrid's bite, Salem's bite had given me fangs. We didn't know what my bite would do to a hybrid. Though Salem wasn't a hybrid, I didn't blame him for not wanting to be my first test case.

Michio should be able to determine if I had venom glands, if my bite would envenom Salem with something harmful or fatal. Until then, it was safer if Salem prevented me from penetrating his veins.

We ate a small portion of his packed food supply—hardtack crackers, deer jerky, and pine nuts—and washed it down with sips from his animal skin water bladder. Then we slept in a cuddle of body heat until darkness crept through the cave entrance like an unwanted intruder.

Salem dressed quickly, grabbed the club and hunting knife, and swept toward the narrow opening in a gust of leather-scented determination.

"Wait." Panic edged my voice as I dragged on my clothes. "Where are you going?"

"I'm not leaving you, but I'll move faster and quieter alone."

My jaw clenched. "I need—"

"Wood and feathers for arrows. Something to eat. I'll be quick. Stay here." He tossed me a warning glare.

I didn't trust him. Or maybe I just didn't want to be cared for like a breeding woman. Whatever was causing my hands to clench, it wasn't worth arguing over. I'd wait until he left and follow after him.

He ducked through the crack, gave the frozen river and

treescape a swift scan, and in a flash, he was gone.

I shoved my boots on, and with my mother's dagger clutched in my gloved hand, I headed toward the entrance.

And stopped.

Tingling in my gums drew my tongue to my straight, small...*not fangs.* A heavy feeling swelled in my stomach. I yanked off a glove and prodded around my teeth. No fangs. My fingers slid over human canines again and again. What the fuck?

I paced around the cave, my mind swimming and heart racing. The change didn't happen when he bit me again. That was hours ago. It happened when... I glanced at the serrated crack he'd vanished through.

Hybrids couldn't retract and regrow their fangs. Neither could Salem nor my fathers. Their teeth were set in place, sheathed only by their lips. Why were mine different? Was the answer connected to Salem? We hadn't been separated since my fangs first appeared. Did they only extend when he was near?

Anxious to test the theory, I ducked through the crack and stepped into the blistering cold. My breaths huffed in white clouds of vapor, and my eyes prickled against the bite of the wind. I probed the landscape, and all I could see was black. I didn't know which direction he'd went or how far away he hunted.

I pulled in a breath, and the frigid air cut through my lungs like a knife. I should wait for him to come back. He had the compass to guide him. I had a head full of flustered thoughts and an impulsive tendency to run off and get lost. Fuck.

Slipping back into the cave, I pressed my back against the rear wall and sank to my haunches.

About an hour later, the tingling in my gums returned, and my canines lengthened. The sensation was subtle, a little sensitive, like growing a fingernail.

As my fangs reformed, I stared, unblinking, at the murky hole in the cave. A moment later, he stepped through.

That was when I knew he wasn't just the trigger for

unlocking a latent ability. He was the Achilles' heel that could lead to my failure.

If my fangs were crucial in saving humanity, I needed him at my side.

If my fangs prevented me from succeeding, I would have to choose.

FOURTEEN

Salem must've noticed the turmoil in my huddled posture, because he froze at the entrance of the cave. A huge gray owl dangled lifelessly from one hand, his club gripped in the other, with a bundle of sticks pinned beneath his arm.

When he found my eyes in the dark, he dropped his burden and jolted forward, his silhouette cutting through the chamber in a blink.

"What's wrong?" he asked from inches away, his chest pressed against my bent knees.

A voice in the back of my mind urged me to keep the revelation about my fangs a secret. "I need to pee."

"Why didn't you go when you stepped outside?"

He'd seen me? But my fangs hadn't emerged. Maybe it depended on whether or not I could see him?

"You caught that nearby?" I nodded at the owl on the ground behind him.

"There are a couple owls in the woods across the river." He narrowed his luminous eyes. "I'm faster and hungrier."

"No beavers?"

"You needed feathers, and you're stalling." He gripped my chin, the sparkling silver of his irises so bright it felt like a spotlight tracking my every move. "Tell me what spooked you."

"I really need to pee."

A flash of anger set his jaw before he grabbed my waist, tossed me over his shoulder, and bolted out of the cave. Cold air morphed into frigid misery as he moved with inhuman speed across the river and through the trees. He set me down, and my boots wobbled on rocky ground, my breaths coming too short and heavy for someone who hadn't taken a step.

"Careful." He held my elbow and kicked a jagged rock out of my path. "Talk while you're peeing."

I turned away and shoved through the undergrowth, searching for a reason to not tell him about my fangs. Maybe I didn't want him to stay with me because of a supernatural connection through teeth and veins. I wanted him to want me for *me*. But he'd already told me he wasn't letting me go. He could've abandoned me the moment we were freed and zipped home to his *utopia*.

As I pulled down my pants and peed, I felt his watchful, patient gaze grow more watchful and less patient. "Dawn."

"My fangs retracted." I retied my trousers and stepped toward him.

"When?" He reached for my hand, glancing at my mouth.

I explained the disappearance and reappearance of my teeth on the walk back to the cave. He didn't speak, didn't look at me, his gaze sweeping the frozen shadows of the limestone cliff. But the furrow in his brow told me he'd heard.

Inside the cave, he plucked the owl feathers and helped me fashion arrows. Due to lack of time and dry firewood, I couldn't cure the shafts. But I compressed them through bending, making them as straight as possible while he sharpened the ends into points.

"Tell me what you're thinking." I used the heel of my hand to bend a shaft of wood and watched him out of the corner of my eye.

"It changes nothing."

"I disagree. My birth was foretold three years before it happened. Annie, my sister's ghost, told Jesse there will be no human race without me."

"I know the prediction, Dawn." He fit a feather into the slit I'd cut in the shaft. "The whole fucking world knows."

"Yeah, well, no one knew I'd grow fangs. Fangs that can only be meant to bite…someone. Fangs that only emerge when *you* are nearby. What does that tell you?"

"How many humans and hybrids have you been around since your fangs first appeared?"

Just Salem and our faceless captors. That wasn't a big enough sample to assume my reactions were only connected to Salem.

"You're right." My shoulders loosened. "I'm jumping to conclusions."

He cleaned the owl, wrapped the meat in a scrap of leather, and stored it in his pack. When I ran out of feathers, I had twenty-four arrows. That done, we packed up and followed the river southeast.

For the next two nights, we plodded over the unforgiving terrain. Another cave on the Yukon River provided shelter during the day. He caught a second owl, and I made more arrows. But we didn't encounter a human, a hybrid, or any signs of intelligent life. I continued to knot tree limbs and stack stones, anticipating my fathers tracking me. Though the closer we drew toward camp the more I hoped they'd stayed put and awaited my return.

On the third night, the wind grew stronger, more bitter, bringing with it a torrential hell of sleet and heavy snow. We plowed through it for miles, my hair whipping against my face, icy droplets clinging to my lashes, and my cheeks and lips cracked and abraded.

Salem kept a hand clenched in the furs on my back and guided me along the treed shore of the river. It was too dark and blustery, the poor visibility making the billowing snowdrifts unwieldy to navigate. He wanted to carry me, but he was already burdened by the huge backpack.

Sheets of freezing rain permeated my cloak and fur pants, weighing me down and soaking through to my skin. The vicious trembling in my muscles slowly ate away my strength. Each step required more energy, more willpower. I was running out of both.

A couple hours later, the glacial cold stiffened my joints. Icy water seeped into the neck hole of my cloak and trickled down my spine. I no longer felt my fingers, face, and toes, and my movements grew clumsy. The shivering had subsided, but I struggled to fill my lungs with air. I just needed to sit down for a minute and gather my strength.

I sensed him move in behind me and pitched my voice over my shoulder. "Leafff me lere…here." Why was I slurring? "Find slllelter. Come back fler me."

He would travel faster without me. He'd have to. My vision blurred to blackness. The howling sounds of the wind faded. My knees liquefied, and I started to sink toward the ground. Before my face hit the snow, he caught my waist, lifted me against his chest, and wrapped his coat around my body.

The last thing I remembered was his fierce demand. "Hang on."

FIFTEEN

I woke with a parched mouth, head fuzzy and my body dry, warm, and nude. The pillow beneath my cheek was made of steel and sinew, and I burrowed in as the rest of my senses slowly roused.

Heat crackled at my back with the scent of musty wet earth and burning wood. A fur rug lay beneath me on the floor. My fingers and toes were stiff but thawed. There was no wind. No stinging ice on my face. It was too good to be true.

Opening my eyes, I stared into luminous silver aglow in a flawless face that was all sharp bones, black brows, and sinful lips.

I propped an elbow on the pillow—which was Salem's chest—and took in the rustic log walls, raw wood flooring, and yawning rafters overhead. Our clothes, overcoats, and boots spread over a long table—the only furniture in the huge space.

No windows. No pounding sleet against the exterior walls. The blizzard must've passed. How long had I been asleep? Had he found one of those public use cabins built in the old, old world? Numerous hunting cabins were tucked in remote corners of Canadian wilderness, but finding them without a map was damn near impossible.

I turned toward the source of heat at my back and sighed at the glorious sight of the low-burning fire in the hearth. "Where—?"

"Drink first." He reached for a tin cup sitting near the fireplace and sipped from it. "Careful. It's hot."

He held the handle as I slowly swallowed the piney-citrusy concoction, avoiding the green stems floating in the cup. Pine needle tea was high in vitamin A and C, a fantastic booster for the immune system. I would've expected something like this from Michio, but knowing Salem made it warmed my chest even more than the tea.

"Thank you." I set the empty cup aside, curled into the softness of the fur pelt beneath us, and luxuriated in the heat of his nude body wrapped around me. "Where are we?"

"About fifty miles south of the river."

Shit. That wasn't the direction of my camp, but I couldn't bring myself to feel anything but gratitude. "You carried my dead weight for fifty miles."

"You weigh nothing." He brushed a lock of hair behind my ear and tugged me closer, chest to chest. "As the blizzard died down, I tied and bent tree limbs in this direction. If your fathers are out there—"

I kissed his beautiful mouth, pouring every ounce of appreciation into the press of our lips. "I owe you my life."

Pulling back, I searched the shadows cast across his face. He looked tired, thinner, his eyes bruised and heavy-lidded.

"Have you eaten?" I stroked his sunken cheek.

"I cooked some of the owl meat, but I need…" He met my gaze. "I need blood, and you're too weak—"

"You never take much. I won't miss it."

With a groan, he rolled me to my back and pressed his nose against my neck, his hand wandering over my chest. "I can't feed without fucking you, Dawn. You need to rest."

The hard length of his cock pulsed against my hip, and I wanted him inside me with a desperation that shocked me. I was too exhausted to do anything but sleep, but that didn't stop me from hooking a thigh over his hip and pulling his heavy body on top of me.

You don't trust me, and we'll talk about that.

I hadn't trusted him, but every moment I spent with him disintegrated more of that wall I'd held between us. He could've left me on the frozen river. He could've bitten me while I slept. Instead, he'd proven his loyalty a thousand times over.

"I trust you." With my hands framing the masculine angles of his jaw, I wrapped my legs around his hard ass and arched against his erection. "I'm yours."

That was all the encouragement he needed. Bathed in the warmth of firelight, he fucked me with aching tenderness, sank his fangs in my throat, and brought us to orgasm softly and thoroughly. Then he fed me roasted owl meat and forced me to drink another cup of tea. Belly full and heart at peace, I followed him into a deep sleep.

Hours later, I woke in darkness. The fire had smoldered into embers, and a chill settled through the cabin. With my nude backside exposed to the frosty air, I lay sprawled over his chest, staring at the glowing remnants of wood and listening to the rapid beat of his heart. It wasn't an amplified sound of his veins, but the pace was too erratic, the muscles beneath me too tense.

I lifted my head to see his face, and my nose came within inches of glinting steel. My pulse detonated as I stared at the long-pointed blade angled beneath his throat.

SIXTEEN

My stomach hardened with dread as I met Salem's wide eyes. His fangs were bared, his throat jogging against the press of lethal steel. No glowing veins, but someone stood behind me, holding a fucking sword. Could it be…?

Heart pounding, I slowly lifted my head and followed the edge of the blade toward the handle, the Celtic engraving on the hilt, huge freckled hand, red-leathered sleeve of a coat…

"Da!" I jumped up, overcome with relief.

"Put some fecking clothes on." Roark's jade eyes stayed on Salem, his fangs elongated and sword arm stiff and unyielding as he held the sharp tip beneath Salem's jaw.

"Lower the steel, Da." I slapped my hands over my chest and groin, my cheeks flushing with heat. "Salem isn't a threat."

Spinning toward my clothes, I collided with a brick chest. Arms came around me, wrapping me in a fur blanket and the familiar scent of hickory.

"Dad!" I stared up at Jesse's copper eyes, yanking my arms from the pelts to hug him as tightly as he hugged me. "Tell Roark to lower the sword. Salem saved my life." I pulled back. "Where's Michio?"

"North of here, hunting for you." The deep voice came from the dark silhouette behind Jesse.

The brown eyes, broad shoulders, and mocha skin of my best friend sent me hurtling from Jesse's arms and into Eddie's.

"You made it." I draped the furs around my body and held his beautiful face in my hands. "The women? Did they—?"

"All safe back at camp." He leaned down and planted a wet kiss on my cheek.

A low growl rumbled from the floor behind me. "Get your fucking mouth off her." Salem lay nude and dangerously pissed off with his neck arched beneath the sword.

"Da, release him!" I grabbed our clothes from the table and darted to Salem's side, shouting over my shoulder. "Turn your backs so we can dress."

"Not taking me eyes off the fecking hybrid." Roark's voice grew rougher, angrier. "Wha' in the bloody hell were ye doing all cozied up with me naked daughter?" he roared, pushing on the sword and producing a trickle of blood on Salem's neck.

Heat exploded through my body in waves of fury. Before my brain could catch up, I was crouched over Salem's chest and hissing at the man who raised me.

"Jaysus ballsac!" Roark stepped back, eyes bulging and locked on my mouth.

Then Jesse was there, hands gripping my jaw and throat with a fanged scowl on his face as he glared at my teeth. He turned that scowl toward Salem, who rolled from beneath me with lightning-fast reflexes. In the next breath, I was ripped from Jesse's grip and shoved behind Salem's flexing frame.

The air crackled with dry heat and tension as Eddie and Jesse stood in a face-off with Salem, boots planted and arrows nocked and trained on Salem's head. Roark raised the sword, his eyes possessed with emerald fire.

"He's not a hybrid, and if you harm him, I will never forgive you." I shoved at Salem's arm, stepping around him and adjusting the furs on my body. "If you kill him, I will follow him into hell. Lower your fucking weapons!"

Jaws clenched and throats bobbing, each man eased his weapon to the floor.

"Explain the fangs and lack of clothes, lass, before I go off me bloody nut." Roark pinned me with a look that would normally make my knees wobble.

"After I'm dressed." I turned away and dropped the furs,

which prompted a snarled Irish curse and the shuffle of multiple boots.

Salem snagged my clothes from the floor and thrust a finger at someone behind me. “Turn around!”

“I don’t trust you.” Eddie’s voice strained with tension.

I grabbed Salem’s arm before he did something stupid and spoke with my back to Eddie. “I trust Salem with the lives of every person in this room. Give me some privacy.”

“You’ve never needed privacy before,” Eddie said, his tone laced with suspicion.

Salem’s arm went rigid beneath my hand. Damn jealous man.

I tightened my hold. “I need it now, Eddie. Turn around.”

The chill in the room stood still for an eternal moment before the creak of boots sounded Eddie’s capitulation.

Salem held my gaze as we pulled on our pants. When I reached for the bandana to secure my breasts, he yanked it out of my hands.

“You’re not wearing that ridiculous scrap of nothing,” he whispered.

He shoved his wool sweater over my head. I pushed my arms through the sleeves and breathed in the masculine scent wafting from the soft fleece. I might never take this sweater off. Especially if it meant he had to go shirtless.

Trailing a finger down the ridges of his chest, I felt the tension coiling beneath his skin. He was unusually quiet. No doubt preparing for the impending conversation about his mother and the intimacy of our relationship.

You’re asking me to enter the domain of the great warriors after I deflowered their precious daughter? They’ll castrate me.

“You still have your balls,” I mouthed, grinned, and poked his abs.

He didn’t smile back, his expression fierce as his attention returned to the men behind me.

I stole a greedy glance at his powerful legs and cock encased in black leather, his deliciously nude *V*-shaped torso, and the noctilucent glow of his twilight eyes. Then I shifted toward the rest of the room.

Salem threw more wood on the fire as I stalled for another few seconds. Eddie leaned over the table with his back to me, hands planted on the wood surface and head lowered. He wore his usual fitted leather from neck to boots. His black hair was clipped close to his perfectly-round skull, his shoulders broad and rigid. I wanted to rub his back and promise him he had nothing to worry about.

A few feet from him, Jesse and Roark stood shoulder to shoulder, their heads bowed together and facing away from me as they whispered in tones too low for my ears. Jesse crossed his arms, stretching the seams across the back of his black leather jacket. Roark was taller and broader than Jesse, and always so damn imposing in his red leather duster that bulged on the side where his scabbard hung. The sight of them together was enough to make any man or hybrid tremble, let alone a daughter about to spill confessions about sex and bloodlust.

I gulped, cleared my throat. "You can turn around."

Eddie swept forward first. "What happened to Jeremy?"

I rubbed a hand over my mouth and shut my eyes against a spike of grief. "He didn't make it." When I opened my eyes, I gestured them toward the fire Salem had stoked to life. "I'll start at the beginning, but maybe we should wait for Michio." I looked at my fathers. "Can you sense how far away he is?"

Jesse glowered at Salem then narrowed his eyes at me. Evidently, he didn't want Salem to know he, Roark, and Michio shared an unexplainable connection that allowed them to sense one another's auras and pinpoint their locations. It wasn't common knowledge, but it wasn't a secret either.

"C'mere." Roark dragged me against his chest and buried his nose in my hair. "I've been a bleedin' header with worry."

"Effin' and blindin' nonstop, were ya?" I laid on the Irish accent, grinning up at him.

"Aye." He cupped my face, his eyes gentle and brimming with love. "Jesse threatened to give me a bocky leg if I didn't pull me shite together."

"I'm sorry, Da. I have so much to tell you."

"Eddie. Go retrieve Michio." Roark released me and lowered to the floor beside the fire, propping an elbow on his bent knee. "He's a thirty minute hike northwest."

Eddie's nostrils flared, his gaze aiming daggers at Salem. Then he pivoted in an angry swirl of leather and stormed out of the cabin.

"Your BFF doesn't like me." Salem tucked a lock of hair behind my ear, his mouth twisted in an impish smirk.

Refusing to encourage adolescent rivalry, I disregarded the comment and sat on the rug facing Roark. "Is Michio alone?"

His sharp green eyes ticked between Salem and me, narrowing into distrustful slits as Salem lowered beside me with an arm across my lap and not a sliver of space between us.

"Doc's with Link and Hunter." Roark brushed a blond dreadlock from his scruffy face.

I nodded, relieved. Link and Hunter were two of my fathers' closest friends.

"Start talking." Jesse sat against the wall beside the hearth and stretched a leg out behind Roark.

"Right." Roark gave me the full force of his Irish glare. "Start with the part when ye lost your thick-as-a-plank mind and legged it from the protection of your soldiers, making a holy show of yourself."

Oh boy. I sucked in a strengthening breath and plunged into the events of the past two weeks. Jeremy's decapitation, the prison in the mansion, the hybrid children, the regular meals, and our baffling freedom. I skipped over the sex and biting, as well as Salem's stalking and background, fully aware I was only delaying the inevitable.

"Did he force ye?" Roark asked, quiet and deadly, and nodded at the fresh bite mark on my neck.

"No." My voice hitched. "Of course not."

Roark pointed a look loaded with malice and fangs at Salem. "When, exactly, did ye shag our daughter?"

"Da!" My spine snapped straight. "Stop it."

"They were locked in a cell together for ten days." Jesse stared at the fist he held against his bent leg, his eyes stark and unblinking. "You know when it happened, Roark."

"Girl meets boy," Roark muttered, "and all rational thought flies out the fecking window."

My hackles raised. "It's not what—"

Salem clutched my thigh and met their eyes. "Dawn and I had sex on the tenth day."

A tide of red crawled up Jesse's neck, and he lurched to stand. Roark caught his hand and pulled him back to the floor.

"Our captors released us right after we, um…" I gestured between Salem and me. *Yeah. Awkward.*

"Wha' triggered the fangs?" Roark released Jesse's hand to grip his knee. "Was it…?"

When we had sex? When I came all over Salem's cock? When he bit me and fucked me into oblivion?

"Evie should be here." Jesse laced his fingers behind his neck and lowered his head, his voice grim. "She'd know what to say, how to handle this."

I met Roark's anguished eyes and swallowed around the lump in my throat.

The discomfort in the cabin became a big hairy presence, as if all their pain grew legs and bristled with arrows and we were watching it stagger between us, vomit blood, and crash to the floor in a fit of convulsions.

The silence became unbearable, but I couldn't find my voice.

"The first time I bit her…" Salem linked our fingers together. "She grew fangs."

"The first time?" Jesse cut his copper eyes at Salem, his mouth pinned in a murderous line.

"Dad." I bent across Salem's lap, blocking Jesse's line of sight. "His bloodlust works the same as yours, okay? It's keyed off from exertion, loss of blood, and…sex. Except one difference. His…uh, partners never turn, never grow fangs. I'm the only one."

Jesse and Roark shared a look I couldn't interpret. A moment later, their profiles swiveled toward the wall behind me.

"What is it?" I glanced over my shoulder and returned to them. "Is Michio here?"

"Soon." Jesse sat back and raked his fingers through the streaks of gray at his temples. Then he squinted at Salem. "You have fangs but you're not a hybrid. When you bite, it's sexual. You move like us. I assume you heal like us."

Salem nodded.

Roark stroked his trim beard, the dusting of silver along his jaw shimmering in the firelight. "Who's your ma, lad?"

My breath caught in my throat. *They know.* Hell, all the clues were there. Salem was the right age to be Elaine's son. He had traits that could've only been passed down from Michio's bite. And while I didn't know what Elaine looked like, Roark and Jesse had watched her transform from nymph to human to evil bitch.

"You already know." I glared at Roark. "Why are you making him say—"

"Elaine." Salem squared his shoulders and faced my fathers head on. "I'm Salem of Elaine."

Grooves formed in Jesse's forehead, his lips curving down as he studied Salem's face. "Your father is Tallis."

Salem's head jerked back, brows arched. "How did you know?"

I tried to look at Salem through Jesse's eyes, but I didn't see the swarthy Australian man I'd heard so much about.

"You have his bulky stature." Jesse braced elbows on his knees, head cocked as he regarded Salem. "The shape of your nose. The way your mouth rests in a smirk." His lips twitched with a small, private smile as he took in Salem's jaw and torso. "The bastard couldn't grow hair on his face or chest. I used to give him hell for that."

My chest swelled, and I tightened my grip on Salem's hand.

"He got Tallis' cocky arrogance, too, yeah?" Roark rested a hand on Jesse's nape and gave it a squeeze. "Our Aussie boyo would've been delira and excira to know he had a son."

When Salem gave me a confused look, I said, "Delighted and excited. Your dad would've been happy—"

"Where is she?" Jesse's voice whipped through the cabin.

"She's dead." The silver in Salem's eyes burned white-hot. "I killed her eight years ago."

Roark flinched. Jesse dragged a hand down his face. Then they both leapt to their feet, eyes on the door.

Michio. My stomach knotted with excitement and dread as I rose with Salem at my side. I was dying to see Michio. I was also about to dig up vivid memories of his rapist. We were all thinking it, postures straight and breaths held as the handle on the door turned.

It swung open as he reached it, and Michio strode in, bringing with him a gust of brutal cold before he shut the door. The others weren't with him, but I wasn't surprised. He'd probably run like the speed of light as the words left Eddie's mouth.

He scanned the room, and when his dark eyes connected with mine, deep creases faded from his face.

"Dad." My legs burned to go to him, but Salem's grip on my waist kept me in place.

As Michio moved to close the distance, Roark stopped him with a hand on his neck and spoke low in his ear. His Japanese heritage radiated from his brown eyes as they tapered, sharpened, flickered from Jesse to me and locked on Salem. Roark's hand tightened around his throat, lips moving at his ear.

I knew when Roark reached the part about Elaine. Michio's face contorted, his fangs extended, and shadows churned in his eyes as he glared at Salem.

SEVENTEEN

The agony scoring Michio's face produced a simmering burn in my chest—a burn that spread to my throat as his jaw worked in a threatening way. His shoulder bag dropped to the floor. His cheekbones sharpened, and his haunted eyes regained focus, zeroing in on Salem.

Roark cupped Michio's cheek, touched their heads together, and continued to whisper at his ear.

The few times Michio had spoken about Elaine, it'd been clear his biggest torment was self-imposed guilt. My mother had been imprisoned at Hoover Dam, alone, pregnant, and just down the hall while Elaine had her despicable way with every part of him. Though he'd been raped mentally and physically, he felt like he'd betrayed my mother. Over the years, Roark had become his therapist as much as his lover, but despite Roark's wisdom and support, we all knew Michio still fought demons.

Right now, he seemed ready to fight a demon in the flesh.

"You look like her." He glared at Salem.

"He's not her." I stepped in front of Salem in a show of conviction.

I would never put my back to a man I didn't trust, and Michio knew that. But the angry creases in his expression told me he didn't like it. At. All.

Beside me, Jesse stood tall and alert, his attention fixed on Michio, brows pulled together and hands balled at his sides. My heart constricted at the grief reflected in his eyes, but I was also thankful. In the wake of Elaine's torture and the loss of my mother, my fathers always had one another.

Salem's fingers wove around mine and squeezed, and I was grateful for that, too.

Roark whispered words I couldn't hear as he dragged a hand down the front of Michio's black coat and thumped a fist over Michio's heart. Whatever Roark told him softened Michio's expression and loosened his shoulders. Michio closed his lips, shielding his fangs. By the time he met my eyes, I was already moving.

When I reached him, his steady fingers framed my face, tilting my head to press our foreheads together. We stood like that through a tranquil rhythm of breaths before he said, "I missed you a little too much."

"Missed you, too, Dad." I gripped his hands where they held my face. "And not just because I desperately need you to help me figure things out." I flashed my fangs with a smile.

"It's happening." He regarded my teeth with an amalgam of emotions burning in his eyes.

"*Something* is happening." In the form of fangs and glowy veins, the latter of which I hadn't disclosed yet.

He held my cheek against his chest and kissed the top of my head. I wrapped my arms around his waist, and Roark moved in, enfolding us. Footfalls approached, and Jesse appeared on my other side, closing the circle.

Across the room, the wood floor creaked with movement. The fire crackled and popped, and I assumed Salem was tending it, giving us privacy.

"Evie would be so proud of the woman you've become." Michio splayed a hand against the back of my head, holding me tighter. "You took out the last breeding facility in North America."

"And ye endured captivity," Roark said, his accent thick with pride.

"And survived the brutal Yukon terrain." Jesse wrapped his fingers around my nape.

Michio pulled back and cupped my jaw, his eyes honey warm. "Our fierce, beautiful girl."

I needed their approval like I needed air, and my lungs stretched to capacity as I breathed in their words. Here, in the protective embrace of their love, my world clicked back together.

"How did you find her in that blizzard?" Michio looked from Roark to Jesse.

"We followed her breadcrumbs." Jesse smiled at me.

"Actually..." I stepped back, breaking the circle. "I didn't leave the trail."

Crouched by the fire, Salem glanced up from the cup of pine needle tea he was preparing. His gaze subtly roamed over my body, and I longed for his intimacy with a physical ache in my chest.

Clutching the neckline of my borrowed sweater, I stretched it to my nose and inhaled his masculine scent. "Do you want to tell them what happened?"

He rose and prowled toward me, one hand resting in the pocket of his leather pants, the other holding out the tin cup of tea.

"Thank you." I accepted it and took a sip, relishing the citrusy flavor.

"We got caught in the blizzard." His shoulders pulled back, and the orange glow of the fire bounced off his defined chest. "She lasted hours out there, plowing around snowbanks taller than her before hypothermia set in." The corner of his mouth lifted. "She's stubborn."

"Den' we know it." Roark folded his arms across his chest. "Just like Evie."

I shook my head. "I was fine."

"Until your blood pressure crashed, and you lost consciousness." Salem scowled at me.

I closed my eyes as the beat of my heart rushed through my ears. Beats I wouldn't have if he hadn't been there.

"You removed her wet clothes," Michio said.

When I opened my eyes, I followed his gaze to the clothes drying on the table.

Yep. Clothes were removed because of hypothermia. Not

because we were having sex right before they showed up. My cheeks inflamed.

"Yes." Salem hooked a thumb in his pocket. "I gave her warm tea when she woke. Kept her as warm and dry as possible."

My mind immediately snagged on *dry.* He'd fucked me, and I was soooo *not* dry. Our eyes connected, and his lips twitched, making my lips twitch, and holy shit, my fathers were watching. Salem cleared his throat, and I quickly spoke over the sound.

"He bent the branches." I peeked at my fathers' hard expressions. "*While* he carried me fifty miles to this cabin."

"I needed the exercise." Salem grinned.

"Yeah, as much as I need more overprotective guardians in my life." I smiled over the rim of the cup.

Michio approached Salem, his movements seemingly casual, but I knew every step was measured and deliberate. He slid off his coat, setting it on the table he passed, his narrowed gaze never leaving Salem.

"Thank you." He paused within arm's reach of Salem, hands folded behind his back. "For keeping her safe."

"Don't thank me." Salem regarded him with undaunted intensity. "I did it for myself."

I straightened, confused by his response.

He and Michio bandied stares like predator and prey, only they both had fangs and neither were capable of cowering.

"Explain what you mean." Michio held still, not a twitch in the loose garments that draped his tall frame.

"I'm not letting her go." Salem mirrored Michio's stance, clasping his hands behind his back.

"Wha' do ye want with her?" Roark circled.

Jesse silently stalked from the other side.

"Don't gang up on him." I stepped between Salem and Michio. "Let's sit down. I have more to tell you."

"Answer the question, lad." Roark stood behind Salem, arms crossed.

"You don't have to answer," I said under my breath.

That earned me scolding looks from all four men.

"I enjoy her company." Salem gripped my hand. "Her laughter. Her ferocity and tenderness. My interest is simple. I care about your daughter, and I want *every* opportunity to show her how much."

I squeezed his fingers as my heart ricocheted off my ribs.

Michio zoomed in on our laced fingers and returned to Salem's face, squinting with enough scrutiny to make a normal man squirm. "The epithelium in your eyes doesn't have pigment. And there's no melanin in the stroma." His dark brows pinched. "The result should be albinism—red eyes. Or Tyndall scattering—blue irises. But you have neither. It's as if the layers of your eyes have been altered? Or damaged?"

Salem had mentioned his worst exposure to the sun was when he looked at a sunrise. Was that the cause of his spectral eyes?

"They were brown when I was a child." Salem rubbed the back of his neck.

My jaw dropped. "Really?"

"Like your mother's." Michio's voice was flat, his expression blank.

"Yeah, I, uh…I have a reaction to the sun." Salem cast me a sidelong glance and shoved a hand through his hair. "Dawn's right. I think we should sit. It's a long story."

Two cups of tea later, I lay on the rug with my head on Salem's thigh, struggling to keep my eyes open.

"No more tea." He moved the cup out of my reach and stroked my hair. "You're going to overdose on vitamin C."

Roark and Jesse reclined against the wall, shoulder to shoulder and eyes closed, but I knew they were listening to every word.

Michio sat across from us, bent over a leather-bound notebook from his bag, the pages scribbled with notes about Salem. The moment he'd pulled out his graphite pencil, my concerned father disappeared and Dr. Nealy took over.

The scientist listened with rapt attention as Salem walked through the past twenty years. The sun's lethal effect on his body. His abusive childhood and murder of his mother. His curiosity about me that led him to tracking me and getting captured. My ability to hear and see whatever was slithering through his veins. Then he demonstrated my connection to him by stepping outside. My fangs retracted the moment I couldn't see him and reemerged when he returned a few minutes later.

"How old were you when you tried to look at the sun?" Michio looked up from his notebook, the pencil paused mid-scribble.

"Fifteen." Salem's fingers tightened in my hair.

What? I'd assumed Elaine forced him look at the sun, but he was twelve when he killed her.

"Why did you do it?" I asked. "Knowing what it would do to you?"

"Stupidity." He scowled at the floor. "I wanted to see it."

My heart broke. I reached for his hand and tucked it between my cheek and his thigh with my head on his lap.

"When your eyes healed, they lost the structural coloration?" Michio asked.

"Why are you so focused on his eyes?" I lifted my head.

"Aphids and nymphs had all-white eyes." Michio scratched a note on the paper. "That was a different cause and effect, but I wanted to eliminate a connection."

"My eyes looked like this when they healed." Salem nudged my head down, guiding my cheek back to his thigh. "My eyesight is normal. *Human.* I don't have night vision." He tugged on a lock of my hair. "Or x-ray vision."

I pinched his leg. "I can only see *your* creepy veins."

"Have you bitten him?" Michio's cautious voice drew my attention to his stern gaze.

"No." I rolled to my back and spoke to the rafters. "There have been a few times when I…well, I would've bitten him if he hadn't stopped me."

"During sex?" Michio asked, without a hint of emotion in his voice.

Roark and Jesse tensed in my periphery.

"Yes." My face heated.

Michio set the paper and pencil aside and leaned forward, clasping his hands in front of him. "There are circumstances we'll never be able to explain. Like the way Evie sensed things, felt things deep inside her. Maybe it was intuition or the work of some external force, but whatever it was led her to the cabin…" His eyes shifted to Salem. "Where she found your mother. It led her to Jesse and called her across the ocean to Roark and me."

"What are you saying?" I sat up and brushed the hair from my face.

"I'll run tests and examine your teeth when we return to camp, but I already know that the one thing we're searching for won't be found under a microscope." He looked at Salem and back to me. "What does your gut tell you when you see his veins?"

"To bite him." I picked at a hole in the matted fur rug. "To go after those silver things in his blood. To…extract them?"

"Extract them or destroy them?" Salem tilted his head to study my face.

"I don't know." I rubbed my gritty eyes. "I'll pay better attention next time." My entire body felt heavy and lethargic, no doubt working in overdrive as I recovered from hypothermia.

"Have you bitten or been bitten by a hybrid?" Michio asked Salem.

"Both."

"What happens?"

"Aside from blood loss?" Salem cocked his head. "Nothing."

"Tell me about your relationship with the hybrids you live with." Michio picked up his notebook.

"They have varied personalities like humans." Salem sighed. "But all hybrids have the same nature. They're very passive until they scent a human…"

His voice faded in and out. My eyelids grew heavy, my

head nodding. As I moved to curl up on the floor, Salem's arms came around me. He pulled me across his lap and tucked my head against the warm skin on his chest. It didn't take long for the vibration of his timbre to lull me to sleep.

When I woke, I was in the same position. The fire had dwindled to a low-burning flame, and Salem and Michio were still talking. As I started to drift back to sleep, my attention snagged on the table, now overflowing with wet coats and packs.

I perked up. "Is Eddie—?"

"He's back." Michio nodded at the space behind me. "Sleeping."

I turned in Salem's arms and spotted Eddie, Link, and Hunter stretched out on bedrolls by the door. On the other side of the room, Jesse and Roark hadn't moved. Their eyes were closed. Roark's head lay at an angle on Jesse's shoulder, his hand resting over Jesse's on his lap.

Warmth spread through my chest. I didn't know until now how much I'd always wanted that for myself. A shoulder to sleep on. A hand to hold. A man to give my heart to.

I relaxed against Salem's chest and mumbled, "What's the plan?"

"The sun sets in two hours." Salem pressed his lips against my forehead. "Then we head to your camp."

We. A happy hum resonated deep in my gut.

EIGHTEEN

Three weeks later, I sat beside Eddie on a concrete rooftop and lifted my face to the pinkish-orange sky as the sun sank behind Yukon's Volcano Mountain. Sleeping with Salem during the short daylight hours had filled me with longing for *this,* the emotional warmth of sunshine breathing life into a cold dead world. So I'd left him asleep, exchanging the comfort of his arms for a stolen moment of UV rays.

"Is it weird to have your teeth come and go like that?" Eddie stared at my mouth and passed the hot cup of acorn brew we were sharing.

"A little, I guess." I slid my tongue along straight human teeth and shrugged. "I'm getting used to it."

"At least Salem can't sneak up on you."

"True." I sipped the bitter coffee-like beverage and flexed my legs where they dangled over the edge of the roof.

We perched on the corner of a three-story *L*-shaped building. It'd been a hospital in the old world. Now it served as the western bulwark of our temporary camp. Behind me, a hodgepodge of rock and wood walls encircled what was left of a rural Canadian town. The fencing was weak in areas, and the exterior barricades between the crumbling stone buildings could be climbed given enough time and determination. My soldiers had been toiling for weeks, cutting down trees, and reinforcing the perimeter.

Thirty-six human men and four women resided here before we showed up. Our group of two dozen soldiers and twenty female survivors more than doubled the population. But once the border around the settlement was secured, we would head back to Hoover Dam and leave the pregnant women here.

Eddie raised a pair of binoculars and scanned the shadows that started to form across the frozen tundra. "Michio wants to bring Salem home with us."

"I know." I set the cup aside and shivered against the rapidly declining temperature.

My hooded tailcoat was made from patches of sweaters in an assortment of earthy colors. The sleeves hung past my hands and the layered wool flared around my knees. Since my return to the camp, I'd acquired a badass wardrobe. Two of the survivors from the breeding facility were seamstresses, and they'd discovered a stockpile of fabrics in one of the old buildings. Surrounded by wool, flax, alpaca, and leather, they'd fashioned numerous pieces for me, tailored to fit every dip and curve of my body.

Today I wore a brown leather corset over a flowing white blouse and fitted trousers. My favorite accessories were the chunky utility belts that draped around my waist, each customized to carry things like a compass, my mother's dagger, and rope. The first time Salem saw me in this outfit, he removed it piece by agonizing piece and fucked me against the wall of our makeshift bedroom.

My thighs clenched at the memory of the predatory hunger in his eyes, and I felt a sudden urge to race back to the room and wake him with my mouth around his cock. He hadn't let me pleasure him like that since my fangs appeared. I didn't blame him, but dammit, I loved to feel him against the back of my throat. I needed to figure out a way to suck him without biting.

"Michio seems to like him." Eddie lowered the binoculars, his brown eyes narrowing as if he could read my thoughts.

"Yeah, Michio likes him the way a scientist is fascinated by a bug under a magnifying glass." My exhale escaped in a white cloud of steam. "Salem's reached his limit with Michio's probing and pricking. He wants to go home. *His* home."

After a battery of blood tests and medical exams, Salem and

Michio had arrived at an inconclusive debate. The strange silver things in Salem's blood didn't show up under a microscope or trigger any known medical causes in Michio's tests. Salem believed it was *me*, that my genetic makeup allowed me to see something that didn't medically exist. Michio wanted to marshal more figures, data, and facts.

He asked Salem to come home with us, where he could study us with better equipment and analyze to his heart's content. When Salem politely refused, Michio concurred with, "You're right. The answer isn't in a lab."

The line between science and faith was one that Michio struggled with since the day he met my mother.

But not all of Michio's exams were inconclusive. He found venom glands in my fangs, but no venom in my body. No baby either. The pregnancy tests were negative. As it turned out, those tests weren't needed. Salem's fertility test confirmed that fangs and inhuman speed weren't the only traits he shared with my fathers. He was also infertile.

When Salem heard the results, he'd said, "Good. One less thing to worry about." But I'd recognized the disappointment in his eyes and felt it carve out a hollow place inside me.

"If he returns to Alberta…" Eddie rubbed his neatly trimmed goatee, his chocolate eyes soft and calming. "Where does that leave you, Red?"

"I don't know." I stared at the darkening sky. "We haven't discussed it."

Salem would be awake soon. I glanced over my shoulder at the camp below. Armed with crossbows, guards patrolled the exterior walls. A quick scan confirmed every sentry was appropriately positioned. A few men smoked cigarillos. Others stole peeks at the women who strolled along the broken street that ran down the center of the camp.

"He's going to take you from me." Eddie hooked an arm around my back.

I relaxed against his broad chest. Eddie was leaner than Salem, but powerful and dominant in his own right. Other than my fathers, he was the only man who ever stood up to me. Until Salem.

"Don't be a drama queen." I rested my hand on his where he balanced the binoculars on his thigh. "We haven't even talked about the future."

"I don't like him." His arm tightened around me. "I don't trust him."

"Spoken like an overprotective brother." I grinned.

"Hmm. I would be the *older* brother in this scenario. That makes me wiser. Definitely better looking. I got all the good genes."

"You're one day older, dumbass. And you're a guy, so that makes you brain damaged by default."

I stared down at our joined hands, my pale skin glowing against the smooth brown of his. We looked nothing alike, but we were cut from the same cloth. Inseparable since birth, we were synonymous in our ideals, manifestos, and determination.

"What's next for the Resistance." I traced the bumps of his knuckles. "More fighting? More killing? We've taken out all the breeding facilities in North America. The troops I sent across the globe already found the same success before we left for Canada. But it's such a small battle in a huge war."

"We slowed down their breeding," he said.

"We can barely keep our tiny camps secure."

Overrun and persecuted by hybrids, we couldn't rebuild and prosper as a species until every single one of those bastards was eliminated. Michio still hoped for a cure, and while he spent every waking hour pouring over formulas and blood results, I was out there killing and fighting the very thing he wanted to save.

"We keep fighting." Eddie jabbed a finger at the soldiers behind us.

"To what end? We've been fighting for so long. Fighting to eat. Fighting to breed. Fighting to free twenty women from a Yukon nest. Fighting to walk down the damn street in any city across the world. The tedium of the mortal coil is taxing, you know? I'm beat down, worn out, and…" I shivered against a rude gust of wind. "And I'm fucking cold. Aren't you?"

"Yes, but…" His eyes hardened into brown glass. "You're not quitting."

"No." I pulled away and rolled back my shoulders. "I'll never quit. I just think maybe there's a better, *smarter* way. Like I'm overlooking something fundamental."

"You're thinking about the prophecy."

I nodded. "I won't win this war by flinging arrows at random hybrids. The solution is bigger than that."

"Well, you get all fangy around Salem for a reason, right?" He raised the binoculars and gave the obscure landscape another sweep. "You should just bite him and see what happens."

I hummed a frustrated noise that sounded more like a growl.

"What does Michio think?" he asked.

"He told me to follow my gut."

"And?" He glanced at me and returned to the binoculars.

"My gut is a clueless bitch."

"That doesn't sound like you." He shifted toward me, giving me his full attention. "Why do you say that?"

I wondered for the umpteenth time about the captors at the mansion. Why did they put Salem and I together? What was the purpose of releasing us after we had sex? It didn't make sense. I could take an army back there and investigate, but I suspected the property had been abandoned the moment they freed us. Deep down, I knew I wouldn't find answers there.

Don't look back.

My mother had lived by that mantra, and I tried to do the same. My destiny was forward, and he had a body built for wicked things. Whether he was beating my ass in a wrestling match, thrusting inside me, or sleeping in a tangle of bedding, he made me feel protected, adored, and frighteningly possessive.

"I have this strong instinct to bite Salem," I said. "*Just* him and no one else."

"You sure?" He yanked down the collar of his shirt and bared his throat. "I don't tempt you at all?"

"Nope."

"Well, that's a relief." He flashed a pearly-white smile then sobered. "So what's the problem?"

"I also have this nagging feeling that my bite will wipe out those silver things in his veins. Michio thinks they're ribbons of venom, that I can actually see the infection in Salem's blood. But it all congregates around his heart and…" I pressed my fingers against my chest and rubbed the ache there.

"You think your bite will kill him."

"I don't just think it. I feel it." I hugged my arms around my waist. "I need Salem to make the decision."

"That *really* doesn't sound like you."

"I'm not explaining it right. I need him to offer it, to *want* it." I tented my fingers against my lips and gathered my thoughts. "There's a tangible connection between us. Not like the visceral threads my mother felt with the aphids. This is different, more subtle. So imperceptible, in fact, I've only become aware of it in the last couple days. Though I'm certain it's been there all along. The more I concentrate on it the more I sense it."

"Like now?"

I closed my eyes and focused, but Salem was too far away. I couldn't feel shit. "No. When he's nearby, I can trace the connection like the veins in his chest. But something always blocks me from reaching the end of the link, like he's mentally stopping me from touching his heart."

"Okay, that sounds…" His laugh cut off at my hard glare. He cleared his throat. "What does this have to do with biting him?"

"It's connected. Don't ask me why or how. I just know if I bite him, I would be forcing my way through his veins and into his heart. I don't think he would survive." I wasn't sure I would want to survive if I killed him. "But if he opened our connection fully…"

"You mean, if he trusted you enough to bite him and fuck

his soul?"

"Nice, Eddie." I rubbed my head, regretting saying anything. "This is why I haven't mentioned this to him. He'll think I've lost my mind."

"This is what you say to him..." He raised the pitch of his voice. "Listen here, you oversized pain in the ass."

"Off to a great start," I deadpanned.

"Shh." He shoved a palm in my face. "You tell him, 'Open your heart or I'll destroy it.'" He swept an arm toward the horizon, his voice high and dramatic. "I have a world to save."

"Now you're just making fun of me." I shoved his shoulder. "Speaking of hearts, when are you going to win Jizzy Lizzy's?"

"I wish you'd stop calling her that." He returned to the binoculars, panning left to right.

Elizabeth was the resident beauty at Hoover Dam. She'd taken Eddie's virginity and his heart—and that of every other boy we grew up with. *Yes* and *more* were her favorite words, especially when she screamed them into a pillow.

"How many asses are you going to kick when you get home?" I grinned.

"All of them." He started to lower the binoculars and jerked them back up, his entire body going rigid.

"What is it?" I jumped to my feet and followed his line of sight to the northern wall and the pitch-black landscape beyond. "Eddie?"

"I swear I saw movement." His fingers clenched around the wide lenses. "Between the green shack and the old bank."

"I stationed two guards there." My pulse spiked. "We haven't patched that section of wall."

I spun, swiped our bows from the roof floor, and tossed his to him.

"It could've been a play of light." He shouldered his quiver and freed an arrow.

My gums tingled, and I parted my lips just as my fangs came in.

"Damn." He stared at my mouth. "I'll never get used to that."

I raced toward the fire escape on the exterior of the building. When I reached the ledge, my gaze collided with Salem's luminescent eyes.

He stood on the bottom platform, club in hand, and his black leather trench coat buttoned to his chin. Fuck me, he looked sharp and dangerous and sexy as hell, but…

"I need to see your neck." I ran down the rickety steps, skipping several and stumbling forward, with Eddie pounding after me. "Hurry!"

Did any nearby hybrid make his veins light up? Or just our captors? I assumed the former and wasn't taking any chances.

Tucking the club beneath an arm, Salem's fingers flew over the buttons. He opened the top of his coat, baring his throat. The sight of his glowing veins sank my heart to my stomach. It was the first time they'd appeared since we were freed from the mansion.

He looked down at his chest and back to me, a question in his black brows.

"Sound the alarm!" I grabbed an arrow and took off toward the north wall.

NINETEEN

Adrenaline flooded my veins and red-lined my pulse as I sprinted through the snow. How many hybrids were trying to breach the fence? Had they already broken through? Fuck! It would take me a couple minutes to reach it—minutes we didn't have.

A blur of black streaked by and vanished between the buildings up ahead. My fangs retracted, and my heart thundered in my ears.

The clanging sound of a bell sent people scattering around me. The women darted inside the hospital, and the men gathered weapons, looking at me for direction.

"Hybrids on the north wall." I picked up my gait, lungs heaving. "Flank both sides of the weak point. Close quarters formation. Fast and discriminating fires. Don't you dare hit Salem. I need three on the south gate. Find my fathers!"

I continued to bark orders at the soldiers I passed, my legs burning with exertion and fingers locked painfully around the bow.

Eddie caught up, outrunning my shorter legs. "Did you see his veins? That's how you know?"

"Yeah. Did you?" I cut a corner, narrowly dodged a rusted barrel, and my fangs reemerged.

"Saw his neck." He positioned his bow and nocked an arrow as we closed in on the wall. "No veins."

Maybe Salem was right. The anomaly was me. *My* freaky vision. But he was a freak, too, because amid the mayhem of clashing bodies up ahead, Salem was the only one who stood out, his vascular throat glowing like a beacon.

Hybrids poured in through the newly smashed hole in the wall, slamming into my soldiers and tackling them to the ground. I counted nine intruders before I lost track. Thirty yards from the battle, I positioned myself with an unobstructed field of fire and targeted the closest hybrid.

With a steady breath, I drew back an arrow and let it fly on my exhale.

The shot went wide, as did my next three attempts. More soldiers swept in around me. It was too dark to make out faces, but the clank of Roark's sword and my fathers' shouts drifted from the center of the melee.

I volleyed arrows with deliberate slowness, my nerves eroding with the fear I'd hit one of my own. Salem moved in my periphery, swinging the club and sending the deadly spike through more heads than any of our arrows. There was no question whose side he was on, yet none of the hybrids attacked him. They weren't just avoiding him. They were giving him a wide berth.

My mind raced as I tried to focus on my targets. I finally hit one in the eye before two others broke the front line and darted in my direction.

"Dawn!" Eddie spun toward them, his arrows missing their inhumanly fast movements.

My hands trembled as I lined up the next shot. I would never hit both of them in time, but dammit, I tried. Feet braced apart and breaths even, I nailed one in the eye, aimed for the second one, missed. *It's okay, it's okay.* I aimed another shot. Oh fuck, I was too late.

Fangs bared, he leapt toward me from a few feet away. My heart stopped, and my arrow slipped.

Someone slammed into my attacker from the side. They rolled through the dark and landed against the side of the shack. The spiked club hung from a bloody hole in the hybrid's skull.

Salem freed his weapon and turned toward me. The veins in his neck dimmed, faded into nothingness. *No more hybrids.* A visual sweep confirmed the fight was over. I let out a huge breath and lowered the bow to brace my hands on my knees.

"That's all of them," I shouted to the soldiers and met Salem's eyes. "Thank you."

"You okay?" He prowled closer, scanning me from head to toe.

"Yeah. You?"

He nodded and turned toward the approaching footsteps.

Silhouettes emerged from the dark—Eddie, my surviving soldiers, my fathers. I wanted to run to them and hug them with relief. But bodies littered the ground, three of them writhing and convulsing. I recognized the faces. Three of my soldiers. *Bitten.* We only had about a minute before they would turn.

I ordered several men to repair the breach in the wall and joined Michio beside Kip, one of the bitten soldiers. Roark quickly moved between the other two, murmuring Last Rites. Jesse stepped behind Roark, tomahawk raised to end the men's lives before the infection took over. My chest squeezed.

Salem touched Jesse's arm. "I'll do it."

I looked away, but couldn't tune out the wet *thunks* when that spike pierced through bone and brains.

Kip lay on the snowy ground before me, delirious and jerking with seizures. When venom attacked the body, it was violent and painful. And agonizing to watch. Especially as I thought about the wife and husband he had at home, anxiously awaiting his return.

Roark crouched beside me, his hands on Kip's chest, and whispered prayers of absolution. I removed my mother's dagger from my belt and fisted the handle, prepared to spare Salem another kill.

Michio gripped Kip's hand, wearing the expression of a doctor who desperately, passionately wanted to save lives, no matter how infected or irreparable. I stared at the dagger in my hand, listening to Kip's final breaths, loathing myself for not keeping him safe.

My worldview was shaped by my fathers, but my motto was adopted from my mother. *Stay alive. Seek truth. Don't look back.*

Killing Kip kept us alive. Once I plunged the blade, I wouldn't look back. But was I searching hard enough for the truth? What if I could cure him and return him to his loved ones? I didn't feel an urge or craving to bite him. Contrarily, the thought made me sick. But it was just one bite.

"One bite." I met Michio's eyes and pressed my fangs against my bottom lip. "And we'll know."

"Is that what your gut is telling you?" His brown eyes filled with hope as he searched my face.

I shook my head. "Seek truth, right?"

He closed his eyes, opened them, and stared at Kip, who foamed and frothed at the mouth.

I turned to Salem. "Can you hold him after he turns?"

"You're *not* biting him." His nostrils flared. "It's too fucking intimate."

"I'll bite his wrist and think of you."

I stood, shifting to the side as my fathers pinned Kip to the snow-covered ground.

"Move out of the way if you're not going to help," I said to Salem.

He flexed his hands, gave a reluctant nod, and knelt above Kip's head, gripping the man's shoulders.

"Eddie?" I found him standing off to the right, an arrow nocked and aimed at the writhing man, having already anticipated my order. "Thank you."

I lowered beside Salem and pulled back the collar of his coat. His strong neck worked through a swallow. I stroked his throat, relishing the warmth of his skin as I waited for the veins to light up.

The wait felt like hours, and a bitter taste washed over my tongue. My stomach twisted and clenched at the notion of drinking Kip's blood. Was this my body's way of throwing a cold light of reason on this plan? Before I could consider that, another light flooded my senses.

Salem's veins burned hot against my hand, each capillary so evenly lit and prominent it was a scientific wonder. There was no explainable light source, and I realized his epidermis wasn't transparent. The glow radiated so brightly it simply shone through his skin.

"Dad," I said to Michio, gliding my hand down Salem's throat, captivated by the way the veins reached toward my touch. "Do you see this?"

He followed the movement of my fingers, eyebrows furrowing and releasing. "No."

I looked at Roark and Jesse, and they shook their heads.

Lowering my chin, I released a heavy sigh and moved to Kip's wrist. "Do I aim for a vein?"

"Your fangs will find it." Salem watched me intently, displeasure sharpening his cheekbones, evidently still sour about me biting another man.

Kip growled, bucking against the hands holding him down and snapping his altered canines, his hungry eyes fixed on me.

I raised his wrist to my mouth and bit hard and fast. The pungent taste of blood rushed over my tongue and down my throat. I swallowed quickly, pulling on the vein and fighting nausea.

I couldn't see Kip's arteries, but holy hell, Salem's glowed brighter than ever, bulging and pumping beneath his skin. I sucked harder, and the silver things in Salem's veins froze in place. I was doing that? Affecting their movement? I tried to redirect my focus to Kip, but I was utterly absorbed by Salem's blood. The need to bite him was powerfully vicious, tightening my fingers and commanding the movement of my jaw.

"Dawn." Michio's voice sounded muffled, distant, beneath the pounding in my ears. "Dawn!"

The skin against my lips burned feverishly hot, so hot I yanked my fangs from Kip's wrist. His exposed flesh grayed, crackled, and sank against his bones, his eyes staring heavenward, lifeless.

A chill gripped my spine. "What—?"

Kip's entire body collapsed, disintegrating into a heap of clothes and…

I covered my mouth, whimpered. There was nothing left of him.

Nothing but ash.

"I killed him. I did that." My breaths came fast and deep, but I couldn't draw enough air. "I killed him."

"Dawn." Michio reached for me.

I spun away and wretched, emptying my stomach and splattering the snow in red.

TWENTY

Warm water lapped around me, and the scent of sandalwood soap softened the air. I stretched my legs in the old bathtub, one of those wrap-around inserts in the bathroom connected to the hospital room Salem and I had been sharing. The heated bath numbed the violent shivering in my body. But instead of enjoying my first soak in months, I felt guilty about using precious resources. Guilt piled on top of more guilt.

He was a hybrid. No longer human.

Roark had repeated those words and rubbed my back as I vomited my horror into the snow. Yes, Kip had already turned. Yes, I'd planned to kill him before I got the brainiac idea to save him.

But I couldn't erase the memory of Salem's incredulous stare and stiff posture after he watched me reduce the man into ashes. In that moment, I knew exactly what he was thinking. That would be him if he stepped into the sun. That would be him if I bit him.

I expected him to leave, to pack his shit, return to the safety of his utopia, and hope to never see me again. But he didn't.

Silhouettes paced beyond the crack of the bathroom door. Salem and my fathers congregated in the connecting room, speculating the pros and cons of my bite. Michio did most of the talking, his words too low to carry into the bathroom.

A candle dripped on the vanity, dancing shadows across the cracked tile walls. Michio had carried me in here and filled the tub from the pipes, violating the hot water restriction. It required a lot of energy to heat the tanks, but he deemed this an emergency and demanded I take a bath.

I couldn't hear Salem amid the murmur of voices, but my fangs were present. We'd tested the metamorphosis of my teeth over the past few weeks and discovered that any of my five senses could trigger the transformation. It was also subconscious. If I felt his touch while I slept, smelled him, heard him, my fangs formed. I didn't have to be mentally aware for my body to sense him and react. It was a total mind trip.

The sound of Jesse's voice drew my attention, and I leaned closer to the door, resting my forearms on the ledge of the tub.

"She would never agree to bite us," he said.

Oh, fuck no. Who the hell even suggested that?

"She doesn't need to bite us to test the theory." Michio's whisper sounded closer to the door. "Everyone in this room carries significant homoplastic traits of a hybrid and if…"

He moved out of hearing range, but I could guess the rest of that sentence because I'd already arrived at the same conclusion. Salem and my fathers might've been human, but they shared the same strengths as hybrids. *And weaknesses.* If I bit them, odds were they would turn to ash.

I slumped into the water, dipping my chin beneath the surface, and massaged my pounding head. My fangs killed hybrids. That would be useful in hand-to-hand combat. But I didn't have venom in my blood or fangs, nothing to extract and use as a mass weapon.

The fangs meant fuck all. It was the unearthly connections that tripped me up. My bloodlust was linked to Salem. When I bit Kip, the venom in *Salem's* veins reacted. How was Salem connected to the hybrids? How was I connected to Salem? I'd shared all of this with him and Michio while waiting for the bath to fill, but they didn't have answers.

A knock sounded on the door.

"Dawn?" Jesse's voice drifted through the crack. "How're

you doing?"

"I feel like I've been put in time-out."

He grunted. "You were vomiting and shaking—"

Shadows moved in the crack, followed by Michio's voice. "There's food and tea out here. When you come out, make sure you drink both bottles of water. I want you to sleep—"

"Wait." I sat up, splashing the water over the edge. "Are you leaving?"

"You need to rest." Michio sighed, his tone softening. "I love you, and right now, my priority is your mental and physical wellbeing. Eat, get some sleep, and find us when you wake."

Was it even time to sleep? The sun set around four o'clock. It was probably six now. But I'd been sleeping during the day with Salem. Except I didn't today. I'd slipped away to see the sun.

"Okay." I gathered my wet hair over my shoulder. "Love you, too."

I considered letting the water out of the tub, but it was still warm. Maybe Salem would indulge in this rare treat with me. I waited for the retreat of footsteps, the dimming of voices, and the click of the exterior door. A moment later, he stepped into the bathroom.

He paused beside the tub, fingertips resting in the front pockets of his fitted trousers. The weight of his hands inched the waistband low enough to give me a glimpse of smooth skin and carved abs. Heavy stitching detailed the shirt that hung over his torso in shades of black. Thick leather cuffs encased his wrists.

I wasn't the only one who'd acquired a new wardrobe from the resident seamstresses. The whole outfit accentuated his sleek muscles, dangerous power, and lickable fanged mouth. If those women couldn't resist taking his measurements, dressing him up, and drooling over the sexy result, I didn't blame them one bit.

Leaning back in the tub, I met his arctic eyes. "My fathers left you alone with their naked daughter."

"We've been sharing a room for three weeks."

"But they sleep on the opposite side of the hospital and don't have to think about it." I ran my palms over my thighs. "They knew you'd come in here after they left. Did they tell you to keep your hands to yourself?"

"No." He perched on the edge of the tub and tested the water with a finger. "If they had, I wouldn't have been able to give a convincing argument."

He grabbed my hand and pressed it against the hard length in his pants. I tightened my fingers around him, and a torrent of heat rushed between my legs.

"After seeing your gorgeous ass in battle," he said, low and gravelly, his cock twitching in my hand, "watching you expertly handle that bow, and knowing the most beautiful woman alive was nude and waiting one room away, it was all I could do to not shove your fathers out the damn door."

My toes curled. His compliment on my weaponry skills meant more to me than his assessment of my looks. I'd trained my entire life to be as efficient with the bow as Jesse, and while I was nowhere near his level, I appreciated Salem's praise.

"Sixteen hybrids are dead." I moved my fingers to the button on his pants. "Most of them fell beneath the spike of a cannibal club."

"Maybe so, but you were incredible out there, Dawn."

My faced heated beneath his gaze. "Join me in the bath." I peered up at him through my eyelashes, fumbling with his fly.

He caught my hands, his eyes smoldering and mouth parting. I wanted to lick the fangs that dimpled that devious, sexy-as-hell bottom lip. More than that, I wanted to bite that lip and suck the fuck out of it.

"We're not having sex." He stood and pulled off his shirt.

My stomach clenched. "Is this about what happened with Kip?"

"No." He removed his pants, holding my gaze. "I'm faster and stronger than you. You don't need to worry your pretty head about biting me."

"Then we're having sex."

I didn't want to beg, but his cock was right there, huge and long and beautiful. I never thought I'd stare at a man's genitalia with such awe and hunger, but it really was a magnificent cock. Thick and hard and capable of giving so much pleasure, it was an extension of his allure, a symbol of the overwhelming effect he had on me.

He slipped into the tub behind me and positioned me to lie back on his chest and thighs. His mouth touched my ear, caressing my skin with a seductive breath. "Relax."

Relax? With his erection sliding against my pussy? I reached between my legs and gripped his shaft. My inner muscles throbbed in anticipation as I positioned him at my opening.

His fingers shackled my wrists and pinned them at my sides. "Behave."

"Why?" I ground against his cock, but there was no leverage in this position.

"If I make love to you, I'll bite you, and I've already bitten you today."

Make love. Did I hear him right? Did he even realize he said it? The question hung on my tongue, but I decided not to make a big deal out of it, afraid he'd tell me he didn't mean it.

"You bite me multiple times a day all the time." I angled my neck to see his eyes. "It's just a sip."

"Don't move your hands." He released my wrists and trailed his fingers along my hips, drifting up my chest, his breath warm and erotic against my neck. "You had a traumatic night." His lips brushed the sensitive spot beneath my ear, licking, nibbling, as he cupped and kneaded my breasts. "I'm going to make you come. Then you're going to sleep and be peaceful."

"What about you? I want to—"

His fingers slipped through my folds and penetrated me knuckles-deep. I moaned and dug my nails into the hard flanks of his ass, jerking my hips against the thrust of his hand. The water slapped the walls of the tub, his bicep flexing as he worked me into a panting, heaving puddle of lust.

He ground his cock against my ass, and his breathing quickened, the stroke of his fingers growing harder, sinking deeper.

"Ah, Salem." I was primed and swollen, pulsing and ready to explode. "I'm there. Right there."

He shifted his thumb, circling it against my clit, and I came undone. Electricity burst through my core and rippled through my body in sparks of scorching heat. I shouted his name, twitching and writhing and choking on my breaths.

My brain turned to pulp, my body boneless and humming with tingles. Fuck, that was good. So good I couldn't imagine living without it.

When I caught my breath, I lazily rolled over to face him. "Your turn—"

"No." He captured my mouth in a gentle kiss, leisurely licking, his tongue plunging and rubbing against mine. Then he kissed a path across my cheek and whispered at my ear, "I never thought I'd live to see the dawn." He cupped my jaw and held my face inches from his. "Absolutely breathtaking."

My heart skipped. *This man and his words.*

"You have no idea how happy you make me." He guided my cheek to his chest and stroked my hair.

"You make me happy, too." Impossibly so. I didn't want to lose him.

His cock was still hard, but the water was cooling, and he was already moving to pull the plug. We dried off. I drank the bottled water and picked at the roasted radishes and nuts. Then we blew out the candles and curled up on the small mattress in our makeshift room.

Boards covered the window to prevent light from sneaking in. Layers of wool wrapped us in a tangle of shared body heat. Thanks to that delicious orgasm, my muscles were loose and languid, my insides uncoiled. Calm. Drowsy. *Peaceful.* Exactly how Salem wanted me, the generous bastard.

I think I love him.

"You're coming home to Alberta with me," he breathed

against my hair.

My eyes popped open, unseeing in the dark. *What about my fathers? The Resistance? My fangs? How well do I even know you?* "Are you telling me what to do?"

"You're coming home with me?"

"You can't just raise the pitch of your voice at the end and make it a question."

"So it's settled. We leave tomorrow at dusk."

TWENTY-ONE

Despite the satisfied state of my body, sleep didn't come easily. When I finally succumbed, slumber was as restless and wary as my thoughts. I drifted in and out of consciousness, obsessing over my confusing feelings about Salem, my purpose as Eve's daughter, and where to go from here. A few hours later, I gave up on the nap and untangled my limbs from Salem's warmth.

He rolled to his back, and his shadowed hand reached for my face, tenderly caressing my cheek. "Do you want to talk about it?"

A conversation was exactly what I wanted. With the three people I trusted most.

I rose from the mattress and pulled on my clothes in the frigid darkness. "I'm going for a walk."

The bedding rustled with his movement.

"Alone," I said. "I can't think in the presence of all your…sexiness."

He laughed. "Now you know how I feel."

Dressed in a simple shirt and trousers, I shoved on the boots and buckled my mother's dagger to my belt. "I won't be long."

I left him with a kiss full of promise and made my way through the lower level of the old hospital, sans fangs.

The maze of corridors stretched into darkness, and a strange odor emanated from some unknown source. Maybe mold in the peeling wallpaper? Or rotting wood beneath the chipped linoleum floors? I snagged a candle from a wobbly table and lit the wick.

The flame cast an eerie glow through the graffiti-painted hall. *Aphids are near* spanned one wall from floor to ceiling, the drippy words faded from twenty years of wear. I turned the corner, shivering at the array of messages spray-painted in hurried handwriting.

They will hear you.

Have you seen my little girl?

I didn't want to die.

I'd encountered a lot of desperate graffiti in my travels across North America, all chilling reminders that the world had plunged into ten kinds of crazy when the virus hit.

Broken hospital equipment and the rusted metal bed frames lined the corridors. No people. It must've been around ten o'clock. Most of the residents would've been tucked into their rooms for the night. Ten of my soldiers would be patrolling the perimeter of the camp, ready to come off their eight-hour rotation.

Up ahead, one of my men stepped in from outside and stomped the snow from his boots. When he spotted my approach, his posture straightened, shoulders back, and head lowered. "Ma'am."

"At ease, soldier." I closed the distance. "Are my fathers out there?"

"No, ma'am." His bearing relaxed. "They came in about twenty minutes ago. Check the meeting room."

"Thanks." I headed toward the west wing of the *L*-shaped building.

A few minutes later, I entered what had once been a hospital conference room. Illuminated by several kerosene lamps, Roark and Link bent over a long table covered in maps. Empty bottles of Bushmills held down the corners of the drawing they were discussing.

Link's wrinkly bald head popped up, his smile partially obscured by a grizzly beard. "Hey there, Mini Evie."

"Hey yourself, old man." I set the candle on the table. "What are you looking at?"

Roark lifted an arm, a silent invitation to dive in for a hug.

I pressed against his side, slipped my hand around his broad back, and stared down at the map of the Yukon Territory. A trail of *X*'s followed the Yukon River and marked paths north and south.

"You're supposed to be resting." Roark kissed my head.

"Couldn't sleep." I traced the scribbles on the map. "You're going to look for the mansion?"

"Aye. Salem drew his route from Alberta." Roark roamed a finger along the map, his accent deep and tired. "To his end point here. We'll start with his directions since the hybrids that chased ye and Jeremy made a complete haymes of yours."

Link folded his arms across his chest, black eyes pointed at me. "You didn't seem too confident about the path you took through the woods."

I studied the map and shook my head. "No, you're right. The mansion could be in any direction from this point." I tapped the shaded area on the faded paper and pulled my hand away. "I don't want to go back there. Just let it go, Da. We'll—"

"Feck no." Roark's eyes hardened into emeralds in the soft light. "Those fangers held ye for ten bloody days, and I want to know why." The snarl in his accent and tension in his jaw told me he didn't just want to interrogate them. He intended to kill them. "Ye and Eddie will take half of the soldiers with ye back to the dam." Roark glared at the map. "The rest will come with us."

Us meaning all my fathers. They never traveled without one another.

The thought of returning to the dam without Salem produced a stabbing ache in my chest. His demand to bring me home with him was one of the reasons I couldn't sleep. I should've outright rejected the idea of going to Alberta, but I hadn't, and that confused the fuck out of me.

"Where's Michio and Jesse?" I asked.

"Ye just missed them." Roark glanced at the door. "They should be in our room." His eyes narrowed on my face.

"What's wrong?"

"I need some advice." I stole a glance at Link and returned to Roark. "Can we talk? In your room?"

"That rings of boy trouble." Link smirked. "This is why I never had kids."

I flipped him the finger.

"Den' know wha' you're missing, ye ugly dosser." Roark slapped Link on the back.

"I'll take your word for it." Link's chuckle followed us into the corridor.

A short walk down the hall led us to the room my fathers shared. The door stood slightly ajar, illuminated by the soft glow within.

"Father Roark?" One of the female residents poked her head out of the room across the hall. "Can I trouble you to help me move my mattress? There's a draft, and I'm having a hard time sleeping."

Her silk robe slipped off her shoulder, and she didn't bother adjusting it. She didn't try to hide the perusal of her gaze up and down his body either.

Disgusting. The girl wasn't much older than me and was more than capable of moving a mattress by her own damn self. I gave her the stink eye, but she didn't notice. She was too busy eye-fucking my dad.

"I'll just be a second," Roark said to me and stepped into the woman's room.

If she touched him… Ugh. It wasn't my concern. I spun, shoved through the door of my fathers' room, and slammed to a stop.

Michio held Jesse against the wall, breathing heavily, chest to chest, with his face buried in Jesse's neck. Both were fully clothed, but Jesse's hands were between them, gripping, stroking, and—

I gasped, stumbled backward, and ran into the door.

They flew apart, and I dashed toward the corridor.

"I'm sorry." *Fuck, fuck, fuck.* "I should've knocked."

In the hall, I shut the door behind me and slumped against

it, cursing my stupidity. I pressed my cold fingers against my flushed cheeks and startled when Roark emerged from the room across from me.

Hands on his hips, he squinted at my expression. "Ye look mortified. Wha' did ye—?" His gaze floated to the door behind me. "Oh." A smile struggled to break free on his lips, and he rubbed a hand over it. "They were supposed to wait for me."

"TMI, Da!" I started down the hall. "I'll come back."

"Wait." He gripped my shoulders and positioned me against the wall beside the door. Then he peeked into his room. "Bloody hell, put some clothes on."

Oh my fuck. I covered my face and jolted forward to make my escape.

Roark grabbed my arm. "I'm only codding ye. And *them.* I like to see their faces turn scarlet."

"That's mean."

"Trust me, lass. They'll find it amusing by night's end."

After the conversation we were about to have, I wasn't sure how much smiling they would be doing. I followed him into the room.

Two mattresses were pushed together in the corner and piled with blankets. Michio sat in a chair beside it. Jesse reclined at the center of the bed, his back against the wall, and legs crossed at the ankles. He patted the space beside him.

I quickly removed my boots and curled up against him like I'd done millions of times since I was little.

"Rosalie needed help with her mattress." Roark shut the door and locked it.

Jesse half-grunted, half-snorted. "You finally set her straight?"

"I politely told her to feck off."

Feck off was Roark's polite swear word, which meant he told her exactly that. I pinned my lips together, grinning.

Michio perched on the edge of the chair, elbows on his knees and hands clasped together against his mouth. "You're supposed to be sleeping."

"Too much on my mind." I shifted closer to Jesse, making room for Roark.

"She needs her oul fellas' brilliant advice." Roark scooted in, jostling the bed under the weight of his muscled frame.

Michio leaned back, propped an ankle on a knee, and tilted his head, eyes sharp.

Oh, man. That look made me feel like a preteen again. Sandwiched between Roark and Jesse, I wrestled with the sudden silence. *Just spit it out.*

I pulled in a breath and released it slowly. "He wants me to go back to Alberta with him."

"No." Jesse shot to a sitting position, twisting at the waist to glare at me. "You're not—"

"Let her talk." Roark shoved a blond dreadlock from his face.

Roark and Jesse shared a tense stare off before Jesse stabbed a hand through his graying copper hair. Then he leaned against the wall and tucked an arm around my back.

"I think I love him." With my legs stretched out, I tapped the toes of my wool socks together. "I think he might feel the same way."

"You *think* you love him?" Michio asked quietly. "You don't know?"

My eyebrows twitched as I considered the answer. Our chemistry was indisputable, and I trusted him with my life. But… "If I followed him to Alberta, I don't know if I would be doing it because I care about him or because I care about humanity's future." I traced a finger along the straight edge of my human teeth. "Without him, I don't have fangs. I won't learn the truth behind their purpose. If my fangs are necessary in saving mankind, I must stay with him. If they're some kind of opposing force against the prophecy, I need to let him go and"—I rubbed my breastbone—"that really, really hurts."

Michio stared at the wall above my head, his gaze distant. "Humans don't make decisions based on logic." He blinked and met my eyes. "We make decisions based on whether we love what the logic tells us."

"Are you saying I can only make decisions based on emotion?"

"It's the way we're wired, Dawn, from birth to death." He glanced from Roark to Jesse to the floor, and the corner of his mouth lifted in a private smile. "Love is mankind's greatest power. It's more crucial to our evolution than canine teeth and opposable thumbs. It chooses what to cling to, who to raise children with, and where and how far to go in life. I'm saying that the pain in your chest means the decision has already been made for you."

The ache behind my ribs clenched tighter. I turned toward Roark, who was uncharacteristically quiet.

He tapped a finger against my breastbone. "If it's deep inside ye, if it's wha' ye want very badly, you'll break your own rules—"

"Vows." Jesse coughed against his fist.

"Right." Roark lifted my medallion, his thumb stroking over the fang, stone, and rosary bead embedded in the metal. "If ye love him, nothing and no one will be able to keep ye from him. Not the prophecy. Not God." His gaze found mine. "Not even your fathers."

"Bullshit," Jesse growled. "We don't know that man. We have no idea what his motivation is."

My molars crashed together, and I shifted to face him. "Is it so difficult to believe he might love me?"

"No." His eyes widened. Then his face slackened, and he pulled me to his chest. "Christ, I already know he's madly in love with you. It's just…I don't like it. This life is already so goddamn hard. I don't want a relationship to make it harder for you."

"Is that what you thought when you met my mother?"

"No," he said furiously.

"A prophecy couldn't keep you away from her." I pushed away from his chest and pointed at Roark. "His vows didn't stop him. And…" I turned to Michio, my voice rising. "You were her captor. I don't even understand how that worked out. But it did."

What was my point? I gripped the back of my neck, my chest heaving, overcome with the urgency to make them understand.

Then it dawned on me. I was arguing *for* my relationship with Salem, not against it. I wanted it, wanted *him*, with an intensity that scared me.

"I love him," I whispered and saw my fear reflected in my fathers' expressions. My attention narrowed on Jesse. "You left your Lakota brethren, the only family you had, to follow my mother across the ocean. Did you question that decision?"

Jesse closed his eyes and breathed deeply. "No, never. I loved her." His eyes opened, glistening in the lamp light. "Love isn't just vital. It's what vital means."

I folded my arms around his neck and lay my cheek on his chest. Michio moved to the bed and curled around Jesse's back. Behind me, Roark rested his brow on my shoulder. For the next hour, we debated the pros and cons—mostly the cons—of me running off to Alberta with Salem.

My fathers were scared, their voices vibrating with emotion, so I threw Michio's words back at him.

We make decisions based on whether we love what the logic tells us.

As they asserted their opinions, I curled up between them and recalled the stories about my mother.

The loss of her children and husband.

Grieving. Alone. The only surviving woman in the world.

Her dangerous trek to the Allegheny Mountains.

The pub where she met Roark.

Imprisonment on Malta.

A gunship to Iceland, and the battle with the Drone.

Her return to West Virginia where she cured Salem's mother.

More women. Endless blood donations.

Her fall from Hoover Dam.

"Everything my mother did was a risk," I said, interrupting their discussion. "If she hadn't taken those risks, if she hadn't followed her gut *and* her heart, I wouldn't be here. *We* wouldn't be here."

No one spoke. I looked into three pairs of grief-stricken eyes, knowing they shared the same memories. We didn't move for an eternity, alone with our thoughts but together in the solace of family.

"Give me six months," I said in a strong voice, issued from a place of strength and love. "I'm leaving tomorrow at dusk."

TWENTY-TWO

The next night, I stood inside the south gate of the camp with a heavy heart and a fluttery buzz in my stomach. Residents and soldiers gathered with candles in hand and hope in their eyes. They didn't know the specifics surrounding my departure, but they trusted my motivation. As the daughter of Eve, I would never abandon my obligation to humanity.

"Give Shea my love." I wrapped my arms around Eddie's shoulders.

"I will." His voice was rough as he brushed his lips against my brow and stepped back. "See you in six months, Red."

Beyond the gate and out of hearing range, Salem sat atop a black Appaloosa, surrounded by saddlebags crammed with food, arrows, and survival supplies. He also carried a concentrated mix of flax seed, beet pulp, and grains for the horse.

I didn't want to leave my fathers short a horse, but I'd lost that argument. If we stuck to the roads and trails, it would take Salem and I three months to hike to Alberta. By horse, we could complete the journey in half the time.

Six weeks to ride to Alberta. A three-month stay with Salem. One month to ride to Hoover Dam. Along the way, maybe I'd find a car modified for gasification. An engine converted to a wood gasifier took dry wood, hay, or coal and turned it into fuel. Transportation like that would drastically reduce our travel time.

The three-month limit was a detail I hadn't mentioned to Salem. Cowardly on my part, but I hoped it would give us enough time to figure out our connection. I also planned to use the months ahead to convince him to return home with me.

Salem had drawn a map for my fathers, indicating the location of his home and the route we would take to get there. He also promised to send a messenger to Hoover Dam once we were settled to let them know we arrived safely. The messenger would make treks with letters, keeping communication open until I returned home.

I gave Eddie a parting smile and moved toward my fathers.

"Six months," I said to Jesse, hugging him with all my might. "If you locate that mansion, watch the shadows in the front room, and please, *please*, be careful."

"Take a soldier with you," he whispered at my ear.

"Leave it alone, Dad."

We'd talked about this last night. It was Jesse's last ditch effort to have some control over my decision. But Salem had promised I didn't need armed guards. If I loved him, I needed to trust him.

"Stay alive." Jesse stepped back, copper eyes stark and unyielding.

"I love you, too," I said softly.

Michio was next, his hug just as tight. "When you write to us, tell me about his relationship with the hybrids."

"I will." I was nervous about how Salem would keep a pack of hybrids away from me, but I was also wildly curious to find out.

"Seek truth." Michio kissed my brow, then my nose, and let me go.

"I love you, too." I bowed my head.

The final hug crushed my ribs.

"Can't breathe," I choked.

Roark loosened his embrace slightly, his accent thick. "I won't breathe till I see ye again."

"Stop it. This isn't any different than my Resistance missions." Throat tight, I leaned back and placed my hands on his scruffy cheeks. "Say it, Da. Say the words."

The mantra was my mother's, and we repeated it every time I left.

He closed his eyes and pulled me in for another hug. "Den' look back."

"I love you, too."

After I mounted the horse with my legs hugging Salem's hips, I mentally chanted, *Stay alive. Seek truth.* I didn't look back, despite the hard stares searing between my shoulder blades.

As Salem steered us away from the camp and across the frozen dark terrain, I rested my cheek against his strong spine. Leather and wool covered him from the chin down, but with my ear so close to his torso, I would hear his veins if they glowed.

I clung to the pillar of his body, rocking with the sway of the horse. Our connection hummed between us like an electrical charge. It burned hot and bright inside me, sparked along an invisible wire, and fizzled into the wall of his back, fading into nothingness.

Six months. I had time to open his heart, to talk to him about it, to figure out the mystery behind his veins and my fangs. I was afraid, though. Afraid I would fail. Afraid I'd trusted him too fast and too deeply. I'd never traveled this far away without Eddie and my soldiers. I'd never traveled alone.

But my mother had. I gripped the medallion around my neck. She'd crossed the Atlantic in a shipping container. Climbed through a volcano in Iceland. Endured a cage in the back of a truck through the snowy Rocky Mountains. I wouldn't, couldn't have done those things by myself.

"You're braver than me, Mom," I whispered.

The man who held my heart gave a disapproving grunt. "You're braver than you know, Dawn."

TWENTY-THREE

Nights passed without incident. The endless roads stretched into darkness, the bitter wind a relentless whip against my face. Salem pushed the horse hard, pausing only to find shelter at dawn and sleep a few hours until dusk. I didn't complain. I might've slept easier back at the camp, but in my travels with the Resistance, I'd grown used to the hardship of nomadic life.

On the sixth day, we lay in a listless tangle of limbs and pale light from the lantern. Tucked in a hay-strewn stall of an abandoned barn, he'd woken me with his powerful body curled around my back and his hungry cock buried between my legs. Several orgasms later, the lingering bliss of sex and the warmth of his bite slowly circulated through my blood, lazy and satisfying.

Keeping to the broken pavement of old roads made it easier to find shelter before the sun rose each day. Rural towns and melting rivers frequently crossed our path, though we hadn't encountered a hybrid or human since leaving the camp. The farther south we ventured, the warmer and more populated our route would become. We were only two people, though. I tried not to envision us battling a bloodthirsty horde.

The relatively mild weather combined with his exceptional hunting skills had saved us from dipping into our limited food supply. But one torrential blizzard could put a deadly wrench in our luck. We needed to keep moving south.

I glanced across the dirt floor toward the rotting door of the barn and the darkness creeping through the cracks. "We should get going."

"Mm." He pulled my back tighter against the heat of his chest and kneaded my breasts. "I'm not ready to give this up."

We had at least five more weeks of *this* before we reached Alberta. He'd made love to me every day. Though we never spoke the words, I was certain he saw the sentiment in my eyes as clearly as I saw it in his.

He brushed my hair from my neck and traced his tongue across my skin. I purred and stretched as his hand molded around the curve of my waist.

"You have no idea how beautiful you are." His breath feathered across my cheek, stoking a fire beneath the words he whispered daily.

"You'll just have to keep telling me." I grinned, squirming beneath the tickling nibble on my neck. "Until it sinks—"

The amplified *lub-dub lub-dub* of his heart galloped in my ears. The hairs on my nape stood up. I twisted in his arms, and the illuminated maze of his veins filled my vision.

"Hybrids." I launched to my feet and grabbed the bow.

"Get dressed." He swapped the bow in my hand with my clothes.

In rushed silence, we dragged on leather pants and linen shirts. His mouth formed a tight line, despite the calm movement of his fingers as he fastened a corset around my torso.

"Forget the damn thing." I tried to bend away, reaching for the bow at his feet.

"Hold still." He pushed me against the wall, his hands flying over the hooks on the busk. "Your fucking shirt is see-through."

I hissed through my fangs, but two seconds later, he had me clasped up and heaving for air. We quickly shoved on boots and coats, my gaze glued to the brightening glow of his throat. Panic surged through my blood.

"Stay here." He turned toward the door.

"No fucking w—"

The ground vibrated, and a strange noise rumbled in the

distance. I froze and met his eyes.

"Is that…?" I cocked my head, listening as the vibration grew louder. "A stampede of horses?"

He shook his head, his expression cast in shadows.

The sound was a low, heavy, continuous growl, like thunder or…

"Cars." Goosebumps rose along my spine as I grabbed the bow and quiver. "We can't outrun a fucking engine." I spun, seeking the best place to fire off shots. "We'll have to fight them, Salem. We need to—"

He grabbed my bicep, snatched the bow and arrows from my hands, and tossed them out of reach. "It'll be easier if you don't fight."

"What?" I jerked in his iron grip, going nowhere. "Are you crazy? They're coming!"

He swung me around, pinning my back to his chest and curling his fingers around my throat. "Shh."

The purr of engines rolled up to the barn door, shaking the ground with a mechanical rumble.

"Now would be a good time," I said with a strangled voice, "to fill me in on your plan."

"Deep breath, baby." His timbre was soft against my ear. Too soft. Too calm.

"Salem?" I struggled in his arms, a wasted effort. "What's going on?"

The engines shut off. Car doors slammed. The tread of boots approached the door.

My heart banged against my ribs. Salem must've had a plan, one that required me to be scared and unarmed. I needed to trust him.

I don't trust him.

The door swung open, and a blond man in his late-twenties strode in. He held his head down, blue eyes up, as if he were used to ducking through doorways, because holy shit, he must've been seven-feet-tall. Dressed head-to-toe in layers of furs and black leather, he carried a long sword on his back and a fanged scowl on his pale yet strikingly handsome face.

Hybrid.

He looked utterly terrifying, like a Viking bred for blood and death. Why were we just standing here? The only tension in Salem's body was in the clench of his hands as I bucked and thrashed. What the fuck was going on?

An assortment of deadly knives and axes clanked on the hybrid's belt as he closed the distance. Salem didn't move, his breaths steady, the magnified sound of his heart thumping along at an even keel.

I pressed back against his chest, clawing at the hand around my neck. "Let me go, dammit."

He tightened his grip on my throat and waist. "Erebus."

Every muscle in my body locked up. "You know him?"

Was this seven-foot Viking one of the hybrids that lived with Salem? Or did Salem know other hybrids? Why did Erebus look so pissed off? And why wasn't he attacking me with mindless hunger?

"Salem." Erebus stopped a few yards away, his glower pointed at Salem. "This was not the fucking plan."

"What plan?" I renewed my fight to break Salem's suffocating hold.

In a fluid motion, Salem swept me to the ground, face down, with my wrists pinned behind my back.

Ice-cold shock stole my voice, and blood rushed from my face to my feet, prickling my skin with dread.

"Change of plans." With a hand on my wrists, Salem fisted the other in my hair, using his grip to twist my neck and angle my face toward the other man. "Dawn, this is Erebus. The man who delivered our meals in the mansion."

TWENTY-FOUR

The fist in my hair brought tears to my eyes, but it was Salem's words that spilled them down my cheeks.

Erebus... The man who delivered our meals in the mansion.

Our captor. I closed my eyes as my heart shattered. Not *our* captor. *My* captor. Salem was in on it.

"You know him." I exploded in a fury of kicking and jerking beneath Salem's restraining hands, my tears mixing with the dirt pressed to my face. "You were fucking in on it!"

Erebus crouched beside me, the blades on his belt glinting in the lantern light, and his eyes on Salem. "Need help?"

"Rope." Salem released my hair to reinforce his grip on my arms and legs. "Help me tie her, and watch out for her fangs."

"What? No!" My struggling worked the tear-soaked soil into my nose and mouth. "Why are you doing this? I trusted you!"

"Shh." Salem stroked my hair, and the tender touch only further enraged me.

"Don't shush me." I twisted my neck and tried to catch Salem's arm with my fangs. "You lying son of a—"

He gagged my mouth with a strip of leather and tied it at the back of my head. "You're right about that, sweetheart. Elaine was a bitch."

As I sank my teeth into the strap, the full force of his deceit hit me directly in the gut. In the mansion, we'd had a rocky start, sparring and circling each other for days. But he'd never gagged me, never so blatantly ignored my questions. I felt sick, violated, and utterly betrayed.

His furrowed brow darkened his eyes, his mouth tipping down at the corners. The depth of his treachery wasn't clear, but as he bound my wrists behind me, I lost my grip on the ridiculous hope that this was all a game or a misunderstanding.

I rolled to my side, watching with a splintering ache in my chest as he and Erebus embraced each other in a hearty hug. The kind of hug shared among close friends, not business acquaintances.

I'd been duped. Played a fool since the day I ran into that mansion. Hell, maybe Salem had orchestrated the chase that had landed me there. I'd suspected as much the day I met him, but I'd ignored my gut to follow my dumb, guileless heart.

With my hands bound and mouth gagged, I should've been contemplating the severity of the situation, like them killing the prophesied daughter to destroy any hope for mankind's freedom. But I couldn't focus past the lancing pain of Salem's duplicity against me and the relationship I held so dear.

Had I imagined every passionate moment between us? Had he tricked me into falling in love with him so he could use me for some heinous purpose? I'd been convinced he cared about me. How could I have gotten that so wrong? Even now, I refused to believe it was all a farce. He couldn't have faked the connection between us. I simply couldn't accept he felt nothing for me.

"Do you know how hard it was to not storm into that prison cell and deal with this myself?" Erebus gestured at me and glared at Salem. "Why isn't she dead?"

I stopped breathing, my eyes blurring as I searched the hard lines of Salem's face. He was supposed to kill me?

"I decided to keep her." He straightened, his brutal expression etched in marble.

"Keep her?" Erebus snarled past his fangs and narrowed ice-blue eyes. "You decided to keep the daughter of Eve? Defeats the fucking purpose, don't you think?"

What purpose? To kill me and be done with the foretold threat against their species? I sat up and bent my knees, planting my boots on the ground. I would never outrun them, but if they took me outside, I had to try.

"We'll talk later. We need to get moving." Salem lifted me to my feet with his hands on my waist. "Don't leave anything behind," he said to Erebus. "There's a carbon-steel knife in her pack. Put it in a safe place."

Tears gathered on the rim of my lashes, and each blink sent a droplet down my face. Why would he care about my mother's dagger? And why was he rubbing my back as he led me bound and gagged toward the door. He was fucking with my head. Wringing my stomach. Gutting my heart.

We stepped outside, and the glacial wind instantly froze the moisture on my cheeks. Other than the rope on my wrists at my back, he didn't restrain me, didn't even touch me, as if to say, *Go ahead. Try to run.*

I scanned the perimeter and shuddered at the number of eyes staring out of the darkness. The human-shaped silhouettes were tall, masculine, and bristling with fangs. At least two dozen hybrids. But none moved to attack me. Did Salem have some sort of power or influence over them?

They sat atop huffing horses. Others stood around the six massive trucks parked in an intimidating line in front of the barn. Were they even trucks? No two vehicles were alike but they all looked downright menacing. Painted black and covered in armor plates, they were equipped with gasified fuel tanks on rear and side carriers, scowling steel grills that could plow through a building, and the biggest, baddest all-terrain tires I'd ever seen. It would take a large forest to produce the fuel needed to move that much weight. But there were no visible weapons mounted on the exteriors. They seemed to have been customized for the sole purpose of safe transportation.

Salem guided me to the vehicle parked second to the front of the convoy. It resembled a tank on four wheels. The only windows were on the front cab. The rear appeared to be a self-contained, armored pod.

He opened the back door, revealing something out of a

medieval fairytale. Thick cushions made of silk covered the floorboards. Tufted velvet padded the interior walls, the fabrics boasting rich shades of red and black. An array of meats, fruits, vegetables, and wine spread over a built-in table. Dim electric lights glowed from handcrafted wood panels along the roof.

It was a palace on wheels. A symbol of majesty and power. A modern royal carriage fit for a dark prince with an aversion to the sun.

Was this a glimpse of his *utopia*? How could anyone afford such luxury in this world?

My hands fisted in the rope. I didn't want any part of it.

The aroma of grilled meat reached my nose, rushing saliva against the gag. The food had been freshly prepared and served on silver fucking platters. If it was meant for Salem, the hybrids had been expecting him. They had known where to find him.

All of this was planned.

My stomach roiled and cramped as I stared up at him with so many questions wetting my eyes.

Who are you? What do you want with me? I loved you, and I don't even know you.

He brushed the dirt from my cheek, his hand warm and painfully gentle. "We won't stop again for a while. Do you need to pee before we leave?"

Yes, and given the coiling, fucked-up state of my insides, I might very well shit myself. And hurl all over my boots.

Footsteps sounded behind me, and I glanced over my shoulder.

Erebus led the Appaloosa out of the barn. He and the horse were weighed down with our belongings, including my bow and arrows. I twisted my wrists against the rope, trembling with the urge to flee. Fuck it.

I ran, darting between the vehicles and around the horses. My legs burned and my boots pounded and slid over snow as I sprinted north across the open tundra. North toward my fathers. Far away from Salem and his plans, his hybrids, and his fancy...*fuck-I-don't-even-want-to-know* armored carriage.

The blustery air froze my lungs. My tongue dragged against the gag, my wrists scorching against the scratchy rope. I must've run a quarter of a mile before I dared a peek over my shoulder. The barn, vehicles, and horses blotted the bleak horizon. No one chased me. Not the hybrids. Not Salem. Adrenaline fired through my blood and fueled my muscles.

I redirected my focus forward and slammed into a wall of leather and muscle. The impact knocked me on my ass, and I blinked, dazed.

Salem stood over me, boots shoulder-width apart, hands clasped behind his back, and expression eerily composed. The flap of his black trench coat whipped like a flag in the wind, the veins in his throat outshining the moonlight.

My corset felt like a steel band around my ribs as I fought for air. How the hell did he sneak up on me? Why did he look so calm?

He knows you can't outrun him, you idiot.

As if to punctuate that thought, he gave me his back, stepped a few feet away, and urinated in the snow. "If you don't pee, Dawn, it's going to be a miserable trip. We're not stopping for eights hours."

Because opening that back door would kill him.

Not my problem. I stumbled to my feet and took off in the other direction. The stomp of my boots echoed through the icy darkness. Only *my* boots. He didn't chase? I glanced back at the snowy landscape. No Salem. Even with his superior speed, I should've spotted him. Unless...

I jerked my head forward and skidded to a stop. Too late. I collided with his chest and fell back.

He caught my arms, halting my downward tumble. I bit down on the gag. Did he fucking teleport?

"You're wondering why you can't perceive my movements." He knelt before me and reached for the fastening on my pants.

I shuffled backward, chest heaving at the audacity of his touch.

"Come here." He flicked his finger, pointing at the spot in front of him as lightning flashed in his eyes. "I'm going to help you with your pants so you can pee. And I'll tell what you want to know." He rested his hands on his thighs. "I'll tell you everything."

As if I could believe him. But at this point, I had nothing to lose. The threatening look he pointed at me said my pants were coming down the hard way if I ran again.

With a shivery breath, I stepped forward.

He pushed the trousers to my boots and waited until I squatted before he spoke. "I'm faster and stronger than a hybrid. Far faster than the human eye can detect."

I emptied my bladder and stood, every muscle in my body trembling from the wind and his words.

"You can't run from me." He pulled up my pants, his fingers warm and soft along my thighs. "You can't bite me. Can't fight me. I will always win."

The truth of his statement sucked the air from my lungs. He was bigger, deadlier, and faster. I was helpless against him, and that was the scariest feeling in the world.

He ducked his head to tie my waistband, and a sliver of skin peeked above his collar, glowing with veins.

Do it!

I opened my jaw and slammed my fangs toward his neck. But instead of making contact, the air was knocked out of me. Vision fled, and the sensation of falling overpowered my senses. Plummeting. Flying. It happened in a blink, and when the world stopped spinning, I was sitting in his armored chariot, surrounded by opulent fabrics and vented heat and Salem. He perched on a cushion across from me, liquid-steel eyes pinning me in place.

My heart thundered. Did I black out?

He read the question in my expression. "I carried you here, but you didn't sense it, did you? I'm fast, Dawn. Too fast for your awareness."

How was that possible? What was I supposed to do with that information? I looked around, didn't spot any weapons.

Not his club. No eating utensils. Nothing I could use to stab through his eyes. Not that I could wield any weapon with my hands tied behind my back.

The rear door was locked with a steel bar on the inside. Not only had he hurtled me across a quarter mile distance in a fraction of a second, he'd also barred the door. A bar I had no chance of removing if he was that damn fast.

Was I even capable of killing him? If I got that door open during the daylight, I could fry him. But the thought crushed my chest with unbearable pain. Maybe I could do it out of desperation or fear. I'd tried to bite him just a moment ago. If I'd turned him to ash, would I have regretted it? I still felt something for him, something twisted and complicated that entwined through my heart. I didn't know how to untangle that.

I'm a stupid, lovesick girl. Perhaps too stupid to live.

I was supposed to be the prophecy. The prediction must've been flawed or misinterpreted. Though it had been drilled into my head since I was born, I'd always had my doubts. But I'd never questioned it as much as I did now, sitting beside a man who had imprisoned me not once, but twice. How could I save an entire race when I couldn't even save myself?

The engine rumbled to life, and the transport rolled into motion.

He bent toward me and slid off my boots, slowly, carefully, while holding my gaze. I couldn't look away, couldn't move, my entire body frozen in heartache and bewilderment as he massaged my feet. Why was he caring for me? I needed to hate him. He'd lied to me. Bound and gagged me. Hell knew what else was looming on the horizon.

The floodgates reopened, dripping the evidence of my turmoil down my cheeks.

"Don't cry." He shifted to sit beside me and wiped the tears from my face. "I'm going to tell you what's going on and answer all your questions. You're not going to like it, but Dawn…" He cupped my jaw and stared into my eyes. "Nothing changes. This…" He gestured between us. "This is what matters. Everything else is just logistics."

What did that even mean? I glared at him, seething against the gag.

He pulled off his boots. His coat was next. Then his shirt, leaving his chest bare and crawling with gleaming veins over sinewy muscle.

"I'm going to remove the restraints." He turned me on the seat and lowered his mouth toward my bound hands.

I tensed but didn't fight him as he bit through the rope. The instant it fell away, I reached up to remove the gag.

"Wait." He clasped my wrists, lowering them to my lap and rubbing around the red marks on my skin. "You have a lot questions and a helluva lot of hostile things to say." He smirked. "I can see it all behind that golden fire in your eyes. Let me talk first. I need to explain some things."

With my stomach twisting in knots, I pushed my tongue against the gag and gave a jerky nod.

He untied the gag, and I wriggled my jaw, my attention fixed on his veins. The urge to bite him tingled through my gums, but I breathed through it, pinned my lips, and waited for him to speak.

Lowering his chin, he stared at his chest. "I can see what you see. I can see my veins and hear the amplified sound in my head."

I opened my mouth to call him a cocksucking liar, but the warning look in his fluorescent eyes muted my voice.

"I've sensed hybrids this way for as long as I can remember." He traced the largest, brightest vessel in his chest, unerringly following its path to his heart. "No one else has ever been able to see or hear my veins. Until you. And these silver things? It's venom. Not mine." He met my eyes. "It's the venom I've consumed from hybrids."

"How do you know?" I gasped. "Are you drinking—?"

"Shut up." A muscle in his jaw bounced.

I sat back, nostrils flaring.

"The hybrids traveling with us aren't attacking you," he said, "because I've bitten all of them. Drained them to the point of near death. In doing so, I freed them."

Freed them from the mental programming? Salem could lift the Drone's harness on the hybrids' brains?

"They're not cured." He stroked a thumb against his leather-clad thigh, his brows pinching together. "They still crave blood and sex, still have that need to proliferate and spread the infection. But their minds are free to make decisions. They can mentally fight the instinct. Some of them have been with me since my early teens."

He freed their minds, and in return, he gained their loyalty.

My pulse went crazy. Salem was closer to a cure than Michio had ever been able to create in a lab, yet Salem had kept this from my fathers. Why? He could've saved…

"You could've saved Kip and my other soldiers." My eyes widened, welling with tears. "Did you send the hybrids that breached the wall in the camp?"

"No. I had nothing to do with that."

But he could've cured their minds. Except it would've drawn too much attention from my fathers, and they wouldn't have let him go. Not if he carried a key to the cure. That was why he'd hidden this from them. So instead of saving the hybrids that attacked us, he'd killed them.

A gruesome thought hitched my breath. "The hybrid children—"

"It doesn't work on children. I have to drain a dangerous amount of blood to remove the programming. I've tried." He braced his elbows on spread knees. "And failed."

"You told me you never killed a hybrid child."

"I've never killed one intentionally." He stared at his bare feet, unblinking. "Until the mansion."

Why did he kill them? Why were they even there? I gripped my forehead and rubbed my head as a thousand questions pounded to the surface. The one that mattered most escaped my lips. "What do you want?"

He looked up, his eyes shining like molten moonlight. "I want to fuck you, cherish you, and protect you for the rest of our lives."

Not the answer I expected, and it left me stumbling over my tongue. "That's…I-I don't understand."

"Neither do I."

I flinched, clutching my throat. "Do you love me?"

"I don't know what that means."

Acid burned in my stomach, heating my voice. "Would you die for me?"

"That's ridiculous. No one's dying."

"It's hypothetical, and you fucking know it. Answer the question."

"Eat." He gestured at the spread of food and wine. "We're going to be in here for five days. Plenty of time to talk."

"What? Traveling by car, we should make it to Alberta by tomorrow."

He leaned back on the cushion and tilted his head. "I don't live in Alberta."

TWENTY-FIVE

My entire body turned cold, despite the electric heat wafting from some unseen vent in Salem's ostentatious chariot.

He doesn't live in Alberta.

He'd drawn a map for my fathers, indicating where I would be and how I would get there. He'd also told Michio nothing happened when he bit a hybrid. Pretended he couldn't see or hear his glowing veins. Claimed he never killed a hybrid child. Concealed his ability to move faster than hybrid fast. And sat in that prison with me for ten days, making guesses about the identity of our captors.

All lies.

Omissions.

Deliberate fabrications.

Why? Because he wanted to fuck me and protect me? Bullshit!

"Where are you taking me?" My breath came fast and shallow, constricted by the damn corset pinching my ribs.

"That's the one thing I can't tell you." The frown that pulled at his perfect lips suggested he regretted his answer.

He could choke on a dick. My chest heaved, and a sudden flush fevered my cheeks. I yanked off my fur cloak and tackled the hooks on the corset. *I can't breathe. Fuck, I need air.*

He knocked my hands away, swiftly unclasping the busk. "To protect those who live in my home, the location must remain a secret."

"To protect them or yourself?" I tossed the corset and

rubbed a hand over the thin shirt to soothe my tender ribs. "It's not the only thing you refuse to tell me." Glaring at him, at the exposed strength rippling his chest and arms, I loathed his arrogant beauty and superiority. "Would you die for me?"

He reclined beside me, stretched an arm across the cushion behind my shoulders, and tilted his head to look me directly in the eye. "No. I die for no one."

For all the pain shattering through my chest and burning up my throat, I was motionless. Composed, even. I'd needed to hear that response, and now I could process the situation from a detached standpoint, one that wasn't craving his love with every beat of my heart.

"Who are your friends?" I asked hollowly, numb.

"They work for me."

I wasn't surprised. He wasn't the kind of man who followed orders. He commanded with all the power of a ruthless tyrant.

Tears sparked at the backs of my eyes but didn't catch. "Tell me about the mansion."

"You need to eat." He set a plate of charred meat and potatoes on my lap.

The knot in my stomach protested, but I needed mental and physical strength. Hunger would be counterproductive. I selected a cooling slice of meat, chewing and swallowing without tasting it.

He mirrored my movements, eating from his own plate and savoring every bite with a satisfied look on his face. "I knew you would target the Yukon breeding facility before you led your soldiers there."

Made sense. It was the last nest in North America. But if he didn't live in Alberta, how and when did he start tracking me?

"So I set up a trap in the mansion." He chewed, swallowed, and stared at his plate. "I orchestrated the chase that led you there. You killed a lot of my men."

"You killed Jeremy!"

"The hybrid children killed him."

A bite of potato lodged in my tight throat. "Those *men*,

the hybrids that chased me… They were infected. Mindless with hunger—"

"They were acting. I'd removed their programming."

I thought back to the hybrids I'd encountered that day. The one that had called me *Daughter of Eve* right before I put an arrow through his eye. He could've attacked me and hadn't. And the others that had fallen on top of me, pulling at my clothes. I'd been outnumbered, weaker, yet only one had bitten me. And I'd killed them.

"The hybrids that chased me through the forest…" My chest squeezed. "They could've outrun my horse."

Why hadn't I questioned that at the time? Maybe I did. So much happened that night.

"They could've outrun you," Salem said. "Could've slipped through the gate that circled the mansion. Could've killed you at any point. I'd instructed them to steer you toward me without harming you."

"Some of them died." The twinge behind my ribs wasn't regret. It was more complex than that. Confusion. Sadness. *Anger.*

"They owed me their lives," he said, without a hint of emotion.

I shoved my plate at him, unable to eat any more. "Erebus asked you why I wasn't dead yet. Do I owe you my life, too?"

He set our food aside and propped his bare feet on the opposite cushion, crossing his legs at the ankle. "You're different."

"How so?"

"The plan has always been to eliminate you. My friends have tried for…" He pulled in a deep breath. "For a long time."

I tensed. "How long?"

"Since you started leaving the dam without your fathers. When you created the Resistance and ran missions."

I was fifteen then. "They've tried to kill me for four years?" I asked incredulously.

"You're not an easy target. Always surrounded by soldiers

or locked behind walls."

"Because every hybrid on the planet has a hard-on to fuck me, bite me, or kill me." I narrowed my eyes. "In light of your *super* superhuman speed, you could've blinked past my defensive line or slipped into my camp while I slept, tore out my throat, and flashed away before anyone saw you."

"I tried."

My heart shriveled, the pathetic miserable thing.

"Do you remember the nest you took out near the Oregon coastline?" he asked quietly.

I curled my fingers on my lap. "It was one of my first missions." My brows pulled together. "We didn't run into any problems. I had a lot of soldiers back then."

"Fifty soldiers. You camped in a deserted parking lot that night."

"In an old gas station."

He nodded. "Your army stood watch, protecting their precious leader while she slept inside. Alone."

"You were there?" My fingernails stabbed into my palms.

"I knelt over you in the back room of that building, prepared to end the prophecy that kept my friends in a constant state of restlessness. I'll be honest, Dawn. I didn't give a fuck about the war. Still don't. I'm happily oblivious in the protection of my home. But back then, I was still trying to build a place for myself, with people I trusted—"

"Hybrids."

"Hybrids I'd freed. And they were uneasy with you roaming the planet. They saw your missions as a sign. The coming of the prophecy. Your mother ended aphids with a thought when she became pregnant. What is your trigger, and how will you wipe out the hybrids? As long as you're alive, you're a threat. But their attempts to kill you ended in failure."

"You decided to deal with it." My voice strangled. "Except you didn't."

"I couldn't." He leaned closer, so close he stole my air. "I felt this."

The connection between us ignited in my chest, shooting electricity along an obscure line, fusing us together on a level that transcended physical space. His eyes heated, his fangs lengthened, and for a moment, I thought he might grab my neck and devour me. Would I try to stop him? The violent need to pull him closer was an instinctual craving in my gut.

His breaths quickened as he watched me, as if his tenuous control combated his desire to fuck me and bite me.

"You can feel this thing?" I waved a hand over the charged space between us, unsure what to call it. "I feel it, too, yet on your end"—I flattened my palm against his hard-packed chest—"it's closed off."

He jerked away and dragged his hands down his face, his shoulders slumping forward. "I don't know why you'd think I'm closed off, because I feel the connection lighting up my fucking insides." He seemed to realize his posture contradicted his claim and sat straighter, chest open, and arms at his sides. "It's the reason I spared your life in that gas station. And why I didn't kill you in the basement prison."

My entire body started to pull toward him, missing the connection, needing it back.

Don't fall for it. He's a world-class liar.

"Then why set the trap?" I shoved my hair out of my face and leaned in, shaking with anger. "Why go through all the trouble of capturing me? Walking me back to my camp like a doting boyfriend?" My voice rose to a shriek. "Hanging out with my fathers like we're one big happy fucking family?"

"Are you done?"

"No! I will never get over the embarrassment of giving my virginity to such a mendacious, secretive, poisonous snake. You're a frontal lobe disorder, and you have all the appeal of a lobotomy. But you need one, seeing how your emotional and social struggles are placing a demand on you. Do you live to appease your friends? Is that why I'm here? Is my death still on the menu? Are you procrastinating the bloody finale? Or maybe you want to get your dick wet a few more times before you rip out my throat?"

In a speed too fast to perceive, he yanked me beneath him, chest to chest, with a hand on my throat and his hips between my thighs. "I could've fucked you the moment I tranquilized you in the mansion. What I told you in the cave was the truth. You made me care about you. Fucking you just to fuck you no longer mattered. I wanted you to trust me then, and I still do."

I shoved my throat against the collar of his hand, every muscle in my body straining with the heave of my breaths. "Why didn't you just tell me the truth? That's how you win a person's trust, you shit-spouting sod!"

"The truth wouldn't have brought us here," he seethed, tightening his hold on my neck. "Your fathers would've killed me, and the mystery behind our connection would've been lost forever."

"So here we are, back to you saving your own life and destroying mine. Why didn't you just take me from the mansion?"

"I wanted to meet your fathers." His fingers twitched against my throat. "I wanted to see if Michio could tell me anything about my genetics. I like them, Dawn. And knowing they're not looking for you while I transport you home is a bonus."

My fathers believed I was free, doing my thing. They weren't worrying, at least not more than usual.

I deflated beneath Salem, all my steam used up in that pointless explosion of rage. I was spent, crushed, with nowhere to go. No match for two-hundred pounds of inhuman strength.

He must've sensed the tension leaving my body, because he released my throat and moved his hands to my head, bracing his weight on his elbows.

"It wasn't just our connection that hypnotized me when we were fifteen." He stroked my hair, his gaze following the movement. "I watched you sleep for hours in that old gas station. Your red hair slipped through my fingers like fire, your skin warm and soft to the touch. I longed to see the legendary gold of your eyes. You were so young, yet you looked terrifyingly fierce and radiant, even in sleep, as if you'd somehow harnessed the sunrise and wrapped it around you."

An ache sparked behind my eyes, my throat swelling with conflicting emotion. He'd touched me? Watched me? And hadn't killed me.

"I almost took you that night." His face tightened, sharpening his cheekbones. "I didn't have a safe place to keep you. So I left just before dawn." His fingers clenched in my hair. "That was the dawn that burned the color from my eyes."

I trembled beneath him, warring with the desperate need to wrap my arms around him. Instead, I grasped for a reason to push him away. "You shot the dart that sedated me after Jeremy was decapitated."

"Yes." His expression hardened. "I carried you to the basement."

"You were never drugged? What about the night we were released?"

"Erebus waited for my signal. Three bangs on the door, followed by *my* order to let me out. One of my guards accompanied me while I carried you thirty miles from the mansion so that he could make the tracks in the snow that led north."

I closed my eyes. The message Salem had said he was given—*Fuck the daughter of Eve and you'll be freed*—was just one more lie in an arctic hell of lies. After everything he'd told me, I wasn't surprised, but I couldn't stop the betrayal from constricting my heart.

"What was the purpose of the hybrid children?" I met his crystal gaze. "Killing them goes against the hybrids' instinct to reproduce."

"Erebus took them from the breeding facility. I suspect he used them to scare you, but it wasn't part of the plan." His jaw flexed. "I didn't know he would bring them down there, so I killed the creatures to let him know what I thought about that."

Holy fuck. "Will he retaliate? How much control do you have over your *friends*? If they want me dead—?

"No one will touch you." Eyes ablaze with hellfire, they burned with enough promise to melt my insides.

I stared at him in stunned turmoil as he lowered his head and licked my mouth. Our lips brushed, and that simple touch shoved me off-balance. My traitorous body vibrated on the edge of insanity, my hands locked at my sides through no force but my own.

I was too emotionally weak to push him away, every part of me longing for the man I'd fallen in love with. The man who listened to my childhood stories, carried me fifty miles in a blizzard, and praised my skill with a bow. The man who touched me with protective familiarity.

His mouth was wet silk, his breath warm and intoxicating. He didn't hurry to deepen the kiss. He sampled and tested, every flick of his tongue deliberate, coaxing, intended to seduce. The iron length in his pants jabbed against my hip, but he didn't grind or thrust, his muscles clenched with restrained hunger.

I returned the kiss with vigor, rocking against him and gasping as heat flooded below my waist and lower. I needed…

He was a manipulator, a lord of seduction. He would lure me with his sinful tongue and pacify me with his cock. Then what?

I tore my mouth away. "You said you'd send letters to my fathers."

"Write the letters, and I'll have them delivered." A renegade smile stole across his lips, and his fingers slid through my hair, gripping gently, possessively.

"For how long? I told them I was only staying three months."

His quicksilver eyes turned to stone. "You never mentioned that."

No, I hadn't. I flashed my fangs in a humorless smile.

"We'll rectify that." His voice deepened to an authoritative masculine rasp. "When the time comes, you'll write them and tell them you're staying."

"For how long?" I repeated the question with a growl.

"Forever."

"What?" My heart slammed against my ribs. "You can't keep me from them."

"I can do whatever I want."

With a surge of panic, I shoved at his chest. For a flickering second, I thought I'd actually moved him. The heat of his body vanished, replaced with a sweep of cold air. Before I realized what was happening, he'd stripped us both of our pants and impaled his cock between my legs.

My head fell back on a soundless scream, my mind chanting objections while my body liquefied beneath his ruthless thrusts. I tried to mentally pull away. The slapping wet sounds were just two people fucking. The electric tingles in my chest meant nothing. He was nothing.

But he was in me. His tongue in my mouth, his cock in my pussy, his soul in my chest, and his eyes locked on mine. He was a fiery spark in a cold dark place. Burning, consuming, and violent with passion. He rode me into the cracks of the cushions, grinding my shoulder blades against the metal floorboard, and never looking away.

My struggling was pointless. I tried to bite him, but his reflexes were faster, always more agile. He maneuvered around my fangs as fluidly as he drew my pleasure, pounding me with endless energy and eating at my mouth with aggressive abandon. He grunted through labored breaths, his hands caressing and gripping.

Then his fangs flashed, and he bit my throat, reopening the marks that were always there. *His* marks.

I continued to fight, but at some point, my hips started working with him instead of against him. I grew frantic, urgent, bucking and crying out, controlled by delusional love and seeking release.

The moment his thumb rolled my clit and our eyes reconnected, my pussy contracted, raging with a burst of sensations that overtook my body. I came so hard I lost my voice. He plunged in deep and froze, his cock swelling and spurting inside me, hands cupping my face, and pupils dilating in a sea of molten glitter.

As we lay in a breathless pile of boneless limbs, my muscles twitched with the remnants of adrenaline and ecstasy. I hated myself for not being strong enough to resist him. I hated him for turning my body against me. I hated him for lying to me. For twisting our connection into something I resented. For killing Jeremy and letting my soldiers die. But I hated him the most for instilling in me the fear that I'd never see my fathers again.

The following days cultivated my hatred. He seduced me over and over, a master tempter toying with my wounded soul. He never had to force me. He was too good, and I was weak and disgusting. He fucked me until my insides chafed and my blood sang. Then we ate, and he fucked me again.

The convoy made a couple stops each day. The trucks were refueled. Our food was swapped out, and I was blindfolded, stripped, and taken outside to relieve myself. Nudity made me less inclined to run, but the purpose was hygiene. Constantly coated in the scent of sex, Salem bathed us both regularly, standing beside the truck with a cloth and container of warm water, permeating the air with the aroma of vanilla musk. I doubted he let anyone see me naked, but I didn't know. With my eyes veiled, I listened for familiar sounds, hints of my location. The only clue was the gradual rise in temperature. We were heading south. Far enough south that coats weren't needed in the winter.

On the fifth day, the convoy stopped, and Salem opened the door for the first time without blindfolding me. "We're home."

I wiped sweaty palms on my leather pants and tugged at the green silk corset, my chest and shoulders nude in the humid air. I felt exposed, vulnerable, borderline trashy in this outfit, but it was the only clothes he'd given me today.

Insides fluttering, I climbed out, my boots wobbling as I stepped though a dimly lit underground parking garage.

"Don't be nervous." He placed a hand on the small of my back and led me across the vast space toward a steel door.

Electric bulbs flickered on the ceiling. The fissures in the concrete floor had been sealed with layers of glue-like tar. Hundreds of parking spots spread out around me, but there was only a few dozen cars and trucks, all decked out with the same armor and rugged bumpers as those in the convoy.

On the other side of the garage was a windowless door large enough for a truck to pass through, reinforced with thick steel bars. If the double gate wasn't enough to prevent escape, the twenty armed hybrids that guarded it would stop me. No one was entering or exiting unless they allowed it.

Erebus and several other hybrids swept in behind us, expressions expectant and eyes alert as they followed us to the door.

The urge to reach for an arrow curled my fingers. I didn't have my bow or my mother's dagger. Nothing to defend myself except the fangs digging into my bottom lip. I was prey, encircled by a pack of predators, and Salem was leading me into their den.

As we approached the door, a strange rhythmic noise thumped from behind it. I tilted my head, brow furrowing. It sounded electronic, almost metallic, like something out of one of those music players I'd heard as a child.

I stopped at the door, pressed my hand against it, marveling as the dull thump vibrated through my body. "What is that?"

Salem laughed and shook his head.

"Welcome to my utopia." Eyes gleaming, he opened the door.

TWENTY-SIX

The door swung open, bringing with it a muffled discordance of electronic thunder. The sound throbbed in a continual tempo—*boom boom boom*—forcing my heart to submit to the pounding rhythm. Where there was music, there were people. *Hybrids.* The hairs on my nape shivered.

I'd been around acoustic instruments at the dam and through my travels. But this was different, more barbarous, vibrating the floor with deep droning thuds and pulsating through my body. A trickle of fear slid down my spine, but curiosity kept me moving.

With Erebus's towering shadow behind me, Salem led us through the door, down several flights of concrete stairs, and into a corridor floored with white and black patterned carpet.

Salem didn't touch me, but his long-legged strides slowed, accommodating mine. Black leather stretched across his powerful legs, his t-shirt too tight for my greedy eyes. I hated him. I craved him. My entire body hummed at his closeness.

How did he define my position in his domain? How would his friends react to my presence? I wasn't his equal here. I didn't look like a prisoner either. The absence of restraints gave a false sense of freedom. He didn't need to bind my hands or muzzle my fangs. His speed and strength made him a more effective force than chains, shackles, or gags.

If, by some miracle, I managed to slip away from him, I'd never make it past his armed hybrid guards. They stood at every corner of every corridor. Crossbows, axes, swords, and fangs—I saw every shape and size of crude weaponry from the parking garage to the bowels of his lair. Mouth dry, I flexed my hands and forced my feet forward.

Dark textured paint coated the walls, illuminated by recessed lighting in the ceiling. The deeper we moved into the underground structure, the louder the music thumped.

"Do you have unlimited electricity?" I kept my arms at my sides and shoulders back. "The lights and the music…is it all running off generators?"

Hoover Dam was a hydroelectricity facility, powered by water. It practically ran itself. But this, wherever I was, had been updated in the new world.

"I have engineers." He raised his voice to speak over the increasingly loud music coming from around the corner. "They deal with all that."

No surprise. Hybrids were resourceful. They had the speed, intellect, and governing power to establish small cities while humans hid in camps and fought to survive.

"Have you been building this place since you were fifteen?" I asked.

"Yes." Pride glimmered in his eyes.

I hated to admit it, but I was impressed. No wonder I hadn't seen or heard of him until recently. He'd been busy.

Up ahead, the corridor opened into a spacious room. Plush furniture fringed the perimeter, flickering with shadows from the movement around the corner.

"How many hybrids live here?" I dragged my boots along the carpet, stomach tightening.

"Around seventy or eighty at any given time."

The music blared as we approached the threshold. The air was smoky, redolent of cigarettes, a waft of alcohol, and the ominous scent of blood and sex.

As I turned the bend, I counted thirteen males and four females. At least one of the women was human, her mouth agape as she lay nude beneath a rutting male right there on the rug in the center of the room. My muscles heated, preparing to fight for her, but the thrust of her hips and the blissful look on her face rooted my boots to the floor.

She was older than me by at least five years, as were the other human women. That meant they were born pre-virus, cured by my mother, and immune to the hybrids' bite.

All the women were either fucking or bending their necks beneath a fanged mouth. Some were joined with multiple males in positions I'd never dreamed, their bodies rocking and grinding to the rhythm of the music.

I didn't know what I'd expected, but it wasn't this. My skin flushed at the raw eroticism of the scene, but the presence of women had a deeper effect, sprouting a seed of dread in the pit in my stomach. I'd envisioned only males living here, like a secret brotherly order. A naive assumption. Of course, there'd be women. Salem hadn't become a skilled lover by fucking his hand.

Venom seared through my chest. I swallowed, breathed, and fought to smother my jealousy. Irrational emotions would not get me out of this.

The layout of the room was reminiscent of a lobby in one of those old abandoned hotels, with corridors leading off in every direction. But instead of broken chandeliers, dusty furniture, and scattered debris, the yawning space was lavishly maintained, glittering with fancy light fixtures, rich woods, and plush fabrics.

Paintings hung from the walls. Thumping bass shook the crystal decor. Sweaty bodies tangled together on elegant furniture and rugs. A long mahogany bar and dozens of couches and armchairs provided areas to sit and chill, where the rest of the males congregated.

I'd never been in a place so luxurious and clean. I was afraid to put my boots on the polished marble floors.

Salem stepped forward, and the hybrids stirred. The rutting stopped. Every head in the room swiveled in his direction.

"You're back!" someone shouted.

An uproarious burst of cheers drowned the electronic beats. Then the music shut off, and the hybrids straightened their clothes, continuing their hooting and hollering as they raced to greet Salem. A few feet away, they slowed. Quieted. Their eyes locked on me.

Silence blanketed the room. The impulse to curl in on myself pulled at my shoulders.

Glares upon glares, the hybrids perused me head to toe. Recognition hardened their eyes, but their drawn brows and tense muscles suggested they hadn't expected the daughter of Eve to be here, let alone to still be alive. Even the half-dressed human woman tossed me a loaded glance. But beneath the males' aggressive postures, there was something else. Interest. *Hunger.*

Unease clenched my stomach, my nerves wrung so tight I fought the urge to heave. And run.

Beside me, Salem stood tall and commanding, back straight, hands clasped behind him, his entire demeanor uncompromising and alpha to the core. With one silent stare, he prompted every head in the room to lower. Some of the hybrids took a step back.

"Salem!" a husky female voice shrieked from the hall on the right.

The slap of bare feet marked the woman's running approach. A tall blonde shoved through the pack of males and leapt onto Salem's body in a cloud of flower-scented soap and transparent pink silk. Her legs and arms wrapped around him, and her lips peppered his face.

Prickles swept up my neck and burned my cheeks. He stood unemotionally still beneath her affection, but I knew he'd fucked her. She was way too touchy-feely for this to be anything else. Was she his girlfriend? One of many? I felt sick, agonizingly bitter, and spinning toward rage.

"Macaria." He clutched her waist, forcing her legs to lower to the floor as he set her away.

"Oh my fucking Eve, I missed you." She slid back in, molding her curvy body against his side.

My pulse howled through my ears, my skin afire with unholy fury. I wanted to stab something in her eyes and crush her skull beneath my boots.

"I missed your bite." She dragged her tongue along his

neck. "And your gorgeous cock." She cupped him through his leather pants.

Red blurred my vision, and a feral growl erupted from my throat. The unnatural sound startled me as much as it did her, her gaze flying to mine and opening wide as she noticed me for the first time. Just as quick, she jerked toward me with a scornful snarl hissing past her human teeth.

I thrust forward, baring my fangs inches from her face as I reared back my fist—

Salem roared, the deep guttural sound so hostile and terrifying it reverberated through my bones and wobbled my knees.

The very air shuddered, and every mortal in the room cringed with instinctual terror. The potent aggression morphing Salem's face scared the piss out of me, but I stood straight and blanked my expression, refusing to wither.

The woman—Macaria—stumbled back, cowering beneath the cover of her hands. "I'm sorry, Salem. I forgot myself."

Murderous rancor tore through my insides like jagged shards of glass. But I couldn't kill her. Eve help me if I did. Eve help them all, because that woman was human, younger than me, and not infected. That made her fertile, rare, and indispensable. She was the most integral commodity to mankind.

Salem, now composed and unnervingly quiet, gripped my arm and guided me to the center of the large sitting area. The residents turned but remained where they were, leaving a ten-foot space between the pack and their leader. The hybrids' unquestionable allegiance was a reminder that Salem had bitten them, freed their minds, and in return, earned their devotion.

My heart beat erratically. What was he planning and would I survive it? He'd said he wanted to protect me, but trust was no longer a component in our relationship. His friends wanted me dead.

He released my arm and didn't spare me a glance as he commanded the room's attention with the blinding, unforgiving cast of his gaze. "You're all wondering why the daughter of Eve is alive and standing among us. She's here because that's what pleases me."

Restlessness rolled through the room. Erebus towered over them all, his blue eyes hard and vigilant. I tried not to fidget, but fuck me, I felt too many heated stares on my throat.

"She's no longer a threat to your species." Salem tilted his head, and his messy black hair fell across his brow. "She'll remain here indefinitely, living among us. She's human, with human weaknesses. If she tries to attack you, do not engage. You can easily sidestep her without contact. That is *exactly* what I expect you to do."

My chest heaved with indignation. I was a battle-honed warrior, the leader of the Resistance, and this motherfucker talked as if I were nothing more than his pet.

"What about her fangs?" a male voice asked from the crowd.

The hard lines of Salem's jaw sharpened. "Steer clear of them."

That's right, assholes.

I might've been physically weaker and slower, but my bite would reduce them to ash. However, the likelihood of attacking a hybrid, pinning him down, and imbibing his blood before he disabled me was slim to none. Salem and my fathers had to hold down Kip for eternal seconds before I'd turned him to ash.

Something clicked in the back of my mind. I didn't feel the urge to sink my fangs into hybrids. Couldn't use my mouth as an offensive weapon in battle. Didn't have venom to extract and harness as a cure.

Because I'm not meant to do any of those things.

My heart raced as I recalled Michio's lessons in evolution. Were my fangs an anti-predator adaption? A function of aposematism, where prey animals deterred predators from attacking by mimicking a species with badass defenses? The hornet moth looked like a wasp, but it had no stinger. The red milk snake resembled the venomous coral snake, but it was harmless. I had fangs like a hybrid, the razored points serving as a warning—*Stay away. I'm poisonous*—but I couldn't overpower a predator.

How did this fit in with prophecy? If my fangs were simply a defense mechanism meant to keep me alive, I could buy that. My mother had evolved in unimaginable ways after the virus hit. But my fangs only appeared when I sensed Salem. And there were the other vexing issues involving our connection and my urge to bite him, and only him.

As I focused on the dull charge in my chest and followed the electric link to the wall of darkness that was Salem, I had an epiphany. He hadn't been closing off our connection. It was my instincts telling me, long before I knew he moved like the speed of light, that I needed him to *let me* bite him. I could seduce and fight and strike to exhaustion, but I would never be fast enough to puncture his vein. But if he gave me his vein willingly, it was game over.

How the hell would I convince him to do that?

The night I told my fathers I was leaving, Roark walked me out of their room and said, "1 Corinthians 13:2... *Though I have the gift of prophecy, and understand all mysteries and all knowledge, and though I have all faith, so that I could remove mountains. But have not love, I am nothing."*

He was telling me that love conquered all. But could it vanquish darkness? Only a week ago, my connection with Salem was a symbol of our love. Now it was shrouded in toxicity. His end was deceitful and manipulative, and mine was bitter and full of contempt.

I needed to fix this, and it started with forgiveness.

My hackles went up at the thought.

"What happens if she bites us?" someone asked from across the room.

"Her fangs won't just kill you." Salem's eyelashes twitched against his cheeks. Then he met their gazes with an unwavering gleam. "You'll turn to ash."

Whispers rose, and he slashed an arm through the air, silencing them instantly.

"Heed my warning." He regarded them with the dangerous eyes of an underworld lord. "If anyone touches her or so much as breathes in her direction, *I* will kill you."

I didn't sense him remove my pants and boots. Didn't realize he'd bent me over the arm of the nearest couch until it was too late. One second I was standing beside him, and the next I was naked from the waist down and screaming in shock beneath the merciless ram of his cock.

He fucked me dry, without preparing me. Fucked me in front of a room of hybrids. Fucked me like I was an object without voice or feeling. He was staking his claim, pissing on his property, and shredding my soul.

It was impossible to fight him off. With a hand shackling my wrists behind me and the other on my jaw, he held my mouth shut in a vise grip and restrained me beneath the hammering stab of his cock. I couldn't tell him no, couldn't lash at him with fangs. All I could do was strain against the arm of the couch and take it.

Tears blurred my vision, but I was horrifyingly aware of the audience—the rising pace of their breaths, the shift of their boots, and the heat of their eyes. At the edge of my periphery, a swirl of pink silk flashed away, followed by the fading slap of Macaria's feet. I should've been pleased by her absence, but the pain from Salem's disgusting performance overshadowed everything.

Physical and emotional agony twisted me inside out. His violation was shockingly brutal, the loss of control petrifying. Then his fangs broke the skin on my throat and pierced my vein, robbing me of my sanity. What had felt like pain only moments ago was now a languid molten river of lust. He violated me, but what was worse was the betrayal of my body against me. Pleasure curled through my insides, tightening my nipples, soaking my pussy, and hijacking my senses.

The corset cinched my ribs. My hips rolled uncontrollably, and my inner muscles clamped around him, greedy and wanton. He rode me to the edge of orgasm, thrusting with barbaric possessiveness. He would push me over any second, force me to spasm on his cock, and I wouldn't be able to stop him. I was so close, right there, and I fucking hated him.

He slid his fangs from my neck and adjusted the angle of his thrusts, unerringly hitting the spot that set me afire.

I came, reluctantly and violently, sobbing my humiliation against the grip of his hand.

"Mine." His voice was smoke, smoldering and deadly, then louder, roaring as he spilled inside me. "She's mine."

In the next breath, I was plunging down a dark tunnel. He'd swept me out of that room, and when the sensation of falling halted, he stood in a regal suite, cradling my body against his chest.

I pushed at him, shaking and devastated. He set me on the edge of a bed, stripped off my corset, and wrapped me in a soft blanket. I swayed, shivered, reduced to a mess of swollen flesh and mangled emotions, my heart raw and crushed to pulp.

A knock sounded on the door. As he retreated across the room to open it, I tried to gather my wits, but everything was fuzzy, my blood doused in adrenaline. I still hadn't caught my breath.

"Spread the message to every resident," Salem said.

Erebus stood outside the door, his blond head lowered in deference. "Anything else?"

"Her things—"

"There."

I followed Erebus' gaze across the room to the packs in the corner near a steel safe. My bow and arrows lay on top, surrounded by… *Holy shit.* Opulence was the best word to describe this ginormous bedroom. Curvy upholstered sofas, exotic statues of half-naked women, an entire wall of artfully-displayed weapons, such as old-world guns, bullets, missiles, and torpedoes—all of it pulled together with strong contrasts of colors and materials.

Curtains draped the walls and silky textures covered every surface, giving the space a warm sensual feel. Countless cushions invited one to curl up and lounge, sleep, and fuck. A pleasure palace built for a sex god. *Or a rapist.*

My face heated with renewed fury. "Is this my room or yours?"

His conversation with Erebus had ended, and the door was shut behind the casual lean of his body.

"Mine. Now ours."

"What about Macaria?" Acid lanced my tone. "Or your other women? How many girlfriends do you have?"

"You're free to roam my home. It's yours now." He prowled through the room, tiptoeing his fingers along the back of a sofa. "But I expect you to sleep here. With me."

"How many women are you fucking?"

"Meals are served in the dining hall—"

"Stop ignoring my question." I ground my teeth.

"Stop acting like a child." His eyes blazed as bright as the sun and ten times as hot.

I pulled the blanket tighter around my nudity. "When my best friend gave me a platonic kiss on the cheek, you acted like a rabid dog. That woman"—I thrust a finger at the door—"humped your leg and grabbed your dick! But *I* am acting like a child?"

"You're my girl," he said matter-of-factly, as if that was the answer to everything.

"I'm not your girl. Especially not when you're fucking other women. How many whores have you claimed in front of your loyal followers?"

A muscle bounced in his cheek, and that hurt. It hurt so goddamn much.

My throat thickened, burned. "You raped me."

"I call it…" His lips twitched. "Surprise sex."

I sucked in a sharp breath. "Don't you dare fucking trivialize it."

"You didn't say no."

"You had my jaw clamped shut!"

"You came all over my cock." He reached into his pants. "Want to see the evidence?"

"Fuck you." I shook from head to toe, my voice

weakening with tears. "You made me. You…" I swiped at my cheek, despising my emotions. "You hurt me."

His face fell, and those glowing eyes shuddered. In a blink, he knelt before me. I tried to jerk away, but he gripped my hips, my wrists. His hands were everywhere, evading my slaps and effectively subduing me into a sitting position on the bed in front of his crouch.

"I won't apologize for claiming you." His fingers cinched around my hip and hand. "I did it to protect you. None of those men will bother you now."

But he'd claimed and protected other women, too. I couldn't focus past my jealousy. It was a vile wretched poison in my blood, eating me alive.

"Stop thinking about them." He held me tenderly and petted my hair, twisting up my emotions. "You're the only one here. The only one sleeping in my bed."

I clung to his words, the sweetness of his touch, and strengthened my resolve. A battle loomed on the horizon, but I was a fighter. Only this time, I wouldn't win with arrows or blades. He was too fast and physically powerful.

I needed to win his heart. *His vein.* Then I would give him a bite that turned the darkness to ashes.

The bite of dawn.

TWENTY-SEVEN

The next two months burned like a lazy flame on an endless wick. Salem and I spent most of the time in his room, our bodies joined in mutual lust while I pretended to rekindle an emotional connection corroded by lies. It wasn't easy.

I'd become a doormat, cuddling in tangled sheets with my rapist. But my end game required the ruse. I needed to win his heart and calculate every move so that he didn't steal *my* heart again.

I lay beside him in bed, curled around the relaxed muscles of his thigh and torso, both of us nude. He'd fallen asleep only moments ago, stretched out on his back with his fingers woven through my hair. With each steady draw of his breath, his arm slowly surrendered to gravity, his hand slipping from my hair and falling limp on the mattress behind me.

A nearby candle cast a lethargic gleam of yellow across the menacing angles of his face. According to the electric clock on the wall, it was just after five in the morning. But time was irrelevant in this underground world. Sleep set its own schedule, and right now, I was wide awake.

I still felt the disorientation of being cast underground in this complacent life. I didn't have to hunt for my food, sharpen and clean weapons, or strategize defensive maneuvers. Freedom from war was softening me, but it didn't seem to have the same effect on Salem. He reigned over his utopia through intimidation and hero-worship, using the residents' adoration and fear of him to maintain order.

Gazing at his perfect face, I wondered how many had ever

seen him like this. When his jaw was slack, lips parted, and lethal gaze hidden from view. I loved to watch him sleep. He didn't look as threatening. Though his masculine beauty was always daunting.

A silk blanket gathered below his hips, exposing the root of a soft cock nestled in short dark hair. The sharp ridges of his abs widened into a broad hairless chest, his skin impeccably smooth and tight over pronounced muscle. I wanted to drag my tongue along the irresistible valley that divided his six-pack, nibble on his flat nipples, and nuzzle the hollow of his throat. A quiver awoke in my core, my fingers twitching to touch every inch of his dangerous sexiness.

I hadn't forgiven him. That wasn't what this was. My desire for him was an unemotional beast that I kept separate from my heart. Mostly.

Careful not to wake him, I gingerly brushed soft inky hair from his brow. He never cut the strands, never needed to shave. He'd told me his follicles stopped growing after puberty. If he shaved or trimmed, the hair returned to the length it'd been. Eternally frozen in time. Neither my fathers nor the hybrids shared this characteristic with him. What if he was immortal? What if I bit him and nothing happened?

Every time I thought of his death, a masochistic twinge pinched my chest, as if my heart cared more about protecting him than itself. I crushed that sentiment with the reminder that he'd made me lie in the letter I sent to my fathers. *I'm happy and safe. Alberta is cold. Salem is amazing, blah, blah, bullshit, and more bullshit.*

I shifted my touch to his throat. His breathing remained even, his dark lashes unmoving against his cheeks. The veins in his neck lifted and bulged beneath my fingers, and the rushing sound of his blood hummed in my ears. He didn't stir as I traced the vascular path to his heart, marveling at the ribbon-like streams of venom in his arteries.

A week after I'd arrived here, he'd led me to the parking garage where his friends had held three feral hybrids. He hadn't lied about the effects of his bite. As he drained the mindless creatures to near-death, I watched the silver ribbons slide down his throat. It only took seconds for the hybrid venom to bleed away from his digestive system and enter the veins in his chest.

When the hybrids had awoken from a coma-like sleep hours later, they were as grateful and loyal to Salem as all the others. Salem was their savior, their god. A god that could see and hear his own veins. But he couldn't make his blood flutter beneath his hand like I could.

I glided my palm over his chest, beckoning the venom in his blood vessels. The silvery foreign bodies swarmed toward my touch like staticky glitter, begging me to open his vein and extract them. I knew, without a shadow of a doubt, this was what I was meant to do. The venom in his veins had reacted when I bit Kip. They were the very essence of the hybrid infection. The *heart* of it. Whatever the Drone had injected in Salem's unborn body had connected him to the hybrids, and I was connected to Salem.

My mother had a direct link to the aphids. My link to the hybrids was through Salem. If I imbibed the venom in his blood, I would kill him and sever the connections forever. Maybe that would wipe out the entire hybrid race or—if there was any mercy left in the world—it would cure them.

But I'd given up trying to bite Salem without his consent. My constant attempts had ended in frustrating failure. It also didn't help my effort to win his heart.

Pretending to love him was critical. There was a perilous line between faking it and becoming it. If I fell for him again, if I requited any of the feelings I drew from him, I wouldn't be able to destroy him.

I lowered my mouth toward his throat. With no intention of biting him, I simply wanted to taste his skin, lick the strong lines of his neck. He smelled clean from his shower and so sinfully male I couldn't stop myself from indulging. Just a press of my lips, a delicate kiss. I moved carefully, silently, an inch away—

His eyes flashed open, and in one imperceptible motion, I

lay on my back beneath him, staring into the furious fire of his gaze.

"Are you prepared to kill me?" The cruel whip of his voice left a clawing echo in my ears. "Have you thought through what that would feel like? Your skin covered in my ashes? Your fangs stained red with my death?"

A knot formed in my throat. I hadn't let myself imagine those things. I couldn't.

"I just wanted to kiss you," I whispered, filling my eyes with the truth.

Half the truth. I wanted the kiss to lead to feelings. His feelings, not mine.

He searched my face, and his expression softened, pupils dilating. His hands found my hair, and he growled, a low rumbling sound of pleasure. The vibration penetrated my chest and gathered between my legs, throbbing with promise.

His head lowered. Our lips rubbed. A touch of tongue, a release of breaths. Then we kissed, slow and gentle, hands caressing, legs entwining. He growled again, and this time, it was louder, resonating through my veins and awakening my blood. Pulses of warm moisture saturated my pussy, my inner muscles clenching, opening me, preparing for him.

He swelled against my inner thigh, hot and rock hard. His tongue collided with mine, but the kiss kept its own pace, measured and deep, burning with unhurried passion. When he lined up his cock and sank into me, I felt so possessed by him, breathless, the bond between us purring with electricity. He took his time, rolling his hips with drugging strokes, weaving his fingers through my hair, and kissing my lips, my neck.

His bite followed, melting my veins with liquid fire. Then he cradled my face in his hands, stared into my eyes, and rocked us into a growly, grinding, deep-reaching climax that left me adrift on a cloud of dark ecstasy. Nothing existed but Salem.

He looked at me as if I were his sunrise, his sunset, and everything in between. His thumb absently stroked my cheek, his gaze intense yet adoring as it rested on my lips, traced the line of my nose, and fell into my eyes. His irises shimmered with fragile emotion, and it was in moments like this when I thought I had him.

I glanced at his neck, at the alluring vein that summoned a twinge in my gums and begged me to bite him.

"No." He pulled out of me and rolled to his back, glaring at the carved beams in the ceilings. "You're hell-fucking-bent in your determination to kill me."

"I'm not! I—" Shit, I'd ruined the moment. What the hell should I say? Partial honesty would be better than lies. "I crave you." I sat up and leaned over him. "Imagine if you weren't able to bite during sex. That's how I feel. I have this insane overwhelming need for your blood and have *never* quenched it. Not once."

His jaw tightened, and he pulled the blankets over his waist. "You're willing to kill me to scratch an itch?"

"It's not an itch, dammit. And we don't know that my bite would kill you." I cupped his flexing cheek, nudging his gaze to mine. "Open your heart, Salem. Give me your vein. If you let me in, it won't—"

"Never." He shot from the bed and strode through the room toward the wall of cabinets, rifling through our clothes.

His gorgeous ass flexed in the candlelight, and I had to force my gaze away to concentrate.

My fangs were an off-limit topic. Right up there with his relationships with other women. Since my arrival here, I'd counted three human women, fifteen hybrid females, and at least sixty hybrid males. The female hybrids were guards, but I'd also spotted them when they were off-duty, fucking and biting male hybrids in the common room—the lobby I referred to as the orgy room.

Then there was Macaria, haunting the halls in her lingerie. After the message Salem had dispersed the first day, she didn't so much as look at me. I didn't know if the other two human women were as friendly with Salem as Macaria. All the women kept a safe distance when I was with him.

He refused to talk about the female residents, but my

vicious jealousy wouldn't let it go.

I slid from the bed and approached him. "Have you fucked the female guards?"

He pulled on a pair of cotton shorts, eyes on his task, lips in a flat line.

"Did you let them bite you? I've seen them fuck, and they always bite. Must be nice."

"They don't turn their partners into dust." He shoved his feet into a pair of joggers.

"So you let them bite you?" I grabbed a shirt and trousers from the drawer and pulled them on, my voice rising. "Are you still fucking them?"

Without a glance in my direction, he strode from the room and shut the door. My fangs retracted, and my hands curled into fists.

I hated his refusal to explain his relationships with other women. I hated the hope I harbored for his monogamy when we were together. I hated the passion-filled hours I spent in his arms, basking in the notion that if he was with me, he wasn't with anyone else. Most of all, I hated the moments he wasn't with me, because all I saw was him with someone else.

A steel safe sat across the room, taunting me with its hidden contents. My bow and my mother's dagger were locked inside. Why, when so many other weapons were within my reach? Ancient guns hung along the wall like a museum display. Knives and forks sat among the dishes on the coffee table from last night's dinner.

It wasn't like I could storm out of this place in a rage of gunfire and arrows and…forks. Me against seventy hybrids and Salem? That wouldn't end well.

He knew what the dagger meant to me. Maybe he thought I wouldn't try to escape without it, that I wouldn't leave it behind.

But there was no escape. I was powerless prey among inhuman predators.

At least he hadn't locked up my medallion. I fingered the metal disk against my breastbone. My mother had been pregnant when my fathers gave it to her. She was wearing it when she took her last breath. She'd seen her death coming and confronted it with spectacular courage. If she could do that, I should be able to face this thing with Salem.

The door to the hall opened, my fangs popped out.

He stood in the doorway, stiff and still as a predator. "Come with me to dinner tonight."

My breath hitched. Every evening, he ate dinner with dozens of his friends in the dining hall. As much as I needed to meld myself into his life and his heart, I refused his daily offers to join him. I hadn't gotten over the humiliation of being publicly fucked against my will. Couldn't bring myself to eat with those women who had seen Salem use me in such a degrading way. I hated my weakness, and I hated Salem for making me feel vulnerable.

I wasn't as brave as my mother.

I gave him my answer with a shake of my head.

His expression turned to stone, and the slam of the door vanished my fangs and cracked a sizzling fissure in my chest.

Fuck him and his self-righteous anger. And fuck me, because through all my chafing animosity, I couldn't stop my body from heating in his presence. Couldn't stop my heart from pumping harder and my soul rejoicing whenever I saw him. I craved him, yet I was no closer to forgiving his lies than I was two months ago.

One thing he hadn't lied about was my ability to roam his home alone and without restraints. So I left the room to wander down the main passageway, populated only by the guards at this hour of the morning.

All corridors led to a central hub, like spokes on a wheel. At the center was the industrial kitchen, dining room, and orgy room. I'd counted ninety doors in the corridors. Ninety private suites. Over the past weeks, I'd slipped into a few rooms that had been left unlocked, looking for windows or escape routes.

Of course, there were no windows in this underground hotel. The only way out was through that parking garage. If this place went up in flames, not even Eve would be able to save me.

I quickly passed through the empty orgy room and turned into the hall that led to the garage. My fangs hadn't emerged, so Salem must've been jogging out of hearing range.

Given his aversion to daylight, I understood why he'd built underground. The residents lived down here without sunshine, but I knew they came and went frequently. Someone had to gather food and supplies. And three humans weren't enough to satisfy seventy-some hybrid appetites.

I hadn't seen the sun in two months, but I'd felt the heat of its rays and needed that sensation now to warm the chill of Salem's absence.

My brisk walk took me up the stairs and into the parking garage. I strode toward the massive door on the far side, giving a taunting wave at the twenty hybrid guards. They didn't move, didn't smile.

They also didn't stop me when I reached through the thick bars of the inner gate. Didn't twitch a muscle as I pressed my palms against the exterior door. Warmth seeped from the steel to my hands, and I sighed. Sunshine was just a door away, right there on the other side. It was torture, and I delighted in it several times a week.

What did the landscape look like beyond the door? A sandy beach? A rolling field of silvery grass? Or the crumbling concrete of a fallen city?

Holding my hands to the steel, I rested my forehead on the inner gate and angled my gaze toward the nearest two hybrids. "Are we in Florida?"

One of them didn't twitch—the normal reaction. The other hybrid clenched his fingers around the crossbow. He must've been a new guard on this post and wasn't familiar with my heckling.

"How about Mexico?" I arched a brow.

Nothing.

I listed more warm locations, threw in the Nine Circles of Hell and Disney World, and was met with the usual silence.

"If you let me go…" I looked at the new guy. "I can give you power, wealth, and women." I talked out of my ass, because none of my realistic offers ever worked. "Isn't that what every man wants?"

Rigid and unyielding, the guards didn't blink.

"Come on." I stomped a foot dramatically. "You guys have no rhythm. Your combined personalities are that of a leech, living in a cold sunless void and feeding off a dead man. I can give you colonies of flesh to fuck and bite. Just open this door, and I'll let you hang out with me. Who knows? My awesomeness might rub off on you."

I swore I saw the bounce of a smile from the male in the back corner.

"See?" I pointed at him and returned my hand to the heat permeating the door. "That guy knows what I'm talking about." I shifted my gaze to the new guard. "I don't know your name." I didn't know any of their names. "But your fly is down." It wasn't. "Is that…are you wearing unicorn underwear?"

He didn't glance down, didn't even look at me. None of the guards did. Neither did the residents. In two months, no one had spoken to me or acknowledged me in any way. Salem's message in the orgy room had been more than effective. It'd made me invisible.

Being invisible was really fucking lonely.

Maybe I should accept Salem's offer to join him for dinner. Except the women would be there. I couldn't be around them without seeing red. Not until I knew he was with me and no one else.

"I'll give you a choice." I scanned the guards, my voice echoing through the garage. "You can let me go and never hear from me again. Or you can stand there like slack-jawed meatslappers and listen to my tedious babbling and half-baked offers. I mean, I have all the time in the world to string together obnoxious insults loaded with truths. I can make this really painful for you."

My fangs descended a fraction of a second before I sensed

movement behind me. I turned, and my gaze crashed into glowing silver.

Salem stood ten feet away, arms relaxed at his sides, and a crooked smile on his lips. My blood hummed, heating my skin.

How long had he been here? On the opposite side the garage, the door to the stairway was closed. I would've heard it open. His guards hadn't fluttered an eyelash at his approach. He must've been here before I arrived.

"You knew I'd come here." I held one hand against the steel door, reluctant to let go of the sun's warmth.

"You like to distract my guards." He prowled toward me, bare chested with shorts hanging low on his narrow hips.

My pulse kicked up. "They're really good conversationalists."

He reached my side and studied me with a strange private smirk on his face.

"What?" I anchored a fist on my hip.

He shook his head, his smirk stretching into a wide grin.

"Tell me." I reached out to tweak his nipple.

He caught my wrist and used it to angle me toward the huge door. Slipping behind me with his chest to my back, he gripped my other hand, raised our arms through the gate, and held our palms against the sun-warmed steel.

"I love your mouth." His lips brushed my ear. "Your patronizing sarcasm." He nibbled on my neck, sending a shiver to my toes. "I love your twisted little smile and the force of nature in your sunlit eyes. Don't even get me started on your staggering beauty." His fingers curled around mine against the door. "I love everything about you, Dawn of Eve."

Sincerity rasped through his whispered words. His forehead lowered to my shoulder, his breath stroking tenuously. He was softening toward me, opening himself and giving me affection without pretense.

I pivoted in the cage of his arms, my hands rising to his chest, palms pressing against muscle that was stronger and hotter than the steel at my back. My legs felt unstable, and I swayed toward him, searching his eyes, uncertain.

"You love me?" I whispered.

His lips separated on a breath, and his strong fingers framed my face with startling tenderness.

An answering emotion swelled in me, deeply-rooted and powerfully moving. He was going to say it. His affirmation was right there on his beautiful lips.

His hands twitched against my cheeks. A shadow rolled over his eyes, dimming the glow and darkening his expression. *No, no, no.* What was happening?

The warmth of his touch vanished. The door to the stairs swung open, and he was gone.

TWENTY-EIGHT

"Come on. You can press more weight than that."

I seethed at the rasp of Salem's voice, my arms shaking violently beneath a hundred-and-twenty-pound barbell.

"I'm benching more than I weigh, motherfucker." I lay on my back, straining with agonizing effort to push the bar high enough to return it to the rack.

My muscles burned and trembled. I couldn't…push…up… The last of my strength waned. My fingers lost purchase, and the bar tipped down.

Salem caught it in a flash of motion and set it easily on the steel supports with one hand, the fucking showoff.

With a ragged exhale, I collapsed on the bench beneath me, my arms dangling toward the concrete floor. The stench of my sweat permeated the workout room, the labored sound of my breaths stirring the stale air. The residents shared this huge space and all its fancy equipment, but right now, Salem and I had it to ourselves.

He stood above me, his face upside-down and hovering over mine. With a gentle finger, he caressed my cheek and tucked a wet strand of hair behind my ear.

"Beautiful." His gaze was as bright as a summer sky as it kissed along my cotton-covered breasts, short shorts, and bare legs, before returning to my face. "Sometimes you make it so fucking hard to breathe."

My own breath lodged in my throat.

It'd been three weeks since he'd left me speechless and floundering in the parking garage. Three weeks since I'd asked him about other women or demanded he let me bite him. I'd left that garage focused on one thing—his almost confession of love.

Every day since, I pushed and prodded and begged. *Do you love me? Please, tell me. I need you to say it.* His reaction was always the same—a longing look in his eyes, the declaration teetering on his lips, followed by complete and total shutdown.

I didn't need to hear the words. I needed him to accept them.

As I stared up at him now, I saw the same intensity in his gaze that had been there the past few weeks. Hell, it'd been there all along, in the mansion, at the camp, and every moment we spent together in his utopia.

He loved me.

I'd let the cruelty of his betrayal cloud my understanding and make me believe otherwise. What I hadn't stopped to consider was his true motivation. He'd captured me because he couldn't kill me. Lied to me out of fear of losing me. Forced me sexually and publicly to protect me.

He'd pursued me with all the gracefulness of a devil, his morals that of a conquerer. But he loved me, in his own way, in his own words.

I want to fuck you, cherish you, and protect you for the rest of our lives.

His love was coarse and twisted, dark and reluctant, but it was real. I saw it in the adoring way he watched me. Heard it in the catch of his breath every time I met his eyes. Felt it in the unconscious strokes of his fingers in my hair. Tasted it in the self-giving sweetness of his kisses.

When he fled the garage that day, I realized he didn't just love me. He loved me so much it terrified him.

I knew he'd never been in love before and had never received the love of another person, not even from his own mother. The fucked-up part was *I* had loved him and never said the words. Instead, I'd made countless attempts on his life. No wonder he shut down when I demanded he admit his feelings.

Love might've conquered all, but in his case, the notion was literal. It wouldn't just conquer him. It might disintegrate him to ashes.

A burn ignited in my chest, as it always did when I thought of his death.

He knelt beside the top of the bench, his torso level with my head and his upside-down face inches from mine. His fingers found my hair, combing through the strands with aching affection.

I love you. Fuck, I just needed to say the words.

He lowered his mouth to mine, the brush of his lips patient and unassuming. This wasn't a kiss that led to sex. It was his language of devotion. Each tender stroke of his tongue told me I was beautiful, cherished. The desperate intensity in his eyes said I was essential and loved.

I love you. I needed to say it and sound like I mean it, while *not* meaning it.

The soft glide of his fingers across my collar bones whispered a thousand apologies. His touch ghosted over my breasts, mourning emotional scars. He traced my ribs, silently promising his protection, worshiping me, loving me.

I love you. If I could fake it, it wasn't real. If it wasn't real, I wouldn't have to choose.

Except I couldn't fake it. I'd tried. Fuck, I'd tried every second of every day for months. Didn't matter that his betrayal had tarnished our connection. My love for him had survived, burning as strong as ever at the core of our bond.

My heart was bruised, my trust beaten to hell, and if this were only sex between us, I'd take him into my body without thought or attachment. But it wasn't.

His fingers feathered across my skin soothingly, humbly, and without pretension, and my blood sang. The breathing fundamental marrow of my soul was so deeply infused with his I was powerless against it.

"What are you going to do, Dawn?"

I locked onto his gaze, my voice shivering. "What?"

"Are you going to love me without conditions? Or kill me to save humanity? You can't do both."

Every muscle in my body stiffened. It was always going to come down to this. A choice between him and the future of mankind. How could the prophecy be so cruel? It'd stolen my mother and devastated my fathers. How many more people needed to be sacrificed?

I had to believe there was another way. If Salem would just let go of his fear and offer his vein, I could beckon the living venom in his blood. I knew implicitly that my fangs were meant to extract it and sever the links. I could do it slowly, cautiously. I would stop if it hurt him. He didn't have to die.

"You have my heart." I sat up and stared into his eyes with conviction. "If you give me yours, I won't destroy it. I'll be careful."

"Do you know how fucked up that sounds?" He rose and paced across the room, shoving his hands through his hair. "You have no evidence, no scientific proof—"

"We have no evidence or proof that my bite would kill you." I stood, shoulders back, voice strong. "We have to try."

Devastation contorted his expression. He didn't want to tell me no. I saw it in his liquid gaze, his need to give me what I wanted warring with his fear of the consequences. I knew he was thinking of Kip's combustion beneath my bite. I wasn't just asking Salem to risk his life. I was asking him to risk the lives of every hybrid beneath his roof. According to the prophecy, I would end them all.

But this time, he didn't say no.

I inched toward him with cautious steps, my pulse hammering from the wretched conflict in his gaze. I ached to soothe him and quickened my gait, reaching with hands sliding up his bare chest.

A purr vibrated in his throat, and his arms encircled me, pulling me to him with his lips on my forehead. "What are you doing to me?"

I caressed his sculpted chest and bulging shoulders. He allured me with his beauty and tantalized me with his ferocious personality. But it was this, the exquisite way we gravitated toward each other, that made me weak in his presence.

The more I touched him, the quicker his breaths came. His head lowered, brushing his cheek along mine, and lower still, until his throat hovered a bite away.

My gums ached, pulsing a throb through my teeth. He'd bared his throat, every sinew in his neck straining taut. Was he offering or teasing?

Heart pounding, I clutched his shoulders and leaned in. My fangs scraped his skin, and his body went utterly still. I was at the precipice of decision, waiting for him to make the next move. Would he flash out of the room or press closer against me?

He twitched ever-so slightly, just enough for my fangs to dent his throat without breaking skin. I didn't move, didn't breathe.

Then I felt it, the moment the silence went from hopeful to despondent. His muscles tightened, and his entire demeanor blackened, shutting down. Warmth fled from his body, and in the next blink, the only thing I held was cold empty air.

I stared at the swinging door and the vacant hall beyond. Salem was long gone and had taken my heart with him. But I had his. I rubbed my breastbone. The connection between us was overly-sensitive, but it was also persistent and unbreakable. He could run to the other side of the world, and he wouldn't be able to escape the raw emotion that melded us together.

I returned to our bedroom and didn't see him again until that night when he delivered my dinner.

"Come to the dining hall with me." He lingered in the doorway.

A pillar of power encased in black leather, he owned the very air that surrounded him. But his expression was guarded, his eyes looking everywhere but at me.

My hesitation made his jaw flex, and he left without my answer, shutting the door and vanishing my fangs.

Could I blame him? I wore a ratty sleep shirt with no intention of leaving the room. Turning away from the door, I stared at the spread of food he'd brought. The meat probably smelled delicious, but the only thing I smelled was the stench of my weakness.

I wanted him to overpower his fears and risk his life, yet I couldn't even face a room of women he'd fucked. Not fucked? Was still fucking? Images of him thrusting inside Macaria twisted my stomach. I needed to grow up and let go of my jealousy. He loved me, and we wouldn't move past this deadlock unless we *both* made an effort.

An hour later, I waffled and stalled in front of the full-length mirror in the en-suite bathroom. A black lace corset cinched my waist and pushed my breasts up and out in fleshy mounds. The satin skirt gathered up in multiple places, creating billowing drapes that swished with my steps. The seductively high-low hemline looked like a miniskirt in front that ruffled to a floor-length back.

When the seamstresses in Canada had given me this outfit, I'd balked. I had no use for fancy shit. But somehow, it'd made its way into my pack and into Salem's room. I suspected he had something to do with that.

I pulled my knee-high boots over bare legs. A few sweeps of my fingers fluffed the waves of red hair that fell over my shoulders and curled around my ribs. I pinched my cheeks and dabbed beet juice on my lips for a splash of color.

When I stepped back and took in my reflection, my breath caught. I looked different. *Good* different. Borderline hot. Maybe hot enough to prompt Salem to whip me out of that hall of horrors and back to the bedroom, where this painful corset would be shredded beyond repair.

I was scared to go in there, but I needed to do this. I wanted to and not for the reasons that should be driving the daughter of Eve. This should be a calculating mission, but it wasn't. It was just me, longing to put a smile on his face, aching to make him happy.

A deep breath lifted my breasts to my chin and shot a

twinge of pain through my ribs. Sweet hell. No more breathing.

I walked stiffly down the corridor toward the central hub. The orgy room came into view first, the air vibrating with music and thick with the scent of blood and sex. Hybrids flowed out of the dining room, laughing and smoking and corralling the outnumbered females. The women smiled and flirted back. Two of them were human. No sign of Macaria.

Salem wasn't among them, confirmed by the absence of my fangs. I continued into the dining area. No one looked at me directly, but I felt the scorch of their gazes on my back. My skin prickled, and my stomach fluttered with nerves as I wove around the tables, searching faces for the only one I cared to see.

Why hadn't my fangs lengthened? Where the fuck was he? I would've passed him if he'd returned to the room.

I swept over the space again, and panic rose. My palms grew clammy.

Erebus sat at a corner table, his blond head standing out above the others he ate with. He didn't look my way, but I sensed him watching.

I strode over to him, scanning every hybrid in the room. "Where's Salem?"

He didn't acknowledge me. No one twitched an eyebrow in my direction.

Salem wasn't here, and neither was Macaria.

Denial straightened my spine. He was a liar, but he loved me. That couldn't be faked. He wouldn't betray me.

He already did!

But not like this. Not with another woman.

He never said he was monogamous.

The barbed hooks of doubt rooted into my heart.

I backed away from the table, lungs heaving, hands trembling. Dread knotted so viciously in my gut every breath was an agonizing stab of pain.

The room carried on with a din of merriment, every male and female eating and conversing as if I didn't exist. I clutched the medallion against my bodice and walked out on unsteady legs, swiping my tongue over my teeth and urging my fangs to appear.

Despite the ball of fire in my throat, I held my chin high, passed through the orgy room, and into a hall I'd only entered a couple times. My fangs remained absent, and my blood burned hotter. The instant I slipped out of view, my composure crumbled. My face pinched painfully, my breaths wheezed, and my legs hurtled me forward.

I'd never been to Macaria's room, but I'd paid attention. I knew which passageway she took and which door she slept behind. I sprinted there now, the roar of my heart drowning the sound of my boots.

Choking down distress, I stopped at the last room on the right and gripped the handle. *Locked.*

Solid wood stood between me and whatever waited on the other side. I raised a hand to knock, my arm shaking violently. Before my fist made contact, a sound muffled through the door. A masculine grunt.

My fangs elongated. *No no no!* I couldn't unclench my jaw, and the razored tips pierced my lips. Blood rushed over my tongue. Wet warmth trickled down my chin, and tears smeared my vision.

Another grunt sent my fist against the door. I knocked hard and fast and covered my mouth to stifle a guttural sob, the pressure inside me so unbearable I couldn't think straight.

My gasping breaths cut off as the door opened.

Salem stood on the threshold, shirtless, pants open and barely hanging on his hips, his face taut and white with shock.

Sharp ringing bludgeoned my ears, and a horrible pained noise tore past my lips. "Why?"

"Dawn." A choke, thick with regret.

This isn't happening. This isn't happening.

I pulled my hand away from my mouth, my fingers covered in blood. I needed to see. Locked in tunnel vision and focused on a single goal, I slapped and shoved around him. I had to know.

"No, Dawn. Stop. Listen to me." He gripped my bicep, halting my movement, but he was too late.

Across the room, Macaria lay nude on the bed, blonde hair fanned over tangled sheets, legs spread, with her hand between her thighs.

I no longer felt the fingers on my arm, couldn't taste the blood on my lips, couldn't hear the scratch of his pleading voice.

Everything inside me went silent.

Can't feel.

Bloodless.

Can't breathe.

Darkness.

Don't care.

Empty.

TWENTY-NINE

I returned to the bedroom in a fog. My feet moved. My lungs cycled air. My heart pumped blood. But I didn't feel it. I felt nothing.

Baneful whispers ravaged my insides, feeding on the remains of my soul, but I closed off my mind to it. As long as I was numb, it wouldn't hurt.

In the room, I curled up against the safe that held my bow and dagger and stroked the cold metal. The demon with black hair and silver eyes sat on the floor a few feet away. His discontent flexed in ripples of muscle. His mouth moved, and strong words quaked the air.

Words.

Lies.

Filth.

He'd chased me back to the room and tried to rinse off his filth in the shower, but it was in his blood, his genes. He was his mother's son.

Tears of disgust pooled in my eyes as I stared at his monolithic bearing, calculating sexual allure, and lethally beautiful features. How naive to have thought he was mine. How despicable that I'd even wanted him at all. He was my tormentor, my ruination, and my greatest enemy.

Wet hair stuck to his sharp brow. Beads of water glistened on his vein-less chest. He was shouting and pointing at my mouth, his face inflamed, but my hearing fell into periodic exhaustion.

"Are...listening...I didn't..." His voice pulsed in and out.

"Can…veins…your fangs…"

I liked the stretches of quiet. Lowering my shoulders to the floor, I curled on my side with knees to my chest. The intermittent silence was strangely peaceful, like a steadying breath before death.

Cold fingers touched my face, breaking my isolated peace. His hands were acid on my skin, his toxicity penetrating my pores and finding its mark in my chest. The horrendous jolt of my heart felt like flesh being torn apart and laid waste.

How was my heart still beating? I would rather die than endure the anguish that gnawed at the edges of my calm. The affliction of his evil wanted to devour me. It wanted to burrow deep inside and make me suffer. I couldn't let it in.

"Dawn! Snap out of it," he said, the desperation in his grip jerking my gaze to his. "I can't see my veins. Can you? And your fangs…" He pulled my lip up, his eyes wild and feverish. "They're gone."

I dragged my tongue across my teeth with the energy of a snail. My fangs weren't there. His chest and neck didn't glow. Unless seventy-plus hybrids died or fled to the surface, the connection between them and him was severed. Fried to ash like the bond I'd shared with him. If I had any fucks to give, I might've contemplated the poetic righteousness in his self-destruction.

"I don't see your veins," I said flatly, pulling my face away from his touch. "Did your hybrids die?"

"No, and I don't care about that. I can't…" He pushed me to my back and pressed a palm against my breastbone. "I can't sense our connection." His breath was shallow, his hand trembling on my chest. "I can't feel you."

I stared up at him in cold desolation. "You broke us."

"No!" He clutched at my hair. "I didn't—"

"You didn't stick your dick in that woman?" I rolled to my side and gave him my back.

"Don't do this," he commanded loudly and with enough aggression to rattle the ceiling. "You're *not* giving up on us."

I laughed, the sound hollow and crazed, echoing from an

empty cavern. "*You* gave up on us the moment you walked into her room."

He continued to make noise, spewing desperate hostility, his restless movements vibrating around me. I tuned it all out and focused inward, seeking the solace of numbness. Eventually, I would have to pull myself out of this and face a crucible of violent emotions. But not yet. Right now, I just needed the deadened relief of detachment.

I didn't mean to breathe, but air passed through my lungs as my body mindlessly did its job. Breathing was painful though, constricted by the steel frame of the corset.

He droned on about how beautiful I looked all dressed up, his voice haunted by remorse. Then my clothes were gone, and I lay on the bed, enveloped by blankets and the scent of the deceit.

Erebus delivered our meals and exchanged whispers with Salem, without a glance in my direction. Salem never left my side. He didn't stop touching me, didn't shut up. Maybe all that growling would burn out his voice box. Maybe he'd put himself out of his misery and walk into the sun.

Days came and went. Maybe weeks. The loss of hope for the future held me in a timeless vacuum. I didn't use my voice or move my limbs. There were eternities when I didn't open my eyes.

Why couldn't I move past this? The loss of our connection cut me to the core, but was it worse than a normal broken heart? Maybe my need for him was biological in some way, and its absence had weakened me to the point of near death? I should've been pissed and raging, but I had nothing inside me. I had no fight left. So I let him carry me to and from the bathroom, bathe me, brush my teeth, and force nutrients down my throat. At some point, he stopped putting clothes on me.

He could do his penance and look at me with oceans of regret in his eyes. There would be no forgiveness. Not from the lifeless creature I'd become. I was suspended in a permanent state of detachment where I didn't feel bitterness, suffer pain, or fear death. I also didn't care enough to devise my own end. It would've been too much effort since he never left my side.

He paced around the bed, his hair spiked every which way from constant tugging.

"It's been ten days. Ten fucking days." His gaze darted over my body where I lay nude and unresponsive on the mattress. "What can I do, Dawn? What can I say to make this better?"

"Give me back my fangs." My voice was hoarse with disuse. "So I can rip your throat out."

He froze beside the bed. Didn't matter what I said. The fact that I'd said anything put way too much hope on his face.

"I'd give you your fangs if I could." He propelled toward me, straddling my hips and cupping my face. "Fuck, I'd give you anything. My vein. My life. Just please come back."

"Little too late." I bared my human teeth in a wooden, lifeless smile.

"I'm so sorry." He rested his forehead against mine, his voice thick with self-loathing. "So fucking sorry. I fucked up, but I'm going to fix this. Just talk to me."

I'd already given him more words than he deserved, and the urge to buck off his weight grew stronger by the second. But my struggling would excite him. *Any* sign of life would encourage him.

I closed my eyes and retreated inside myself, where feeling was lost beneath an endless sky of black.

"No." His fingers slid into my hair, fisting the strands with careful possession. "Come back to me. Fight, Dawn. Please! Yell at me. Hit me. Give me your insults." His breath grew harsher, fangs bared. "I fucking need you."

My heart gave a painful thump, striking a spark against our dead connection. My eyes flew open, but I felt nothing more. There wasn't enough strength or desire to reignite the bond. All the power in the world wouldn't fuse us back together.

Cold and unmoved, I sank into the mattress and shut out the feeling of his weight on my legs.

"What have I done to you?" He rolled to the edge of the bed and dropped his head in his hands, the taut lines of his back etched in pain and guilt. "What have I done? I never intended this. Never wanted to hurt you. I went to Macaria…"

Her name on his tongue shot a fiery burn through my chest. He continued talking, but I blocked out his voice, fighting to hold back the distress that pushed through my defenses.

He lurched from the bed, arms stiff at his sides as he charged through the room, wearing only a pair of shorts. His hands shot out, demolishing everything in his path. Chairs hit the wall. Stone statues shattered across the floor. Cushions exploded in a blizzard of feathers.

His temper numbed me. It occupied him and put distance between us. I needed that distance.

He glanced at me, his expression lost. Then he switched back to his rage. Roaring past his fangs, he turned to the wall of cabinets and slammed his fist through one of the doors. The first hole of many over the following days.

The shifts in his moods measured the passing of time. Some days, he smothered me in the stench of his grief, stroking my hair, my face, and every inch of my body as he begged for forgiveness.

I felt nothing.

Other days, his desperation vibrated with anger. Anger at himself. Anger at my unresponsiveness. It detonated in more damaged furniture, his knuckles destroyed and bloody. But he always healed.

I didn't. My soul was rotting, making me weaker, more lethargic. It became harder to pull back from the dead thing I'd become. I didn't care.

Day by day, his voracious need to repair the irreparable turned more frantic and reckless. His touches grew heavier, bolder, and more intimate. He kissed my slack lips, caressed my chest, nuzzled my thighs.

I was numb.

He put his mouth between my legs and licked me endlessly.

I was empty.

He fit his cheating cock inside my body and rutted. Pressed his mouth to mine. Rubbed my clit. Bit my throat. Demanded I come.

I was dead.

He fucked me repeatedly, twisting himself into a suffering miserable beast. He refused to orgasm without me, and his failure to bring me pleasure brought him to his knees, cursing and moaning his pathetic wretchedness.

I turned away and hated myself for being so cold. I hated myself for regretting my coldness. But I would hate myself more if I forgave him for hurting me so badly.

The room lay in ruins. Every painting and priceless artifact shredded and smashed. Debris scattered the floor. Holes riddled the walls and furniture. He didn't seem to care, kicking shit out of his way as he paced his usual circuit.

"I have something for you," he said after Erebus delivered one of our meals. The bed dipped beneath his weight. "Look at me, Dawn."

I closed my eyes.

His sigh billowed between us, his face inches from mine on the pillow. He put a paper in my hand, and my fingers tightened around it. An envelope. I knew it was a letter from my fathers.

Warmth tingled through my cheeks. Then the numbness returned.

"Open it." His voice was hushed, reverberating with hope.

I opened my eyes, found the envelope sealed with candle wax. Anything my fathers had written—good news, bad news, declarations of love—was a threat to my carefully constructed walls. If the pain crashed in, it would be the zenith of my ruination. I wouldn't survive. I wouldn't want to.

But I had to read it. Had to know they were alive and well.

With a dispassionate breath, I broke the seal and read the letter composed in three different penmanships. The demon watched me obsessively with those traitorous eyes as I skimmed over the tender statements, the soft things, and looked for clues, hidden meanings behind words that might suggest my fathers knew about my situation.

I found nothing. They thought I was in Alberta, believed I was happy, and expected me home in two months.

Folding the letter with unfeeling fingers, I extended it toward a nearby candle. Keeping their warm words would tempt me to read them excessively. Memories of them would consume me. I held the paper in the flame, watched it catch fire, curling the edges and engulfing it in a mesmerizing glow.

The demon ripped it from my hand and stomped it out on the floor. Stepping back, he glared at the charred smears of ashes, his eyes unblinking and bleak. When he lifted his head, all trace of desolation was gone, replaced by the strife and ruthlessness that surged through his vile blood.

"Is that what your mother would've done?" He narrowed hard eyes.

No. She'd carried a letter from her dead husband across the world, leaning on his words for strength.

"I'm not my mother," I said without emotion.

"No, you're not. Your mother was a fighter." Words meant to cut like the sharpest blade.

I felt nothing.

"You were a fighter once." He bent toward me, bracing his arms on the bed beside my head, his tone challenging. "I took that from you. I know I did, and I will never be able to express how regretful I am. But it's time for you to take it back. It's time for you to fucking fight."

Truth dripped from those masculine lips. The same lips that pleasured other women.

A stab of agony splintered my chest. "I want to leave." I looked him dead in the eye. "Let me go."

"That's not fighting!" He straightened, his entire body flexing with frustration. "That's running."

"Fighting you gains me nothing." A nasty smile twisted my mouth. "You have nothing I want. *You* are nothing."

He pulled in a sharp breath. "I was scared."

"You're dead to me."

"I went to her room because I was fucking terrified."

My chest squeezed and I rolled away. "Then carry your pathetic ass back to her."

In one quick yank, he was in my face, hands in my hair, and bloodshot eyes afire with a thousand tortured emotions. "I love you."

"No." Breathing became harder, more painful. "You don't get to say that."

He pinned me to the bed with his weight and searched my face. "I love you."

"You love me so much you fuck other women." I stared through him with dead eyes, my voice thin and hollow. "How many others are there? No. You know what? I don't give a fuck."

"You haven't listened to anything I've said." He held my head in his hands, stopping me from looking away. "Macaria—"

"Did you put your dick inside her?"

"Listen—"

"Yes or no?"

He looked me in the eye, a damaged, tormented ghost of a gaze. "Yes."

Everything inside me shut down. He shouted words, but I didn't hear him, didn't know how long he carried on. None of it mattered.

Then something strange happened. He put on clothes and stepped out of the room. A moment later, he returned, dressed me in trousers and a shirt, and set me in an unbroken chair amid the clutter of wreckage. The door opened behind him.

"I didn't want to do this." He leaned over me, blocking my view of whoever stepped into the room. "You've given me no choice."

I stared up at his severe expression and was unimpressed.

Until his hands swept over mine, and he stepped back. I

jerked my arms, a useless effort. The motherfucker had tied me to the chair.

My pulse kicked up, and the sudden scent of flowers turned my stomach. “What are you—?”

He shifted to the side, revealing the intruder. Blonde hair. Long curvaceous legs. Fearful blue eyes.

Macaria.

THIRTY

"Another manipulation?" I yanked at the rope that tied me to the heavy armchair, my breath arriving hard and fast. "You're a fucking monster."

Shoving his lover in my face was low, even for him. But effective. Of all the tricks he'd tried over the past couple weeks, the sight of Macaria was the hammer that struck through my precious detachment, cracking open my chest with an outpouring of pain.

A pale pink dress hugged her hourglass figure and exposed mile-long legs, the fit intended to make a man fantasize about what lay beneath. But the demon didn't need to fantasize. He'd seen it all, and so had I.

The waves of her golden hair and big doe eyes transported me to that night. Her, spread out and nude on the bed. Him, opening the door with his fly unzipped.

A keening noise escaped my mouth, and his brutal gaze latched on to it.

"Every time I say her name, you withdraw. No more shutting down." His voice rose to a thundering volume. "We're doing this right here, right now."

I looked away, my stomach rolling and turning inside out.

He stirred in my periphery. A shift of air. The speed of sound. When I glanced up, he stood a few feet away, with a fist in her hair and a dagger against her throat.

"Salem?" Her face scrunched up and tears leaked down her cheeks. "Why are you doing this?"

Tricks.

Lies.

Manipulations.

Except the determination on his face was the same look he wore when he'd killed the hybrid children at the mansion and the attackers at the Canadian camp. His unblinking stare promised death.

I sat back and calmed my breathing as she squirmed and nicked her neck on the blade. He wasn't being careful with her. And why a knife? He never used one. His fangs were more efficient.

And more intimate.

He knew that his mouth on her throat would shove me into total darkness. I tried to go there now. *His cock was inside her.* I tried to block out the view of his body pressed against her back. I needed to look away from his fingers in her hair. I couldn't shut down, couldn't stop my heart from pounding, begging me to do something.

Because the horror in her eyes was genuine. It leaked in huge drops down her face. Whatever this was, she wasn't in on it.

She was a human woman, so very rare and important. I might've failed in my prophesied role, but I would never sabotage a chance for the human race to reproduce.

"Let her go," I whispered, dragging my gaze to his face.

His eyes connected with mine, flaring with desperation. "Tell me to kill her, Dawn. I'll give you her blood. I'll give you anything you ask."

I believed the part about killing her. She wailed and clawed at his arm, and he didn't react. Didn't give a shit about her. This show was all for me.

"Let. Her. Go." I gritted my teeth.

He released her, and she grabbed her throat, weeping uncontrollably. Tears flooded my own eyes.

Prowling around her, he didn't take his gaze off me. "Tell Dawn what happened the night I came to your room."

A dull knife plunged through my heart, opening a gaping wound and bleeding agony through my body. There was nothing to wrap around me. Nothing left to protect me.

I felt everything, and it hurt. Fuck, it hurt so damn much.

"Tell her!" He pointed the blade at Macaria, seething with impatience. "And don't fucking sugarcoat it."

"H-He…knocked on my door. I—" She looked at him with watery eyes, sniffling. "I didn't expect you."

"Tell Dawn," he roared, thrusting a finger in my direction. "Tell her why you didn't expect me."

My molars snapped together as I glared at him with what could only be terrified pain in my eyes. I didn't fear him. I feared the words he would force me to hear.

"I didn't expect him b-because…" She wrung her hands in front of her. "He didn't come to me anymore." Her breath hitched on a sob. "Since you arrived, he had nothing to do with any of us."

"Lies," I breathed, the air thickening around me.

The demon stopped prowling, his expression hard and barren as he stared at the floor.

"I have no reason to lie." Her chin trembled. "I used to be his favorite. Then I was nothing."

My hands balled into fists. I hated her. Hated that she knew him so intimately. Hated that I felt her anguish, became one with her misery. She was a beautiful woman, and he'd reduced her to a pitiful heartbroken creature. Like me.

He was a cancer to love. I could fight him, kill him, but the damage was done. There was no cure. I would never be free of him.

"Tell her about the sex," he said hoarsely and flung the blade at the far wall.

Icy prickles raced across my cheeks. "No—"

"I can't." She shook her head.

"Tell her," he shouted.

She flinched, and a flush of anger stormed across her tear-stained face.

"He came in. Demanded I remove my clothes." She stared blankly at the smashed wall of cabinets. "He was so…*cold.* Disinterested. Wouldn't even touch me." She blinked rapidly and swiped at her fallen tears. "But I missed him. Wanted him. So I touched myself. He used to like it when I did that."

My own tears welled up, singed with bitterness and jealousy. Those sentiments disgusted me. I shouldn't have felt anything for him. I couldn't even look at him.

"Keep going," he said quietly.

"I couldn't..." She wiped her sniffling nose on the back of her hand. "Nothing I did aroused him, and he wouldn't let me touch him." She peeked over at him and looked at the floor, whispering, "He didn't get hard."

Twenty-years-old and he couldn't get an erection. How embarrassing. I should've laughed my ass off. Should've laughed so hard my face reddened and my insides stitched. But all I felt was despair, and it poured down my cheeks in rivers. He wasn't interested in her, didn't want her, so why in the name of all that was holy did he fuck her?

She cleared her throat and tilted her head toward him. "Do you want me to tell her—?"

"Yes." His jaw clenched.

I didn't think the stabbing pressure in my chest could get any worse. But there it was, threatening to double me over beneath the unholy pain. My nose was runny, my eyes gritty, and my throat swelled with fire. I just wanted this to end.

She rubbed her palms on her dress. "He stroked himself to get hard, but as soon as he was inside me..." Her breath hiccupped. "He couldn't— H-he lost his erection."

Standing a few feet away, he lowered his head and clasped his hands behind his neck. The dejected posture was as uncharacteristic as the notion of him going soft during sex. He was the essence of virile masculinity, power, and superhuman stamina. So what had happened? Some kind of emotional or mental impairment? I didn't know what to do with that. I didn't want to care, but I couldn't stop crying.

"I repulsed him." Her face fell. "He wouldn't look at me. Wouldn't touch me or—"

"Stop." I turned my soggy glare to him. "You've hurt her enough. Let her go."

Rather than ending this nightmare, he studied me for a daunting moment. For what reason? To watch me break down so spectacularly I would forgive him? That was never going to happen.

I reined in my tears, and he turned away.

Striding toward the door, he motioned for her to follow. "Are your things packed?"

She nodded, wrapped her arms around her waist, and shuffled after him.

"Wait." I jerked against the rope. "Where is she going?"

"To the surface." He reached for the door, chilling the air with his cold-hearted demeanor. "She'll be blindfolded and dropped somewhere so that she can't find her way back."

She hugged herself tighter, her lips pinned and trembling. He was dumping her like a piece of trash? Why was I surprised? Only a moment ago, he was prepared to kill her.

"You will *not* just leave her somewhere outside." I thrashed harder at the restraints. "Fucking untie me!"

"Not yet." His tone was firm.

"You son of a bitch." My voice shook with the hammer of my heart. "If you leave her out there alone, she'll be raped and bitten by nightfall." I hardened my eyes, blinking away tears. "Escort her to the nearest human camp. They'll protect her."

Her head shot up, wide eyes locked on mine.

"That's what you want?" He regarded me with suspicion.

"That's what *you* should want. She's a person, not an instrument to use in your games."

"This isn't a fucking game," he bellowed. Then he collected himself and dragged a hand down his face. "I'm trying to fix this."

"*This* can't be fixed, but you'll make it a whole lot worse if you don't protect her." I trembled to rip off these damn restraints and punch his stupid face. "Escort her to safety. Promise me."

He pushed a hand through his hair and nodded. "I promise."

Without a look in her direction, he opened the door.

She moved to follow him, curling in on herself, chin tucked, shoulders hunched. The bastard had done a number on her self-esteem.

"Macaria," I said and waited for her to turn to me. "Only *you* define your worth. His inability to see you is his own dysfunction." I sucked in a tear-clogged breath, taking my words to heart.

Her face paled, and she looked around the room as if seeing the destruction for the first time.

"He destroyed it while spinning in rabid circles, chasing his limp dick." I tried to laugh, but it came out strangled. "You're better off without him. He lives in a flaccid world of tiny-fisted tantrums and erectile problems. I doubt he could get it up if his dick was tied to a bird in mid-flight."

She covered her gasping mouth, and her eyes flew to Salem.

I felt the weight of his glare and pretended to ignore it. I was kicking him when he was already down, and I hated myself for it. But I was tied to a chair with my fucking heart on the floor. What he'd done to me was so much worse than any insult I could throw, and right now, insults were all I had left.

"There'll be hundreds of men fighting each other for the chance to love you," I said. "Hot-blooded, better-looking men who know how to pleasure a woman. Just…" My chest swelled with a rising surge of grief. "Stay alive and don't look back."

She lowered her hand to her throat and stared at her feet. "I get it now."

My lashes twitched, and a rogue tear tracked down my cheek. "What?"

"I get why he loves you so much." She straightened, shoulders loosening as she whispered, "Thank you."

She slipped into the hall, passing Erebus and vanishing out of view. He stepped into the room and bent his neck to listen as Salem gave him instructions for her escort.

I twisted my hands in the rope, dreading the conversation that would follow. No doubt he'd kept me restrained to exercise control over me and force me to hear his remorseful pleas. I wouldn't be able to block him out just like I couldn't dry up the tears now that they'd fallen.

Misery sat in my chest, a bludgeoned heart that beat away the numbness. It cracked and bled, and I knew the pain had only just begun.

THIRTY-ONE

I waited in the darkness of my broken heart, where there was no sun, no life, no future. It was so much worse than the absence of hope. It was death while still breathing.

Without him, I was empty, soulless, no longer living.

With him, I was a trampled, abused, pathetic version of myself.

There was no escape.

He closed the door and rested fingertips in the front pockets of his trousers. His porcelain face would've been flawless if not for his gaze, which flashed like lightning in a storm of lies.

Lowering his chin, he regarded me from beneath the shadow of his brows. "Tiny-fisted tantrums?"

"And a limp dick." Tears thickened my words.

"You're back." His shuddering breath was distant thunder echoing from nowhere and everywhere.

I was more lost than ever. "I'm not coming back."

He stalked toward me and the thunder grew louder, rattling my bones and fisting my heart. It was him, working his way inside me.

"All those times I asked if there were other women…" My voice carried so much resentment it crackled the air.

"It was only her. Just the one time."

Despite his hushed whisper, I cringed at the asperity of his words. I didn't want to believe him, but he spoke with such helplessness I knew he wasn't lying. Didn't matter. One time was one time too many.

I needed to understand why. "Before that night, you could've told me you were monogamous. Are you cruel just for the thrill of being cruel?"

"I didn't understand the concept. I'd never been…faithful? Is that the word? I'd never been with just one woman, in a relationship, and I was spinning off balance." He closed the distance with humanly cautious speed and knelt at my feet. "I was scared. I saw my faithfulness as a weakness. You were emasculating me faster than I could run."

Every word was the swipe of a blade, the pain inside me far from undiminished. "It's called love, you stupid cheating asshole."

"I didn't know that at the time. I've never felt anything like this before." He gripped the arms of the chair, his hands inches from my bound wrists. "You were on an assassination mission, seducing me with your eyes and manipulating me with your body."

"I was not." The lie fell flat.

He arched a brow, igniting a quiet storm between us. After an agitated silence, I caved.

"Yeah, okay, I tried to fake it." I flexed my fingers along the arms rests. "I tried to make you love me without reciprocating. But that's no reason—"

"I saw the trap a mile away and couldn't stop myself from falling in. I was already dangerously in love with you." His eyes blazed until the fire outshone his grim expression. "I was ready to die for you, to give you my vein and let you turn me to dust. I was ready to sacrifice my life and the lives of my friends because I love you."

"Words." Venom ripped through my body and struck my wounded soul. "All of it bullshit. You say one thing but—"

"That day in the workout room, I bent my neck to you. I offered you my life." A flood of emotion swirled in his gaze. "Do you remember what happened?"

The pain inside me strengthened, and the tears fell. "I hesitated. I couldn't do it."

"Yes." A whisper. "You couldn't bite me because you

loved me." Silver eyes burned with wonderment. "That's when I knew. It wasn't just my life I was sacrificing. It was yours." He looked at me with slanted brows, a demon bewildered by love. "What happens to a woman when she kills the one who holds her heart?"

"She saves mankind."

"And destroys herself."

The impact of his words propelled me to an imaginary place where I wasn't born as a prophecy and my only purpose was to love and be loved by a dark prince. The notion awoke a deep-seated longing that strangled the breath from my body.

"You didn't want me to destroy myself," I choked. "So you stuck your dick in Macaria. What did you think would happen? That we'd be cured of love?"

"Yes."

That one horribly powerful word hit the spot where my wounds bled and he was everything.

"I went to her," he said, gripping my bound hands, "because I thought it would make me hate myself more than I love you. That you'd see my inadequacy and hate me, too." The light in his eyes dimmed. "If you hated me, you wouldn't destroy yourself when you saved the world."

A sobbing breath erupted from me, but he wasn't finished.

"I failed on all counts." His voice was soft, yet feral in its self-loathing. "I annihilated our connection. Took away your fangs. Destroyed my ability to free the hybrids. I fucking despise myself, and I still love you more."

"Don't—"

"I love you more than I can bear."

The horrendous twist of my heart threatened to wring me into a mewling broken mess. He wasn't the only one at fault in this. I was bad for him. Instead of turning him into dust, I'd reduced him to a limp-dicked shadow of a man who'd tried to force me to hate him. *Because he didn't want me to destroy myself.*

I'd loved him. I *still* loved him, and every bleeding breath in my body wanted to sympathize with him. I had to force myself to remain angry with him, because dammit, I wanted him so fucking much. The man, the demon, his tenderness and cruelty—I wanted it all. I was a glutton for abuse. A victim of my own insanity.

But I wouldn't forgive him. He'd gone to another woman instead of coming to me. He broke us in the worst way possible. The very thought made me angry. So fucking angry I let the vicious heat of hatred curl and coil until it exploded.

"You're disgusting," I seethed.

He nodded. "I don't deserve you."

"You deserve no one." I thrashed in the chair, grasping for hurtful words. "You're an infection of stupidity."

He caught my chin and leveled our gazes. "I know."

"Don't you dare try to soften my anger."

"I'm not. I'm agreeing with you."

"You don't get to agree. You don't get opinions. You…you…" My voice cracked. "You fucked my trust in the ass. You…you fucking broke my heart." *No air. Can't breathe. Pull up, pull up, before you drown.* "I can't believe how cruel you are."

"I'm sorry." He cupped my face, eyes bare and glassy with moisture.

"Your words mean nothing." I jerked from his hold, every inch of my body laboring against the pain. "You're the highest order of cruel. Meta-cruel. Trans-cruel. Superhuman cruel."

"Are you finished?"

"No. You're so catastrophically cruel it goes beyond the scientific laws of cruel and into a whole different hell of cruel." Tears streamed down my face. I hurt so badly I couldn't even concoct a good insult. "You're a carcinogen of cruel and—"

"You're done."

"Untie me."

He stared at my wrists, hesitated, then bit through the rope. "Where do we go from here?"

"*We* aren't going anywhere." I stood and searched the

debris for my tennis shoes. "*I* am."

"No." The remorseful man from a moment ago disappeared, and in his place stood the captor who'd tricked and lied and cheated. "I won't let you run."

"I need to rebuild my strength." I found the shoes and shoved them on. Then I jogged out the door.

I spent most of the next week running the corridors. Toning soft muscles. Exercising my pain. And thinking. Sometimes he ran with me. Most of the time, he left me alone. He didn't touch me, didn't pressure me, but he always slept beside me.

For reasons I didn't understand, I accepted every offer to join him in the dining hall. I didn't dress up. The hybrids continued to ignore me. The females were there, but all the faces were new. He'd sent the others away. I tried not to let the thoughtfulness of that action worm into my resolve.

I was stuck in a holding pattern between lethargy and action. I'd gone from utter shutdown to keen awareness, my mind on a never-ending race for the truth. Maybe he'd betrayed me for the right reasons. Maybe he loved me so much it gave him brain damage. Maybe I was missing some earth-shattering answer to everything.

Love was supposed to conquer all. The prophecy was supposed to save the future of humanity. I felt completely obliterated by both.

I thought about all of this. Then he and I talked about it endlessly. Agreeing, arguing, we had the same conversations over and over and could never move past the cold hard facts.

Our metaphysical connection was broken.

My fangs and ability to see his veins was lost.

I couldn't forgive him.

He refused to let me go.

So I ran the halls. I ran to channel the emotional pain, clear my head, and escape the source of my misery. But no matter how far I ran, he was with me, prowling at the edges of my mind. When he was physically near, my body ignited, humming and throbbing with remembered pleasure.

I would always crave him, and though I'd reached a level of civility in our interactions, I wouldn't, couldn't have sex with him. He didn't get to have that part of me. Of course, he could take it, force it, but he didn't.

Being with him while not *being* with him was a special kind of hell. I loved him, but I couldn't forgive him. He loved me and told me a hundred times a day. I was miserable. He was miserable. Something had to give.

One month later, the darkness lifted.

He let me go.

THIRTY-TWO

I pressed a trembling hand against the huge door in the parking garage and absorbed the warmth of the steel. Four months ago, I'd left my fathers beneath a dark cold sky in a quest for truth. It seemed only fitting that I would return to them in daylight, sun-kissed and glowing with answers.

Except I had no answers, no cure, no momentous solutions for humanity's future. I'd fallen so far off my path, I didn't know who or what I was anymore.

My time with Salem had changed me. My skin was pale. My eyes were bruised. I'd lost my fangs, my hope, and my heart. I would never be the same. I didn't want to be. That naive girl was dead.

An engine sounded behind me. My transport was ready. I released a ragged breath that felt nothing like relief. Where was I? How far would I have to travel? And the question that hung the heaviest in my mind… Was I strong enough to say goodbye?

When he'd woken me this morning, all he'd said was, "Get dressed and go to the parking garage." Then he was gone.

I'd arrived a few minutes ago to find my belongings in the truck we'd ridden in from Canada. I'd checked the packs, strapped on my bow and my mother's dagger, and waited for the comforting sense of completeness. It never came.

Erebus sat in the driver's seat, observing me dispassionately.

Salem was nowhere to be found.

He's setting me free.

I'd spent the last month demanding he let me go. Now I

was here and instead of shouting at Erebus to speed me away from this doomed place, I was avoiding that truck. Scanning the garage for Salem. Fighting back tears. I couldn't breathe. All I felt was stomach-cramping pain around a hard knot of *this-doesn't-feel-right.*

Michio had told me to follow my gut. My gut trusted Salem four months ago when I left the Canadian camp. He cheated on me, and my gut wanted to give him another chance.

No way. I could never, because… Lessons! Learned!

A loud clank sounded, vibrating through the door. I jerked my hand away from the steel. Hybrid guards unlatched the locks and rolled the interior gate to the side. I shuffled back, eyes wide and breath stuck in my throat.

With a heavy metallic groan, the steel door began to roll skyward, folding back along overhead tracks.

Frozen in shock, I stared at the crack of light along the bottom, watching as the opening grew bigger and brighter. I stole a glance at the truck beside me and found Erebus' steely blue gaze. *No blindfold?*

He didn't move, didn't blink.

They were going to let me see the location of their home? If I recognized the landscape, I could bring my fathers back. They might not be able to catch Salem, but they would kill his friends and destroy his home.

Protectiveness spiked through me. Despite everything that had happened, I had no interest in retaliation. I would fight anyone who tried to come after him.

I turned back to the rising door. If I knew where he lived, *I* could come back. Was that why—?

"There was a popular saying in the old world." The deep rumble of Salem's timbre rose above the screech of the door.

I spun around and found him standing in the darkness ten feet away. His hands were shoved in the front pockets of his leather pants, his shirt stretched tightly across his defined chest. Elbows tucked against his sides, shoulders forward, he stood stiffly, uncomfortably, a posture so horribly unnatural. So anti-

Salem.

Sunlight and heat spilled in behind me, slowly climbing up the backs of my legs. As much as I wanted to see the view outside, I couldn't take my eyes off him.

"According to the saying…" He watched the yellow glow stretch across the concrete and reach for his boots. "If you love her, set her free. If she comes back to you, she's your captive forever. Restraints optional."

My chest squeezed, my lips twitching between a smile and a full-on sob. "That's not how the saying goes."

"Close enough." He retreated a few steps, chased back by the creeping light. His gaze locked on mine. "I'll wait for you."

Longing and bitterness surged through me, my chin trembling with a battle of emotions. "I'm not coming back, Salem."

He nodded, a jerky movement taut with pain, his eyes aglow beneath dark brows. "I'll wait forever."

Please, don't mean that. I couldn't bear it.

The door finished its climb, forcing him to slip deeper into the garage, enveloped by shadows. The heat on my back beckoned me, making it easier to turn away from him.

Golden sand scattered a dirt ramp. I ran toward it, raced into the blinding light, and gasped. The sun blasted my vision and smothered my skin in heat. The sensation was so overwhelming I wobbled with wheezing breaths. It. Was. Amazing. I stood there for long moments, absorbing the fresh air and lifting my face to the glorious blue sky.

The sun sat high over an endless desert. A few concrete towers rose up around me like jagged pikes in the sand. The landscape, the dry heat, the mountain range in the distance—all of it was familiar. My heart banged against my ribs. Was it just my hopeful imagination or…?

I pivoted to the garage and stumbled back, my gaze tipping up, up, up at a massive wall of broken concrete. The structure sat atop Salem's underground home, its distinctive curved shape and ginormous size a known marker in the ruins of Las

Vegas.

No fucking way. I was only forty miles from home!

I looked at my surroundings with new eyes and recognized some of the crumbled piles of concrete. When the last of the humans abandoned this arid city twenty years ago, the desert took back what belonged to it. The monolith towering above me was one of the few ruins that still looked like a building. The front of it did anyway, which was punched with square holes—the glassless windows of what had once been a luxury hotel. The entire backside was missing, as well as huge chunks from the upper stories. It looked as though the hand of Eve had reached down from the heavens and snapped off random pieces.

With my back to the distant smudge of mountains, I faced east, the direction of Hoover Dam and my family.

Four months ago, Salem had taken me from Canada and brought me home. All this time, I'd been home.

With a lump in my throat, I ran back into the garage and found him where I'd left him. Shoulders stiff, hands in his pockets, he watched me approach with liquid fire in his eyes.

"Why did you build here?" I stopped just outside arm's reach and mirrored his pose.

"The city was abandoned, and there are miles of underground tunnels."

"That's not the only reason."

"No." A muscle in his cheek bounced. "I needed to be near you."

The cruel things he'd done to me had left permanent scars. But this, the gut-wrenching injustice of leaving a man I would love for the rest of my life, was an infected wound that would never heal.

I couldn't stop myself from walking to him. His arms opened, and I kept walking until I was crushed against his chest, held tightly in his embrace, and breathing air that would never smell this good again.

It wasn't the scent of deceit. It was fiercely genuine. He'd smelled like snow in a blizzard. The aroma of pine needle tea and a wood-burning hearth. It was laughter, dreams, a gentle hand in my hair, a spark in my chest. It was the smell of his deep sigh when he kissed my neck. It was love. Selfless love. Strong. Warm. And it was in me, in every breath.

With a burst of hope, I focused internally, searching for the connection that had once hummed between us.

Silent. Dead. It wasn't coming back.

I wrapped my arms around him, breathed him in, and memorized every rock-hard edge of his torso, the sturdy strength in his spine, and the feel of his jaw resting on my head. And I cried. Loud, shoulder-shaking, sniveling tears of bitter anguish. I cried so hard I couldn't form a coherent word. But I didn't need to.

He stroked my hair, his chest heaving in a way I'd never felt before.

"Go," he whispered, and it sounded like *Stay.* Then louder, harsher. "Go!"

I untangled my body from his, and his hands went back in his pockets, every inch of him curled in and rigid.

He did this to us. Turn away. Start walking. Don't look in his eyes. Don't—

I looked up and found those translucent depths saturated with moisture, so stark and ravaged I felt his agony down to my bones and deeper still. I longed to kiss him. I ached to stay. I wanted to choose the trampled, abused, pathetic version of myself over empty, soulless, and no longer living.

But staying meant giving up on humanity. There was nothing left here to save us. Out there, I still had my soldiers, my fists, and my arrows. Out there, I could channel the anguish into a greater purpose.

I forced my legs to move, sobbing as I stepped into the light where he couldn't chase me. By the time I reached the passenger door of the waiting truck, I was weeping violently. The sun itself couldn't penetrate the tears in my eyes. They were a downpour of raindrops against a cloudy sky, heavy, angry, and uncountable.

Sliding into the passenger seat, I shut the door and caught

his reflection in the side mirror. He prowled restlessly along the edge of the sunlit floor, hands in his hair, glaring at the band of light. Trapped like a caged lion.

"Go," I said to Erebus. *Before I change my mind.*

He hit the gas and drove up the ramp and into the sun. I swiped at my tears, eyes on the mirror, watching with unbearable heartache as Salem fell to his knees at the shadowed edge of his darkness. He'd deliberately sent me off during the day. He couldn't run after me, and I would be safely tucked within the walls of Hoover Dam before the sun set.

As we drove away, the steel door began to lower, and an explosive crash vibrated from within the garage. A horrible roar followed, and I looked away, gripped the edge of the seat, and cried some more.

The desert stretched out around us, but I didn't see it. Couldn't see anything past my wretchedness.

The Viking beside me kept his fangs shut and eyes on the sand.

Eventually, I pulled myself together, dried my face, and turned to him. "What's stopping you from killing me?"

"Salem's public claiming protected you in our home. Now…knowing how important you are to him, I would never hurt him in that way." His fingers tightened on the steering wheel. "None of us would."

"That's…" I shook my head. "That's pretty serious loyalty."

"All those feral hybrids you take down with your arrows?" He shot me a glare. "They have fears, hopes, dreams. They feel everything a human feels, but they're trapped. Enslaved by a mental harness. Imagine that. Imagine feeling and thinking while having an infection in your brain that overrides your actions. Your father, the doctor, he knows. He was imprisoned by the same mental programming. Your mother helped him break free. That's what Salem did for us. He freed us."

I swallowed and stared blankly at the windshield. "If I don't kill them, they'll wipe out the human race. Fighting is the only way I know."

"Find another way."

"Find a way that doesn't involve defending our lives?" I asked incredulously.

"Salem got us this far." He gestured between us, as if to indicate that we could share space without killing each other. "But I'm still a slave to these." He flashed his fangs. "Still haunted by the kind of urges that keeps a man awake at night."

I shivered. "But you have the bloodlust under control, right?"

"Mostly." He shifted his bulky weight in the seat. "Try not to cut yourself or...bleed in any way for the next two hours."

My breath caught. That was why Salem didn't let me leave his room when I had my period. I knew the scent of blood affected *him*. But the others? Holy shit. Seventy-plus hybrids in an enclosed space frothing and foaming at the mouth for my blood? *That* blood? I fought down nausea and shoved away the thought.

We drove through the remains of the day in silence. The ride from Vegas to the dam was a short breath compared to how long I'd been traveling. The journey that had taken me to Canada, the mansion, and Salem's home had lasted a year.

It'd been a year since I'd seen Shea, slept in my own bed, and visited my mother's garden.

But as the rocky landscape of home emerged on the horizon, I felt emptier, colder. Meaningless. I glanced at the side mirror, and a hollow echo of my former self stared back.

This isn't the way.

"Stop the truck," I whispered.

"No. I was instructed to take you directly—"

"Stop the truck! I just..." I closed my eyes and rubbed my head. "I need to think."

He slowed to an idling stop.

Just over those cliffs, a thirty-minute drive along a winding road, and I would be home. I would return to the fighting, the struggling, the endless cycle of pointless hell. The Resistance barely kept current generations alive. An army of arrows wasn't the solution for the future of our species.

Find another way.

"You're going back to him," he said matter-of-factly.

"No. Shh."

A sigh billowed beside me, followed by the silence of the engine.

Keeping my eyes shut, I forced myself to relax in the seat and just breathe. In. Out. *I'm missing something crucial. What is my purpose?*

Annie's ghost had predicted the creatures would evolve. My mother exterminated the aphids. The spiders were the next wave of evolved creatures, but their infertility wiped them out. Annie's prophecy referred to the hybrids.

I wasn't fearless and powerful like my mother. I couldn't wipe them out with a thought. I was human—a stupid girl who couldn't hold on to her fangs or protect her own heart. I might've had a rebellious spirit once, but I'd never been brave enough, strong enough to be called a savior.

Maybe I wasn't meant to fight with arrows and fangs. Maybe I wasn't meant to fight at all.

I opened my eyes and studied the rugged lines of Erebus' face. I'd hunted and killed his kind my entire life. It was what I'd been bred to do, and it hadn't brought mankind any closer to salvation.

"Why are you looking at me like that?" Erebus narrowed his eyes.

Find another way.

I'd never tried to learn what it was to be a hybrid.

I'd never shown mercy.

What if I was meant to save *his* kind?

The prophecy said my mother wouldn't be able to save future generations from the infection, but her daughter could.

Without mankind, the *hybrids* were the future generations.

My heart raced. Was that it? Was that the answer? They were the ones I was supposed to save?

Adrenaline charged through my blood and quickened my breaths. I yanked on the door handle and jumped out.

"Wait." Erebus followed suit and stomped around the front bumper. "Get back in the truck."

I held up a finger and wrapped an arm around the empty drum of my chest.

The surrounding desert stretched toward the massive cliffs in the east. A gray sky cast the barren landscape in monstrous shadows as it pushed the sun into the horizon behind me.

Nothing but darkness ahead. Daylight would return, but if I climbed back in that truck, if I let him drive me home, I would be heading backwards, starting over from the beginning. The fighting. The resisting. The death. Only this time, I was a hollow shell of the person I was before.

The answer, the future, was not at Hoover Dam. Salem was right. I was running. But the solution wasn't with him either. Had I stayed, I would've eventually been seduced by his presence. I would've submitted to the ache in my heart and forgiven him in my weakness.

I needed to forgive myself. My manipulations had hurt him as much as he'd hurt me. I needed to forgive myself for putting my agendas and my heart before his. I needed to forgive myself for not figuring out the connection between my fangs and his veins. I needed to forgive myself for loving him despite it all.

For once in my goddamn life, I needed to do something right and through that, find absolution.

"If you don't get back in the truck," Erebus said, taking an assertive step toward me, "I will force you. We're out in the open, and there are always hybrids in this area."

I knew that, but I wasn't returning to that truck.

"You used to hunt me." My boots crunched the sand as I walked toward the bleak horizon. "Was that an instinctual thing?"

"You lead an anti-hybrid army hellbent on exterminating us. The instinct to kill you is a *practical* thing."

"Is?" I glanced at him over my shoulder. "You still want

me dead?"

"Get in the truck." He thrust a rigid finger at the door.

"You told me to find another way."

"The longer we stand out here with your scent fumigating the air, the more dangerous this little rest stop becomes." He scanned the darkness, the lines on his face growing tighter. "We'll talk in the car."

"That's just it. I've been talking and searching and wracking my brain for years. I still don't know what makes me special or what I'm supposed to do about it. I've fought, and I've lost. I fucking lost my heart." Images of Salem shot a fiery burn through my chest, the pain unbearable and never-ending. "There's one thing I haven't tried."

I dragged my boots through the sand, my fear alive and crawling across my skin as the surrounding shadows grew darker, thicker. I'd left my bow in the truck, but I didn't need it. The dagger hung on my belt.

Stay alive? My mother had broken her own rule.

"I don't know what you're doing," he whispered. "But you're making me fucking nervous. Salem will rip—"

"Then leave." I wrapped my arms around myself, my entire body shaking beneath the frightening weight of what I was considering. "Or stay. Tell him you dropped me off, but stay. I need your help."

Something scratched in the surrounding darkness, the vast terrain echoing every sound. A rustling footstep. Then more. They might've been fifty feet away or a mile, but they were coming.

Erebus quietly charged toward me, his hard gaze locked on the pitch-black landscape.

"Stop." I freed my mother's dagger and pressed the tip against the inside of my wrist as terrified tears flooded my eyes. "I'm not going to fight them."

"Are you insane?" He reached for me.

I swiped the blade across my forearm, a small cut, but painful enough to steal my breath. And deep enough to bleed.

He slammed a hand over his nose and stumbled back, his

eyes hard and furious.

"Run!" His fangs elongated from beneath that huge hand, his breaths seething as his tenuous control unraveled. "Get in the truck and lock the doors. I don't want to bite you."

"You can't infect me." Blood pulsed through my veins, hammering in sync with the frenzy of my heart. "No more running. No more resisting."

I turned the blade toward my other wrist and pierced the skin. Fire blazed up my arm, and I sobbed from the pain. From the almighty fear. I was so fucking scared my legs gave out.

I dropped to my knees and stared at the rivers of blood, fingers squeezing the hilt of my mother's dagger. The same dagger she'd used to bleed her own wrists and cure the nymphs. My gut was rock hard with terror, but there was no conflict there. This felt horrifyingly right.

Erebus pressed the back of his arm against his nose and paced stiffly, angrily, ten feet away. Axes and blades clanked on his belt, but he didn't reach for them. He didn't want to kill the hybrids, and neither did I.

"Your blood doesn't cure us," he growled.

"No, it doesn't." The rise of my tears strangled my voice. "But my death will."

"What?" His eyes blazed with rage. And hunger. "How do you know?"

My mother hadn't wanted to get pregnant after the virus hit. She'd fought the notion of bringing life into this miserable world. But the moment she became pregnant and sealed her fate, she was able to wipe out the aphids. In the end, it was the promise of her death that had exterminated them.

I'd tried killing hybrids with weapons. Tried to stop their breeding. Tried to bite them. Tried to bite Salem. Tried to conquer it all with love. "My death is the only thing I haven't tried."

His face contorted, seemingly warring with biting me, stopping me, and killing me himself.

The approaching footsteps grew louder, and my pulse

roared faster.

My fathers were going to be devastated, but they understood the predictions better than anyone. The prophecy was all-knowing, all-powerful, and couldn't be circumvented. It took my mother, and it intended to take me. It already had. I died the day I lost my connection to Salem.

Salem.

A sob rose up, violent in its attack.

He would've spent the rest of his life waiting for me. Alone and miserable. But he didn't have to. He could move on. He'd set me free, and I wanted to do the same for him.

My heartbeat exploded, shooting tremors of panic through my limbs. I held firm in the sand and forgave myself for my weaknesses. I forgave myself for everything.

Silhouettes emerged from the darkness. Fangs. Snarls. Raving, feral hunger.

It was time to do what I was meant to do. Time to show mercy, forgive Salem, and offer my blood.

It was time for me to die.

THIRTY-THREE

Nightfall pressed in from everywhere as I knelt in the sand, shaking with the compulsion to run. Dizziness swept through me, and the sound of my heartbeat thrashed in my ears.

Four hybrid males raced out of the darkness, eyes wild and fangs stark in the moonlight as they arrowed directly toward me.

Whenever a hybrid came across a human woman, his instinct was to fuck and impregnate, bite and infect. But I wasn't a normal human woman.

Forty feet away, thirty feet…they slowed. The moment they recognized my red hair, they stumbled to a halt. Their shock at seeing the daughter of Eve on her knees and without her bow stunned them to a halt. But the hesitation wouldn't last long.

They believed I was the single biggest threat to their species. They wouldn't bite to infect me. They would bite to kill.

"Erebus…" My terror was so acute I no longer felt the throb in my wrists.

He stood to the side, breathing rabidly through his mouth, eyes locked on my bloody arms.

Violent shivers raced through me, my skin sweating and chilling. *I don't want to die.* "Don't let them rape me, please?" Tears filled my eyes. "Let them drain me, but don't let them…remove my clothes."

He growled low and pained, slashing his fangs like twin blades. "I can't come any closer. I can't!"

It didn't matter to me if he bit me. Why did he care? Maybe he didn't want to be part of this, even if Salem never found out.

One of the hybrids crouched, head cocked, sniffing the air.

"This is a trick." The hybrid's voice was thick with hunger, expression feral. "You're hiding something, Daughter of Eve."

They feared me as much as I feared them, but their instinct to bite would win.

"My blood isn't poisonous. Those are just rumors." I dropped the dagger and held out my blood-slicked arms as tears coursed down my cheeks. "I want to save you."

Distrust rippled through them, but it only lasted a moment. Their resistance snapped in a crash of guttural roars, and they launched.

There was no slow-motion play-by-play, no breathless suspension in time. The attack was lightning fast and brutal in its impact. They slammed into me. My back collided with the ground, and air whooshed from my lungs. Their fangs were everywhere, ripping into my wrists, puncturing my thighs through the trousers, and piercing my neck. I screamed against the pain of violent repeated stabbings, my entire body a fiery conflagration of agony.

Instinct propelled my arms and legs to thrash, to fight. Uselessly. It was too late to change my mind. Too late to run. *OhfuckOhfuckOhfuck. I'm going to die.*

I should've told Salem I forgave him. Should've told him I loved him. I would never see him again, and that overwhelming regret added a rush of manic desperation to my fear.

Heavy sobs choked my screams. I couldn't see past my tears, couldn't breathe through the unholy pain. My back bowed off the ground, every muscle taut and shaking. It was death I feared, so much more than this physical torment. What if this was a mistake? What if I wasn't supposed to die? I hated the doubt. Once I was gone, I would never know if I'd done the right thing. It was a torture worse than the brutal teeth tearing the flesh on my throat.

The scent of iron soured the air. My body grew cold, my skin clammy. My breathing shallowed, silencing my cries. Strength drained with the loss of blood, and the ferocious sounds of snarling and sucking dimmed. When hands began clawing at my clothes and exposing my lower body, I silently begged for death.

No no no. I cried without sound, too weak to fight. *Please don't hurt me there.*

The hybrids fed in a haze of senseless hunger. They were beyond reasonable thought and wouldn't be able to stop themselves from fucking me.

Erebus' growl sounded somewhere near my feet. A struggle broke out on top my legs. Heavy weight shifted and rolled. But I couldn't lift my head. I lay listless and broken in breathless horror as bladed teeth sundered my flesh and emptied my veins. I ached for total numbness, petrified that the last thing I'd feel would be the utter devastation of being raped to death.

But nothing touched or penetrated between my legs. Erebus seemed to be fighting them off, even if he couldn't overpower his own need. At the blurry edge of my periphery, his blond head hovered over my thigh, his fangs lodged in my skin as he fed with angry agonized noises.

Another mouth returned to my throat, ravenous in its assault. I no longer felt the blood soaking my neck. But I knew the moment he punctured something vital, felt the snap of one or more arteries in my throat. I lost the last of my muscle control. My head lolled. Breathing became a full-body effort until there was no more air, no sound of my heartbeat, no pain, no sense of anything.

Had the hybrids stopped biting? Something had happened, something big, but I floated away from it, drifting in desolate nothingness. *Dead.* This was what death felt like?

A pulse of golden light swelled in the darkness, moving closer, brighter. This was it, and I wasn't ready. But I couldn't look away. The glow was all around me, enveloping me in phantom arms and extraordinary warmth that couldn't be measured or physically felt.

Particles of transparent yellow gathered inches before me, and slowly, enchantingly, formed an image. Waves of gilded hair cascaded around an exquisite feminine face with delicate bone structure, lips bowed into a graceful smile, and golden eyes. *My* eyes.

I recognized her, not from the carved statues and paintings created in her image, but with a fundamental part of me that loved her innately and unconditionally.

"Mom." I spoke without voice or breath, the soundless word reverberating in a realm I didn't understand.

"My beautiful girl." Her hand was a strobe of light, pulsing with power and blinding my senses as she touched my cheek. "I love you more than life."

I couldn't move, didn't feel my body. "Am I dead?"

"Yes." Her voice was a booming heartbeat, but neither of us was breathing.

"Was I enough?" I searched her face, enthralled. "Was I enough to save them?"

"You've always been enough. So much more than enough." Her aureate eyes burned impossibly brighter. "You saved them."

A blissful sensation of peace radiated from her ambient light. But something vibrated at the edges, scraping against the perimeter of growing darkness that shrunk my mother's aura.

"I love you." I ached to reach for her and hold her to me, but my arms wouldn't work.

"I'm so proud of you." She flickered, her face blurring and dimming.

Wetness dripped over my lips and filled my mouth. Thick. Dark. Richly flavorful. There was so much of it. So much... *blood?* Why did I taste blood?

"Bite." Her face faded, and the warmth of her glow lifted away. "Bite him."

"No!" My heartbeat exploded to life. "Mom, please don't leave!"

"Bite me." Another voice replaced hers, a deeper, more familiar resonance of sound. "Fucking bite me!"

Freezing cold swept over me, and her beautiful face vanished in a blanket of darkness. In its place was a different face, paler, sharper, masculine. *Salem.*

Soul-deep elation warred with a horrible stab of fear. Why was he here? Did he die? Where was my mother? What was happening?

I coughed up the coppery fluid in my mouth, choking as more pooled in my throat. Where was all the blood coming from? The night sky pressed against me. I was still in the desert. Why was I so cold?

"You're dying!" he screamed, eyes furious and teeth snapping. *No fangs.* "I won't be able to bring you back again. You need to bite me. Right now!"

I lay numb and lost in a cloud of confusion, watching his mouth move. Where were his fangs? What happened to Erebus and the other hybrids? I tried to ask, but the words gurgled beneath a river of blood.

Was Salem cured? Or dead? My vision was so distorted I didn't trust it.

He turned his neck and held the tip of my mother's blade against a cut in his throat. More blood splattered my lips, and a rushing sound thrummed through my ears. My heartbeat?

Lub-dub, lub-dub, lub-dub.

The echo amplified, pounding a frantic drum in my head.

His heartbeat.

Blinking rapidly, I tried to clear my vision, and there, shimmering in the darkness was a tracery of glowing branches, bulging and throbbing beneath his skin. The silver ribbons of hybrid venom swam through his veins, beckoning me. *Bite, bite, bite.*

I licked my lips with a heavy tongue and caught the tip on something sharp. I did it again, and that was when I felt it. The ache in my gums. The razored points of my fangs. And the vigorous spark of our connection. It didn't just spark. It ignited, blazing a scorching charge along the live wire between us.

I wanted to cry with happiness, but my eyes weren't working. My body wouldn't respond. His bare chest slid against my soaked shirt, and a soft material wadded against my throat. Was I alive? If I had a pulse, it was weak. Too weak to come back.

He pressed his neck against my fangs. "Bite me, goddammit!"

No! My mother had died for me. I wouldn't let anyone else exchange their life for mine. Especially not Salem.

I forgive you. My voice carried no sound, my lips refusing to move. *I love you.*

The connection between us flared with so much heat it penetrated the coldness of my body. I clung to the sensation.

"Bite me!" he roared, a vicious echo of my mother's words.

Bite him.

Why? My mother had said the hybrids were saved, and Salem didn't have fangs. He was cured!

He gripped the back of my head, pried my mouth open, and shoved my face hard against the wound on his neck. The instant my fangs broke his skin, the urge to drink overtook me, the flavor of his blood too tempting. I couldn't stop my jaw from moving, from pulling the life-giving essence of those silver ribbons into my body.

I sucked hard, harder, suddenly ravenous to consume him. Searing heat coursed through my veins. My lungs filled with nourishing air, and my nerve-endings stirred to vivid life. As I fed with delirious desperation, I became more aware of his weight on me, the length of his body entangled with mine, and the deep sound of his groans. He grew heavier, tenser, breathing, and giving me breath.

He tasted like survival and love. Each drop energized me, thrusting me into a dreamscape where I was stronger, blindingly happy, and whole.

The hammer of his heart began to slow, and mine sped up, strengthening and stretching. My insides sang with euphoria, and every molecule in my body pulsed with vitality as the healing properties of the hybrid venom hummed through my blood.

Afraid to drink too much, I slowed my feeding to a lazy suckle, swirling my tongue across his skin. Strength returned to my arms, and I clutched his back and head, hugging him to me. Sweet mother, I loved this man. I loved him so fucking much and never wanted to let him go.

He held me just as tightly. His hips rocked against mine, and his shallow breaths trickled into a raspy groan. His cock swelled in the confines of his pants, and he lifted his lower body away.

I grabbed the hard flex of his ass and pulled him against me, aching to feel how my bite affected him. The potency of our connection and the feverish fusion of our love curled around my soul, stitching and healing the broken pieces.

His muscles tightened, and he tried to push away, seemingly fighting his climb to orgasm. I wasn't aroused, my insides too over-stimulated as I continued to heal. But I wanted his relief. Craved it. So I continued to pull on his vein, each hard suck coiling him tighter against me.

He dropped his hands in the sand. His entire body locked up, and he released a hoarse grunt that shot electricity along our connection, jolted my heart, and stole my breath.

Then everything blinked out in an explosion of light.

THIRTY-FOUR

The first thing I felt was peace, calm and warm in the stillness of the air. I lay on a mattress and slid a hand across soft fabrics, seeking Salem. The sudden intake of someone's breath snapped my eyes open.

Huge brown eyes stared back, followed by a soft smile. "Baby girl."

"Shea!" Warmth spread through my chest. "I missed you so much."

She engulfed me in a tangle of long black curls and strong arms. "Oh honey, you had me worried out of my mind."

"I'm sorry." I breathed in the comforting scent of her skin.

She smelled like safety and family. I was home, and that realization brought a thousand pressing questions.

As she hugged me, I didn't feel a twinge of pain. Someone had dressed me in cotton pants and shirt. Probably Shea. With a swipe of my tongue, I probed my teeth. No fangs. I touched my neck, and the skin felt smooth and soft. No wounds or scars marred my bare arms. The hybrid venom in Salem's blood had well and truly healed me.

"Where's Salem?" I asked.

"He's here."

Arrows lined the concrete walls, and a black and white painting of my mother hung over my bed. I never spent much time in my room, and now it felt spartan and empty.

"I need to see him," I said. "Is he—?"

"Alive and safe."

I released a heavy breath.

"He drove you here last night." She ran a gentle hand through my hair. "He and a blond man."

"Man? You mean Erebus? Do they have fangs? The hybrids…are they—?"

"Slow down." She caught my face in her hands. "I know you have questions. Just…let me look at you before your daddies storm in and take over."

Her mocha skin creased with concern as she studied my eyes. She might've been my mother's best friend and Eddie's biological mother, but she'd been a mother to me in every way that mattered.

I gripped her wrists, and a sudden sheen of tears blurred my eyes. "I died, Shea."

"I know," she said softly. "Salem told us everything."

Everything? I doubted that. Even so, there was one thing he didn't know.

"I saw her." More tears gathered, clinging to my lashes. "She…she spoke to me."

Shea was a strong woman, one of the strongest people I knew. So when that brave chin of hers quivered, I lost it. A sob bubbled up and brought with it a gush of emotions I could no longer contain. She held me as I cried, and the sound of her tears made me weep harder.

I told her about my death, the brilliant light of my mother's aura, the words we'd exchanged, and the peacefulness she'd radiated. My voice wavered through the details, and when I reached the part about the dimming light and the rush of coldness, a sharp inhale sounded behind me.

I glanced over my shoulder and found my fathers standing inside the open door. By the tormented looks on their faces, they'd heard every word.

"We'll catch up later, baby girl." Shea cupped my face and pressed a kiss to my forehead. "Go easy on them, okay?"

Me go easy? If Salem told them everything, that advice should've been directed to them.

She headed toward the doorway and squeezed Jesse's hand on her way out.

I climbed out of bed, shocked by the energy and strength in my legs as I hurried toward them. They didn't grimace or smile or move to hug me, their postures rigid. The mere fact they weren't yelling at me gave me pause.

"What's wrong?" I scanned them from head to toe, taking in their bulky frames, rugged trousers, and heavy boots.

Nothing looked out of place, but everything about them felt... *off.*

Roark flexed a hand at his side, and I zoomed in on the torn skin on his knuckles.

Oh, no. I stepped toward him and grabbed his wrist. "Please tell me Salem wasn't on the other end of this."

He pinned his lips together, green eyes flashing with unreadable emotion.

The blood around the broken skin had dried, but the wound hadn't healed. My heart thundered.

"You're not healing?" *Could it be?* I looked up at his mouth. "Let me see your teeth."

His lips twitched and pulled back. No fangs.

I gasped and dropped his hand, careening on unsteady feet toward Jesse and Michio. They bared their straight human teeth before I asked.

"Holy shit." I clutched my throat. "Did you revert back in every way? Your strength, speed—?"

"Take it easy." Michio gripped my arm and pulled me in for a hug. "We lost our fangs and all other hybrid traits just after dusk last night."

"When I died," I whispered. Hope flared inside me. "What about the hybrids?"

Jesse erupted in a burst of motion through the room. "You sacrificed your life?" He swung back, copper eyes ablaze with fury. "Did you think, for one fucking moment, what your death would've done to us?"

"Yes." I raised my chin, shoulders back. "It was the only way. I had to die for them."

"Them? The hybrids?" he shouted. "How the fuck did you know that?"

"The punishment for sin is death." *Except I lived.*

"Sin?" Jesse glared at me in furious disbelief. "What sins?"

"Romans 3:23." Roark rested his fingers on his chin, his expression grooved with pain and wonder. "For all have sinned and fall short of the glory of God."

I'd listened to Roark's teachings my entire life and sometimes leaned on aspects of his beliefs, but religion had nothing to do with my decision to die. Faith, however, had been the determining factor. Faith in my mother, myself, and mankind.

"I've made a lot of mistakes," I said quietly. "I was too proud to forgive. Too cruel to show mercy. I tried everything to fulfill my role as the prophecy, when all I needed to do was just be humble, scared, and *human*."

"Christ, Dawn." Jesse embraced me, but it only lasted a moment. He released me to pace through the room, rubbing his face.

"Did it work?" A ragged breath crept into my resolve. "What happened to the hybrids? Are Salem and Erebus cured?"

"They're cured." Michio's soft voice drifted over my shoulder. When I turned, he said, "We've sent out patrols and haven't found a hybrid within a twenty miles radius."

"But there are scads of confused, newly-cured humans." Roark cradled my face in his big hands. "God accepted His lamb's sacrifice, and he fulfilled another prophecy by raising her from the dead." His eyes softened, and he pressed my cheek against his chest. "Ye saved them, me beautiful girl."

My heart leapt to my throat.

"We don't all share your beliefs, Roark." Jesse paced around me, his glare burning up my cheeks. "Salem told us what he did to you. After that traumatic experience—all his lying and cheating—self-injury can feel like a way of waking up from the numbness." He stabbed a finger at the door. "He sent you away, and you—"

"He let me go!" Heat rushed across my skin, and I pulled away from Roark to face Jesse head on. "I didn't make the decision to die because I was a scorned woman. It wasn't some dramatic fuck-you to Salem. It wasn't even suicide. *I* didn't end my life. The hybrids did."

"You didn't fight back!" Jesse roared. "That isn't the girl I raised."

"Jesse." Roark narrowed hard eyes at him.

"No, Da." I touched Roark's arm. "He's right. I didn't fight back. When I left Salem, I was devastated and hopeless and miserable. Maybe I wouldn't have made such a morbid decision under different conditions. But I did it. And it. Felt. Right." I turned toward Michio and pressed a hand against my gut. "It felt right, Dad."

Michio wrapped his arms around me. "Jesse knows that. We all do. Doesn't mean we like it."

"But they're cured." I gripped the back of his shirt. "My death cured them, right?"

"We'll know more tomorrow when the rest of our scouts return." Michio rubbed my back. "Per Erebus' account of the events, he and the other hybrids lost their fangs the moment your heart stopped."

"What about Salem? Why was he there?" I was beside myself with anxiousness to talk to him and see him and hold him.

"He wanted to make sure you arrived home safely." Michio rested his hands on my shoulders. "He said when he left Las Vegas at sundown, he still had his inhuman speed."

"Did he tell you he could run faster than sound?" I asked.

"Yes, and he managed to run most of the distance—"

"Until I died." I'd stolen his power and strength, had truly emasculated him in every way. My heart sank.

Michio closed his eyes, nodded.

Jesse sat on the edge of the bed and put his head in his hands. Roark joined him, gripping the back of Jesse's neck and staring at the floor.

Michio met my gaze. "Salem was almost there when your heart stopped. He ran the rest of the way at human speed. He could still see his veins and knew the hybrid venom hadn't left his blood. So he cut himself, tried to make you drink from his vein."

"Hoping the venom would cure me." I rubbed the unmarked skin on my wrist. "He saved me. All this time, those silver things in his blood—"

"They were never meant to save humans or hybrids." Michio kissed my head. "They were meant to save *you.*"

"Why did I lose consciousness a second time…after I bit him?"

"Your fucking jugular was ripped out," Jesse said, his voice rough. "Your body shut down to heal the damage."

A knot hardened in my throat. "What if I'd bitten him while he still had hybrid traits?"

"I suspect you would've carried the venom inside you until you needed it," Michio said. "Maybe it would've prevented you from dying. Maybe you would've died from blood loss, and the venom would've brought you back. With regard to Salem…I don't know. Biting him when he was wholly human is probably why he didn't turn to ash. We'll never know for sure."

Wholly human. A sudden thought accelerated my pulse. "What time is it? Has he been outside?"

"The sun doesn't come up for another thirty minutes," Michio said.

"Where is he?" I darted toward the door.

"Elaine's old room," Roark said.

"What?" I spun around, my blood rising to a boil. "Why would you put him there?"

"Seemed fitting." Roark flexed his swollen knuckles. "The lad's bloody lucky to be alive."

For fuck's sake. I ran out of the room and down the corridor cast in the yellow glow of overhead bulbs. The comforting scent of limestone and old cement tinged the air, an aroma deeply ingrained in so many wonderful memories.

My fathers didn't follow me as I darted from tunnel to tunnel, passing numerous closed doors. The residents were still asleep, but not for long. The sun was coming. I picked up my pace.

A moment later, the final tunnel dropped me into a long hall. One of Eddie's fathers, Paul, stood outside the room that had been gutted and left untouched for twenty years.

His huge eyes widened, his smile bright against his dark skin. "There you are!"

I gave him a fierce hug. "Did you take good care of Shea while I was gone?"

"I try." He laughed. "You know how it is."

The trials and tribulations of a relationship? Yeah, I knew. I also knew the effort could bring the purest form of joy.

"We have a lot of catching up to do, but my priority is in that room." I nudged him down the hall. "I'll take it from here. Tell Eddie Senior I'm starving and expecting a huge breakfast."

"You got it." He ruffled my hair. "Good to have you back, kiddo."

I watched him lumber away and opened the door to the room.

Two men leapt to their feet, and my gaze went unerringly to the one who held my heart.

Salem stood in a shadowy realm all his own, cloaked in seductive darkness where nothing existed outside of him and me and the connection thrumming between us. No more backward glances. No more distrust. Everything faded away, leaving only the man with the spectral eyes that devoured me head to toe. I did the same, stepping closer to peruse the masculine lines of his perfect form.

My breath caught at the sight of his face. Broken skin swelled around his translucent eyes, his nose bent and bruised. Roark had done that to him, and I'd taken away Salem's ability to heal the damage.

"I'm so sorry." I covered my mouth. "And this room…" I grimaced at the cold barrenness of the space. "They shouldn't have put you in here."

"I don't care about the room. Come here." His command was deep, uncompromising, and deliciously Salem.

I moved toward him, glancing at the other man, and stopped. Erebus grinned at me—a grin that bulged beneath angry lacerations. He sported the same swelling on his eyes and nose, and his arm wrapped around his ribs as if nursing other injuries.

"Did Roark hit you, too?" I asked him, clenching my hands.

"I did." Salem's eyes flickered with challenge.

"Why?" My stomach pinched with guilt. "I asked him to stay with me. He's the reason I wasn't raped."

"He fucking bit you. He's damn lucky to still be breathing."

Same thing Roark had said about Salem.

I turned back to Erebus and found his blue gaze amid the nasty contusions. "Are you…free? Did it work?"

"I'm human for the first time in my life." His fang-less smile outshone the bruises on his face. "I've never felt more alive. I'd hug you—"

Salem's growl reverberated through the room.

"I'll have to settle on simply saying thank you." He bowed his head.

My own fangs hadn't returned in Salem's presence, not that I expected to ever see them again. They'd served their purpose.

A floating sensation lifted through me. "Thank you, Erebus, for staying with me last night."

"You're welcome."

Both men wore borrowed clothes, their hair wet and wounds cleaned. I could only imagine how much blood they'd been covered in—mine and theirs.

"You're not a captive here," I said to Erebus. "You're free to go. Or stay. Breakfast is usually served at seven."

"I'll stick around for a bit." He gave Salem a grin and a chin lift and left the room.

When the door shut behind Erebus, I drew a deep breath and turned to Salem.

He loomed at the back of the room, his black hair messy

from tugging, his gaze overly bright and glossy. It wasn't the gashes on his face that made him look broken and tortured. It was the stiff way he held himself, the vigilance in which he tracked my every move, and the breath he held as if the tiniest movement might spook me into running. Now that we were alone, his entire demeanor spoke of uncertainty.

I looked him directly in the eye. "I forgive you."

His relief was palpable, parting his lips and loosening the muscles in his face.

"I love you." I stepped toward him. "I've loved you since Canada, and I'm sick to my soul for waiting until now to tell you."

"Dawn…" he croaked, moving toward me.

I met him halfway and launched into his arms.

"You let me go." I hugged him fiercely, burying my nose in his neck and inhaling the scent I thought I'd never smell again. "Yet here you are."

"I never said I wouldn't follow you. I intended to watch you from afar, to keep an eye—"

"Stalker." I kissed him. I couldn't help myself.

He crushed me against him, arms gripping oh-so tightly, and kissed me back. Then we were spinning, and my back collided against the wall, my body pinned in the best way possible. The powerful flex of his muscles wasn't as strong as it had been. The roll of his tongue wasn't as lightning fast. But the connection between us blazed hotter than ever.

I'd risen from an emotional numbness and physical death with a clarity that made every touch feel like the first. The slide of his tongue against mine zapped my nerves to life. Everywhere our body made contact—lips, arms, hips, chests—was a static shock. The hungry rush of his breath, the heat of his skin through his clothes, the scrape of his whiskers—

"What the—?" I wrapped my fingers behind his neck to prevent escape. "You have stubble."

Hardly enough to call it a shadow, the hair growth was indiscernible to the eye. I lifted on tiptoes and pulled him to me, rubbing my cheek along his and relishing the scratchy burn.

"I take it you like it." He chuckled, and the sound shivered deliciously across my skin.

"I love you." I kissed him, slowly, melting into his embrace and cursing every inch of cotton that separated us. "I missed you so much," I breathed into his mouth. "I've been so numb and stupid and stubborn I couldn't feel you. But I feel you now, your heat all around me, the power in your body, your love sparking through our connection." I licked his lips, bit along his chin, and returned to his mouth, twining my tongue with his. "Do you hate me for making you so human?"

"I fucking love you, Dawn." He yanked me back for another kiss, bruising my lips.

I pulled back. "When I bit you, did you know you would live?"

"I knew *you* would live. I could see the venom in my veins." He captured my mouth.

This man had been ready to die for me, and his kisses would forever remind me how close I'd been to losing him.

I broke the kiss again. "When I lost consciousness, there was an explosion of light. Did you see that?"

He gripped the backs of my legs and lifted me up the wall, wrapping my thighs around his waist and holding me in place with the press of his body. "Your bite had an uncontrollable effect on me."

"You were hard." My eyes widened. "Did you come? Is that what I felt?"

"Yeah." He slid a hand into my hair, holding my face as he pressed his smile against my lips. "Not the first time you made me come in my pants. Probably not the last."

I laughed. "Our love is stubborn and messy."

"It's trial and error." He licked my mouth, nibbling and exploring.

"And forgiveness and acceptance."

"Command and conquer." He bit my lips.

"Dusk and dawn." I bit him back.

"I want you," he said as a tremor shook through his body.

"Mm. I want you to see the sunrise."

"I see it, and she's never been more beautiful."

The strong thud of my reborn heart rushed through my ears. What if the sun could still hurt him?

"We can view it from my mother's garden," I said. "There's an overhang there—"

"All right." He trailed fingers across my cheek. "Show me this dawn that will never be as stunning as the one I have."

THIRTY-FIVE

With a flutter in my belly, I led Salem toward the statue of my mother amid the blooming vegetation. The garden sat on the roof of the generator room at the bottom of the dam. No one was here this early in the morning. Just him and me and lots of hidden alcoves to quench the hunger burning along our connection. Every time he turned those gorgeous glowing eyes in my direction, he was in danger of finding out exactly how much I missed every hard inch of him.

But the real danger lay to the east, behind the red-rock canyon. The sky paled above the open rafters of the garden. The sun would be up any minute.

I halted just outside the cover of an overhang and the door that led inside the dam. If his skin started burning, protection was a two-second sprint away.

He tipped his head back, taking in the colossal wall of the Hoover Dam. "I knew it was big, but damn."

"That's what she said."

"She says a lot of things." His lips twitched.

I waved a hand up and down my body. "Five feet of pleasure and a ball of energy. I'm dripping with *come* backs."

He laughed, eyes gleaming. "Now that you've turned all the hybrids into humans, maybe you can turn all aspects of life into sexual innuendos and earn a living as a roadside entertainer."

"Maybe I will." I trailed a finger down his shirt, relishing the hard indentations beneath. "Innuendos will always be appreciated, because life itself is sexually transmitted."

"You're on a roll." He hooked a finger in the waistband of my pants and tugged me to him.

I circled my arms around his neck and kept an eye on the eastern ridge behind him. "For my next trick, I need a bed and a volunteer."

"I like the sound of that." He kissed my lips. "Where's your bed?"

"Hmm." I pretended to look around. "You'll have to think outside the box."

"All panties aside, I'd rather think inside your box."

"Nice." I nibbled along his jaw. "Maybe you can be the sidekick in my entertainment venture."

"I'll do anything you want as long as I'm with you."

"You might change your mind. I'm kind of a pain in the ass."

"I'll go slow and use a lubricant."

I burst into laughter. "I'm definitely keeping you."

"Good, because I'll never let you go again."

I pressed against him in a satisfied catlike stretch, absorbing the feel of his strength and heat. Then a different kind of warmth spread over me, and my gaze lifted to the blush of orange above the cliff. "Dawn's coming."

His face cracked into a wide grin, and he opened his mouth.

"Don't say it." I touched a finger against his lips. "I walked right into that one." Stepping back, I turned him toward the sunrise. "Look."

Shoulders back, chest out, chin high, his beauty took up a lot of space. It wasn't just his brawny physique. It was his sense of assurance, dominating presence, and larger-than-life aura. Just standing beside him filled me with a frisson of intense emotions. Excitement, longing, fear…

"I'm scared." I stared unblinking at his profile, waiting for the first ray of light to touch his face. "I stole your superhuman strength. If I left you unprotected with your only weakness—"

"I have you, Dawn, and you're all I need." He wrapped an

arm around my back, tucking me against his side. "If karma had its way, I wouldn't even have that."

"Karma is like sixty-nine. You get what you give."

He chuckled, kissed my hair, and squinted at the glowing ridge.

"You gave me life." I watched him closely, arms locked around his waist, breath suspended as sunlight bled into the canyon.

His chest rose with a heavy inhale, the flawless porcelain skin around his bruises resplendent in the fiery glow of dawn. He didn't shield his eyes, didn't sizzle or burn. He absorbed the full force of the sun with his head tilted back and lips parted.

I touched his neck. Smooth, warm, *human* skin. I smiled so big my cheeks hurt. "Say something."

"It feels like you." He closed his eyes, his timbre low and raspy. "Blinding. Extraordinary. Alive."

I hugged him tighter and turned my gaze to the golden spears piercing the persimmon sky. "I was born right here. Right where we're standing. This view was the last thing my mother saw."

"You were part of the view, right?" He absently stroked my hair, eyes on the sky. "Didn't she see you?"

"Yeah. She was holding me."

"If the last time I closed my eyes was with you in my arms and the sun on my face…" He looked down at me, his voice gravelly. "I'd die a happy man."

An overwhelming feeling of peace swept over me. "I love you."

He framed my face in his hands, his eyes warm and bright with the depth of his love. "Thank you for giving me this." He was quiet for a moment, his thumbs tracing the curves of my cheekbones. "I lived my entire life without love or light. Now I have both, and no matter what happens, I will never stop feeling them."

I brushed my lips against his, and slowly, tenderly, the kiss deepened, wobbled with breathlessness, and moved to the bench beside my mother's statue. For the next hour, we sat side by side, lost in the sun's warmth and each other. I told him about my conversation with my mother, but all other events of the prior night were left where they belonged—in the past.

Eventually, my fathers showed up, bringing breakfast and news of more cured humans. The five of us sprawled on the patch of grass beside my mother's memorial, eating fried eggs, shredded potatoes, and jerky.

The garden used to hold a patina of gloom for me, a place haunted with the deaths of my mother and Darwin. But new memories, brighter moments, were quickly casting a great light of hope on my entire world.

"I love him," I said around a mouthful of food.

"We know, lass." Roark stretched out a leg in front of him and wiped his mouth.

I narrowed my eyes at three faces that had relaxed significantly since I first woke. "That means you have to love him, too."

"Dawn." Salem stiffened beside me.

Jesse draped an arm over his bent knee. "Now that the Resistance is obsolete, what are you planning?"

I swallowed. "We haven't talked about—"

"I'm asking him." Jesse looked at Salem.

When Salem didn't answer, I peeked up at his face.

Thoughtful reflection glowed in his eyes as he held Jesse's hard glare. "We'll put down roots and build. Plant seeds and harvest crops. Work hard and sleep well. Pursue our dreams during the day and come home at night to dream some more."

Good answer, beautiful man. I slid my hand in his and laced our fingers.

"Come home where?" Michio set his plate aside and clasped his hands in front of him.

"Wherever Dawn is," Salem said without hesitation.

"That won't be Canada." I feigned a dramatic shiver. "Or underground...anywhere."

Salem breathed deeply, his bruised face awash in sunlight. "I can live with that." A smile stretched across his mouth. "Our home is out there waiting for us."

"It's the tallest building in the biggest city." I rolled the idea around in my mouth, testing the flavor. "Surrounded by the bustle and rebuild of life."

"It's on a sandy beach with every window open to the ocean." He grinned wider, squeezing my hand.

"Hard to plant and harvest food on a beach." I rested my head on his shoulder, my mind spinning with dreams. "It's on a grassy hillside, overlooking fertile acreage waiting to be planted."

"Where are your oul fellas in these scenarios?" Roark arched a blond eyebrow.

"Someone has to tend the crops." I bit down on a smile. "I hear the Irish know a thing or two about planting potatoes."

"Ach, ye little harpy." Roark reached across our spread of food in the grass, knocking over cups and bowls to muss my hair into a tangle on top of my head. Once he had me in reach, he cupped my face and deposited a kiss on my forehead. "You're stuck with us."

When he settled back beside Jesse, I looked each one of them in the eyes and asked, "You'll leave the dam? You'll leave…" I glanced around the garden and settled on the carved statue of my mother.

"Evie isn't here." Jesse twisted a blade of grass between his fingers, eyes on the statue. "She's in our dreams, in *your* dreams, wherever that takes you."

"And us." Michio tilted his head, briefly glancing at Roark and Jesse. "We'll be with you."

THIRTY-SIX

My insides buzzed with hope and excitement as I approached my bedroom door and reached for the handle.

Salem hadn't slept in two days, so after breakfast, I'd dropped him off at my room and left to shower in the bathroom down the hall. On my way there, I'd been stopped by Eddie, Shea, and a dozen others, smothering me with cheers and chatter and blinding smiles. Their happiness was infectious, and I carried it with me through my shower and back to the room.

As I turned the handle on my door, Link rounded the corner and entered the hall, pointing his black eyes at me.

"You avoiding me, Mini Evie?"

"Doesn't everyone, old man?" I grinned and released the handle, giving him my full attention. "Did you just return?"

He paused a few feet away, hands clasped behind his back and bald head glinting in the glow of the overhead bulbs. "Yeah."

"And?"

A smile broke through his scruffy beard. "You put me out of work, little girl."

"No hybrids?"

"Nope. We'll keep looking, but you know as well as I do this was a worldwide cure." His eyes crinkled. "Like mother, like daughter."

"Was that a compliment?" I pretended to gasp.

"Yeah," he said gruffly. "It was long overdue."

With that, he turned back down the hall and vanished

around the corner.

Such a strange man.

Smiling, I quietly entered my bedroom and closed the door. A single candle illuminated the most gorgeous eyes and muscular body I'd ever seen. He sat on the edge of my bed, shirtless and bent forward, with his elbows on his spread knees. His head lifted, and the impact of his smile weakened my legs and kicked up my pulse.

"You're supposed to be asleep." I stepped toward him, tempted to remove my shorts and tank top and give him another reason to stay awake.

"I can't sleep without you." He straightened and opened his arms.

The darklight that burned between us sparked anew. I climbed on to his lap, straddled his hips, and melted against him. The kiss that followed wasn't tentative or coaxing. It began with a savage snarl on his lips that thrust us straight into the future. And south. Way down south where our bodies ground together in hard unapologetic hunger.

"You should sleep." I panted into his mouth.

"You should be naked." He tore off my top.

My fingers dug into his back, and my hips rocked with the roll of his. The mattress squeaked to the rhythm of our need, and the room vibrated with the sounds of our impassioned kisses.

His stubble scraped down my jaw as he slid his mouth to my throat, licking and nibbling the spot that had been ripped open only one night ago.

My head fell back beneath the tingling caress of his tongue. "Do you miss your teeth?"

With a toe-curling growl, he stood, lifting me with him. "Sweetheart, I still have teeth."

He tossed me on the bed and yanked off my shorts, leaving me completely bare beneath his burning gaze. My heart couldn't race fast enough as he prowled up my legs and buried his face between my thighs.

I writhed beneath his diabolical mouth with neither grace

nor breath. The closer I approached combustion, the hungrier he became, working his tongue in and around my folds until I came with a howling scream.

He caught my hips and continued to kiss me in the most intimate way possible. Evidently, he wasn't tired, and I couldn't fight. I didn't want to. I came when he sank his fingers inside me. I came when he sucked on my clit. I came every time he made me, cursing and bucking and pulling his hair.

I'd been lost and found, claimed and conquered, and just when I thought I had nothing left to give, he showed me exactly how he could use those human teeth. Biting my clit with the right amount of pressure, I came again with a hoarse cry.

As I caught my breath, he removed his pants and kissed his way up my body, covering every inch of hypersensitive skin in his path. When he reached my face, I cupped his jaw and brushed my lips over the swelling around his eye, down the crooked break in his nose, and across his tangy-wet mouth.

"You're a wicked man." I licked his lips. "Do you know how long it's been since I've come?"

He slid his hands in my hair and nudged his hard length between my legs. "Forty-four days."

He'd fucked me a month ago in his attempt to pull me out of my terrible desolation, but neither of us had found release during those miserable two weeks. Excluding last night, it'd been forty-four days since his last orgasm, too.

"Your turn." I wriggled beneath him, pushing at his chest. "Now that I don't have fangs, I can put *my* mouth on *you.*"

He pressed his face against my neck and groaned. "I'd never last."

"Are you worried about your stamina now?"

"Admits no man ever." He playfully bit the juncture between my neck and shoulder. "But my recovery time is probably going to be…human."

"The horror." I reached down between us, wrapped my fingers around his thick cock, and stroked. "I might actually be able to walk when we finish."

"Don't count on it." He caught my hand around his length and positioned himself at my opening.

"Wait." I clenched my fingers around him, eliciting a sexy-as-hell growl from his lips. "Given all the changes your body has gone through, it's possible you're fertile now. Do you want to get tested first?"

"No more tests. No more science."

"What happens happens?"

"Absolutely." He thrust hard and vigorously, instantly setting a pace that owned me from the inside out.

My hands flew to the muscled flanks of his ass. "Fuuuck!"

"You feel so damn good." His lips captured mine, and all thought evaporated. "Tight and perfect and mine."

He filled me up and stretched me out, pounding me into the mattress and grunting against my mouth.

I missed this. The shocking drive of his hips, the sinful friction of our grinding bodies, the feverish way he possessed my lips. I missed every touch, every response, so fucking much.

His hands swept over my pleasure-soaked skin, triggering a rush of sensations that took me to the pinnacle of bliss. He stared directly in my eyes, and the fervency of his love blazed through our connection, fighting my body for possession of my soul.

He was my heaven and hell, my death and rebirth, and every vibrant heartbeat in between.

"I'm yours." I came in an explosion of heat and friction, screaming *Yours* until my voice was raw.

His pupils widened, and his thrusts became erratic, his heavy breaths tumbling into husky groans. When he came, it was all there in his gaze, his wonderment and pleasure and eternal devotion.

If he didn't have the same stamina as before, I didn't notice. He was Salem in every way that mattered.

He was my forever.

THIRTY-SEVEN

Five years later

The scent of fresh earth filled my lungs as I hurried down the grassy hillside, shielding my eyes from the eastern sky. The soft amber glow kissed the smile I couldn't stifle. The sun itself had barely risen, and already the surrounding farmland stirred with harvesters, all of them too busy to lift their heads and notice my excitement.

Twenty-seven years ago, my mother had lived on this land, smack in the middle of old-world America, with her husband, Joel, and my siblings, Annie and Aaron. Her neighborhood was long gone, but I hoped she'd be proud of the village we'd erected in its place.

Building where my mother had once called home made this location special, but it wasn't the only reason we'd chosen it. The winters here reminded us of Canada. The summers were reminiscent of Hoover Dam. The in-between seasons were mild and peaceful, the best foundation for new memories.

Most of the homes gathered around the main road, encircled by swaths of crops and pastures dotted with horses and cattle. There were no ugly walls to keep out hybrids. There were no more hybrids. The infection had died worldwide the moment my heart had stopped.

Of course, there would always be threats. Wolves and wild cats and the random armed asshole who thought he could steal happiness from those who had earned it. But those predators were trappable—and easy to kill if it came to that. I ran the security, trained the guards, and maintained order among our ninety-two townspeople. My fathers called me the town sheriff.

My feet hit the dirt road, and I raced past the huge oak tree at the center of town. A dozen small buildings lined the main path. Soon there would be more. So much more.

I approached the one room hospital. Michio would already be inside, preparing for his day as the resident doctor. But I didn't stop.

My fathers lived just outside of the village, a five-minute ride by horseback. They'd built a log home on the other side of the lake, claiming they wanted peace and quiet. As quickly as our community was growing, I suspected their location would be surrounded by homes and more farmland within a few years.

I passed the town's only church—a tiny thing with a triangular roof. Roark might've been the resident priest, but he counseled and married folks of all faiths and beliefs. He also liked to sleep in, so I didn't bother peeking through the shutters.

When I reached the largest building, my legs burned and my lungs labored for air. I skidded through the doorway and found the front room of the town hall empty. I ran security out of the space on the right, but the building was primarily used for meetings.

Jesse's timbre drifted from the back room, followed by a feminine voice I didn't recognize. I strode across the wood floors, down a short hall, and around the corner.

A dozen heads turned in my direction. Most of the faces I didn't recognize. Three wore familiar smiles.

Jesse, Erebus, and Salem sat around a large table with men and women from… another village?

With the help of Erebus and Jesse, Salem had found great success in governing our town, from organizing an efficient structure of engineers, carpenters, and farmers to ensuring plans ran smoothly and timely. Towns like ours sprouted up everywhere. Many struggled to keep up with population growth and reached out to Salem for advice. I suspected this was another one of those meetings.

The strangers in the room bowed their heads and didn't meet my eyes. A common reaction, one that made me feel awkward and isolated. It was probable that some of these men and women had been hybrids and saw me as some kind of savior. But I was just a woman, a human with fears and dreams just like them. Though I'd freed them, it was up to them to build a future for mankind.

Salem found my eyes, his sunburned forehead creased in concern. "Everything okay?"

"Yep. Sorry to interrupt." I hadn't realized he'd already be in a meeting. My excitement could wait. "I'll come back."

I slipped out of the room, through the building, and stepped onto the main road.

Five years ago, Salem had told me he didn't want a fertility test. I never mentioned it again. After so many years of unprotected sex, I'd assumed *what happens happens* wasn't going to happen.

Footsteps sounded behind me, and before I turned around, strong arms wrapped around me from behind.

"You look absolutely beautiful this morning," he whispered at my ear.

A shiver raced through me, and my lips pulled into a smile. "I'll never get tired of hearing that."

He stepped around me, keeping me tucked close, and searched my eyes. "Something's on your mind."

I pushed my hands through his thick black hair, tucking the longer strands behind his ears and sliding my fingers along his whiskered jaw. He still couldn't grow a full beard or hair on his chest, and other than the occasional sunburn, his porcelain skin remained gloriously, flawlessly beautiful.

"Kiss me." I lifted my mouth and hummed the moment his lips met mine.

The kiss lasted forever and not long enough.

He pulled back, eyes narrowed with suspicion. "Something

happened."

I nodded. "*What happens* happened."

His brows pulled tight then released with the catch of his breath. "Are you…? We're…having a baby?"

"Surprise." I bit my lip.

"How?"

I arched a brow.

"No, I mean, how do you know?" He paced around me, raking a hand through his hair. "You took a test?"

"Michio gave me a kit a while back." My stomach fluttered with nerves. *Is he upset?* "I've been feeling a little queasy, so when I woke this morning, I took the test."

He caught my hand and held it a long time as he gazed up at the two-story house on the hill. The pitched roof, numerous windows facing the lake, and the little porch with the bench he'd built. Our house. *Our home.*

When his eyes came at last to our joined hands, he lifted them to my flat stomach, lowered to one knee, and spread our fingers over the life within.

"I had a lot of dreams, Dawn." He touched his forehead to our hands. "This was the one that scared me the most. The one I didn't think we'd ever experience."

My heart soared, and my eyes welled with tears.

He rose, took a step back, and gifted me with a smile that rivaled the beauty of the sun. I reached for his hand, but he scooped me into the cradle of his arms instead. Then he carried me through town, up the hill, and all the way home.

His eyes flickered with electricity, the glow of happiness burning behind them. They were a color without color. Not white or clear, but bright and deep. The exact shade of love.

The kind of love that conquered all.

OTHER BOOKS BY PAM GODWIN

LOVE TRIANGLE ROMANCE

TANGLED LIES

One is a Promise

Two is a Lie

Three is a War

DARK ROMANCE

DELIVER SERIES

Deliver #1

Vanquish #2

Disclaim #3

Devastate #4

Take #5

Manipulate #6

Unshackle #7

Dominate #8

Complicate #9

DARK ALASKAN ROMANCE

FROZEN FATE

Hills of Shivers and Shadows #1

Cage of Ice and Echoes #2

Heart of Frost and Scars #3

DARK COWBOY ROMANCE

TRAILS OF SIN

Knotted #1

Buckled #2

Booted #3

STUDENT-TEACHER / PRIEST

Lessons In Sin

STUDENT-TEACHER ROMANCE

Dark Notes

ROCK-STAR DARK ROMANCE

Beneath the Burn

BILLIONAIRE REVENGE

Dirty Ties

OLDER WOMAN / YOUNGER MAN

Incentive

DARK HISTORICAL PIRATE ROMANCE

King of Libertines

Sea of Ruin

ABOUT PAM GODWIN

New York Times, Wall Street Journal, and *USA Today* bestselling author, Pam Godwin, lives in the Midwest with her husband, cats, retired greyhounds, and an old, foul-mouthed parrot. She traveled the world for seven years, attended three universities, married the vocalist of her favorite rock band, and retired from her quantitative analyst career in 2014 to write full-time.

Her interests veer toward the unconventional: bourbon, full-body tattoos, and tragic villains. Equally peculiar are her aversions to sleeping, eating meat, and dolls with blinking eyes.

EMAIL: pamgodwinauthor@gmail.com

www.ingramcontent.com/pod-product-compliance
Lightning Source LLC
Chambersburg PA
CBHW020458310726
48979CB00016B/2701/J

* 9 7 8 1 9 6 6 5 3 7 1 3 7 *